A *Mother's Secret*

Also by Renita D'Silva

Monsoon Memories
The Forgotten Daughter
The Stolen Girl
A Sister's Promise

A Mother's Secret

RENITA D'SILVA

bookouture

Published by Bookouture

An imprint of StoryFire Ltd.
23 Sussex Road, Ickenham, UB10 8PN
United Kingdom

www.bookouture.com

ISBN 978-1-910751-94-7
eBook ISBN 978-1-910751-93-0

Renita D'Silva has asserted her right to be identified
as the author of this work.

This book is a work of fiction. Names, characters, businesses,
organizations, places and events other than those clearly in the
public domain, are either the product of the author's imagination
or are used fictitiously. Any resemblance to actual persons, living or
dead, events or locales is entirely coincidental.

For Ryan Anand D'Souza

For wisecracking and advising, arguing and inspiring.
For being. For everything.

Chapter 1

Durga

Gaddehalli, India

An Old Ruin

'Come child, wake up, we've reached your ajji's village.' Aunt Lathakka's gentle but persistent voice pierces Durga's sleep-fogged brain. She becomes vaguely aware that the rocking motion of the bus, which had lulled her into slumber, has stopped. She is conscious of chatter around her, of mild pressure on her arm, of being half-dragged, half-carried down the steps of the bus. Durga blinks, seeing a cluster of cottages mushrooming from pebble-peppered earth, flanked by velvet fields, and, glowering from the top of the only hill, an old ruin.

The bus rumbles off, raising an avalanche of dust. The few passengers left inside, who'd helped prevent her jumping off and trying to escape coming here, wave from the windows, their rotting yellow teeth framed against the rusty railings. 'Bye, Durga. Be good now.' *Be good now.* The caution Durga has heard all her life.

A lone rickshaw languishes under a peepal tree at the base of the hill, the driver slumbering on its hood, his legs stretched out over the front wheel, feet resting against the trunk of the tree. Aunt Lathakka, the family friend chosen to accompany Durga on the long journey to her grandmother, walks towards the rickshaw driver, beckoning Durga to follow. Durga, wiping sleep from her eyes and cowed by the ruin scowling down from the hill, is too worn out to protest.

Someone yells, 'Hey, Lo, you are wanted…' and the rickshaw driver jerks awake, squinting inquiringly at them.

A small crowd has gathered, Durga realises, as she turns to look at the retreating bus, wishing she had resisted Lathakka's attempts to get her off it. She inhales the tang of body odour and oil, chilli powder and coconut, as the crowd presses close, their hot, curious breath on her neck, her cheeks.

'Why are they all here?' Lathakka asks the driver.

'Hardly anybody comes to our village. You're a novelty.' He stretches languidly, scratching his sweaty head. 'Where do you want to go then?'

'The mansion.' Lathakka jerks her chin upward, indicating the ruin, a brooding blue bruise blotting out the sun. 'Durga is going to stay there, with her ajji, Sumathiamma.' Her voice sounds determinedly cheery.

The gathered crowd, which, necks craned, is watching them agog, steps back as one. Dazed gasps. Traumatised shudders. Loud exhalations. A man swears. Women chant the names of gods. A little boy bursts into tears. The vendor dispensing tea and vadas, rice and fish curry, from a makeshift stand by the road, an expert at pouring frothy tea from a height, misses, the tea splashing everywhere, filling the grime-stained air with the cloying scents of cardamom, over-boiled milk and freshly minted scandal. The water in his rice pot, bubbling beside the pyramid of fly-infested vadas, dries, and the curry looks set to burn as he stares with the rest of the crowd at Durga and Lathakka, as if they have sprouted two heads and elephant trunks for noses.

'You do know that it is haunted? Cursed? That a madwoman lives there?' The rickshaw driver is the first to recover.

'But…' Lathakka begins, only to be cut off, rudely, by the driver.

'There was a fire at the house many years ago. When the breeze careers down from the hill, it brings the acrid hint of ash, and if you listen carefully you can hear the tormented cries of the dying occupants.' The driver's voice has dropped dramatically and Durga, along with the assembled crowd, inches closer, the better to catch his words.

'At certain times, if you go close enough to the ruin,' he adds, his mouth smeared with spittle and trepidation, 'you feel like you are suffocating from flame-licked smoke, as if your skin is on fire.' The crowd nods in agreement. 'Anyone who dares to step foot in there is sure to go mad.' The driver tucks his lungi in decisively.

'Why?' Durga asks and is speared by the collective gaze of the crowd.

'*Why?*' The rickshaw driver shakes his head, melodramatically throwing his hands heavenwards.

'Someone hanged themselves there. His body was only discovered, swinging from the burnt rafters, rotting and barely recognisable, when some boys ran up to the house as a dare. They smelled him first then saw a column of flies suspended from the ceiling, moving back and forth in the slight breeze,' a balding man from the crowd explains, eyes wide.

'No, it was his wife who found him – it turned her completely mad!' The old woman standing beside the balding man jabs him with her bony elbow. Her words are squelchy, her lips and mouth stained red and dripping with paan, like the jaws of a feeding vampire.

'So does this mean she was only half-mad before?' The rickshaw driver snorts, swatting at the mosquito daring to alight on his arm.

'On nights when the ruin is lit up by the ghostly orb of the full moon, it seems you can spy the phantoms of all the souls who died there, gliding through the rooms,' the vendor, who has temporarily suspended pouring tea, pipes up.

'Oh the goings-on in that house,' says an ancient-looking lady, resting against the peepal tree trunk, her toothless gums clicking as they laboriously masticate paan. 'Just because they were rich, just because they owned everyone in the village, they thought they could do anything.' She spits with a resounding thwack into her spittoon, chasing away the buzzing flies that have congregated. They settle again, a black pestilence crowding the orange-brown gloop, once she sets it back down.

What did they do? What were the goings-on? Durga wonders.

'The madwoman will bring seven years of bad luck. She'll put a spell on you,' says someone else, the crowd finding their voices as their consternation grows, their astounded gazes fixed on Durga.

'Durga's ajji, Sumathiamma, is there and she's fine.' Lathakka, Durga's chaperone, finally speaks up, her voice faltering in the face of such vehement astonishment.

'Ha! Who said so? Only an insane person chooses to live there, with ghosts and the madwoman for company,' the rickshaw driver declares. 'I go once a week with provisions, in broad daylight, and never stay long enough to be cursed or possessed. I have not seen the madwoman yet or any spirits, thank God.' The driver strokes the picture of Lord Vishnu hanging from the front mirror of his rickshaw and kisses the hand that touched his god to ward off the evil spirits he might have conjured just by talking of them. 'Sumathiamma is as mad as the old woman she looks after!'

'Shhh… she's perfectly fine, I'm sure,' Lathakka says, trying and failing to inject some assertiveness into her trembling voice as she glances at Durga.

They have sent me to live with two madwomen, Durga thinks, swaying on her feet with tiredness. *I don't even care; I just want my ma and da to be okay.*

'Nobody in their right mind will go there – except Sumathi-amma, who doesn't count as she lives there. And the nuns. And me with supplies of course.' The rickshaw driver spits.

'Nuns?' Lathakka asks.

'They look after the madwoman during the day, administering her medicine and such. Not that she can be cured… She gets violent, you know.'

'Oh.' Lathakka looks at Durga again.

Durga stares at the ground, at all the shiny smooth pebbles, thinking how well they would have fit into her catapult – the new one; her earlier, better one having been destroyed in the accident – angry with herself for not bringing it along.

'Good luck, girl. May the gods be with you,' the rickshaw driver says fervently. The crowd grouped behind Durga joins in, so it grows into a loud, reverberating rumble. 'Good luck.'

She pictures pelting the gathering with stones from her catapult, all these hangers-on running from her, screaming in shock. It makes her feel better, her heart, which she hadn't even realised was beating too fast, settling somewhat.

'So will you take us there?' Lathakka asks the rickshaw driver, peering up at the ruin.

'No way. It will be dark by the time I start back down the hill. Do you think *I* am mad as well?'

After much bartering, the rickshaw driver finally agrees to take them for three times the usual fare, greed winning out over the dread of curses cast by raging madwomen and the fear of being haunted by trapped ghosts.

And before Durga can protest, they are hurtling towards the ruin in the rickshaw. She shivers, huddling closer to Lathakka and resting a tentative hand on her knobbly fingers as they bump over the potholes on the dusty, untarred road. Her aunt smiles down at her, a wan stretch of her thin, colourless lips. Emboldened, Durga tries one more time. 'Do I have to stay with Ajji?'

Her aunt sighs, an exhalation that seems to be coming from her very depths. 'Durga, I am so sorry, we—'

'I'll be good, I promise.'

'Oh, Durga...' Her aunt looks as if she is harbouring a mouthful of bitter gourd. 'With your ma and your da in hospital, it's best for you to stay with family.'

Durga shudders at the mention of the hospital. Ma and Da's bodies, hitched to machines. Pale. Unresponsive. She squeezes her eyes closed to shut out the images but they linger. The rickshaw smells of mould and dust, and as it judders over a gigantic rut, its door flap brushes against her face. She fingers the flap, yearning to tear it in two. But she has promised Lord Krishna that she will be good if he brings her parents back to her. So with great effort she pulls her hands away and sits on them.

'You're sending me away because I'm naughty, aren't you?' she asks, although of course she knows the answer.

Durga has always been naughty, according to the people in the town where she has lived all her life, or 'spirited' as her parents like to call it. The list of her faults is seemingly endless. She asks too many questions. She doesn't know when to stop. If she sees something as an injustice, she lashes out. She hates that girls are not treated the same way as boys, that they have to give in to the boys, allow them first choice in *everything*. She has a fearsome temper. She fights, she swears, she hits. She is not meek and will not give in. She refuses to behave like a girl. This is what her teachers, neighbours, friends and strangers all made sure to tell her parents many times over the years.

'If Durga had been born a boy, she'd have been praised for these qualities,' her ma had huffed. 'She would have been hailed a born leader, and been looked up to and admired.'

'Durga is energetic, that's all. Lively and a bit strong willed. Her maternal grandmother was like that,' Durga's da – who strived to keep the peace – had assured everybody, a note of uncertainty creeping into his voice.

Things had reached a head when Gowriakka's son, Rajesh, had to be hospitalised because Durga pushed him into a ditch.

The townspeople had sent a representative, the most level-headed man in town – Baluanna – who had stroked his oily, balding head, tugged at his lungi and lamented to Durga's parents, 'What a shame! You have one child and she turned out to be like this.'

'She's loyal and has a highly developed sense of justice. Nothing wrong with that,' Durga's ma had replied, her voice stretched thin.

'Ha! Challenging, you mean. Durga has gone too far now, breaking Rajesh's leg. Don't you see that you are doing her harm by defending her?'

'She pushed him because he was making fun of poor Jirjamma, who has lost her mind since her husband passed,' Durga's ma had protested shrilly.

'Rajesh was throwing stones at Jirjamma and calling her names,' Durga had yelled from her hiding place behind the door, where she'd been eavesdropping. 'Jirjamma tripped and fell when one of his stones hit her so I thought it only fair to let Rajesh know how that felt.'

'See,' Baluanna had said to Durga's parents, shaking his head in consternation, 'Durga is not even sorry for what she's done. She has one screw loose in her head. We think you should take her to the mental hospital to be looked at.'

'That's enough! She's fine, just high-spirited,' Durga's da had barked, scowling.

'Well she's getting out of hand. You need to do something and fast, or we will,' Baluanna had muttered, shaking his head and sighing again as he took his leave.

When he'd walked far enough away, Durga had given her parents the slip and followed him. She'd hidden behind the mounds of spices, golden red and blushing orange, olive green and sunny marigold, at the market, trying not to sneeze at the chilli and coriander powder prickling her nose. She'd picked a thumb-sized stone from the mud and aimed with her catapult – the best one she'd made so far, with the V-shaped twig she'd found in Ashwin's mango orchard. When Baluanna had jumped at the pebble pinging his shoulder and turned back to glare at her, she'd laughed, performing a little victory dance before running away.

That night, after her da had given her a talking to and Durga had apologised, her ma had said, 'Durga, it was not right to aim your catapult at Baluanna.'

'Baluanna didn't want to listen to me. He had already made up his mind. Like all the rest of them. They think I'm bad and yes, I know I can be naughty, but it's only when I get angry… I just hate seeing people being made fun of…' Durga had been breathless, her throat dry after her speech.

'They can't understand anyone who's a little bit different from them, that's all,' her ma had whispered in Durga's ear. 'You know, everyone thought Lord Krishna was naughty too when he was little. He got up to all sorts of mischief, stealing buttermilk and whatnot…'

Durga had breathed in her mother's smell of coconut oil and sandalwood powder as she recounted stories of Lord Krishna's antics. 'Lord Krishna was just like you and look how well he turned out,' her ma had said, winking.

'I will pray only to Lord Krishna from now on,' Durga had promised and her mother had grinned, kissing Durga on the tip of her nose.

Now Durga pulls the back of her palm, pinching her flesh between her fingers, twisting it until it turns red and sore, so it matches the ache in her heart. Her aunt awkwardly pats her arm. 'There, there.'

The rickshaw lists precariously as it rumbles over yet another pothole before it rights itself, just. 'I don't even *know* my ajji. I only met her once, and I don't even remember that time.' Durga sniffs and wipes her nose with the back of her hand. She wants to hit someone. She wants to jump out of the rickshaw and run as far away as possible – back to the hospital, to her unresponsive ma and da. Her right leg moves up and down as if to a rhythm of its own and she fixates on it.

Her aunt squeezes Durga's shoulder. 'Your ajji has agreed to have you now.'

❋   ❋   ❋

After the accident, neighbours and friends had taken it in turns to look after Durga's parents at the hospital and have Durga stay with them. But they quickly tired of Durga, their generosity and kindness evaporating like water left out in the sun – for Durga refused to be bossed around; she couldn't pretend to be grateful to her hosts for their hospitality when she'd much rather be bedded down in the hospital beside her parents, keeping a vigilant eye on them.

The little house she'd shared with her parents had to be sold to pay the medical bills. And as Durga's parents still showed no signs of recovery with each passing day, the elders of her town had gathered at Gowriakka's house to discuss Durga's situation.

'Why can't I be present when it is *my* situation you are discussing?' Durga had asked.

'Go play marbles with the other girls,' Gowriakka had said sternly, hands on her substantial hips, not bothering to grace Durga's question with an answer.

'Why can't I play cricket with the boys?' Durga had retorted, imitating Gowriakka and standing, legs spaced apart, hands on *her* hips.

'Why are you so contrary? Why can't you do as you're told for once?' Gowriakka had snapped.

Durga had stayed put, whistling a Kannada pop tune as she'd squinted up at the sky, her feet scuffing the dusty, cracked ground.

'Go on with you,' Gowriakka had huffed, flapping her sari pallu against her face to combat the thick press of heat.

'No,' Durga had said, grinning at Gowriakka. 'I want to hear what you have to say.'

'Well you can't. It's an adult discussion.' With a loud har-rumph and a swish of emerald fabric, Gowriakka had shut the door, locking Durga outside.

'But it concerns *me*.' Durga had pounded on the door several times, letting out a string of swear words.

'Enough, girl, or I will come and whip you right now,' Gowriakka had snarled from inside.

Durga had banged the door three more times for good measure and just as it had creaked open, she had run away.

The boys had been setting up for cricket in the field outside the school.

'Can I play with you?' Durga had asked.

'*You?*' They'd laughed.

She'd snatched their ball, hitting and kicking and biting anyone who tried to get it back, knocking down the tree stumps they had dug into the ground for wickets with the stolen ball. Then, sprinting away with the boys in pursuit, she'd climbed onto the veranda where the girls had been in the middle of a game of marbles. She'd grabbed all the marbles, poking her tongue out at the outraged girls before running away.

Finally, her angst spent, she'd sneaked up to the open window of Gowriakka's house and pressed herself against the wall, where she could hear every word, fingering the smooth coolness of the marbles in her hand, popping one into her mouth and tasting mud and the thousand fingers that had handled it before her.

'We can't keep her with us forever. She's too wild, volatile. And how can we afford it, when all the proceeds from the sale of their house have gone to paying the medical bills?' Gowriakka's voice, sharp as the scrape of chalk on slate.

'We advised them to send Durga to board at a convent when she started exhibiting her mad, uncontrollable streak – perhaps the presence of a punishing Catholic god would have tamed her – but…'

Mad? Durga had thought, almost choking on the marble, the tang of acid and rust in her mouth. *I am not mad,* she'd wanted to yell, but that would've alerted Gowriakka and the others to her presence and she wouldn't have been able to hear the rest of what they were saying.

'I think we should send her to her grandmother,' Baluanna had said, his voice the harsh crackle of sandpaper. 'Luckily it is the beginning of the school holidays. She can spend them with her grandmother. After that, we can decide what to do.'

No! I don't want to go far away from my parents. I don't want to live with my ajji. I don't even know her.

Durga's ajji, who'd famously fallen out with her daughter because of her choice of husband (who was of a much lower caste) and thus the colouring of her granddaughter (dark as mustard seeds), and had refused to have anything to do with her daughter and her daughter's family since. Durga's ajji, who defied everyone by going to live in a haunted house in her old age, to care for a madwoman.

'What if Sumathiamma won't take Durga?' someone had asked.

'As if she has a choice! She's Durga's only relative,' Gowriakka had grunted.

Durga had opened her palms and dropped the marbles so they skittered onto the ground, puffs of apricot dust wheezing in their wake. Then she'd stuck her fingers in her ears and screamed, loud and hard and high pitched, until the door to Gowriakka's house had juddered open, making the settling dust gasp with renewed vigour, and the elders had run out as one, rustling saris and fretting lungis and shock, the women tucking their pallus in, the men's hands coiled into fists, ready to battle whatever evil force had taken their town captive.

❋   ❋   ❋

Does sending me so far away from my hometown, to this ajji I don't recall having met, mean my parents will die? This is the question Durga wants to ask but cannot. The question that dies on her lips on its way out, dissolving along with spit bubbles on her tongue.

Please, Lord Krishna, no.

There are more questions. She adds them to the list she is making in her head.

The List of Questions I Don't Want to Know the Answers to:

1) *Have I been sent so far away from my parents because they are going to die?*

2) *Why does Ajji stay at the ruin if it is haunted, cursed like they say?*

3) *Is Ajji possessed? Mad?*

4) *Now that I am forced to stay there, will I be cursed too?*

She hugs herself hard, trying to inject warmth into the embrace, failing to convince herself that it is her mother who is hugging her.

You'll be alright, Durga, my spirited, amazing girl, she imagines her ma saying, wishing she could hear her voice, its soft, musical cadence, just once more.

Their rickshaw passes a lone hawker peddling paper cones of bhel from the coir tray resting on his sunken belly. The tray is packed with fat white globules of puffed rice, flecked with red onion and green chilli, coriander and tomato, cones fashioned from newspaper jostling for space on one side.

A whiff of spices reaches Durga's nose, making her stomach rumble. She hasn't eaten much since finding out she was being sent away, food turning to glue in her mouth as she worried about what was to come and, mostly, about leaving her parents behind, fighting the fear that something bad would happen to them the moment she left. But the something bad had already happened – and *she* had caused it.

She blinks back tears, looking resolutely out of the rickshaw. Her aunt strokes Durga's back clumsily as they pass tiny abodes, women chatting to each other while they pick stones from rice, tired-looking men squatting in the dirt, smoking beedis and perusing the sky. The children playing lagori in the middle of the mud road clutch their altar of stones and their scuffed ball and dodge out of the rickshaw's path, peering askance at the newcomers who dare disrupt their game.

The rickshaw leaves the houses behind and starts up the hill, groaning and grumbling. The driver urges his vehicle on, muttering to himself, sweat soaking his khaki shirt. Shouts and jeers, catcalls and whoops make Durga and her aunt turn and peer out of the little square of transparent plastic hewn into the black tarpaulin covering the back of the rickshaw. The kids playing lagori have stopped their game and are following the rickshaw at a safe distance. A procession of raggedy, dust-sheathed bodies. Inquisitive eyes.

'Don't you know the ruin is haunted?' one of them yells, as they nudge each other and pull monstrous faces. Durga pulls faces back. Once again she wishes she had her catapult with her, so she could pelt them with stone bullets.

'The madwoman who lives there puts a curse on anyone who dares enter,' another shouts, his eyes dancing with delight at the thought.

Durga turns back in her seat and tugs at her aunt's hand, finally gathering up the courage to ask one of the questions lingering in her mind. 'Is it true? Is this why I've been sent here?'

Her aunt looks down at her kindly. 'No, silly,' she tuts. 'And don't believe that nonsense about curses either.'

'Oh there's a curse all right,' the rickshaw driver huffs. 'No boy child survives in that family. Everyone associated with that mansion is cursed with unhappiness, insanity, death. You must be out of your mind to go there, and I have warned you plenty. But it's none of my business, as long as you pay me three times the fare like you promised.' The rickshaw driver's hair drips with sweat as his ramshackle vehicle brings them closer and closer to the ruin, which looms over the earth-tinged emerald fields, painting the mud below the dark black of clotted blood.

Chapter 2

Jaya

London, UK

Dream-glazed Paint

'I feel angry all the time,' Jaya says, her voice tinged with anguish. 'The grief's easing but it's as if I carry this huge, fuming ball of ire within me. I wake up each morning with a sore jaw, having gritted and gnashed my teeth in the night…' She sniffs, pulling a tissue from the box next to her and blows her nose vigorously.

'Are you angry with anyone in particular?' her therapist Dr Meadows' mellow voice nudges gently.

Jaya chose Dr Caroline Meadows because of her beautiful name – bringing to mind dew-bathed fields dotted with plump black and white cows – and also, of course, because of the string of qualifications trailing in its wake.

'With fate, with everything that's happened.' Jaya's left shoulder itches, the shaggy upholstery of the couch she is resting against irritating her back. 'But mostly… I'm angry with my mum.'

'Why are you angry with your mother?' her therapist asks.

Why? Jaya pictures her mother, her favourite marigold sari dotted with tiny blue flowers hugging her slight frame, the tired lines etched into her gaunt face, her exhausted eyes.

'I...' Where to begin? 'She...' How to put into words a lifetime's worth of upset, love and hurt? How to convey just how much Jaya misses her mother, how much she *needs* her – especially now – while at the same time being so intensely mad at her?

'Okay, tell me this – how would you describe your mother?'

'Solitary,' Jaya says instantly, without having to think about it.

'Why solitary?' Dr Meadows leans forward on her desk, cupping her face in the palms of her hands. 'Call me Caroline,' she'd said at their first session but Jaya still thinks of her as Dr Meadows; it has a nice, reassuring ring to it.

Jaya swallows. 'My mum... She kept people at bay. She had no friends. She rebuffed admirers. She was a quiet, self-contained, prickly person.'

'You said solitary. Not lonely. Why?'

Jaya muses on this. 'She was always on the go. She kept herself too occupied to be lonely, I think. But she was alone. Apart from me, she had nobody. And I always got the feeling she preferred it that way, that she actively sought this distance from people. But, despite my prodding, she never told me why.'

'Did you feel she was too busy for you?'

'No. Never.' Another answer Jaya doesn't have to think about. 'She wasn't warm, bubbly, outwardly affectionate. But she was there for me. I knew she loved me. That I came first, over and above everything else. But… she never answered my questions about her past. She was very closed, remote about everything to do with her history and mine.' Jaya takes a deep breath. 'I loved her. And I resented her.'

'Ah…'

'She was perpetually harassed, juggling two or three jobs, even after I had left home and she'd paid off the mortgage. I thought it was to fill the time. Now I wonder…'

Her mother. Always busy, forever working. Like Ben.

Ben… Jaya is here because of him. To salvage their relationship, which is reeling from sorrow, battered by jagged stabs of loss. She understands that work is Ben's way of dealing with the grief that has ambushed them this past year. But why had Jaya's mother continued to work all hours? What was she running away from?

'It was only ever the two of us – my mum and I,' Jaya says. 'I didn't have a dad or extended family. No grandparents, uncles, aunts, cousins. I pressed Mum about this countless times. But she was cagey and always had excuses handy.' Shrinking from Jaya's questions, sliding into herself, her gaze wide and wary and distant all at once, warning Jaya not to push.

'Didn't she tell you anything at all?' Dr Meadows asks.

'Nothing. And…' Jaya releases a quaking breath. 'And then she died, taking the secret of who my father is with her. Granted, I never met my father, but I had a right to know the truth. She denied me that. She…' Jaya takes another tissue from the box and shreds it.

'You never knew your dad?'

'I don't even know what he looks like. There were no pictures of him in our house, not one.'

'We left them all behind,' was Jaya's mum's paltry excuse. 'There were more important things to bring when we were uprooting our whole life to come here. And here, while we were struggling to make ends meet, buying a camera was an unnecessary expense, taking pictures a luxury we couldn't afford,' her mother had said, in that voice that barred further questions.

'What did she tell you about your father?' Dr Meadows asks.

'Precious little,' Jaya sighs. 'She said that my dad was a labourer who'd worked in Abu Dhabi and procured an opportunity to come here. They'd been here a year when he died of a haemorrhaging aneurysm. She was eight months pregnant with me at the time.'

∗   ∗   ∗

'Don't you miss my dad?' Jaya had asked her mum.

'Of course I do,' her mother had replied, but there'd been no trace of emotion in her voice, her face expressionless.

'But don't you wish you had a photograph of Dad,' Jaya had persisted, 'to remind you of him?'

'I have it in my heart.'

If she hadn't been upset, Jaya would have laughed at the irony of this woman, with her monotone voice, her blank face, her lack of sentiment, talking about storing pictures of a man she claimed to have loved in her heart.

'Well, *I* don't,' Jaya had huffed. 'I'd like a picture to remember him by, instead of him being a faceless unknown man who died before I was born.'

'That's enough now. I thought he'd be around. Didn't think I'd be needing a picture to give you.'

And that had been the end of that conversation. No matter how much Jaya had pressed and begged, no matter how many tears she'd shed, how many tantrums she'd thrown, she'd never got anything more. Several times over the years Jaya had queried her mother's story, all those pat explanations delivered in that flat voice that discouraged further discussion. But the sceptical voice at the back of Jaya's head that questioned her mother's account of their joint past was always silenced, her mother a sealed chest of secrets Jaya had never managed to unlock.

Jaya had pursued it even further once, because she'd had an ace up her sleeve. 'You don't have a single picture of my dad?' she'd asked.

'No.'

'Not one?'

Her mother's mouth had set in that firm line that implied she was getting annoyed, but Jaya had had enough of being snubbed. 'What about his passport?'

Her mother had grimaced. 'What about it?'

'That must have had his picture.'

'I…' her mother had said, swallowing once, twice. 'It was destroyed. A… a fire.'

Something had crossed her mother's face when she'd said that – an expression that had scared Jaya into silence more effectively than her mother's refusal to answer her questions. She had never before seen that look on her mother's face: a searing, anguished distress. She'd had one brief glimpse of it before her mother's face had reset to normal. It had terrified Jaya, this insight into a mother who was not the calm, efficient woman she knew but flailing, petrified. She'd wanted to know what was in her mother's past... and she didn't. She'd told herself her mother was a single woman who'd got pregnant and was pretending to Jaya that she had a dad when she didn't know herself who it was, because a false sense of morality prevented her from confessing that she'd slept around. But it didn't ring true. Jaya couldn't see her mother sleeping around. She was too earnest, too rigid. She had a strong moral code, always, except of course when telling her daughter about her parentage.

* * *

'So you're angry with your mother for withholding information about your dad?' Dr Meadows' gentle voice intrudes into Jaya's reveries.

'Yes. And, unreasonably, I'm also upset with her for not being here for me now.' Another tissue succumbs to Jaya's complicated feelings about her dead mother. 'I feel so alone most of the time. With Ben away with work. And Arun gone...'

She thinks of the smooth, marble headstone she has just left, the marker longer than her baby is ever going to be, sporting the few poignant words that shout out her baby's too-short life: 'Arun Benjamin Campbell. Our beloved angel. Sorely missed.'

She swallows around the lump in her throat. 'I always wanted a big family. To make up for not having any relatives. If I couldn't have a past then I wanted a bustling, noisy future, with at least four children. Ben agreed. But now... Now it's hard to see the way forward. And I feel... I feel as if, if I know who I am, in terms of my past, then I could move on. I… I can't explain it properly.'

Dr Meadows nods. 'You want validation from the only person, other than Ben, who was yours.'

'Yes. That's it exactly. I miss Mum. I want answers from her. I feel like she's abandoned me just when I desperately need her, although I know of course that dying isn't her fault.' Jaya laughs, a wet splutter directed at herself for being so irrational. 'I want Mum back. And… I want Arun back.'

Her therapist waits.

'The day I found out I was pregnant with Arun, I felt able, finally, to leave the missing pieces of my past behind and to look ahead…'

She had stared at the tiny window of the pregnancy test in the cramped McDonalds' loo next to the pharmacy – she hadn't even waited until she was home – the two blue lines winking at her, and she had stroked her stomach where the child she and Ben had created – their future – was growing. She had stumbled out of the loo, eyes averted from the queue that had built up outside, and she had looked benevolently at each little child munching on ketchup-smothered chips, unable to keep the happiness from her face as she pulled out her phone to call Ben. She had grinned at strangers all the way home.

She opens her mouth and tastes the dregs of that hope. It's been six months since she and Ben lost Arun. A horrific period that they have managed to weather – just. But at what cost? Jaya bunches the tissue in her hand. She can't think about that now. This session is about her mum and if she brings Ben into it too, she'll never leave.

The little clock sitting on Dr Meadows' desk ticks down the minutes until Jaya's allotted hour and a half is up. The room exudes patience and pain.

'I often wonder how my mother would have been with her grandson. I picture her face lighting up with that look of pride she wore when she talked about me to others – it embarrassed me and made me inordinately pleased at the same time... You see, she wasn't given to hugs and spontaneous bursts of affection, so I treasured that look, what it meant... I think of her with Arun, and then... And then I thank God that she was spared Arun's loss.'

'In our last session, you mentioned her effects. Have you felt up to going through them like we discussed?'

Jaya thinks of her mother's belongings, gathering dust in the spare room that doubles up as an office in the house that she and Ben bought when they'd found out she was pregnant. They had run through the rooms, holding hands, pausing at each empty nook and writing stories into its waiting walls, populating the toneless air with the multi-hued fountain of their hopes, the dazzling kaleidoscope of their fantasies, colouring the bare walls with the dream-glazed paint of their happy ever afters.

She swallows, tasting sorrow and longing – familiar and bitter. 'I haven't been able to...'

Jaya and Ben had been waiting until Jaya's twelve-week scan to tell her mum. Jaya had memorised what she was going to say; she'd conjured up the expression on her mother's face when she found out she was going to be a grandmother countless times.

Her mother was never to know. By Jaya's eleventh week of pregnancy, she was gone. A heart attack. Sudden. Fatal. Devastating.

What with Jaya being sick every other minute because of her pregnancy, she had not been up to going through her mother's things. Sifting through the debris of her mother's life had felt too raw on top of her unexpected loss. So she had temporarily postponed the task, and the few mementoes of her mother's life had waited untouched in the spare room. And then Arun came. And then he died. And after that… After that, for a very long time, there was nothing. A huge, black expanse of emptiness from which Jaya had only recently emerged.

'You never got to mourn your mother's loss, did you? You were pregnant. You had the baby to look forward to. You were annoyed with her for deserting you just when you were about to become a mother and would need her the most. So you suppressed your emotions, packed them away along with your mother's belongings. They're all surfacing now,' Dr Meadows says.

'I… I just can't face going through her things.' Jaya tears another tissue to pieces.

'Don't you think this is your way of suspending everything? Not making any decisions. Remaining in limbo, cocooned in grief and anger – emotions you are comfortable with and actively seek – so you don't have to move forward into the unknown, face the world, without your son or your mother.'

Jaya flinches at Dr Meadows' words. 'What do you mean?'

'Your mother's things – they represent the metaphorical mountain you have to climb, Jaya. It's holding you back. You need to do this – mourn her properly, put your grief, your anger at her behind you – in order to move on.'

'I don't need to go through her things for that. It's just a couple of boxes. I just… I just haven't got round to it.' She can hear how defensive she sounds.

'Don't you think,' Dr Meadows says calmly, 'you are postponing going through her stuff because you're afraid of finding nothing? No declaration of love. No goodbye. No hint as to the identity of your father. Just nothing.'

'There *will* be nothing,' Jaya barks. 'My mother wasn't sentimental.'

'Sometimes the least sentimental people surprise you the most.'

'Well, not her. She believed in moving through life with very little baggage. She shut the door on her past and didn't open it again, ever – not even for me. She didn't leave anything personal with her will, not even a letter.' The hurt that Jaya had felt then is still fresh. She had hoped for something tangible to treasure, a note in her mother's neat handwriting perhaps. Although why she had expected that when her mother had never been given to sentiment she couldn't say. 'She was so closed, my mum.'

The clock on Dr Meadows' desk beeps. Jaya's time is up.

'This week I want you to go through your mother's things, Jaya. I think you're ready.'

Perhaps Dr Meadows is right, Jaya muses. Perhaps she's put off going through her mother's belongings for so long because she doesn't want to experience once more the disappointment she felt when she was informed of the dry and impersonal contents of her mother's will.

'You'll have to do it at some point. Now is as good a time as any. We'll talk about what you find next week.' Dr Meadows stands and walks across the desk to shake Jaya's hand and see her out.

Chapter 3
Kali

Gaddehalli (Now) and Bannihalli (Before), India

The Smell of Sap

'What are you doing here? I've been looking all over for you,' a voice intrudes into my thoughts, querulous, like a cat that has not been fed on time by its human.

'Well you didn't look very hard, did you?' I snap, annoyed at being disturbed, although I can't for the life of me remember where I am or what I had been doing. 'Why is it so dark? Switch on the light.'

'It's the middle of the night and you've been wandering again. You're outside, in the orchard,' the voice sighs from the blackness.

'Has there been a power cut? Where are Ma and Da?'

Whenever there is a power cut, which happens most evenings, Ma and Da and I sit outside our house, swatting at mosquitoes and chatting with neighbours, our voices and laughter piercing the gloom, the aroma of roasting peanuts and sesame sweets wafting to where I squat cross-legged in the dust, making my stomach rumble. We watch the stars, listening to the frogs croak and the dogs howl and the crickets grumble, the drumbeat of drops from the afternoon's downpour losing their stubborn grasp on the leaves. We taste the darkness, inky and flavoured with shadows, spiced with intrigue.

Faceless voices calling in the dark.

'Come, let's get you to bed.'

I busy myself with my favourite game: matching the voice to the face. But this voice… Its owner's name is evading me. Definitely a woman. But who? Not Vasukiamma. Not Chinnakka or Beerakka.

The smell of sap. The call of owls. I think of the time he came and sat beside me in the darkness. I chatted away, assuming it was Da, and then felt his smile, heard his delighted chuckles as his hand reached out and grabbed mine. 'Manu!' I had screeched, annoyed at being hoodwinked, pulling my hand away and pummelling him while he laughed and tried to dodge my blows.

The neighbours griped about the commotion and Ma ordered me to stop making a scene, and Da asked Ma to shush, to let me be.

Was it today that it happened? Is that why I am here? If so, where are Ma and Da and Manu? Why can't I remember? The smell of sap. Familiar. Nudging at me. What am I forgetting?

'Kali, come. You must be tired after all this roaming.' A hand takes mine, gently tugging and I surprise myself by allowing it to lead me away, the anonymous voice soothing me as I follow in its wake.

I am tired, so tired. I am tucked into bed and as I pull the bedclothes up around my ears, as is my habit, I breathe in the smell of sap on my hands, and I see him.

*   *   *

I spy on Manu as he ploughs his father's field, hiding behind the thick trunk of the jackfruit tree, its prickly fruit digging into my thighs, its sap, yellow gold, bleeding from the bark. As I hide, I bite into raw mango sprinkled liberally with rock salt I brought in my pockets to alleviate its tartness.

Manu is my best friend. I grew up with him, the two of us getting into scrapes together. I never gave a thought to whether he was attractive or not, never looked at him that way. But now that I'm observing him, I realise I love the way his muscles ripple when he pushes his buffaloes forward.

'Every girl in the village has a crush on Manu,' Arathi had informed me this morning, when one of the girls from Sannipur Sewing College came up to me, offering to mend the churidar shawl I had torn on a bush. 'Why do you think all those girls want your friendship and offer to do things for you? They don't act the same with me. It's because Manu is your friend. Don't tell me you haven't noticed how good-looking he is?' Arathi had muttered.

'I honestly haven't,' I'd said.

'I don't believe you.' Arathi's face had settled into a scowl.

I'd ignored her, thinking, joining the dots in my head. It all made sense. Girls crowding around, especially after school when Manu would come up behind me and tug at my plait. I'd hit him for messing up my hair, make him carry my bag, and then we'd fall into step for the walk back home.

'Do you love him?' Arathi had asked, scowl gone, face eager.

I had gagged on the sugar cane I was chewing. 'Love? He's my *friend*.'

I am here because I want to see what makes him so attractive to all the girls in the village, and even far beyond, according to Arathi. I watch him, as flies bite and ants, attracted by the jackfruit tree, creep up my legs. I flick them off, my fingers sticky with raw mango juice and melting salt. But I soon get bored. After all, it is only Manu, annoying Manu – my best friend and the keeper of my innermost secrets.

'Hey, Manu,' I call.

He stops urging the buffaloes on and shades his eyes with his palm. When he sees me, he grins. I have to admit his dimples *are* quite cute and I do love his smile. But, honestly, *the most handsome boy in the village*? Please. 'Thought you might be hungry.' I hold out the remains of the mango and pull out the straggling flecks of fabric-encrusted, sweating salt from my pocket.

'Ew!' He makes a face at the sorry crumbs of salt. 'Don't want *that*.' He takes a bite of the mango and gags on the sourness. I laugh.

'Perhaps I will have some after all.' He grabs my hand to take the salt and that's when it happens – something electric passing between us. When he drops my hand and looks at me, I know he feels it too. I am suddenly aware of my grubby clothes, my torn shawl, my messy hair, my perspiring face. There is something in my friend's gaze that is making me blush redder than the hibiscus flowers waving in the sunshine at the edge of the field.

'So…' he says, wiping his hands on his shorts.

A strained atmosphere seems to have sprung between us. The air that strokes my face tastes of grit and confusion. Did I imagine the current that passed between us? Is this discomfort that has taken over our ease with each other just in my head?

The buffaloes are getting restless. They low and rut their horns.

Manu tweaks my plait and then I am being pulled into his embrace and it feels so very right. In his sweaty arms, the scent of hay and hard work, I am at home.

He plants a soft kiss on my head and releases me. It is as if we have made a pact. He looks into my eyes. This is nothing like how he used to look at me. It sparks an ache within me. I want his arms around me.

I shuffle, looking at my feet, which are encrusted in dirt. What is happening to me?

'Bye,' I say and run away. I know without looking back that he is watching me.

I sprint all the way to the far end of the field and gaze at Manu from behind another tree, no longer bored to do so, as the creaking of the yoke starts up again and he coaxes on the buffaloes in his cinnamon voice. As I look on, he blows a kiss in my direction and I blush, even though I am hidden from view.

That evening there is another power cut. I sit on the wet ground, soft after the late afternoon downpour.

The adults chatter among themselves, munching on paan, calling across the sodden fields.

'Where has your da gone?' Ma asks, swinging the lantern around us, making sure I am safely seated near her before turning it off to conserve the oil. Shadows dance on dusky faces, caves of mouths, yellow teeth.

I etch Manu's name in the wet mud with a twig again and again as the jasmine-scented breeze stirs the coconut fronds above me, raindrops falling on my head. Where is he? Will he not come to sit beside me? He does usually. Getting up to his tricks, threading grass through my plait. Giving me a gift of an earthworm: opening my palm in the darkness and placing the wiggly, slimy thing in my hand, my scream setting off the neighbourhood dogs in a frenzied chorus of barks, my ma snapping, 'What use are your good looks if you behave like a fisherwoman?'

When Ma had gone off on one of her many lectures the other day, she'd said: 'Oh, Lord Krishna, how is my tomboy of a daughter ever going to be married?' Da caught my gaze and rolled his eyes. My ally.

'And you!' she'd yelled, turning on Da. 'You are no help at all. Encouraging her antics.'

Da had looked chastised. Later, he'd taken me aside. 'Come,' he'd said. 'Let me teach you to walk like a lady.'

I'd burst out laughing, spitting juice from the cashew I was chewing. '*You* are going to teach *me* to walk like a *lady*?'

'You need to laugh with your mouth closed, like a *lady*,' Da had reprimanded, trying and failing to mimic Ma's nagging.

'Look,' he'd said, keeping his feet together and weaving demurely around the courtyard like a dainty drunk. 'Just follow me.' He'd picked up several notebooks and set one on my head. 'Try and walk with that book on your head. You need to take small steps, with your legs close together, just so.' He'd placed another one of my notebooks on his head. And together we'd tried to walk the length of the courtyard in a straight line, balancing the books on our heads – not an easy feat with the dog yapping at our heels.

And of course when Ma had returned early from her cleaning job, she'd found us rolling about on the ground laughing, the books spread out around us, pages dancing and mud stained, the dog enthusiastically licking our faces. Ma had shaken her head so hard I'd worried it would fall right off. 'Get off the ground now, Kali. Your clothes are dirty. You need a wash. I don't know what your da is doing down there in the mud either. Don't tell me he's drunk in the middle of the day and encouraging you in your nonsense. What will the neighbours think?'

Now, sitting in the courtyard, the darkness ringing with the neighbours' banter, Ma whispers, 'Where's your da?' as she spits out her paan and starts on another.

I don't care about my da's whereabouts. I want to know where Manu is. Has what happened between us this morning put him off? Is he not going to be my friend any more? My stomach dips at the thought.

And then I feel the air shifting beside me. My hand is taken captive, sending shivers all down my spine. I smile in the darkness, even as I tremble, breathing in his smell of lime and mango leaves and musk.

He writes something in my palm with his finger, and even though it is a game we have played a million times, the other person guessing what the word is, my whole body tingles.

'Is it I?' I speculate, my voice shaking. I can feel him nod. 'L. O. V... Love?'

He nods again, seemingly unaware that my whole body is on fire. Y. O. U, he writes.

I can't speak. I am hot, quivering, unsteady, dazed.

He leans close and whispers into my ear, 'I love you.'

The air around us is electric. I want him to hold me, envelop me in his arms, and he does, the voices of our neighbours washing over us, the aroma of smoke and conjee in the air, the jubilant, thrilling taste of love.

'Manu,' his da calls and reluctantly he lets go of me and leaves.

Five minutes later, there is a whoop and a shout.

'Hey, Jaljakka,' Manu's da calls to my ma, 'my son wants to marry your daughter.'

I freeze although my body is still blazing from his touch. The neighbourhood stills. There is silence as everyone waits to see how this will unfold.

'Have you drunk toddy or what, announcing it to the whole world?' my ma asks, but there is laughter beading her voice. *Look, my daughter is getting proposals already,* she is thinking.

The neighbourhood erupts in a rash of whispers interspersed with giggles. There is chewing and spitting of paan and speculation.

'My daughter is too good for your son.' This time the laughter in Ma's voice spills over.

'Please, Jaljakka. My son is smitten.'

'Oh well, I'll think about it. You need to do it properly though – come to our house with your wife to ask for my daughter's hand.'

'I will, if I can find her,' Manu's da says, laughing.

'Better keep her close, the loveliest woman in the village,' someone yells. 'If I was married to her, I would keep a watchful eye on her at all times.'

Manu gets his good looks, that regal nose, those liberally lashed, bovine eyes, from his mother, Vasuki. A famed beauty.

'Airs and graces that one,' Ma has mocked, her mouth stained with paan and envy.

'What's everyone shouting about?' Da is beside me, whispering in my ear. He smells different, odd. Sweet and salty at the same time.

'Where were you?' Ma hisses at Da. 'Your daughter has just had her first proposal and you missed it.'

'From whom?'

'Manu.'

I feel Da go very still beside me. Then he laughs, a small excuse for a chuckle. 'He's practically her brother.'

'No he's not,' I snap fiercely as the power comes back on with a crackle and a buzz. A cheer goes through the crowd and everyone stands up, a collective rustling and stretching and creaking of knees and groans from the oldies, as they dust themselves off and make to go back indoors. 'No he's not.'

❋   ❋   ❋

'It was love, and it was as natural as anything. We just *knew*. And we thought that, despite their jokey dismissal of our announcement, our parents approved of the match. Why wouldn't they? We were the two best-looking young people in the village. We were of the same religion, the same caste. We were meant to be together or so we thought…' My mouth is dry, my throat parched. I desperately need a drink.

Who am I speaking to? I don't quite know. But I want to go on; I have to, as much for myself as for whoever is listening to my tale.

I am lying down, too tired to sit up. Perhaps I have been ill? Yes, that must be it. That is why my mind refuses to cooperate, to offer up the facts I know are there somewhere in my memory. I have a feeling that what I want to say will slip into the many discreet hidey-holes my mind inhabits these days if I don't speak up. 'Oh how foolish we were. How incredibly naive. We sat at the edge of the field, we munched on pineapples and drank the cool, silver slicked water from the stream and we weaved plans for our future. Little did we know…'

Chapter 4
Jaya

Relics of a Life

Sudha, Jaya's mother, wasn't a hoarder – a few boxes are all that remain of her life. Jaya quietly closes the door to the study, in case her cat Mr Fluff decides to investigate what's going on and resorts to his favourite activity – shredding paper. She can't risk him destroying the few documents her mother treasured and thought fit to keep. With trembling hands, Jaya pulls the boxes towards her, inhaling the musty aroma of ageing paper, stale memories and lost moments.

The first box is a testament to Jaya. Her school reports, and every piece of writing she has ever done. Her mother has carefully preserved all of Jaya's Mother's Day cards, starting with the one proudly displaying her inky handprint (only slightly bigger than Arun's minuscule palm— *Don't think of that now; don't go there*), made with the help of her Reception-class teachers.

Throughout her school years, Jaya had painstakingly designed the cards, the words 'I love you, Mum. You are the Best Mum in the Whole World' penned in her neatest handwriting. The later ones were shop bought, rushed jobs, with 'Love, Jaya' scrawled half-heartedly across the bottom. *Oh, Mum, I didn't know you kept all of this,* Jaya thinks, Dr Meadows' words ringing in her ears: *Sometimes the least sentimental people surprise you the most.*

It had only ever been the two of them. And yet, because of the way Sudha was, loving but sealed off, while Jaya, back then, was all emotion, their relationship was always fraught. Jaya's earliest memory is of racing towards her mother, who was waiting at the school gates with the other mums. But while every other mother squatted down and opened their arms wide to welcome their little ones into their snug embrace, hers had turned away, so Jaya was left hugging her sari-clad legs, only for her hands to be disentangled. 'Come now, Jaya, I can't walk with you holding me so.'

'I want you to carry me,' Jaya had whispered, jealous of the other children in their mothers' arms, her lower lip trembling, holding back her tears.

'You're old enough to walk,' Sudha had said gently before walking away.

Jaya had debated standing there and crying until her mother came back for her and picked her up. But she hadn't even looked back and Jaya, terrified that she would be left behind, had given in, scrambling to catch up with her mum, no hug in sight.

Sudha never once forgot to pick Jaya up from school, like some of the other mums did their children; she always had a hot meal waiting when Jaya got home, despite juggling two jobs, at times even three. But she always kept something of herself back, so Jaya never knew what was going on in Sudha's mind or where she stood with her.

As a teen, Jaya tried rebelling, staying out late, coming home drunk a few times. Sudha was neither angry nor worried. She acted just the same as always. Busy, preoccupied, unflappable. In the end, Jaya had tired of the wild gang she'd got mixed up with and went back to being the good girl she innately was.

When Jaya and Sudha were together, on the rare occasions Sudha was home from work and Jaya was still up, they were silent, each retreating into their own world. Jaya would shout at her mother in frustration every once in a while but Sudha never retaliated and Jaya's anger fizzled out into bitterness and, later, indifference.

When Jaya went for sleepovers at her friends' houses, she envied the easy relationships they had with their mothers, their banter, even their screaming matches. Over time her resentment of the noiseless and, in Jaya's opinion, soulless home she shared with her mother grew so much that she hated it. She couldn't escape fast enough.

＊   ＊   ＊

Jaya came into her own at university. She loved how it was never quiet in the halls of residence, no matter how late it was, or how early in the morning for that matter. While at uni, she ferreted excuses not to go home, preferring to stay on during the holidays or, when invited, to go to her friends' warm, laughter- and even conflict-filled houses instead. Anything, even arguing, was preferable to the oppressive silence in her own home, laden with all the things unsaid between her and her mother, growing every day, fuelled by Jaya's bitterness.

Then she met Ben. At uni she had found her voice and with Ben she found herself.

Back when everything was right with their world, Ben would urge her to visit Sudha. 'She must be lonely, Jaya, and missing you,' he had said, over and over.

'She likes it that way,' Jaya had insisted. 'And she's always so busy.'

Ben is in Chicago, working. Jaya wishes he was here, going through her mother's things with her. When was the last time they did anything together, she and Ben?

Jaya had promised herself that when she was a grown-up her home would never be silent. That it would be lively, bursting with love. But here she is now, alone in a quiet house, weighed down with loss, Ben in another continent. *Nothing* has changed. This could be her childhood home with her mother away working and Jaya pacing the rooms, waiting. Waiting for things to change. Waiting for her mother to open up, to tell her about her father. Waiting for her life to begin. Waiting. Like she's doing now. Once again waiting for her life to start.

'Do you love Ben?' One of the very first questions Dr Meadows had asked of Jaya.

'Very much. He's the only man I have ever loved.'

'And does he love you?'

Hiding her hand behind the cushions of the couch, Jaya had crossed her fingers. 'Yes.' *I hope so. I hope it's not too late.*

She wants to tell Ben about her mother saving every piece of her writing, every card she ever made. She picks up the phone but cannot bring herself to call him. *He's in meetings,* she tells herself. *He would have switched off his phone.* She stares at the phone in her hand. *When did it come to this?* She and Ben have fallen out of the habit of speaking to each other, the intimacy they once shared broken.

She shakes her head to clear it and gets back to the task at hand: unravelling the enigma that was her mother. *Why did it take me so long to do this? And why was I so afraid?*

Finally she is here, squatting in her spare room, among her mother's belongings that span their life together. A life that Jaya resented, which she'd always thought her mother had endured but never really wanted but which, she now realises, meant more to her mother than she knew. She fancies she can detect her mother's scent among her belongings, the faint whiff of curry and coconut oil that was her trademark. *Get a grip, Jaya.*

Remorse nags at her, a sawtoothed splinter wedged in her heart. She should have been a better daughter. Perhaps if she had visited her mother more, if she'd made sure she went to the doctor regularly, made sure she had her checks, the heart attack could have been prevented. Sudha was *young,* unlike Ben's parents. In his early twenties Ben had lost his parents, one after the other, to cancer. They had been older, both of them. Ben was the doted son, their miracle baby who had arrived late in life.

But Sudha… She'd been too young to die. She'd had no health issues. She'd been completely fine until the heart attack came out of nowhere and took her life.

The next box contains photo albums. Much-thumbed pictures of Jaya, a catalogue of her life in snapshots. The few choice things Sudha thought worth keeping, the souvenirs she treasured in the course of her life, chronicle Jaya's existence. *You loved me so much, Mum. More than I can fathom. I kept badgering you about the past, until what you were keeping from me was all I could see. But for you the past didn't matter. Nothing mattered except me. I was your life. This was what you tried to tell me. But I didn't understand. I thought you were being difficult. All my life, I fixated on what wasn't there, what was missing, pushing you away in the process. I never once thought to see what* was *there, right in front of my eyes. Your love.*

Jaya opens her mouth and tastes the truth of it. *Very few have the privilege of being loved like I have been, your whole life revolving around me. I should have accepted it gratefully and basked in it. Instead I chose not to see it, and ran away from your love, throwing away your precious gift like it was nothing at all.*

Sudha was not openly affectionate but Jaya remembers rousing from feverish nightmares and finding her mother by her side, bathing Jaya's forehead with a wet towel, promising, 'Shhh, it's okay, you're going to get better.'

And Jaya always did.

She has hazy memories of waking at night to the feel of a kiss, the sweet warmth of whispered affection: 'I love you, Jaya. My darling child.'

She finds them in the last box: three items, each remarkable in their own way, tucked in the back of an album that documents Jaya's life at secondary school, growing taller than her mother, her face sullen as she navigates the bittersweet milestones of adolescence. The first – a notebook. She flicks it open without thinking, then stops short, her heart tattooing a punishing rhythm onto her chest.

'Dear Diary,' Sudha has written, in her familiar hand. Jaya stares, the words swimming before her eyes. All her life she has ached for this, a glimpse into her mother's intensely private mind, and now… now that she is holding her mother's words, her confidences, in her hand, she cannot read any further than that first 'Dear Diary'.

She runs a hand gently over the book and brings it to her nose, breathing in the odour of moth-eaten memories, of damp and stories and secret lives, before very carefully setting it aside. It makes sense, she thinks. Of course her mother would keep a diary. She was so closed that she would need some sort of outlet for her feelings. Jaya has been offered an intimate peek into her mother's life, her thoughts. A gift, after having given up all hope of ever getting to know the person her mother really was. She'll get back to the diary, but first…

Slowly, her heart still hammering, she goes over the other items hidden in the bulging album and finds her second treasure: a worn brown envelope of photographs she doesn't recognise. She leafs through them, catching a whiff of smoke, the distinctive, charred branding of fire. They are all of a child, a boy, at various stages of development, from baby to around three years old, except for one group picture of a strange family. The little boy is smiling at the camera in almost all of the pictures. Open mouthed, warm-hearted. Happy. Who is this child? Why is he here, among her mother's belongings?

Jaya turns her attention to the group photograph – a family gathered in front of a sprawling mansion. A stern-looking matriarch props up a bald man with a cane. The woman is staring self-importantly, unblinking, at the camera. She is obviously in charge. Standing on the other side of the bald man is a much younger couple. The young man's body is angled towards the woman beside him, his arm around her. He is smiling down at her instead of looking at the photographer. The woman's face is obscured by a toddler, who is squirming in her arms, leaping out of them towards the camera. Jaya looks closely at the toddler. It is the same boy as in the other pictures.

These pictures are all creased where they have been folded and refolded, perused and tucked away, carefully saved and cherished. Why did her mother keep pictures of this little boy, this family? And, more importantly, who are they?

Something about the boy tugs at Jaya's heart. He blurs before her eyes, transforming into the boy she lost. And the devastating sorrow, the crushing loss, is back full force.

She blinks and, with effort, pushes her grief away – something she is able to do now, thanks to her sessions with Dr Meadows. She gently places the photographs of the boy down beside the diary, except for the group picture, which she scrutinises carefully once again, angling for clues. Does she know anyone? No flicker of recognition. No trace of familiarity. She is pretty certain she hasn't met any of them. The women are wearing saris and the house in the background, the landscape, the wide, open sky, is unfamiliar. The house is huge, rambling; the style of it impressive but unlike any she has seen.

She turns the picture over and sees writing on the back. Two lines, in her mother's careful handwriting. Two words actually. *Gaddehalli*, she makes out, *India*. She feels goosebumps along her arms.

Quickly she scans the other pictures: no writing on any of them.

Sudha had not been in touch with anyone from India. It was as if she had reinvented herself to suit the new country she found herself in, shedding her earlier life and culture like an old, too-tight coat that she had long outgrown. And yet she had saved these pictures, tangible links to the past Jaya had tried and failed to get out of her – and, judging by the creases, she'd treasured them, looked at them often.

Why did her mother have these photographs? She had always hinted that she'd come from a poor background, so how was she connected to the mansion? *Gaddehalli*. It obviously meant something to Sudha.

She turns to the third item. Another notebook, even older than the other, its pages falling apart. And, like the pictures, carrying the smoky aroma of fire. Her mother had said that Jaya's dad's passport had been destroyed in a fire. That was the only time Jaya had glimpsed the emotions behind her mother's remote mask. Perhaps she had been telling the truth. Perhaps there *had* been a fire.

Jaya is aware of her heartbeat quickening as she opens the book. Another diary! This one penned in Kannada. She picks up the newer diary again and looks inside – it is written in English. The words inscribed on the back of the group picture of the unfamiliar family are in English too, the language of her mother's adopted country. She flicks through both books. The entries are all undated. Did her mother write the older diary, the one in Kannada, in India, and the second one here? Why write in English when Kannada came more naturally to her, the language of her childhood, her first home?

Sudha had always insisted that they talk in Kannada at home. She had taught Jaya to read and write in the language. When Jaya had started school, she had rebelled against it. 'Why don't you talk to me in English?' she had whined. 'Why do I have to speak to you in Kannada?'

'Because it's my mother tongue. And it would have been yours too if we hadn't come here.'

'But we are here now and I want to speak in English.' Jaya had stamped her foot.

'English may be your first language but it is not mine. I'm not fluent in it like you are.'

'You would be if you spoke to me in English,' Jaya had grumbled, and, when her mother didn't respond, she'd added, 'But why do I have to learn to read and write it? It's like having extra homework.'

'You are learning to read and write Kannada – that is final,' her mother had said in that tone that brooked no argument, her face taking on that unshakeable expression that Jaya was so familiar with.

Had Sudha intended to tell Jaya about her roots sometime in the future? Is that why she'd made Jaya learn Kannada? Whatever the reason, she'd taught Jaya Kannada and for that, now, many years later, Jaya is grateful.

Before Jaya delves into her mother's secret world, she meticulously goes through her belongings, these relics of a life, again. She doesn't want to miss anything. But there is nothing else out of the ordinary – just the photographs of the little boy and of the family, and her mother's diaries. Perhaps, contained in these books, Jaya will find the real Sudha. Perhaps she will even find her father.

Chapter 5
Kali

Black-winged Foreboding

'Kali, here's your medicine,' I hear, as if from far away.

A multitude of small white balls resting on a wrinkled palm, a tumbler of silvery liquid.

'Kali, please take your pills now.' The voice brings to mind waterlogged meadows, gleaming silvery green in the post-monsoon glow.

I hunt for recognition in the voice, for something familiar in the liquid brown eyes. The woman's hair is covered by a headdress. Why? 'You're not my ma. Or my aunt.'

The woman sighs softly. She squats beside me, takes my hand in hers, like Manu used to under cover of darkness. 'No, I'm not.'

I stare at my own hand. Surely there's some mistake? When did my skin get so crinkly? Like scrunched-up paper. Like the marks criss-crossing my face after falling asleep on the bed of coconut fronds by the stream.

I touch one of my hands with the other, noticing how brittle it feels. The skin stretching over my knuckles has folded into itself, looking like it has been pinched a thousand times.

'Have I been ill?'

The woman nods.

'My skin. Is that why I have to take medicine?'

'It's not quite to do with your skin. But yes, taking your medicine will help.'

I watch with fascination as my hand trembles making its way to my mouth, misses, and the woman has to help. I swallow the pills, bitter pellets which stick in my throat. I choke on the liquid that the woman feeds me, some of which trickles down the sides of my chin. There's something niggling in the back of my mind. What is it I meant to ask?

'Where's my ma?' I manage, although that's not quite it. Somewhere nearby a bird calls plaintively. I recoil as the niggle explodes in my head, turning into wails. Mournful. Going on and on. 'Stop,' I scream, rocking to and fro, feeling like I'll burst out of my body. 'Make it stop.'

I know then where I am. What has happened. And I don't want to know. I cover my ears with my unsteady hands. I shudder, begin to shake. I hear loud shrieks that seem so close. My throat is thick, hoarse. My ears ring. And I realise then that *I* am the one screaming.

'Shhh… it's okay, it's fine,' someone says.

But it's not. It's not. This is how; this is where it all begins…

✳   ✳   ✳

It is a sweltering day, an ordinary one, when my life changes.

I am sitting in the dirt outside the ramshackle building that passes for a school, chanting times tables with the rest of the pupils, thinking that at sixteen I'm a bit old for this but

knowing there's nothing to be done when there are not enough
teachers to take individual classes. At least I can let my mind
wander, think of Manu, who is helping his father out in the
fields. I sigh, wanting the comfort of his arms.

I miss Manu when I'm at school. Manu attends the college
in town when his father doesn't need his help in the fields.
When he's attending college, he comes up to the school in
the evening and we walk home together. On the days he's
working with his da, like today, I wait for him by the stream,
and we skim stones and spin dreams for our future together.

Beside where I'm sitting, an ant hefts a crumb and makes
its way across the mud, deftly swerving round pebbly hurdles.

I have fallen head over heels in love, I muse, sampling the
air, aromatic with the juicy pink fragrance of ripening guava.
I fancy I am like the heroine of my favourite book, the one
I discovered in a neglected cardboard box here at school: a
forgotten donation from a visiting do-gooder. The book was in
English, but I was besotted by the cover: a sensuous, beautifully
dressed white woman, the upper part of her face hidden by
the most gorgeous hat, lounging against a white wall and, in
the background, a black man staring at her, mesmerised. I'd
taught myself to read while waiting for teachers to turn up at
school – no one appearing at all more often than not – running
my finger over each word and looking it up in the tattered
Kannada-to-English dictionary until the words made sense.

The book was a love story set in South Africa, between
a white girl and a black boy during apartheid. The heroine
did not care that her love was forbidden, that she would be
ostracised from her community, that she would lose everything

– her pretty clothes, her wealth, her family, the protection of her people. She understood that she was willingly choosing a troubled life by falling in love with the wrong person, but for her it was inevitable.

For me too, I think, conjuring up Manu's face, those eyes that twinkle with mischief and gleam with love for me. 'Loving him is like breathing. I can't stop doing that,' the heroine in the book declared. I sobbed when she and her love were both shot dead – not only for the girl but for all she gave up.

I had stolen the book from school, taking it home boldly one dozy bee-stung afternoon when no teachers had turned up yet again. I've read it enough times to know it by heart, to compare and contrast every step of the heroine's tragic love story with mine. I am holding out hope, of course, that mine will have a happier ending. The book is my guide and my Bhagavad Gita – it inspires and instructs. I use it to navigate the many complications that love brings, the latest being how to get our parents to agree to our betrothal. Should we threaten to kill ourselves?

Since Manu's declaration on the evening of the power cut, nothing concrete has happened.

'It's my ma,' Manu had said the previous evening, chewing on a stalk of grass in frustration and squinting up at the sky, which had darkened with threatening clouds. 'She keeps coming up with reasons for us not to marry… I think she doesn't like your ma. But that has nothing to do with us. It's so annoying. I'm not a child any more. I know what I want. You. Only you.' His voice was soft with adoration for me. 'I want my parents' blessing, but if Ma keeps doing this, I'll threaten to elope…'

I had opened my eyes and looked up at him then. I was lying on the soft bed of grass beside the gurgling stream, my head on his knees. Above me, the sky cracked and fizzed with electric premonition, the air blue with the crisp thrill that precedes a storm. Manu had held my gaze, and then he had bent down and kissed me for the first time, as the heavens exploded and rain fell on us like a blessing from the gods.

A butterfly, gold flecks and turquoise flutters, glides past. The air smells of frying fish and bubbling rice. I stumble on seven times six. Two heads bob up over the mossy, weed-infested brick wall that separates the school compound from the street. Sarlakka and Chinnakka hefting baskets on their heads, on their way home from the market. They set the baskets down on the other side of the wall, right across from me, to catch their breath and have a chinwag.

I hear a melodramatic whisper, 'Have you heard?'

'Heard what?'

I blunder on eight times eight. My ears are angled, set to eavesdropping mode. This is why I sit at the very edge of the semicircle of kids, so I can listen out for gossip. I give up reciting and just mouth the words, so Devaki ma'am, the latest in a long procession of teachers, won't be suspicious. She's concentrating on the younger kids anyway, her eyes bloodshot, her face stressed. I pluck a blade of grass, stick it between my teeth and lean surreptitiously towards the wall.

'…ran away…' is all I hear.

Then a gasp. 'No!'

'She left a note. They must have snuck off in the night. They've been planning this for ages, looks like…'

Suddenly Sarlakka's head pops over the wall, her gaze locking with mine. Her face blanches, going pale. Looking right at her, I feel the first tremor of impending doom. Sarlakka avoids my curious gaze and, bending down to pick up her basket and set it on her head, walks off without a backward glance, ignoring Chinnakka's pleas for more information.

There's a pause. I realise that everyone has stopped chanting the times tables, just as Devaki ma'am says, 'Kali? Is anything the matter?'

I shake my head, trying with difficulty to shake away the unease that seems to have invaded my body. Then I hear a shout. 'Kali, go home at once.'

I am up and running, past the fields, chasing away the crows perched on the coconut tree felled during a thunderstorm. The crows scatter in a demonic cackle, a constellation of black-winged foreboding, upsetting the grazing cows, setting the dogs howling. And all the while I am thinking, anguish pulsing in time to my footfall, *I should have guessed earlier.*

This morning, Da's bullock cart was missing. He had come home late last night and he had seemed happy. Unusually so. He'd smiled as he'd eaten his supper; he'd smiled as he smoked his beedi in the courtyard, the yellow tip punctuating the star-sprinkled dark. And I'd smiled, companionably, right along with him, both of us lost in our own blissful imaginings.

And in the morning, the bullock cart was gone.

✳   ✳   ✳

'Kali… Ow…'

I realise that I am gripping someone's hand hard, muttering over and over, 'I should have known.'

'Kali, please let go, you're hurting me,' a voice says gently.

'I should have looked for the bullock cart, searched for Da. Instead I drew water from the well, filled the bucket, washed my face, ate congee and went to school, just the same as always. I was thinking of Manu. I wasn't thinking of Da...'

'Yes,' the voice, the same one that soothed me moments before, now grates on my overwrought nerves.

'I don't want your pity,' I scream, opening my eyes, only then understanding that they were closed all this while.

Light ambushes me. Stinging yellow. Unwelcome. I close my eyes to shut out the brightness and the knowledge that opens up a yawning abyss of pain within me. I hurt. But... why? It's slipped my mind, whatever it was that caused my pain. I cannot remember.

Chapter 6
Jaya (Now) and Sudha (Before)

Indigestible Truth

Jaya's hand wobbles as she picks up the older diary, the one that smells of ash and damp and stirring secrets. It feels powdery to the touch. She opens it tenderly. The first entry was written when Sudha was a child Jaya understands from skim reading the first few sentences, her mother's handwriting bigger, messier, without the shape and finesse of her later years.

Jaya's eyes tingle as she runs her fingers over her mother's words. Her mother's words!

Why write in two different languages? she wonders again.

Jaya is as ready as she will ever be for this glimpse into the girl her mother once was, the woman she was to become. The guarded, tightly wound woman who never gave of herself completely. Who drove Jaya to distraction. But who loved her so very much.

'Thank you, Mum,' she whispers as she drinks in the childish yet familiar handwriting of her mother's first diary entry and starts to read her mother's words.

✴   ✴   ✴

Dear Diary,

Okay, how do we do this?

My teacher says we should always introduce ourselves when we first meet someone. So…

I am Sudha. I have decided to write to you because… because something happened today which finally gave me the push I needed. I've always meant to do this but never got around to it. Until now. After what happened. Oh, just the thought of it…

I need somewhere, a sacred place where I can be myself. And I have decided that you, Diary, are it. I wear so many faces; try to be someone I am not, almost all the time. It is exhausting.

But even now that I have the courage to write to you, I am worried about what will spill out if I let myself go, confide everything I feel, all that I keep hidden away underneath the many false layers. I am apprehensive about the person who will surface in these pages.

You see, this much I know. And you should too, if we are to be close. If I am to be honest.

I am evil.

My parents don't say it out loud, but I know it's what they're thinking every time they see me, the regret flashing across their faces, the shadow of a dream, of what might have been, before their expressions clear and they smile. Although it is not the beaming smile it could be.

They are faking too, you see. They fake. I fake. We all fake.

'Murderer' is what they are thinking. 'If not for you, your brother would be here.'

The unspoken question: why couldn't it have been him, here, instead of you? Grief and longing for their only son, snatched cruelly from them. They couldn't even mourn him properly, because they had me to look after, the monster they created, the daughter who stole their son, the girl who forever lives in his saintly shadow.

I am wicked. For resenting the fact that I had a twin.

Most of the time, I wish it was me who had died. Me who was the godly one. Then I feel guilty for being jealous of my dead twin. And for wishing that he had never existed, wishing him away even after he is dead. Has been dead for as long as I have been alive.

I have whiled away countless hours spinning a fantasy where I am an only child, born to older parents. Much longed for. Adored. And it's all true, except for the adored bit.

I am forever tainted by my brother's desperately short life, a small flicker casting a very long shadow.

A dead brother who is more alive than I feel at times. More cherished than I will ever be.

Guilt. A bitter tonic I gorge on every single day. When I wake up in the morning, there is that minute of unawareness, of contentment, before guilt rises in my throat. Guilt and shame, that's what I think I am made of. The blood that runs in my veins, the blood that should have flowed in my brother's veins too, is tinted blue I imagine, with – yes, you guessed it – guilt.

Did I know, I sometimes wonder, when he stopped breathing? Or was I blissfully ignorant? Too happy growing and feeding myself in our mother's womb to think of my brother beside me?

Other times I wonder what it would have been like if he had survived.

Would they have loved me completely, wholeheartedly, then, and not grudgingly, doing their duty by me?

I would not have been a living memory of what my parents lost, what I denied them, for one.

I observe other parents with their children, the pride in their eyes. I cannot help but compare them to my own, so lacklustre.

And yet I know I cannot blame them. The blame is all mine.

I love them. My parents. Love them more than life itself. But they… they love the dead more than the living. I understand that part of them died with Sudhir, my twin. The best part.

What am I capable of? This is what I am most scared of. This is why I always give in to my parents. This is why I do not push against the boundaries they impose. If I can kill my twin, who knows what else I can do?

When I was little, I was blessedly unaware of these undercurrents. I loved my parents fiercely and expected the same in return. I would fling my arms around them and be puzzled at the moment or two of hesitation before they opened their arms.

And yet even inside their arms I felt cold. There was a distance, a draught, the air beside me populated with a sigh.

I did not know then that what I was sensing was their loss.

I was five when it sank in. I had coaxed Ma to take me to a fair in the village, drawn by the smell of roasting peanuts and caramelised sugar, by the festive crackle and bang of fireworks and excitement.

I was eating candyfloss, taking huge gulps of the pink fuzz that melted into sweetness in my mouth.

'Look at her eating,' someone said behind me.

Ma was momentarily distracted by the bangle vendor. She had let go of my hand.

'Eating without a care in the world. Just like she ate her brother's share in the womb. He died because of her eating. Destroyed her parents. Poor things. They can't have any more kids. Stuck with the girl. Their own daughter killing their son. They can't even celebrate her birthday as it's the day their son passed.'

The candyfloss turned as bitter as an indigestible truth in my mouth.

It all suddenly made sense. The hesitation my parents showed when they hugged me. The uncomfortable silences when we were together. My birthdays... All we ever did for them was go to the temple, and my ma always cried.

'Why do you cry on my birthday?' I had asked her.

'Because I am happy,' she had choked.

I've tried my very best to right that wrong. To rectify my mistake.

I eat very little as penance for overeating in the womb.

I have always done my parents' bidding.

But now…

Now there is a boy.

He sits in front of me in class. I secretly admire and adore him. The way his hair curls. That shorn part at the nape of his neck, vulnerable, naked, cringing from the kiss of his shirt collar.

Yesterday, out of the blue, he passed me a note.

The smell of moist paper and sweat. The thudding, heart-hammering taste of excitement as I smoothed the scrunched-up sheet.

There was an R, for his name: Ravi. Then a heart. Then S. For Sudha.

He did not turn to look at me. But I watched his neck turn red.

I love him. But I dare not tell him so.

I did not acknowledge his note. I walked out of class, my head bent as always.

I don't know what tomorrow will bring.

I am eager. Impatient. Nervous.

I am happy.

I refuse to feel guilty for being happy even when a little voice in my mind whispers: 'Your brother will never feel like this. Your brother will never know love. Because of you.'

To punish myself, I eat less than ever. I am sure my parents notice how little I eat. But they don't say anything. I suppose they don't care.

I wish they would. Notice. Care.

My stomach is rumbling as I write this. I think with longing of the chakulis my ma keeps in that alcove behind the stove. But I will not sneak into the kitchen and eat them. My brother doesn't even know the crunchy, spiced-cumin taste of chakulis.

My heart thrums with nerves as I think of school tomorrow. He likes me, the boy I have idolised from afar.

A miracle. How did it happen?

This is why I wanted to write to you. To divulge this secret. Keep it safe with you. I was bursting to tell someone.

I don't have friends, you see. I am too dutiful. I don't talk during lessons. I listen to what the teachers say. I rush home as soon as the bell rings.

The other girls are wary of me. The boys make fun of me. Except Ravi.

Ravi has always been a law unto himself. He is good at studies and yet the other boys respect him. This is because he is the best at cricket and lagori. Plus he's good-looking and all the girls like him.

And yet… he likes me.

And I wanted to tell someone.

I don't know why I haven't done this before now, shared with you. You are the friend I have always wanted.

Thank you, friend, for listening.

✳ ✳ ✳

Jaya sets the precious book, this unexpected gift of her mother's past, down very carefully. Tears splotch, tinting the fragile yellow page. She cannot read any more, not just now. She needs to process what she's found out, equate what she has learnt about this sweet, sad girl with the mother she knew. Or didn't know. Not really. Not at all, as it turns out.

Mum, my God. I am so sorry. How could I have been so selfish? So very absorbed in all the ways you had failed me that I refused to see the real you, even after I became an adult. And thus I failed you.

You were always a small eater. A habit honed through a lifetime, I realise now. It irritated me. You made me feel gigantic with your bird-like body, your tiny appetite. And yet you always encouraged me to eat. You never once said anything to put me down.

I yearn to give you a hug. To love you like you weren't loved by your parents. Is this why you were distant with me? Not knowing how to demonstrate what you felt because you had always kept part of you hidden. Because you were always performing, from the time you were a little girl, so that you forgot how to be, so that you were removed even from yourself.

Something claws at the closed door to the study. Frenzied scratches. Mewling. Mr Fluff.

Jaya blinks, coming back to herself. Shadows angle in through the window, swallowing the room. She carefully packs away her mother's things, setting them out of Mr Fluff's reach and then opens the door to the cat, scooping him up and burying her face in his fur, revelling in his warmth, her heart aching for the girl her mother once was.

Chapter 7
Kali

Four Bald Innocuous Words

'Why have you covered your head?' I ask, reaching out to touch the cloth masking the hair of the strange woman hovering beside me.

'It's a wimple. I'm a nun. I'm here to take care of you.'

'Why? Are there no teachers again? I am well able to care for myself, thank you. It's the younger ones who need looking after.' I gather some saliva in my dry throat, as a thought occurs to me, travelling on the wings of expectant anticipation. 'Are you bringing more storybook donations for the school? Where's my ma?'

But even as I ask it, the answer arrives on the heels of distress. My ma is upset. My ma is destroyed.

I shouldn't be here, wasting time, hoping for reading material. I should be taking care of my ma.

I clasp the woman's arm urgently, nails dragging. 'I have to find my ma – she needs me.'

And I am back, slap bang in the middle of that fateful day when my life turned on its head…

* * *

Ma is on the doorstep, huge wails racking her body. The whole village has turned up to watch the spectacle of my mother going to pieces. Some of the women pat Ma's back, stroke her hair. Others hit their forehead, their chest, as they wail along with her. 'Aiyyo the disgrace!'

'Kali,' Ma moans when she sees me, opening her arms, 'Oh, Kali, what will we do?'

I am engulfed in her salty embrace, rocked against her fleshy body. *What will we do?* A refrain that will become the main thing my mother utters over the coming months.

'What happened?' I manage to ask above my mother's howls, and the dread that I have managed to keep at bay balloons, squashing my chest so it is hard to breathe. Hard to think.

'Your da, he's gone.' Ma's cries swell around those few unfathomable words, as she repeatedly hits her head with her fist. And I stand in my mother's wet, spicy embrace, confusion, fear, anger and distress robbing me of words.

At the back of my mind, I had an inkling. The missing bullock cart had nagged at me this morning. Da wasn't meant to be working in the fields today, so why take the bullock cart, and so early? I had wondered before thoughts of Manu took over. But despite that I am shocked, hearing the words out loud. Four bald, innocuous words, capable of changing our lives forever.

'Da?' I whisper, when I am able to speak. 'He wouldn't. Why would he? He's happy…' I think of the previous evening when he was so uncommonly happy. I think of how he usually is of an evening, his brow permanently furrowed in Ma's presence, his back hunched as if flinching from Ma's verbal blows, her relentless nagging. Perhaps he's not happy with Ma. But… he cares for me. He calls me his shining star, his delight. He spoils me. Da *loves* me. He wouldn't abandon me, would he?

I think of how he has taken to disappearing whenever there is a power cut, coming back smelling differently, behaving as if he has something to hide. I think again of the silly, secret grin on his face the previous night, which excluded even me.

The villagers nod and murmur and shake their heads.

Ma moans at the top of her voice.

I sway on my feet.

But it is not over. Not yet.

'He's eloped,' one of the gathered women bites out through clenched teeth as my mother's screeches escalate in tone and pitch. 'With that slut Vasuki.' Her voice is thick with scorn.

No. No, no, no. I look up at the assembled, ogling crowd. Are they joking? *Please let it be so. Please.*

I think of Manu's face, his eyes dark and soft with love as he'd bent down to kiss me, the rightness of his lips on mine. I open my mouth, root around and eventually find the words I am searching for. 'Da bolted with Vasuki? M-Manu's ma?'

Not my Manu. No.

'It's been going on for a while. She left a note,' Chinnakka whispers, goggle-eyed.

'Your da didn't even leave a note. Nothing. He leaves me *nothing* after all these years together,' Ma weeps, hitting her chest.

I run then.

The villagers yell, 'Kali, come back. Your ma needs you.'

But I am flying through the fields and across Anthu's plot, coasting the fallen coconut tree, jumping over the puddles from the previous evening's storm. I fall, taste earth and snot and salt, my breath coming in panting gasps and only then do I realise that I am crying. Huge, breathless sobs. I pull myself back to standing, my hands and feet and clothes muddy, and I do not stop running until I come to the stream.

He is sitting, as I knew he would be, on the damp grass by the bank, skimming stones in the winking water. Fish slither past, a flash of silver scales, and weeds wave greenish violet from the undulating mercury depths.

I come to a juddering, heaving stop, inhaling the wounded smell of ripe guava and raw anguish and betrayal, and I watch him, like I did before, when I became aware of him for the first time. Looking at him hunched on the bank, cows lowing in the fields beside him, I can almost pretend it is yesterday again and our kiss is yet to happen and our future together is intact, untainted by the horrible knowledge that sits between us. I watch him sniff, rub his arm across his nose. He is crying, I realise, tears glinting on his cheeks.

'Manu,' I call, my voice breaking on his name, shattering into a dozen piercing shards.

He stills. But he does not look up. He does not turn. He picks up a stone and throws it into the water with more force than usual. It sinks. He throws another one in. He has made an art of skimming stones. He is the best in the village. He tried teaching me a couple of times. We giggled together at my terrible efforts. 'Not like that, Kali; gently does it.' Now there is nothing gentle about his hurling. He pitches the stones like he means to hit someone.

'Manu,' I call again. He does not acknowledge me. I walk down the verge towards him, sobbing still, unable to stop. He doesn't look up; he just lobs another stone into the water with all the force in the world.

I stand in front of him. 'Please, Manu,' I beg, 'look at me. Don't you care for me any more? Manu?' I reach a trembling hand out towards him.

'Don't touch me,' he growls in a tone I haven't heard before, raging and yet soaked with despair. 'I don't ever want to see you again.' He swipes at his eyes with the back of his hand. He won't look at me.

'You don't mean that.' I don't recognise the voice that escapes my throat, like a mewling, lost kitten.

'Don't tell me what I do or don't mean. Go away. Go.' Like I am a nuisance, a splinter penetrating his skin that he can't wait to be rid of.

I have to ask him. I have to know. In the days to come, I will hate myself for doing this, for grovelling, for sinking so low. But just then... just then, I needed to ask. 'Do you love me?'

Despite his warning, I lay a tentative hand on his shoulder. He shrugs my hand off as if callously shrugging away everything between us. 'What, like your da loves my ma?' he sneers, looking up at me for the first time and I recoil from the hurt and fury in his eyes.

'Leave, Kali,' he says then, his voice softer and incredibly sad. 'Just go.'

And somehow this hurts more than his anger. The hopelessness in his voice, the defeat in his gaze. It is torture to breathe in his familiar smell, sweat and earth and lime, and feel so far apart, so other. My whole body aches, wanting to be held by him. Doesn't he need me like I do him?

'What we had… did it mean nothing at all?'

'How can we be together, Kali? My father… He's devastated by what's happened. If I told him I was serious about you, it would… I can't. I just can't.'

'Then you do love me?' Hope flares in my heart again.

The wrath with which he turns on me makes me stumble backward. His eyes are awash with tears. 'How can you talk about love?' He brushes a palm angrily across his face. 'What is love? Is it what your father has declared for my mother, breaking two families? If so I want nothing to do with it.'

'But we…'

'There is no *we*,' he says, bringing his knees up to his chest and resting his head on them, not looking at me.

'Please, Manu.' I wait there for a beat, two.

'Leave, Kali.'

I wipe at my lips to rub away the memory of his kiss – was it only yesterday?

And I do as he asks.

* * *

'No!' I am screaming my agony, my heartbreak. I reach beside me, my flailing hands wrapping around something. I chuck it, hard, like Manu with his stones. A glass shatters into resplendent shards. It does not help, does not ease the pain. Manu and I fell in love, an innocent blooming, and now my father's illicit, dangerous love has sullied ours, ruined it. I am shattered, unmoored, distraught.

I kick out, sheets tangling. Why am I in bed? Where is my mother? She needs me.

'Kali,' a woman says. 'That's quite enough.'

'No. No, no, no.' The ache of loss, the sting of betrayal, will not be contained. I scratch and pull. I can feel my legs straining against the bedcovers. Then two pairs of hands are holding me down, stronger than me, and it is a relief not to fight, to give in. A pinprick of pain in my right arm, something flowing into me. Then there is quiet, peace, butterflies, times tables… the smells and sounds of a summer afternoon… women gossiping, men farming, children chanting… the heady aroma of paddy and gruel and guava and grass and stories… the taste of fried cashew nuts and syrupy jalebis… and love and lips and warmth… darkness…

Chapter 8
Durga

A Vast Wound

Who in their right mind would live here? Durga wonders, staring at the ruin. *Granted the madwoman is not in her right mind, but Ajji is presumably. Now I understand why Ma was puzzled when she heard that Ajji had moved here to look after an old, madwoman.*

She looks out the back of the rickshaw. The village children have fallen behind, mere dots now, scared off not by the angry faces Durga made at them but by the ruin drawing ever nearer, afraid the madwoman might get them and never let go. Stories of rakshasas, terrifying monsters and curses cast by vengeful ghosts, narrated by the elders in her hometown to scare Durga into good behaviour, resonate in her ears. She sneaks a glance at Lathakka. Her aunt is aiming for an unruffled demeanour but is worrying her sari pallu, bunching it and pulling it apart. She turns to Durga and tries on a reassuring smile. It resembles a tight, pinched grimace. A gust of wind blows into the rickshaw, carrying the sour tang of tamarind, making the flimsy fabric door cover spin and cavort like a dervish.

'We are near the mansion and I can't see any trace of smoke, or smell fire, or hear cries of trapped, wailing phantoms,' Durga says to Lathakka.

'Oh it happens alright,' the rickshaw driver wheezes. 'When the time is right.'

'And what time is that?' Durga retorts, but at that moment the rickshaw bumps over a huge boulder and the driver swears profusely as his head bounces against the roof, the rickshaw grinding to a sputtering halt.

Spying her opportunity, Durga jumps off the rickshaw and, stretching, looks up at the ruin.

'Durga, what are you doing? Don't you run away now,' Lathakka calls, poking her head out the rickshaw.

'And where will she run to? There's nothing out here. The curse will get her before she gets back to the village,' the driver snorts.

What he is saying is true, Durga realises, looking around. They are in the middle of nowhere. Only the ruin sits proud and lonely at the summit. The village is hardly visible from up here, nestling in the hollow at the bottom of the hill, what feels like a lifetime away. A few bushes are scattered among the yellowing grass and stone-littered mud. This close, the mansion is far bigger than she expected. So very huge and so very ruined. It has collapsed inward, into itself. A vast wound.

What happened to make you like this?

Somehow, standing there, breathing in the fruity breeze, nippy this far up the deserted hill, Durga is able to appreciate its long-ago splendour, to conjure up how it must have looked when it was whole, lording over a scant, muddy village of insignificant cottages. The path up the hill, which is wide enough for vehicles, is overgrown now, but it must have been paved once. Durga imagines fancy cars driving up and down in the mansion's heyday, dust staining the expensive paintwork, the smell of gasoline, the taste of adventure.

She pictures a chauffeur-driven car depositing her at the top instead of the rickshaw, women bedecked in golden finery stepping out of the mansion and heaping fragrant sandalwood garlands upon her, sprinkling rose water, offering spiced lemon sherbet and Mysore pak, folding their hands in greeting, heads bowed low. 'Welcome, esteemed guest.'

Durga smiles at the image she has conjured, feeling lighter, despite her tiredness and apprehension. 'You have such a vivid imagination,' her mother used to say fondly. She bends over and hugs herself hard to keep the pain inside, although it wants to escape in tears or, better still, in a stone flung hard, at the rickshaw, the driver, Lathakka.

She picks up a stone, but instead of hurling it where it could cause damage, like she wants to, she aims it with all her strength at the mansion, for existing, for harbouring her ajji, for bringing her so far away from her ma and da.

'Durga, what are you doing? Come inside at once,' Lathakka grumbles and adds, to the rickshaw driver, 'We are ready to start, aren't we?'

He ignores her, languidly scratching his stomach and watching the progress of Durga's tossed stone. It does not go far at all, flopping disappointingly close.

'Ha!' the driver laughs and Durga picks up another stone to chuck at him, to knock the smile right off his face, all her resolutions and promises to Lord Krishna vanishing. The driver ducks, reading her intentions, covering his head with his arms and yelling, 'No! You'll have to walk the rest of the way. I'm leaving if you...'

Something launches from the buckled roof of the ruin, emitting a blood-curdling squawk.

Durga drops the stone, her body trembling, her legs frozen in place. It's a crow, its black wings framed against the rose-grey sky. *Just a bird. Ah, Durga,* she hears her mother's voice in her head. *You and your imagination.* Durga shakes her head to chase away her unease. Her mother's voice gives her the courage to pull aside the flap of the rickshaw and climb back in.

'Are we going or not?' she asks with affected nonchalance, her voice giving no indication of the fright she's just had.

'You pay me four times the amount now, after this,' the rickshaw driver huffs to Lathakka.

'Your charge,' he added with a nod in Durga's direction, 'will suit that place – she's just as mad as the two old ladies up there. She almost killed me.'

'I didn't... You...' Durga moves forward in her seat, her hands itching to lock around the driver's neck.

'Enough.' Lathakka's arm holds her back 'Do you want us to have an accident and die right here? And what will your ma and da do then, when they wake up to find you gone?'

Durga shakes Lathakka's arm off with more force than necessary, thinking, *Will Ma and Da wake up? And when they do, will they be fine? Please, Lord Krishna, please let it be so.*

She slides to the very edge of the rickshaw as, with a groan and an effortful grunt from the driver, it resumes its cantankerous plod up the hill.

*   *   *

'You be good now,' Lathakka says to Durga as the rickshaw rattles to a stop outside the wrecked manor.

Please, Lord Krishna, help me to be good, so Ma and Da can come back to me, Durga prays as she lets go of the cloth covering the rickshaw opening. It flaps back with a small sigh, displacing a small flurry of dust particles into the air.

'I'll need to change that cover,' the rickshaw driver harrumphs as Durga steps out into the dappled light of impending dusk.

Durga looks at the mouldy curtain of his precious rickshaw and realises that she has ripped it in two. *How,* she thinks, *am I so naughty when I'm not even aware of it?*

The setting sun casts the shadow of the ruin across her dust-smeared feet, staining them the bluish black of charred ashes.

'You have to pay me four times the fare and extra for the cover,' the driver says as he lifts his seat to reveal a cavity within, from which he takes out a tiffin box. Durga's stomach rumbles ominously.

'You have come prepared, I see,' an unfamiliar voice mutters as the driver takes a laddoo out of his box and bites into it, raining crumbs onto his dirty lap.

The owner of the voice looks Durga over, her beady eyes lively and piercing, taking in Durga's worn, creased clothes, her fraying chappals, her wayward hair.

The woman is stooped, a wiry mesh of hair capping a face busy with lines. Durga searches her wrinkled face for traces of her plump, bustling mother. 'So,' the woman says, 'you're Nalini's daughter, eh?'

'As you would know if you'd made more of an effort to get to know me,' Durga retorts, tasting anger and disappointment, hopelessness and exhaustion. This shrunken woman is *nothing* like her kind, loving mother. No wonder they didn't get along. No wonder her ma ran away to marry her da. She also, Durga has to admit, does not appear to be either insane or possessed, or even cursed for that matter, although how one would determine that Durga doesn't know.

The rickshaw driver stops demolishing his laddoo to stare, first at Durga's ajji and then at Durga. Lathakka comes forward, wringing her hands, saying, 'Durga, no… Sumathiamma, your granddaughter…'

Durga's ajji laughs throatily, the many lines crowding her face relaxing into grooves etched onto tired, papery skin. 'You'll do very nicely,' she says, beaming at Durga in a way nobody has done for a very long time – since her parents' accident, in fact. And in her ajji's crinkled eyes, the mirth shining out of them so they glow like embers in the orange-tinted dusk, Durga sees her mother.

Chapter 9
Kali

Fairy-tale Mansion

I am being led outside – why? The warm breeze tastes of jackfruit, plump, yellow and juicy. I close my eyes and see meadows, stretching as far as the horizon. Women plant tender green ears of paddy, their hair and backs cloaked by umbrellas of dried, plaited coconut-tree fronds. A lone road is hewn in the middle of the fields, dust rising off it, ending at the base of a hill. At the top of the hill is a house, sprawling as wide as it is huge, glimmering in the sunshine – glamorous, enchanting, out of place. I stand and I stare until I feel a nudge at the base of my back. 'Keep moving, Kali.' And I heft my bag of possessions from one shoulder to the other, my eyes never leaving the mansion on the hill, as I walk towards a future I do not know, towards a life that I didn't ask for, my heart aching for what I have left behind.

* * *

I stopped going to school after my da fled with Manu's ma. Instead I kept vigil by the stream, waiting for Manu, refusing to take seriously his rejection of me the day we both discovered our parents' deception.

But he never came.

I watched his field from behind the jackfruit tree. But the field lay abandoned, and the door to his cottage was resolutely shut.

I went again this morning, before we left to come here, to my aunt's village. I went to the stream, to the field and, when he wasn't at either, to his house. I dared to knock on his door.

No answer.

'Manu,' I called, my voice catching on his name. 'I know you're in there. I want to see you, just once.'

'Go away.' His voice, finally. Hoarse, plaited with pain.

'Please. I'm leaving the village later today. Going to stay with my aunt in Gaddehalli.' I hated myself for begging, for wishing he would bound out of the house and hold me, plead with me not to leave – fight for our love.

A long pause. The air was infused with banana and cinnamon and longing.

Then, 'That's for the best.'

'Lagori,' a child yelled from among the fields to resounding cheers.

Chickens jabbed at the dust around my feet.

'But, Manu, we…'

'There is no *we*, Kali,' he said, his beloved voice stumbling on my name.

A dog howled, echoing my heart.

'Please, Manu. I… I love you. And I know you love me too.' Did I? I didn't know anything any more. I swallowed, tasting salt and entreaty, prayer and hope.

'Goodbye.' His voice barely above a whisper, hitching on a sob.

'Can't I see you?' The last of my self-respect ground into the dirt, pecked at by the chickens.

'Goodbye.'

And it was then, with my heart bleeding into the mud in front of his house, the air sprinkled with the laughter of gossiping women and frolicking children, soft against my hot, teary face, the sky the crushed violet of a bruise – it was then that I vowed never to let my heart be battered like this again. I would not allow myself to fall in love again. Love was ruthless. It reduced you. I would be strong. I would not be vulnerable. I would not beg.

Now I walk through the fields to my aunt's village, awed by the talismanic magnificence of the manor looming above me, giving off an enchanted glow.

I am hurting and devastated, at the lowest point in my life, having been abandoned by the two men that I love the most – both of whom I thought loved me too. I am in dire need of magic and here it is, right in front of me. I am drawn to the mansion and it is as if it has bewitched me, cast a spell. My tiredness disappears, if for a brief while. But reality intrudes of course. I hear my mother sob behind me. I try to ignore her. I will lift above this, all of it, remaining composed, dignified, like this house, sitting regally atop the hill. I'll strive to keep the promise I made myself this morning at Manu's cottage. I will not be like my mother, who has not stopped crying since my da ran away. It is as if she has lost *everything* by losing her husband – her words, her way of sugar-coating the truth. I yearn to yell at her that she did not 'lose' him – he left, with the mother of the boy I love.

Ma's public breakdown is disgraceful to watch, more so than the shame brought by my da's actions. She refused to go back to work – 'How can I face everyone?' – and our money, what little we had saved, stowed in an earthen pot behind the hearth, dwindled until we were living off the charity of our landlord who was loath to ask us to leave but hinted at it several times.

In the end, our landlord sent his wife. She awkwardly patted Ma's back and offered her sympathies. 'You have to vacate this house,' she said, looking more distressed than my ma. 'I'm sorry. The landlord said to tell you he doesn't run a charity.'

Ma wailed, hitting her head again and again. 'Oh fate, why are you punishing me? Rama, Krishna, Vishnu, Brahma, why have you abandoned me?'

In desperation, I contacted Ma's sister, my aunt Nandamma, who lives in Gaddehalli. And that is why we are here, hoisting our scanty belongings on our backs and walking from where the bus dropped us off to Nandamma's house.

I will not let what has happened destroy me, like it is my Ma, I promise myself as we walk. *I will make a life for myself, a good one, so that one day, my da and Manu will look at me and wish they had behaved differently towards me, done right by me.*

The fields thin out and the narrow path widens. Then we are passing dwellings on either side, as if the mud has germinated toadstool-shaped houses. We duck into a passageway and stop in front of a house not much bigger than the one I grew up in, in the village where I left behind the boy I love. My uncle is standing outside the house, truculent, his eyebrows joined in a thunderous scowl. As soon as she sees him, Ma starts weeping again. I cringe in embarrassment. My uncle's expression remains unchanged through Ma's howls.

The whole village has collected in groups to witness our noisy arrival and I am speared by curious, wary, pitying, scornful gazes.

This is becoming a habit, this performing to a crowd.

There is nothing I hate more, I have found in the course of this ordeal, than becoming the subject of speculation, fodder for gossip.

Dusk has fallen, milky blue, and the air that brushes my face is tart with lime. During a break in Ma's cries, my uncle speaks, stormy-eyed, stern-jawed. 'You can't stay here long.'

I look down at my broken chappals, held together by safety pins. My legs are painted orange with a glaze of mud. I stare at my feet until I am certain the flush staining my mortified face has subsided. Then I look right at my uncle and say, above my mother's screams and the collected villagers' sniggers, 'Thank you for having us, Uncle. We won't stay long. I'll find a job soon and somewhere to live.' He looks me up and down, then nods and goes into the house. I let out the breath I've been holding.

The villagers murmur among themselves. The crisp, scorched odour of smoke infuses the air, someone's evening meal burning, abandoned in favour of Ma's ruckus.

'Go and have a wash,' my aunt tells my ma.

Ma's shrieks die into defeated hiccups, interspersed with the odd whimper. She obeys her sister meekly, head bowed, the crushed victim. Show over, the villagers return to their houses, talking loudly among themselves, dissecting us newcomers, not caring if they are overheard.

Once my ma has gone indoors, my aunt sits herself down on the veranda stoop. 'Put your bag down,' she says.

I set it down and sigh with relief, moving my neck to get rid of the cricks.

'Don't mind him. He's moody as hell,' my aunt says, flicking her head towards the house that is to be my home for the foreseeable future, indicating her morose spouse. 'Especially when he's not eaten.' She grins, showing paan-stained teeth and she looks younger and quite pretty, as the worry lines congregating at her eyes and pulling her mouth down are momentarily smoothed. 'Look – he would never have let me bring you here unless I had a job lined up for you.' My aunt extends a hand and squeezes my palm. 'I know how hard this must be for you, to lose your da and also, in some respects, your ma, in one swoop.'

And my love. I lost my love too.

I gulp, trying to swallow my tears. It is this unexpected kindness that is my undoing…

What upsets me tremendously, almost as much as Manu's rejection of me, is the fact that I still miss my da. Despite all he has done, the hurt he has caused, I miss him. I want to hate him and I do despise his actions, but I long for him too, especially now that Ma is like this. We would have shared with each other, commiserated together. We were always a team, my da and I.

A flash of lightning pierces the navy twilight, briefly casting the drab surroundings in a more flattering glow, giving a magenta sheen to the pelt of dust smothering the village. Thunder bursts through a glower of clouds.

'You're so very brave,' my aunt says.

And now I give in. It has started to rain, mirroring the tears showering down my face. I cry for the selfish person my beloved da has shown himself to be and for my ma, who has become someone I don't recognise. I even miss her nagging – anything would be preferable to the weak, defeated victim who has emerged in her place. I cry for my dreams, for the love story I spun, for the catastrophic ending I didn't foresee.

Small drops feed the earth, the concentric circles stippling the ground widening, becoming waves of churning mud in a matter of seconds. The evening is aromatic with the scent of wet earth. Naked children run out into the downpour, opening their arms wide and twirling, their bare feet slipping in the sludge.

'Will I be getting my supper anytime soon?' calls the belligerent voice of Nandamma's husband, my unwelcoming uncle.

My aunt ignores him. 'I had hoped that your ma would start working again and that you could go to school,' she says to me. 'But it doesn't look like it, eh?' She sighs.

I wait, tasting rain and salt, soil and dread.

'As luck would have it, one of the girls at the big house has got married and left the village. They are looking for a servant. I suggested you.'

'The big house?' My eyes are drawn to the mansion. Lights have come on inside so it glows, a radiant beacon flickering through the curtain of rain.

'Yes. But, Kali, you'll have to stay there. Away from your ma, only visiting with us on Sundays. I know it will be hard, especially now that your da—'

'I'll do it,' I interrupt, surprising my aunt, who looks askance at me. 'When can I start?'

To work at the big house. The magical manor that has enticed me since I stepped foot in this village. To be away from Ma's constant snivelling. To not suffer the stab of shame and impatience and guilt. This is it. The chance to start afresh, to reinvent myself. To put into practice the promise I made myself – was it only this morning? – beside Manu's cottage.

I turn to my aunt and smile. Then like the village children, I run into the rain. I whirl around and around, my churidar swelling, while my aunt laughs, a bit unsure, saying, 'Come inside, Kali, have something to eat. I will not be able to cope with two people who have lost their minds. Your mother is more than enough.'

I open my mouth to the heavens, sampling the fruit-scented, hope-flavoured drops and laugh, for the first time since that day when my world shattered.

✳ ✳ ✳

'The big house! I'm going to work at the big house,' I sing. My voice sounds wrong, dry and croaky. I want to clap my hands but they will not do my bidding.

I open my eyes. It is dark – a swelling, undulating darkness like the inside of a well on a stormy night. I am stuck within a nightmare. My hands – I cannot move my hands. I open my mouth and shout, my own voice sounding alien, reedy. What has happened to my beautiful voice? My youth?

'It's okay, Kali, shush now,' someone soothes as my screams echo in the ballooning darkness.

'Where am I? What has happened to me?'

Light. Bright. Sudden.

I blink. Close my eyes and yet the light assaults my closed lids. 'I can't move my hands,' I cry, eyes shut tight.

'That's because you've caught them in the bedclothes, silly,' a gentle voice remonstrates.

I do not open my eyes, allowing the voice to pacify, to ease me into sleep again. Who is this? Not my ma. After my da ran off, it was I who had to look after my mother, me the adult at sixteen, my mother reduced to a wailing child stuck in a never-ending tantrum. I remember feeling unremittingly, constantly angry. Lost without the parents I'd known. Upset at having to abandon my childhood to become the responsible adult. Anguished at losing Manu. Then I discovered that I would be working at The House. The Fairy-tale Mansion. That was a good end to a tiring and upsetting day. A day when I'd said goodbye to all I knew and embarked on an adventure. An adventure that would lead me to…

'No,' I scream, startling out of the doze I was being lulled into, thrashing, struggling. 'No, no, no.'

Chapter 10

Jaya

Mangoes and Moist Earth

Jaya lies in her bedroom, struggling to sleep, her head filled with images of her mother as a young girl. Friendless. Blamed for the loss of her twin. Trying so desperately to please her parents. Confiding about her crush to a diary, her voice coming alive on the pages that catalogued her fears, her yearning.

Ben's side of the bed is now occupied by her mother's precious diaries and the photographs of the little boy. On impulse, Jaya picks up the photographs, flicks through them. Something about the boy tugs at her heartstrings.

She cannot remember sleeping, but she must do, for she has a vivid vision of a little boy playing in an orchard filled with the scent of mangoes and moist earth. The boy dances, carefree, revelling in the glorious, squidgy feel of mud beneath bare feet. His clothes are dirty. He pulls them off. The freedom of fruity air caressing a naked body. A still body. Unmoving.

Jaya jerks upright from where she is sprawled among her mother's things, her heart thudding. The hand she drags across her face comes away tear splashed. The front of her top is wet. Arun…

In her dream, the little boy from the photographs morphed into the baby she lost. Was it the boy from the pictures or was it her son as a toddler, older than she ever knew him, the boy Arun would have become had fate not conspired to take him away? She doesn't know. And why did she dream of an orchard? Fruit trees? Mangoes? Mud?

She shakes her head, rubs her eyes, picks up the group photograph and stares at the little boy who seems to be jumping out of his mother's arms and into hers.

What are you trying to tell me? she asks the boy.

Chapter 11
Kali

A Performance of Predicting the Weather

The sound of someone clapping – or is it banging – reaches my ears. From the way the air smells – fresh, like wet grass – I deduce I am outdoors, sitting on something soft. Splinters of sunshine, polished gold, pierce my languid lids. I am loath to open my eyes, to break this spell. Birds croon from high up among the trees, their song bringing to mind festivities, merriment. A party. I picture winking lights strung on banners, a celebratory feast, saris swishing, bangles clinking, perfume and sweat mingling, hearty laughter, dancing feet, gorged bellies…

And I am off, once again treading the hallways of my youth, a young girl working at the big house, trying desperately to find my way.

*　*　*

It is when I'm polishing the photographs in the main hall of the mansion that the idea comes to me. It is extremely audacious – outrageous even – but then I am a girl who prefers to live in the world of books. I've had enough of fate trying to pigeonhole my life story into a sad ending when I know I am destined for a bigger, better future.

And so, having eavesdropped at doorways and gathered information, when the plan arrives, fully formed in my head, I am awed by the beauty and simplicity of it. Yes, it is daring, but there's no reason why it won't work. It will. It has to…

I have been at the big house, which is what the villagers call the mansion at the top of the hill, a year. Enough time to settle in, to absorb its quirks and its traditions.

There are fifteen of us at the big house: the landlord, his wife, their son, and twelve servants including me, although I haven't seen the son yet – he's been away studying. He's now finished his education, due back home to take over the family business, and the entire household is buzzing in anticipation of his arrival.

I have come to love living in the mansion, nattering with the servants, being one of their gregarious posse. In their company, partaking of gossip, the small highs and lows of our days shared over a cup of spiced tea in the kitchen, I forget, for a brief while, everything that has happened.

The very best thing about the mansion is the library, stacked floor to ceiling with books, the neatly arranged tomes whispering intriguing invitations from the shelves. I immediately made sure the dusting of the books and the cleaning of the library became part of my job, and Radhakka, my boss, who was in charge of the domestic side of things, the cooking and the cleaning, was only too pleased.

What are you hiding between your covers? I muse every time I enter the library. *What lives are you welcoming me to live? Will they be better or worse than mine?*

New books arrive every week, a hefty package delivered by the postman, who always arrives out of breath after trudging up the hill. Radhakka, who has a soft spot for him, as he is her nephew's best friend, invites him into the kitchen and feeds him ginger and cardamom tea and whatever sweetmeat she has concocted for our employers' snack. If I or another of Radhakka's minions so much as look at the spread, we are subjected to Radhakka's famous glare.

'If you continue to eye the chattambades like that, everyone who eats them will get stomach ache. Go on, shoo! Chop the vegetables like I instructed,' Radhakka snaps at us before she turns to the postman, her face softening, a different woman altogether appearing as she smiles and urges him to eat.

I am fascinated by the landlord and his wife. I stand at doors and blend into curtains to eavesdrop and observe their every move. I watch them go about their business in their fancy clothes and their fancy ways, and I dream, scaling the pinnacle of possibility. I want to be part of their hallowed circle. I want their easy authority, the seamless power they wield with such aplomb. I want to be the boss, to rise above the humiliation and hurt my da and Manu subjected me to.

What I have come to realise is that the landlord doesn't do much. He is the figurehead yes, but he leaves most of the running of the household and their various businesses to his wife. He is quiet, introspective and most of the time found sitting in his favourite chair in the library, reading poetry. The landlord's wife is firm but fair, a petite woman with an iron will, who is generous to us servants but keeps us in our place. I want to be like her. She is regal, effortlessly exercising authority and bestowing favours. Neither heartache nor betrayal, I am sure, would dare touch her. Her love would never spurn her. No mother of this poised woman would take to their bed after their husband left, ignoring their daughter and starving themselves into an early grave.

I watch the landlord's wife and I admire her: how she deals with lawyers and accountants, how she handles the bills, how she acts as though her husband is the boss when in fact it is she who is running the house, she without whom everything would fall apart.

One day, I tell myself, *that will be me.*

'Kali!' Radhakka yells from the kitchen and I sprint from my hiding place, back into the heat and noise, the spicy aromas and piquant flavours of the kitchen.

'Where have you been disappearing to?' Radhakka's face is a storm in full progress. 'Here, clean the fish!' Punishing me by giving me the worst possible job.

At night, when I am lying on the hard mat on the floor in the servants' annexe, sharing a room with all the other female servants and surrounded by their snores, I imagine that I am the landlord's offspring, loved and adored, sent to university, lapping up all the knowledge in the world, and that it is my triumphant arrival home that everyone at the big house is preparing for – it is *me* who will take over the family business.

Every Saturday evening, after the evening meal has been served and the dishes washed and put away, the chauffeur drops all us servants off at our homes in the village. The landlord's wife makes sure we are driven home because it is dark, a small kindness she enacts as a matter of course.

As soon as I get out the car every Saturday night, shadow-bruised dust swirling in the car's wake, I take a deep breath and enter my aunt's house. She is usually still at work. My hostile uncle is smoking beedis and staring at the sky, scouring it for rain, making a performance of predicting the weather. I give him my week's wages, which he makes a point of counting, licking his finger and running it through the crisp notes that *I* have earned, branding them with his spit. I leave him and go to find my mother.

Ma is where she always is, lying on a mat in the darkest corner of the house, smelling rank, of grief and unwashed skin. As always, I fight the urge to shake her, to restore her to the mother she once was.

'Is that you, Kali? Come to see your dying ma?'

Barely fifty years old and skin and bones and talk of death. No 'how are you', no 'how is work'. Only self-pity: me, me, me.

Stop being a burden on your sister and her husband. Get up and live, I want to yell. Instead I chew the inside of my left cheek until I taste the hot, sweet tang of blood. 'How are you, Ma?'

'I don't have much time left, Kali,' she whines. 'See what he has done, your da. Destroyed me.'

No, you have done this to yourself. Only you.

I chew my other cheek. Ma starts to sob, lengthy, wheezing moans. My uncle snorts loudly from where he is lounging outside, smoking and eavesdropping on us. Nobody can stand Ma's terribly selfish and indulgent grief. Why can't she see that?

How could I have come out of you? I will never become like you. Vulnerable, weak, reduced, pitiful.

And a traitorous thought sneaks into my mind. *I wish the landlord's wife was my mother. Now she is a role model. Strong. Unflappable. So unlike you, Ma – you who need a man to feel complete.*

On Sunday morning, as soon as dawn burnishes the horizon with a gilt-edged glow, I make my way back up the hill to the big house, the thrill of living there reverberating through every bone. All the other servants are still in their own homes, making the most of their time off. The landlord and his wife are away at a hotel in Sannipur. They go every weekend, leaving after supper on Saturday, when the servants visit with their families, and returning late Sunday evening.

I let myself in using my own key to the mansion, entrusted to me ceremoniously by Radhakka when I'd completed my first year of service. 'Remember,' Radhakka had said gravely as she'd deposited the key into my palm with turmeric-stained fingers, 'this is a sign of your employers' faith in you. Don't abuse it. Many have and they've all been found out and kicked out with no hope of getting a job elsewhere, their life and livelihood destroyed.'

As I turn the key in the lock and push the ornate, carved door open, I can almost convince myself that I am the mistress of this imposing mansion. This is why I return so early on Sunday morning – to feel like this. Like I am the boss and the house is waiting for me to do what I please. I walk the empty, echoing, majestic rooms, taking my time in each one. I save the topmost storey, which houses the rooms of the landlord, his wife, and their son, for last, savouring the moment when I enter their rooms and allow my imagination to run free.

I stand in front of the landlord's wife's mirror and scrutinise my lowly servant's face, lifting my head higher, hardening my gaze, tautening my neck until I have her imperial stance and bearing down pat. I gawk at the landlord's wife's saris, rows and rows of them, a multi-hued kaleidoscope, the expensive material glinting. I lie on the luxurious bed; admire the en-suite bathroom, packed with lotions and shampoos, perfume and soap with exotic-sounding names, smelling edible. I squirt some lotion onto my calloused palms, my hands feeling soft, like a real lady's. I look out the window of the landlord's son's room and stare down the hill at the village, shimmering in a haze of mud.

Look at me, look where I am.

I smell rich and pampered, of borrowed (stolen) perfume, savouring the taste of borrowed (stolen) dreams in my mouth. And for a brief moment, I am able to be outside myself, forget who I am, what has happened, the sorrow I lug around. In that moment, I am happy. Then I spy Radhakka making her arduous way up the hill, stopping every minute to draw breath and I run down to the kitchen, regretfully washing off the perfume and lotion.

And then I overhear the conversation that will plant the germ of an idea that will grow and take me over…

The landlord's son is due back home in a week's time. The household is poised, awaiting his arrival. I am dusting in the far corner of the library, ensconced, out of sight, when the landlord's wife bursts in. The landlord is sitting in his usual chair by the window, his legs stretched out on the divan, a cup of tea and a plate of potato bondas beside him. He has been here all day, working his way through the latest consignment of books, delivered the previous day by the postman – who was treated to masala dosas and spiced tea by Radhakka for his efforts.

'So I was thinking…' the landlord's wife begins.

'Yes?' the landlord murmurs, without looking up from his book, a small smile playing on his lips, whether from what he is reading or from his wife's words it is hard to say.

I surreptitiously flatten myself against the curtains, breathing in the damp, inviting scent of knowledge in the multitude of tomes around me and, thus hidden, shamelessly watch and listen.

'We'll have a party when Vinay gets home. I'll invite all the neighbouring landlords and politicians with eligible daughters. Let's hope *someone* catches his eye.'

The landlord nods absently, pushing his glasses up his nose and bringing his book up closer to peer at the page.

'The thing is,' the landlord's wife continues, sighing deeply, 'that education we are paying so much for has filled his head with nonsense. He tells me he will not marry for money or status but for love. That, though, I suspect,' she says with an arch glance at the landlord, 'comes from you. The romantic in him. After all, he's a poet too.'

The landlord looks up at his wife and smiles. 'Nothing wrong with that.'

I feel a pang at the tenderness in the landlord's eyes when he looks at his wife. I dreamt of being loved like that. I fancied I saw it in Manu's gaze…

'Vinay tells me he doesn't care for position or reputation. I asked him outright if he has found someone unworthy and he sighed and said that nobody is unworthy. Then, when I wouldn't let the subject go, he relented and confessed that he doesn't have a girlfriend. Thank goodness! He wants one, he told me. He categorically does not want an arranged marriage.'

Anxiety colours the landlord's wife's voice the inky black of a roiling sea. In the time I have worked for her, I have come to understand that the lady of the house likes everything – including, it appears, her son's love life – running smoothly and according to one plan only – hers.

A fly buzzes somewhere beside me. A shaft of sunshine angles in, making dust motes glitter like tinsel on top of the yellow-spined shelves.

'I can't sit here and do nothing. We have to act fast, before he finds someone immensely unsuitable.' The landlord's wife tuts. 'That's why I'm planning a party and inviting all the eligible girls around. This way, we are both happy. He thinks *he* is choosing, when I have invited only the girls who I think he should marry. The sooner he is linked with someone of our ilk the better. Before he makes up his own mind and… I shudder to think.'

The landlord nods absently, lost in his poems again.

'He is sensitive. He needs a girl who understands him.'

'Hmmm…' her husband murmurs, taking a bite of his bonda, showering crumbs all over the floor, which I will have to mop later. He does not look up as his wife paces beside him.

'A girl who is intelligent, who likes books. He will not be happy with someone who's just pretty.'

'Uh huh.' The landlord surreptitiously flips a page.

'I think the Maddurhalli landlord's daughter is perfect. She's beautiful and only three years younger than Vinay. And she's studying English at college.'

The landlord finally looks up at his wife again. 'But I thought you said Vinay wanted to choose. How…'

From somewhere within the house I hear Radhakka's strident voice calling, 'Kali! Kali…? Where has that girl got to now?'

I stifle the hysterical giggles that threaten to burst out of me even as the heady taste of stolen moments and someone else's secrets fills my mouth. From the open windows of the library, hot, guava-scented air bursts in, carrying a cacophony of barks, the high-pitched voice of the head gardener chastising his posse, the sputter of a vehicle winding up the hill.

'Oh, it'll be fine. I've met the girl at several parties. She's just Vinay's type. Feisty and not too meek. He likes girls with spirit – I know that for a fact.'

'How?' The landlord shuts his book at last, and his wife beams, triumphant at having won this round in her losing battle for her husband's attention.

'I overheard Vinay talking to Bala, the last time he came home.'

'You eavesdropped on his private conversation with his best friend?'

I shrink further into the curtains. Eavesdropping is not *that* bad surely?

'I was passing by his room – he hadn't even closed the door. They were discussing their ideal woman. Of course I listened!'

The landlord shakes his head and smiles, that soft, sweet smile he reserves just for his wife.

'I'll leave it to you,' he says, before going back to his book.

That afternoon, as I am dusting the photographs of Vinay on the mantelpiece in the living room, it comes to me. *What if…?* I think of what the landlord's wife said, her words going around and around in my head. *Spirited girl, intelligent, someone who likes books… He doesn't care for position or reputation. He will not marry for money or status. He says nobody is unworthy…*

I look at Vinay's smiling face. He is not Manu. But Manu doesn't want me. And to get to where I want to be, Vinay will do very well indeed.

Chapter 12
Jaya (Now) and Sudha (Before)

Rainbow Sky

'I've been going through my mum's things, Ben,' Jaya says into the phone, feeling a sudden urge to rest her head on Ben's shoulder. She closes her eyes and imagines both of them sitting here, like they used to, his arms around her, the kiss of weak sun on their faces as they sip coffee and talk. She cannot recall when they last did this. Everything has become so complicated between them.

Jaya is at what was once their favourite café, sitting at one of the tables outside, watching Londoners go about their business. Some have only just woken up, ambling drowsy eyed and hungover to the patisserie across the road. Couples share brunch and browse the papers, a leisurely start to their Sunday. She feels a stab of longing for the young, carefree couple she and Ben were – it seems so long ago, that hazy time uncoloured by grief, untainted by loss, the future a delightful gift to be unwrapped at their leisure. They would wake to the delicious prospect of a day together stretching ahead, make love and drift off to sleep again among tangled sheets. Then later, ravenous, they'd stroll hand in hand to this very café in search of sustenance and to catch up on what the world had been getting up to while they'd been lost in each other.

They'd met at this café, she and Ben. She had been reading the book she'd just bought from the shop down the street, the book she'd been waiting months for. She hadn't noticed the café filling up, the man approaching, saying, 'Mind if I share this table with you?' One look at his twinkling eyes, the deep grey of an autumn sky, his friendly smile and the laugh lines crowding his mouth, and she was lost.

They'd made it a tradition after that. Having Sunday brunch here to celebrate how they met. Although they hadn't kept up that tradition for months now…

Dr Meadows' face looms in front of Jaya's eyes, her voice echoing in her head: *You need to go through your mother's things… put your grief, your anger at her behind you, in order to move on.*

Dr Meadows is right, Jaya concedes. She woke this morning feeling more rested than she has in months, despite the disturbing dream she'd had of the boy from her mother's photographs… Her heart felt full, overcome by the knowledge of how much her mother had loved her, her head swirling with her mother's words, written when she was just a child. She had brushed her teeth, fed Mr Fluff and then come here, bringing the earlier one of her mother's diaries with her, unable to part from it – this window into her mother's life. And then she'd called Ben.

'I wish I'd been there for you,' Ben says. 'It must have been emotional, going through her things…'

Jaya clutches the phone closer to her ear, biting her lower lip to stop herself crying. She's touched by Ben's words. Sifting through her mother's belongings, reading her words, has made Jaya evaluate her own life, look at it objectively, and she knows that nothing is right in her world. She and Ben are existing, side by side. That is all. When was the last time she and Ben were there for each other? This offer, his kindness, which, not too long ago she would have taken for granted, means more to her than she can put into words. So she doesn't try, telling him instead about her mother. 'Mum had kept a diligent record of my life – every picture, every single scrap of paper I scribbled on.'

When was the last time she and Ben had talked – properly talked – about things that mattered to them?

'Wow, Jaya.'

When was the last time she'd called him while away on one of his trips, which had been nearly every week recently?

'And you know how it drove me mad that she never talked about her past?' Jaya says.

'Yes?'

'I… I found pictures of a little boy, Ben.'

'A little boy? Among your mother's things?'

'Yes. There were pictures of him as a baby and toddler. Carefully saved. And a photograph of a family with this little boy, standing in front of a house, in India. My mum had scribbled a name – of the house, I think – on the back. I didn't recognise any of them.'

'Hmmm… Your mother never mentioned India, or went back there. Apart for teaching you Kannada, she severed ties with her past, didn't she? Something happened perhaps? Involving this little boy?'

The dream from last night; the boy from the photographs. Morphing into *their* little boy… Blue lipped, unresponsive.

* * *

The night preceding the day their world upended, Jaya had given in to the tiredness that dogged her and closed her eyes for a few brief, blissful moments, after having fed Arun for the umpteenth time. She had laid him carefully down in his cot, after he'd finally fallen asleep and she had prayed, 'Please stay asleep. Please don't wake up for a while'.

She was a muddle of exhaustion, a walking zombie. All she'd wanted was to grab a few uninterrupted moments of sleep… She'd been jerked awake by buttery sunlight teasing her eyelids open. Her first thought had been that Arun was with Ben. And then it had come to her: Ben was away on business. She had peered at the clock even as she staggered onto her feet. Seven a.m. She had been asleep for five hours straight. The baby monitor had been beside her like always. How come it hadn't gone off? Usually Arun woke up at least twice in those five hours…

Had she locked the front door, while she was rocking Arun to sleep? The back door? Or had she been too distracted? She had rushed to the nursery imagining all sorts of things: the blankets awry and no baby. But he'd been exactly where he should've been, and he'd looked so peaceful, his little head peeking out from the mess of sheets, his hands curled into fists and resting on either side of his angelic face. She'd breathed a sigh of relief and bent closer. That was when she'd blinked and blinked again as she'd taken in his blue lips, his cold, rigid body…

Her little boy, stiff and pale, not coming to life in her arms, no matter how much she begged him to, kissing him, cajoling him, holding him to her breast, while her milk ran but his heart didn't. His cry had stopped, his life ended, while she was enjoying an extra few minutes of sleep.

'Cot death,' the doctors had said. As if giving it a label would take away the fact of her son not being, not existing.

She blamed herself. For having hoped he would sleep for longer so she could rest her tired eyes. If she had stayed awake that night, sat by Arun's bedside and kept vigil, picked him up and breathed life into him when he gasped for that elusive breath, then perhaps he would be here now…

Night after night, she paced the rooms of their too-big house, reverberating with memories of the hopes she and Ben had had for it.

She loved Ben but couldn't bear to be around him. Ben was love and the promise of a future tinted gold with blissful times. He was also, now, the reminder of what they had lost. And so, no matter how hard he tried to mourn with her, she pushed him away. Shut him out. The endless hours of each day where she was living and her child was not, pierced by grief, dropped through the excruciatingly slow hourglass of her splintered dreams. Her empty arms, which yearned to feel the fragile warmth of her infant, hung loose by her sides. Her milk-heavy breasts ached to dispense their load. And as the dark nights when she fought dark thoughts, the yearning to end it all, to flee to her son's side, to close her eyes and never open them again, ambushed her, she had thought about going back to work, like Ben, if only to keep that inviting urge at bay.

'Do you mind me going back to work?' Ben had asked her – two weeks? four? – after Arun passed. She had squinted up at him, heavy eyed, his words not registering. 'Work is the only thing I can think of that will help, Jaya,' Ben had said, wringing his hands, despair colouring his eyes. 'A way to pass the time. For those few hours, I can forget.'

'Forget?' she'd asked, shocked.

'Not forget exactly. But keep the pain at bay.'

She did not want to keep thoughts of Arun at bay. But she did want to stop the dark thoughts that dogged her. And so she'd called work and her boss, Mel, had said, in a careful voice that tiptoed around her loss, 'Of course, you're welcome back anytime, Jaya.'

She had managed to get as far as the door to her office building. But then she'd seen a group of her colleagues, clutching Styrofoam cups of tea, exchanging greetings and banalities and the thought of doing the same, pretending, dancing around what had happened, was too much…

She had walked right back to the station and taken the tube to the cemetery, where she had felt such a fraud in her work clothes, sitting beside the small polished headstone. She had caressed her son's marker, the cool, hard marble miles away from the soft, nuzzling heat of Arun, waiting for a sign.

There was none. Only her body getting gradually more numb as the day waned.

'You're not in here, Arun,' she'd said out loud and a rook perching on one of the memorial slabs had startled, rising into the air, its black wings spreadeagled, a dark V stabbing the sullen grey awning of sky. That was the moment it fully dawned on her: her son was gone. He was not in the cemetery. He was not in their house either, their home, which sighed and moaned, complaining against the silences in which it was steeped – a house made for laughter, for noise; a house asphyxiated by the deadened pall of grief.

That was the lowest point.

Ben had found her as she held the blade of her sharpest kitchen knife to her wrists, as she watched, with fascination, the scarlet droplets ooze from the red-tipped lips of skin. 'I want to meet Arun in that space beyond. Where all the souls roam,' she had sobbed. 'And this time I will be a good mother. The best.'

'You were a good mother, Jaya,' Ben had cried. 'It wasn't your fault. I shouldn't have left you alone. You were tired, a new mum, hardly getting any sleep. I shouldn't have gone on that trip.'

'I didn't want a nanny; I couldn't trust anyone else to take care of my child. And now… I know that *anyone* would have been better than me…'

'It wasn't your fault,' Ben had reiterated, opening his arms, an invitation that she'd ignored, knowing that if she went inside the fortress of his arms, she would never leave, and she didn't deserve that comfort.

'We lost Arun, but that doesn't mean we have to lose ourselves too,' he'd entreated, his eyes naked, exposed, shimmering. His eyes. Their son's eyes. 'Please.'

And so, Jaya had looked up bereavement counsellors and found Dr Caroline Meadows.

* * *

It's been six months since Arun passed. And gradually, with the help of Dr Meadows, Jaya has learnt to rein in her guilt, to stop blaming herself. She has been able to get past the feelings of hopelessness, the suicidal thoughts, and gone from wanting only to join her son to being able to exist in the present. She is able to sleep most nights. She is back at work, part-time, three days a week. She is working towards looking past what happened to what can be, if she lets it. She is now able to peer around the edges of her grief into the future, one that involves Ben. She and Ben have managed to weather their son's loss. They are surviving, each in their own way. They are together – just. And they are as far apart as they have ever been.

* * *

'Has Ben travelled away with work all the time you've known him?' Dr Meadows had asked in one of their sessions.

'Ben started a new consulting company with his best friend, Mike, when he and I found out we were expecting. The start-up was a lifelong dream but Ben only took the plunge when it sank in that he was going to be a father. Then Arun died and business suffered – the company nearly folded. Ben was always the front man, you see, the one who liaised with clients. Mike is a whiz at computers but not a people person. And the very nature of their business – something technical that I don't know much about – is such that most of their clients are based in the US.' She'd blown her nose noisily. 'After we lost Arun, Ben *needed* to work. It's his way of coping. But he only started travelling abroad again when I urged him to. He didn't want to leave me alone for weeks at a stretch, but I'm better now, firmly in the land of the living and, thanks to you, no longer likely to harm myself...' Jaya took a deep breath. 'He's assured me a million times that he'll stop travelling the moment I ask him to, to hell with the business. But I don't mind really.'

In fact, she almost blurted out, *I prefer Ben being away. That way I don't have to constantly battle the feeling that I am not the wife he needs. That I have changed, and will never again be the woman he fell in love with, the woman he married.*

But there were some things sacred even from her therapist.

※　※　※

A few weeks previously, Ben had asked, 'Shall we try again?'

Jaya had just been drifting off and she had squinted blearily at him, uncomprehending. 'What?'

'A baby, Jaya. We've always wanted a big family. And I... I miss Arun and even though you're right next to me, I miss you.' His eyes were hopeful.

She had wrapped her arms tightly around herself to keep the fury in. 'And you think a baby is the answer? When Arun...'

She had walked away from him then, slept in the room she still thought of as Arun's nursery, on the bare floor, cold creeping into her joints, rendering her body as numb as her heart felt. *Shall we try again?* An innocent, perfectly justified question that opened up, once more, the floodgates of grief she thought she'd exhausted.

In the morning, she woke to sunlight, relentlessly cheery, streaming into the empty nursery, a blanket tucked snug around her. *Ben.* But Ben himself was gone. 'See you next week. Love you.' A note written in his familiar hand, propped against the kettle when she went to make her morning cup of tea.

*   *   *

Now, as she sits alone in the café they used to frequent together, the phone relaying his gentle voice into her ear, and igniting the need to hold him, to feel the comfort of his embrace, she thinks that perhaps all is not lost. They will find a way back to each other. After all, isn't that why she's seeing Dr Meadows still?

She closes her eyes, tuning out the noise and bustle around her and pictures Ben as she saw him last, three days ago, the morning he left for Chicago. The saffron glow from the bedside lamp crowning his hair as he bent to kiss her. His scent of cinnamon and musk.

How long had it been since they'd made love? She couldn't remember. But just then, for the first time in a long time, she'd felt the stirrings of desire. *Take me in your arms now, Ben. Love me like you used to once.*

But he was already turning away, his mind on the day ahead. And she didn't have the energy to act on her fledgling impulse, to grab his hand, pull him down onto the warm bedclothes.

'When will you be back?' she'd asked instead, peering at the bedside clock. Five a.m.

'In a week and then I have to leave for that conference in California – a prospective client will be there.' He'd looked at her, his gaze searching, his eyes asking: *Is that okay with you?*

She had nodded, smiled.

He'd smiled back, his face relaxing, and blown her a kiss as he left the room.

* * *

'I dreamt about him,' she tells Ben now.

'The little boy from the photographs your mother saved?'

'Yes. He became Arun.'

'Oh, Jaya.'

'And I… I also found Mum's diaries.'

'She kept diaries?' Ben ponders. 'You know, that makes so much sense given the kind of person she was.'

'That's what I thought,' Jaya says, touching the diary beside her, this precious gift of her mother's from beyond the grave.

After she ends the call, Jaya stays sitting at the table outside the café, oblivious to the activity around her, her coffee going cold, Ben's words ringing in her ears.

A little girl giggles as she skips down the street, her mother keeping close watch.

'Mum,' the little girl calls, grinning up at her mother and the woman's face softens.

The air that brushes Jaya's cheeks is the crushed mauve of regret, flavoured with the deep gold of yearning. She wishes she could go back in time, be a different daughter, one who had accepted her mother for who she was and loved her unconditionally, like Sudha had loved Jaya. Their relationship would have been so different then…

Carefully, she opens her mother's diary and reads Sudha's second entry.

✳   ✳   ✳

Dear Diary,

So much has happened in the past week. My heart bloomed. And then it sank. I have decided to never let it flower again…

Oh but it hurts. Everything hurts, so much more so than before. Perhaps putting it in writing here will ease the ache.

I will write as if it is all taking place right now, so I can relive the good bits, just once more, before I put them behind me…

Ravi passes me more notes in class the day after that first note, which I had ignored.

This time, when I walk past I look sideways at him just to check whether he is joking, perhaps making fun of me, even though I know he is not that kind of boy. He locks eyes with me and smiles. A small lifting of his lips.

Around us, our classmates chatter and laugh as if it is another ordinary day. But for both of us, it is anything but. Without so much as a word passing between us, we have reached an understanding. He must have heard the rumours about what I did to my twin, and yet… he loves me. He does.

All my life I have waited for something like this. I glide home on a haze of happiness, not noticing, as I usually do, how all my classmates have friends, but I am alone, trailed by the ghost of my dead brother.

Ma is squatting in the courtyard, sifting rice on a coconut-frond thali. She places two cupfuls of rice on the thali and she flicks it upwards in a practiced movement, catching every grain back in the thali, losing the stones.

The dog bounds up to me and gives my face a thorough lick with a tongue that smells of fish. Ma flashes that smile that does not quite reach her tired eyes. 'There's milk and sesame laddoo for you inside,' she says.

I drink the watered-down milk. I do not eat the sesame laddoo, putting it back in the packet like always. Ma pretends not to notice that I never eat it. I take my tiffin box out of my bag, tip the remaining conjee, of which I had taken two bites, into the cat's bowl, and then take it outside to wash in the bucket of water sitting underneath the coconut tree.

Then I gather my books and head for the banana copse. 'I'm doing homework,' I say to Ma, who nods, but doesn't reply. I sit there until the sun sets turmeric gold in a rainbow sky, until the fields surrounding our cottage ripple with shadows.

I go inside when Ma calls. I look at my parents, the light from the lamp playing on their faces. Da is swatting at mosquitoes and Ma is sewing. I love them both so much that my heart hurts. Surely they love me too? Surely the animosity and resentment I think they feel towards me is all in my head?

Somehow the words spill out of my mouth before I have thought them through.

'I don't want to have an arranged marriage like everyone in the village. I would like to marry for love,' I say.

There is a stunned pause.

And even before they speak, before tears fall soundlessly from my mother's eyes, before my da raises his hand and slaps me, before I see the shocked pleasure in his eyes, the recognition of how much he has wanted to do this to me all my life, I know I have made a mistake.

My da slaps me as much for what I just said as for what I have done to them. And in the instant that I see the pleasure in his eyes, the sheer liberation, I know that he wants to do it again, to keep doing it. Even as he forces his hand back to his side. Even as he averts his gaze.

But in that one dazed meeting of our eyes, in that one look, I note the truth. What I have assumed all my life is true. What is unsaid is there, a barrier between us. When he hit me, some of that barrier crumbled, a bit of what is left unsaid was revealed. And although I hurt, I am relieved for the honesty.

'What are you doing?' my ma shouts in the aftermath of the ringing slap. And not one of us, not even she, is sure of what she is asking, and of whom. We are not sure if she is speaking to Da, telling him off for slapping me or if she is asking me, 'What are you doing to us? What are you still doing to us?' Or if she is asking all of us, 'What are we doing bringing this out into the open after all this time?'

My cheek smarts and stings. I want to run away. But I know I won't. I will stay here. I will repent. I will try and please them. I will do as they say. I will not look at Ravi again. Tomorrow, when he passes me a note, I will tear it into a million pieces and fling it away as I walk past him, the pieces fluttering and falling beside him, his heart breaking, but not as much as mine is. And a few days from now, when I see him giggling with some other girl, I will pretend not to notice, even as it drags knives through my shattered heart.

*   *   *

Jaya closes the diary and softly strokes the cover as if, by doing so, she is caressing the girl her mother was, offering comfort to the broken child rejected by her parents for something that happened in the womb, something she didn't consciously do, something that *wasn't* her fault.

How could they?

Her palm itches, desiring to reach across the years and slap Sudha's father, Jaya's grandfather, as hard and as ruthlessly as he hit Sudha. She roots around in her handbag for a tissue, wipes her eyes, and calls Ben again.

'Jaya, have you been crying?' His concern echoes down the line. 'What's the matter?'

The stark memory of her breakdown bridges the miles separating them. Jaya pictures Ben looking at his watch, checking to see if it is too early to call Dr Meadows, calculating how soon he can book a ticket to come back home, images of her with a kitchen knife piercing her arm crowding his mind.

Much as she likes it this way, with him travelling so she doesn't have to make an effort to be wifely, and although he always checks with her if she'll be okay with him gone, she realises, suddenly, that she secretly resents his absence, his leaving her alone in their sorrow-doused house for days at a time… She doesn't want him gone and yet, until recently, she didn't want him there either… But that is changing, thanks to Dr Meadows and, especially now, thanks to her mother's words.

Going through her mother's things, reading her diary, has shown Jaya just how much she needs Ben. They used to talk, about everything and nothing. She misses that. She wants to talk to Ben properly, face to face, about what she is learning about her mother. She wants to read her mother's entries out to him. If he said he was coming back right now, she would seek solace in his arms, the solace he used to offer and she'd rejected, repeatedly, so that he didn't bother any more.

'I just read one of my mother's diary entries. Oh, Ben, she went through so much… I… I hurt terribly for her, but I'm glad I have this glimpse into her life. Although I wish… I wish it wasn't too late…'

With you too. I hope I haven't left it too late with you, Ben.

'Jaya, she knew that you loved her.'

'Did she?'

Do you know how much I love you, Ben, although I haven't said so, or shown you so recently?

'Yes.' Ben's voice is firm.

And it's as if he's answered her unspoken question, the one she is too afraid to ask.

'I can't bring myself to read more than one entry at a time. It's all too much to process.'

'I can imagine. It must be so weird, given how your mum was, to see this whole other side of her.'

'I feel like a voyeur reading. But I am compelled to at the same time… I understand now why she wouldn't tell me about her past, why she put it behind her. I would have too if I'd had the childhood she endured… I feel horrid for pushing her all the time…'

'Jaya, your curiosity was understandable. She knew that. She loved you. You were the most important person in her life.'

She thinks of the guilt she feels for never noticing just how much her mother cared for her, because she was always looking over Sudha's shoulder, wanting a glimpse of the past, which was gone and couldn't be retrieved.

She has been making the same mistake with Ben. He is here, in the present. With her. The only other person who has experienced the same loss as her. And instead of grieving with him, of remembering their son together, she has pushed Ben away.

'I miss you, Ben. Come home,' she says softly, the first time she has said it since Arun died.

'I will. I love you, Jaya.'

The Sunday-morning crowd, the café, the fruit stall, the delicatessen, the laughing children, their stressed parents, the cool air brushing her cheeks, the scent of hot milk and cream cakes – nothing registers except the beloved man thousands of miles away, his tender voice in her ear assuring her of his love despite everything that has gone before.

'I love you too, Ben.'

Chapter 13
Kali

Perfume and Pretty Dreams

'I'm tired. I want to leave the party. I know you need help, but I'm not feeling too good.'

'That's okay, come, let's get you into bed.' The woman – Sumathi? – holds my hand and starts leading me away.

I push her off. 'No, you need to stay. Otherwise the party will be an absolute disaster.'

She shoots me an odd look, and I am confused.

'Where am I?' I ask.

'At the mansion.'

I look at the old, crumbling bricks, the black-stained walls seeping moss and neglect.

'This is not the mansion,' I say, my voice a plea for help. 'It can't be, it can't.'

'Kali…'

'No, no, no… You've got it wrong. You've got it all wrong. Haven't you?'

* * *

The landlord's son, Vinay, is set to arrive late at night on Tuesday. Ahead of his arrival, the landlord's wife pays a rare visit to the kitchen. 'Just for tomorrow night, I would like you to stay back after supper and prepare a meal for Vinay and the driver,' she says.

'Thoo,' Radhakka spits after the landlord's wife has left, chopping onions with unnecessary force. 'Not only do I have to cook, serve supper and wash up…'

'I am the one who washes up. When was the last time you scraped the grease off a bowl?' I want to say, but I quietly continue peeling potatoes. I need Radhakka on my side for what I am planning to do.

'Not a minute to spare, preparing breakfast, lunch, supper, plus all the snacks in-between for the mistress.' Radhakka sets the pan on the gas with a loud thwack. 'And then, instead of retiring for a well-earned rest, I have to cook another two meals, one for the chauffeur and one for the boss! Why can't they eat the same one? "No," declares Ma'am. What her son eats has to be special, cooked with ghee, seasoned with cashew nuts. He probably won't even want to eat!'

'At least she feeds the chauffeur,' Sumathi, who is second in command to Radhakka, dares to say. 'Most wouldn't even think of the chauffeur, let alone ask for a meal to be prepared for him.'

Radhakka turns to her, eyes flashing, throwing the haphazardly chopped onions into the pot. 'Have you finished cleaning the chicken?' And when Sumathi nods, she says, 'Start on the rice then – what are you waiting for?'

Better her than me.

I make my move. 'I could stay up and serve the young master. I don't mind. You can go to bed.'

And just like that, it is I who am now on the receiving end of Radhakka's acrimonious glare. 'I take my responsibility as head of this kitchen very seriously, Kali, and I wouldn't dream of leaving the tired young master in the charge of an inexperienced kitchen maid.'

In her corner by the sink, where she is sifting the rice before soaking it, Sumathi smirks.

Never mind, I think. *He's not going anywhere. There will be other opportunities.*

Opportunity knocks during the preparations for the party to celebrate Vinay's homecoming.

Via the servants' grapevine, I have established Vinay's routine: what time he wakes, what he likes for breakfast, lunch and dinner, and what he does in-between. He has spent most of the two days he has been home sitting with his father in the library, both of them side by side, facing the window but not looking out, reading and not talking.

And although I have dusted and served and cleaned around him and even, one day, purposely spilled a tumbler of water right by him, he hasn't taken much notice of me, unable to be distracted from his books.

But I will not give up, I think, as the night before the party we stay up cooking and chopping, peeling and mashing. There is rice to grind, dough to knead, masalas to prepare, fish to gut and clean, meat to tenderise and marinate, vegetables to slice, ginger to crush, garlic to paste. It is endless, a cacophony of noise, aromas and flowing adrenaline.

The day of the party dawns and we have slept for a couple of hours, if that. Radhakka is stressed and that means the entire kitchen is stressed. 'Every single course needs to be perfect,' she keeps saying, a hundred times. 'Kali, the shape of those laddoos – I said round, not hexagonal!'

Early in the morning, as I am in the herb garden plucking coriander and mint, fragrant and moist with dew, to make chutney for breakfast, I see Vinay standing by the entrance, lost in thought. By the time I have taken the herbs inside to an impatient Radhakka and come back out again, he is gone.

Over the course of the day I see him, engrossed in the activity that is taking place around him, a contemplative smile on his face as he watches workers erect massive tents, mushroom-shaped awnings sprouting from bare lawn in a matter of minutes. He doesn't stay for long, and I am never able to get away in time to coincide with his appearances. But knowing he is leaving the library every so often to come outside and watch the party preparations is enough. I can wait. I am nothing if not patient.

It is while I am adding flaked almonds to the kheer that I see some men hefting a worn-looking statue, some sort of bird with a fish in its mouth, past the kitchen window, and a plan takes shape in my head. I tell Radhakka I am going to the loo and hurry to intercept the men.

'Where is that statue going?' I ask.

'We were asked to get rid of it. It's in the way of the marquee,' they say.

'Hmmm… I think it would look wonderful there by the entrance,' I say.

'But…'

'It will save you a walk.' I smile at them, batting my eyelashes. 'Believe me, we've been watching you from the kitchen and we feel so sorry for you, saddled with the worst job, lugging all those heavy objects and you get no thanks for it. Nobody will notice if you leave the statue over there by the steps instead of hefting it halfway down the hill to the truck.'

They sigh. 'It *is* heavy,' one of them says. 'I suppose nobody would notice.' They nod.

Finally, by mid-afternoon most of the cooking is done. I have a quick wash and change into my emerald churidar, my favourite, the one Ma had stitched for my birthday. I dance outside for a quick look around for Vinay and stop, utterly mesmerised by the transformation. The whole front of the vast house has been decorated with shimmering lights in all the hues of the rainbow. Men are also positioning lights all the way down the hill. I can imagine how it will look later, at dusk, the entire hill twinkling with illuminations.

The gardens look magical, festooned with streamers and fountains dispensing multi-coloured water. Everything is perfect. And then Vinay comes down the steps, looking down the hill towards the village. He has a sweet face and gentle, slightly distracted eyes. He is neither too tall nor too short. He is kind to the servants who have been attending to him, I have heard. (I am not one of them, of course, being on the lowest rung of the servant hierarchy.) He tips generously, is very polite and talks to them, asks about their day.

He is not Manu.

Are you sure you want to go ahead with your plan, Kali? my conscience chides.

I flag a passing servant. 'Why is this here?' I ask, pointing at the statue that the two men were carrying away some hours ago and which is now sitting smug by the steps – thanks to me.

'Oh I… I don't know.'

'When the guests arrive, they'll be looking right at this old thing. See, it's chipped. Can't it be moved somewhere else? It lowers the tone. Imagine you are one of the guests, okay? The valet opens the door for you. You step out of your car, accept your glass of lime sherbet, you turn gracefully and bang – you come face to face with this horrible monstrosity!'

The man looks panicked. 'Wait, I'll get the head gardener,' he says.

'Who wants me?' The small, stout head gardener appears in front of me, wiping sweat off his moustache with the palm of his hand.

'Sir, I think this…'

'Who are you, girl?'

'I work in the kitchen.'

'Then why are you poking your nose over here?'

I stand my ground, although I am cringing inside. 'Look, everything else is perfect here but this…'

'I don't take orders from the kitchen help,' the head gardener says snootily before turning away.

'But you do take them from me.' A voice shot through with steel.

I was so immersed in trying to get Vinay's attention that I didn't notice the landlord's wife coming down the steps. I swallow. This was not part of the plan.

'She's right, you know. Do as she says,' the landlord's wife says.

I release the breath I didn't know I was holding.

The head gardener nods. He doesn't look at me but I know I will pay for this. He will snitch to Radhakka and she'll punish me with the worst jobs for a few weeks. But it is worth it for this. And who knows? A lot can happen in a few weeks. Lives can change.

'On second thoughts, just get rid of it. She's right. It is chipped.'

The head gardener nods again, his head bowed in meek subjugation.

She said that I am right twice. I am giddy with exhilaration. *She agrees with me.*

The landlord's wife looks at me and smiles.

'Well spotted,' she says. 'What is your name?'

Uh oh. I didn't mean to draw her attention to me this early on.

'Kali, ma'am.' My voice shakes.

'Well done, Kali.'

And despite everything, I glow. I have admired this woman from afar for so long. And now she has noticed me, praised me. She turns and walks back inside. And I twirl, laughing out loud, my green churidar ballooning around me, knowing full well the effect I am creating for the man who is now no longer looking towards the village but at me, captivated, I hope. After all, I *am* the prettiest of the servants.

'You have a very infectious laugh, you know.'

I stop spinning, waiting for my groggy head to settle. He is grinning at me.

'Mind your own business,' I say coolly, hoping the landlord's wife was right that Vinay likes spirited girls, praying this is the correct approach.

His smile deepens, dimples tunnelling his cheeks.

'And I'll have you know I don't take compliments from strangers,' I toss over my shoulder as I flounce off, knowing he is watching. I hear him chuckle in response, but I don't turn to look.

That evening, when the party is in full swing, I weave in and out of the assembled guests serving kachoris and vadas, kebabs and samosas, Mysore pak and coconut burfi, topping up chutney and glasses, knowing for a fact that despite the myriad beauties assembled here to meet Vinay, I have secured first claim to him.

I've felt his gaze on me all evening. He looked for me from the moment he came downstairs, dapper in his suit, to greet the guests who had started trickling in, his mother by his side, proudly introducing him to this girl and that, and to their illustrious families. His eyes had lingered on each servant, I noticed, as I watched from the kitchen door, planning my entrance.

I had come in with drinks just as he was being introduced to the Maddurhalli landlord's daughter and he had stumbled during the introductions, his gaze skimming hers to land on mine, and his mother had pulled him up sharply. 'Vinay, this is…'

Now there is a brief lull in the party, with most of the guests in the dining room, and Vinay has managed to escape his mother. He is propped in a corner of the hall with a drink and a plate. Watching me.

I boldly walk right up to him. He smiles. Chandeliers glint soft gold, bathing us in a creamy amber glow. The gentle murmur of the indulged drifts from other rooms, washing like waves over the soft melody of sitars and tablas reverberating from speakers hidden discreetly around the house.

'Sir, I'm sorry about before,' I say, suitably servile. 'I didn't realise you were the young master…'

'So you'll take compliments from me now you know who I am?' His smile is wider now.

Before I can reply, the landlord's wife is beside us, grabbing Vinay's hand, saying, 'Vinay, come, you need to…'

Her gaze lands on me. 'Ah, you're the girl from this afternoon.'

She recognises me? I am thrilled. And worried.

'Well done,' she says. 'Now those people over there were asking for refills of their drinks.'

For the first time since I started working for her, she looks ever so slightly ruffled. And then her words settle in my mind like pebbles sinking to the bottom of a lake. I am, despite my lofty ambition, just a servant. A lowly servant. Why on earth would Vinay want me when the mansion is teeming with high-born, educated, intelligent girls this evening? What was I thinking? That just because I asked someone to move a statue and looked pretty in a fraying green churidar Vinay would prefer me?

Fool. You make a nuisance of yourself with Manu, begging him to love you. And then you come here and instead of putting your head down and working, entertain arrogant notions far above your station…

The landlord's wife is leading Vinay into the dining room. As he is walking away, he looks back, right at me, and winks. And all my doubts dissipate like mist kissed away by morning sun.

Vinay is back less than ten minutes later, accosting me as I am circulating with drinks in the nearly empty lounge, most of the guests either enjoying the buffet in the dining room or boogying on the dance floor set up in one of the rooms off it.

'Miss me?' He grins charmingly at me.

Relief that he's sought me out makes me relax enough to say exactly what I'm thinking. 'So how come you're back so quickly? Gave your ma the slip did you?' Even as I say it I wonder if I'm going too far.

His mouth tightens, sets in a grim line.

Oh no, this is it. I'm going to be sacked.

'Meeting all these people is so tedious,' he says.

Try peeling potatoes and scrubbing dishes and serving drinks, I think.

'Bet you want to be reading poetry right now,' I say instead, smiling at him.

His eyes light up as he beams at me. 'How did you know?'

'I love poetry too. Don't tell your parents, but I read your da's books when I'm supposed to be dusting.'

He laughs long and hard, and when he looks at me, there is an admiring gleam in his eyes. And I know then that my plan, conceived in a moment of impulse, is well on its way to working.

The next day, the outdoor servants set about dismantling marquees, removing the strung lights, packing away the party trappings. It is as busy as it was the previous day, but there is the hungover, pallid sense of anticlimax left in the wake of a successful celebration.

I spent the previous night tossing and turning, wondering if what I had done was enough to win over Vinay or whether it was over the top, worrying that I'd be told I'd lost my job. Vinay had enjoyed my company, he had been enthralled by me… hadn't he? What if it was all in my mind? He had kept coming back to me during the party, despite his mother's summons to meet this girl and that. I'd impressed him with my knowledge of poetry. We'd recited poems to each other, dissected them and discussed what they meant. And I'd found myself enjoying the conversation, forgetting where I was and who I was, until one of the other servants nudged me, or Radhakka stood in my line of vision glaring at me, or Vinay was called away to exchange pleasantries with yet another landlord's daughter. Even so, I was aware of his eyes on me the whole evening.

I woke this morning bleary eyed and anguished and I was relieved when Radhakka, looking even more flustered than the previous evening, barked without preamble, as soon as I made an appearance in the kitchen, 'You need to go to the village immediately. The fishmonger hasn't delivered the sardines we specially requested. The missus is hosting a luncheon for the Maddurhalli landlord's family this afternoon, and sardines are on the menu.'

So the landlord's wife was not taking any chances in her quest to link her son to the bride of *her* choice.

'Of all the days for the fishmonger to fail me! Hurry, Kali! They're eating at one-thirty at the latest. Sardines are the Maddurhalli landlord's daughter's favourite it seems, and even our young master is partial to them.'

At the mention of Vinay, I had turned away to hide the blush that suffused, the memory of the previous day setting my stomach aquiver, inducing nausea.

Did I imagine his attraction to me? Even if he *is* attracted to me, is it enough? Especially now the girl his mother has chosen for him is spending the afternoon with him...

As I walk down the hill into the village, I wonder if perhaps I shouldn't get the sardines, jeopardise the meal... But Radhakka was already skinning a couple of chickens as backup when I left, so all that would happen if I didn't get the fish is that I'd be sacked, my plans for a sunny future disintegrating like laddoos in an eager mouth.

What more do I need to do? I muse as I walk back with the stinking fish. That depends on whether I will be allowed to continue at the mansion… Will I be told to leave when I get up there, Vinay having talked to his mother about the overfamiliar servant girl?

I look up at the house, iridescent in the golden haze. I think of what it can bring me: status and wealth, and more importantly, of what it can take away: the stigma associated with my past, the feeling of worthlessness at being on the lowest rung of the domestic-help ladder and at the mercy of my aunt and uncle. I think of the promise I made to myself as I stood outside Manu's house – to never feel small and insignificant, to never be vulnerable again. And I think, *If I'm not sacked, then I will definitely pursue my plan.*

'Oh there you are,' a voice says.

I jump, almost dropping the fish. I'm sure it will have gone off by now in the heat. *Good. Hope the Maddurhalli landlord's daughter gets an upset stomach.*

'I've been looking all over for you.'

I look up into his twinkling eyes, my heart lifting.

It worked. It did!

'You scared me,' I say meekly, swallowing down my elation, my heart thumping and my legs trembling so much that I fear they won't hold my weight. Although… it wouldn't be such a bad idea to swoon into his waiting arms. No – not while I'm reeking of fish.

'Did I?' He smiles at me as he falls into step beside me, walking alongside me as if we're friends. As if he is not the boss and me the servant who's just trudged down to the village and back because he likes sardines. 'Let me carry that for you.' He holds out his hand.

He is so very nice. It makes what I'm doing, shamelessly manipulating his affections, even harder. Doubts flock my mind like a swarm of birds and then fly away as if they've been startled by a predator in their midst when I look up at the house.

'Do you want to get the stench of raw fish all over you?' I ask archly.

He laughs heartily, a cascade of fireworks. 'I quite like your concern for me, but I'd rather not thanks…'

A loud clang, followed by a vigorous cheer, echoes down to where we're standing, as chairs that are being loaded onto the lorry poised at the top of the hill topple, narrowly missing the servants.

I decide to show him more of the 'spirit' he so adores. 'So which of the girls your mother showed you last night did you fancy?'

His mirth overflows in a series of delighted chuckles. 'Oh you picked up on that, did you? My ma thought she was being subtle…'

Dust eddies in the humid air, smelling of spices and drains.

'I like you, you know. You are so refreshingly different.'

He likes me.

I taste fear and excitement, salt and sweat on my parched lips. Despite my efforts to attain just this, I am overwhelmed.

Inexperienced as I am in the art of flirting, I didn't expect my plan to work quite this quickly.

'But why?' I ask, genuinely curious. 'I'm insubordinate. And adept at insulting you!'

'I like that,' he says, eyes warm, sparkling. 'Makes a change from the procession of blushing girls I was introduced to yesterday. None of them even looked at me, let alone made conversation. You are funny, interesting, intelligent. And you love poetry.'

A bee buzzes close to my face, a stippled whirring, the air around me shifting in a fuss of yellowish black.

'The other girls are oh so coy,' he says.

'Does this apply to the girl who's coming for lunch this afternoon as well?'

He stops smiling, his eyes serious, his mouth grave.

Oh no, I've done it this time.

'There's a girl coming for lunch?'

He didn't know about the guests. His ma didn't tell him. This might work to my advantage.

'I'm sorry. I didn't… Maybe I've got it wrong.'

His hands bunch into fists, his gaze hard. 'My mother. She means well, but why does she have to interfere like this? I'm not interested in landlords' daughters. I want to find my own partner.' He looks meaningfully at me. 'Someone who loves poetry just as much as I do. Someone who isn't afraid to speak their mind.' He grins, his eyes softening. There is such affection in his voice. For me.

Thank you, gods. Thank you.

'That's all well and good,' I say, choosing not to notice what he's really saying. There will be a time and place for that, now that I know he likes me, but not here, with me reeking of fish. 'But excuse me while I drop these sardines off for *your* lunch. Radhakka will be fuming thinking I've dallied – she has no idea how long it takes to walk up this hill in this heat, and I'll likely be asked to gut and prepare the fish as punishment.' I am babbling, I know, relief, honey sweet, making the words effervesce out of my mouth.

'Yes. Get those sardines to Radhakka. I fancy a nice fish curry.' He rubs his stomach and I lunge at him, catching a hint of peppermint and musk.

'I'll give you sardines! Actually I don't mind shaking your hand now.'

'No, thank you.' Guffawing, he jumps away, and I laugh.

'You're beautiful when you're annoyed, but you are magnificent when you laugh,' he says and, instead of joy at the compliment, I feel hurt stab at me. *I wish Manu had said that. Did you care for me at all, Manu?*

Out loud, I say, injecting a smile into my voice, 'Do you go around saying this to all the servant girls?'

'No. Just you.' His eyes glow with emotion.

From the house, a faint, imperious, slightly impatient call carries, 'Vinay, son.' The landlord's wife. And an accompanying, deferential echo from the servants, 'Vinay, saar.'

He grimaces, his face setting in a mutinous scowl.

'See you later – that's a promise.' He winks at me, like he did the previous night, and sprints up the hill.

I am well on my way to achieving what I set out to do. Then why don't I feel triumphant? Why do I ache from the tip of my toes to the hair on my head?

As I had predicted, Radhakka has me gutting and scaling the
fish while she and Sumathi rush about frying chicken, grinding
masalas, grating coconut, pounding ginger, peeling garlic. As I
work, I push aside the melancholy that has taken me captive,
the longing for Manu. I am so close to realising my plan,
I tell myself. And I definitely do not want to be doing this
forever. My arms deserve to be pampered with exotic creams
not plastered with fish scales and bloody entrails.

Once the fish is bubbling in the orange sauce, spiced with
green chillies and heady with turmeric, and the rice is cooking
away, and I have rolled out the chapattis, ready for frying, I
am allowed to leave the kitchen to have a wash and change
before I am deemed fit to serve the guests.

I change, once again, into my best (and luckiest, it seems),
green churidar. I make my way to the kitchen via the elaborate
drawing room, now empty and forlorn, in stark contrast
to last night's bustle and celebration, dust motes already
in evidence despite it having been cleaned to perfection
just the previous afternoon. I am going this (longer) way
to the kitchen in the hope that I will bump into Vinay and
cement his affection for me further, before the Maddurhalli
landlord's daughter gets her claws into him, when I am
arrested by shouts reverberating from the library. I quicken
my step and flatten myself against the door, ear pressed to
the carved wood, breathing in the scent of furniture polish
and intrigue, praying nobody will walk past and ask me what
on earth I am doing.

'Ma, I told you I would choose my own partner and you agreed. You promised not to interfere.' Vinay's mild voice is raised in irritation.

'But, Vinay, son, if you only give Laxmi a chance—'

'Ma, I don't want to be pushed into anything I don't—'

'But you said you don't have anyone particular in mind.'

'Which doesn't mean I don't have the right to choose.'

'Kali,' I hear Radhakka's strident tone calling for me. 'Where has that girl got…'

'Please, son – Laxmi is from a good family…' The landlord's wife's voice is bruised like the underside of bark stripped off a tree. I have never heard her sound like this before.

What is the landlord doing? Is his nose buried in a book or is his distressed gaze gravitating between his wife and his son? Most probably he is just wishing for peace, for a resolution to be arrived at so he can get back to his reading.

'Ma, nobody cares for that any more. And I am not attending today's luncheon. Please make excuses on my behalf.'

'Vinay, you have to come. I've already told them…' A pleading note enters the landlord's wife's voice. Another first.

'Tell them I'm ill.'

'But Laxmi is very nice.'

'She might be. But I'm not interested.'

'Son, you're letting a perfectly good opportunity—'

'Ma, it was torture keeping my smile fixed while meeting all those girls yesterday. I can't face another few hours of fake greetings and smarmy chit-chat today.'

'Son, if you don't attend the luncheon, you're not welcome to accompany us to the hotel this evening.' Anger and hurt are warring in the landlord's wife's voice.

'That's fine. I'll stay here.'

'There'll be no servants – it's their evening off.' Her voice is sharp with hurt.

'Kali…' Radhakka calls, her voice fiery, laced with impatience.

I run before the door opens and someone catches me eavesdropping, dreading the hell Radhakka will subject me to when I enter the kitchen.

'How is it at the big house now that the young master is back?' my ma asks when I sit down beside her, as I do every Saturday evening, counting down the hours until the morning, when I can escape her stifling grief and the hostility emanating from my uncle. I am all the more eager to get to the mansion tomorrow because I know Vinay is home alone, although he doesn't know I know of course.

I am surprised by my ma's acuity. Usually she is so soused in her own sorrow that she doesn't notice anything around her. Or perhaps she does, and I have been unkind and unfair to her, I think, guilt – the emotion most in evidence whenever I am with my ma – piercing me and holding me accountable.

'Oh, there was a party at the mansion to celebrate his arrival. There were visitors again this afternoon, but the landlord's son was ill and couldn't attend. Must have been something he ate,' I say easily.

'Rumour has it he's returned with all these ideas in his head of how he'll marry only for love, how he doesn't care for status. All the girls in the village are preparing to throw themselves at him, given half a chance.' My aunt, just back from work, is sitting by the hearth, the flickering vermilion glow from the embers casting shadows onto her face as she chews paan and combs her hair.

A cockroach scuttles out from under Ma's mat, darting a bit too close to my bare feet, its glossy shell gleaming ebony in the murk. The smell of stale conjee and mouldy clothes assaults my nostrils.

'It'll never work,' my ma tuts. 'It doesn't do to upset the order, the way things are. And whatever that young man says, it would cause the biggest scandal. Destroy both families… Like your da's actions.' Her voice wavers and the tears come, an endless flow.

My aunt catches my gaze and rolls her eyes. In the half-light of the hearth she looks like she is being strangled. Perhaps she is, having to put up with my ma every single day, caught between Ma and my uncle, forever keeping the peace.

'Oh the landlord's wife has no intention of her son marrying a mere commoner.' I try for nonchalance.

'As it should be.' My aunt nods as my ma chokes on her tears.

On Sunday morning I sprint up the hill again, eager to be away from my ma's moans, my uncle's surly disapproval, my aunt's determined cheerfulness, anticipating my 'chance' meeting with Vinay, alone in the big house, another opportunity to charm him. The early-morning air caressing my face carries the music of birdsong, a hint of tamarind and the heat of the day to come. The sky is rosy mauve, layered with mellow gold.

I feel lighter with each step closer to the mansion, the load I carry – the burden of my mother's self-wrought illness, my sense of obligation and gratitude towards my aunt and uncle – receding. When I am with my ma, I remember how it used to be, those evenings sitting in the courtyard, Ma and Da chatting to the neighbours, Manu by my side, teasing, playing, talking, laughing.

I don't want to recall that time, grief sitting heavy on my chest, loss lodged in my throat. So I count down the hours to when I can leave, earlier and earlier every Sunday, it seems, so I can have some moments alone in the big house. I have come to cherish them. In the few hours before the other servants arrive, I can pretend that I'm the queen of all I fancy, the boss. I can pretend to be the woman I look up to, the landlord's wife.

And today I am not alone. Today there is Vinay, and the tantalising possibility that I could very well achieve all of my dreams… My aunt said that the village girls are preparing to throw themselves at him. So why not me?

I let myself in quietly and, once inside, I set down my bag in the kitchen and traipse through the house, breathing in the familiar smell of air freshener and clean fabric, touching the odd ornament, flicking through the pages of a book.

He is not downstairs. Is he still asleep? Or did he go with his parents after all?

I slip my feet into the landlord's wife's chappals, a size too small for my feet, and wander the rooms, the slap of the chappals making a satisfying echo. I trek up the stairs, pausing at the entrance to Vinay's room. The door is closed, and I turn the knob and push it open, my heart a percussionist in the throes of performance.

His bed is unmade but empty. Where is he?

I am not one of the servants allowed upstairs. My job is to help out in the kitchen and vicinity, and to clean and maintain the library. I boldly walk across Vinay's room, touching his pillow, which bears the indentation of his head – so he did stay here last night – and peer out of his window. The view is magnificent. I can look down the hill, all the way into the village, and I fancy I can spy my mother bemoaning her fate in a corner of her sister's house, where she is unwelcome, allowing her life to pass her by.

'You're missing all this,' I whisper to my ma, my words dispersing on the gentle, banana-flavoured breeze. 'You are missing the pleasure of possibility, the joy of anticipation, what you might be if you only allowed yourself the freedom to look ahead instead of languishing in the past.'

Emboldened by his continued absence, I root around in Vinay's wardrobe. Rows and rows of suits – pristine, immaculate. There is a faint tang of musk, the same smell I caught when he bent close to me – was it only yesterday?

Where is he?

I look in his floor-to-ceiling mirror, which takes up an entire wall. I see a girl in a servant's drab dress spinning dreams worthy of a queen. I murmur the words he said to me, the words that have seared themselves onto my heart, making it ache with longing for another mouth to have whispered them: 'You are magnificent when you laugh.'

I laugh experimentally, the sound hollow and too loud in this empty house that seems to be full of echoes and suddenly forbidding. Am I magnificent? I splutter, fake laughter mutating into the real thing.

'Stop dreaming, Kali and get on with your work,' I mime in Radhakka's acerbic voice and laugh even harder.

I am saving the best part for last. And once I have savoured these, my favourite moments stolen each Sunday morning, I will look for Vinay and engineer 'bumping into' him. I walk into the room the landlord shares with his wife. On his side of the bed, his spare reading glasses rest on one of his poetry books – he must have taken his other pair with the smarter frames to the hotel. The landlord's wife's side is neat. An array of perfume bottles, talcum powder and lotions dot the dressing table. I liberally apply all of them, feeling myself transform into a sweet-scented lady of leisure.

If I had all this, I would never want for anything. I would not feel the gloomy dip of my stomach, the nausea that accompanies my visits every Saturday, when I sit vigil beside the prone, thin excuse for a human being my mother has become.

I shrug away thoughts of my mother, daring to encroach on these precious few minutes that I treasure and live for each week, and glide into the bathroom. In the en suite are bathrobes, his and hers, hanging from hooks. I wear hers, of course. It is like a warm, furry embrace. I feel loved. I smell glamorous. I close my eyes and revel in the lavish, pampered luxury of being above petty concerns such as tearful mothers and cheating fathers and lost loves; the heady taste of power and privilege, of having people attend and pander to you; the charged tingle of everyone's awed envy, their goggle-eyed admiration.

I sit on the bed, wearing the landlord's glasses, and squint at myself in the mirror. I am so ensconced in the robe that only my face is visible. I look like an exotic bird with furry plumage and bulbous eyes. '*Now* you are magnificent,' I tell the girl in the mirror.

I pick up the poetry book and attempt to read, although the words swim before my eyes thanks to the myopic glasses.

A snort.

I look up. What was that I just heard? I feel a tickle of fear creep up my spine. What if it wasn't just Vinay who stayed back at the mansion last night? What if one of the servants did too, to look after the young master? Why didn't I think of this earlier? Why didn't I check?

I am in my master and mistress's room, wearing *their* clothes, availing of *their* property. I am trespassing, sure to be accused of theft, especially if I am caught by one of the servants. They will be even more vicious than the landlord and his wife if one of their own has dared to do something they haven't had the courage to attempt.

Do not abuse your employers' trust in you. Radhakka's words when she gave me the key to the mansion echo in my ears.

Another louder snort, and then an eruption of laughter.

I drop the poetry book and stand up very slowly, on jelly legs that are now wobbling with relief.

'You've made my day!' Vinay guffaws, coming into the room.

'You gave me the fright of my life,' I snap, not letting my relief show.

He comes closer, sniffs. 'You smell like my mother.'

I blush.

'Oh, now,' he says, rubbing his hands together in glee. 'This is the first time I've seen you speechless. A moment for posterity, don't you think? But I have to say, you do look fantastic when you flush so prettily like that.'

'Stop it, you. Why are you here anyway?'

'And it is back!' he says, clapping in delight.

'What's back?' I am genuinely stumped.

'Your voice, silly. I thought you'd lost it forever.' His eyes are shining with mirth. 'So is this what you do every Sunday morning? Good job I stayed back then, eh? I wouldn't have missed this for the world.'

'How long have you been watching me?' I inject ire into my voice.

'Long enough to know you've remembered every compliment I paid you.'

I feel colour flooding into my cheeks again.

He comes and stands behind me. I catch the hint of musk again. I quite like it, I decide, breathing in deeply. He picks up the poetry book and flicks through it. 'Ah, this one is my favourite,' he says. And standing there, the two of us framed in the mirror in his parents' bedroom, where I categorically should not be – he in his pyjamas, hair tousled, the shadow of a beard on his face, me in my borrowed bathrobe and glasses, wearing a worried expression, the smell of musk mingling with perfume and pretty dreams – he reads me a poem.

'This is in Urdu,' he says, 'but I'll translate it as I go, so bear with me.'

'That's why I couldn't make out the words,' I muse. 'I thought it was because of your da's glasses.'

He sputters, laughing long and hard. Then he gathers himself, starts reading.

'My darling.

Everything you do, you do with such aplomb.

You look in the mirror and although you are wearing a bathrobe and thick-lensed glasses, you manage to carry it off like a queen…'

I scrunch my nose.

'You smile at me and although your hands are full of fish and your face adorned with sweat, you are the most beautiful vision I have ever seen.'

'Stop,' I mutter. 'That's quite enough.'

He explodes into laughter again, and I wipe the reciprocal smile that dares grace my reflection in the mirror. Once he's stopped chortling, he looks at me and his gaze is serious. 'I will admit that that poem isn't in here. I made it up.'

'I should imagine so. It's absolute drivel.'

More laughter. I make to swat at him, taking even more liberties than I already have.

'But I meant every word,' he says softly and then he is very close, his face inches from mine.

Suddenly there is no air in the room and I struggle to breathe. His earnest, shining eyes, his face with its day's worth of facial hair, its rugged planes, is superimposed with another, a face I have watched grow into its contours, a face I have played with and teased, taken for granted and adored, a face I could draw with my eyes closed – a face I have loved.

'You…' Vinay whispers, but it is Manu's voice I hear, soft with love, mouthing the words I have longed to hear from his lips. 'You enchant me.'

And then he kisses me; his lips on mine, the taste of mint and cloves, his musky scent engulfing me, the heated proximity of his body.

I am not in this room, wearing Vinay's mother's robe and perfume, his father's glasses knocked off my nose. I am by the undulating stream of my childhood village, silver-finned fish gliding past, the rain falling softly around us, a winking, whispering, wet curtain offering the illusion of privacy while the cows moo and the buffaloes grumble and the dogs howl and the thunder performs, the mouth of the only boy I have ever loved communing with mine.

✳ ✳ ✳

The darkness is syrupy brown, molasses thick. It strangles, robbing me of breath, of words. I want to escape this heaving black; I want to find the light, but I can't.

I can't.

I am suffocating. Lost in a winding tunnel of overwhelming gloom that presses down upon me.

I am being punished, I think. *That is why I am floundering, sinking.*

It is wrong, what I am doing.

It is not meant to be.

When I find my voice, it is gritty, glutinous, alien.

'Vinay.' His name a prayer, a song, a call for help. 'What will become of us?'

Chapter 14
Jaya

Inner Voice

'How does reading your mother's words make you feel?' Dr Meadows asks.

'I hurt for my mum. I wish I had seen through the front she put up to the woman inside. I hate that I didn't.' Jaya sighs deeply, tasting regret, the deep navy of the sky mourning the setting of the sun. 'In the corner of my mind I'd always assumed that I would have it out with her one day, woman to woman. I thought I had plenty of time… But time was one thing I didn't have. With my mum. Or with Arun…'

'Your father – does your mum mention him?'

'Not yet. I've only read the first couple of entries. I can't read more than one at a time. I… I'm overcome by emotion, swamped by upset for the girl my mother was. I know that if I read every entry in my mother's diaries back to back, I would know who my dad is. But I don't want to read them in one huge, breathless gulp, like a novel where you're so desperate to know the ending that you miss so much in-between – subtle nuances, the author's carefully constructed clues. I want to savour each entry, contemplate it, try and match what I've read to what I know of my mother. I want to map her life via her entries and reconcile my image of her with them. I want to go slowly, not rush, now that I have this unexpected treasure. I want to know my mother and know her well, to make up for my mistakes, my neglect of her when she was alive.' Jaya pauses, overcome.

Dr Meadows nods her assent and waits, knowing that Jaya is not done.

When she has composed herself somewhat, Jaya says, 'You know, I went through her things once or twice over the years, wanting to find something – anything – pertaining to my father…'

Jaya takes a sip of water from the tall glass sitting beside her, next to the box of tissues. 'I found nothing. She must have known I'd come searching and spirited her secrets far from prying fingers.' Jaya stumbles on a sob. 'She kept every single thing I ever wrote. And she made up for the lack of photographs of my father with a glut of photographs of me, as if, without this pictorial evidence, she might lose me. And her fears had, in a way, been justified, with me, towards the end, hardly visiting her.'

'You feel guilty about that?' Dr Meadows asks.

'Very.' Distress ambushes Jaya's mouth. 'When I did visit, our silences dragged on. There was too much to say and we didn't know where to start, how to fill it…'

'You said she was always working?'

'Yes, but now I see that she made an effort to be home when I visited, rearranging her shifts. She would cook all of

my favourite dishes and even that annoyed me. I felt she'd
gone over the top! How spoilt I was, how selfish!'

'We are all selfish when we're young.'

'But my mum wasn't. She spent her life trying to please.
First her parents. Then her ungrateful bitch of a daughter.'

'You're being too hard on yourself, Jaya.'

Jaya takes a deep breath, salty with tears. 'Growing up,
I was sick of the silence in our house. I wanted to scream,
make some noise. Splinter the silence into a thousand pieces.
I wanted to hear my mother's voice. Her *real* voice.'

'Why did you think her voice wasn't real?'

'I just knew that she was keeping things from me. That there
was so much more to her than what she allowed me to see. It
irked me that she wouldn't share herself completely, especially
when it was only the two of us.' Jaya swallows. 'I even wrote
her a letter once. Left it on her pillow. In the morning it was
gone. My mother never mentioned it and I was so angry that
I didn't either. I found it among her belongings. Treasured.
Creased. Even tear-stained. She must have read it so many
times. But she never gave me a clue even as to whether she'd
received it.'

'What did it say?'

'I remember it word for word. *Mum*, it said. I remember
intentionally omitting the *Dear*. She wasn't dear to me then.'

Dr Meadows waits patiently.

'*Mum*, I had written. *I want to know who you are. The real
you. Stripped of lies and that unshakeable, impenetrable exterior,
like a bulletproof vest.* I was learning to use figurative language
in my writing, you see, hence the simile.' Jaya tries for a smile,

and ends up hiccupping instead. '*I want to see what you're hiding inside. Please, Mum,* I wrote. That was the last time I pleaded with her. Tried with her. Tried to crack her. After that I gave up. Became cold, distant.'

'And now?'

'Now, so many years after I wrote that letter, I've discovered her voice. Her inner voice.'

'And?'

'I understand that she was protecting me by keeping it from me. You see, that's my mum all over – unselfish to the core. Shielding me to the point of pushing me away. Allowing me to misunderstand, bearing the brunt of my anger, my indifference, in order to spare me.'

'Why? What was her inner voice like? Why couldn't she show it to you while you were growing up?'

'I would have gone to pieces if I had heard it then. I saw a brief glimpse of it once, when she mentioned the fire in which my dad's passport had been destroyed, and it shook me to the core. Her real voice, her inner voice – it screams pain.'

Chapter 15
Kali

Trappings of Modesty

'Kali, come – it's time for your walk.'

'Why do I have to walk?' I ask, uncomprehending. 'I have work to do. Radhakka will be angry if I don't finish peeling all those bitter gourds in the next fifteen minutes. And anyway I don't feel like walking. I don't feel like doing anything at all. Least of all skinning these gourds. Their smell makes me feel sick…'

'The fresh air will do you good. Come.'

'The fresh air only makes it worse. You know that, Sumathi. Why are you tormenting me like this?'

✳   ✳   ✳

Vinay kisses me in his parents' bedroom on a sunny Sunday morning and I return the kiss, imagining another boy in another time. He holds me in his arms and baptises my lips with his, showing me the world while my eyes are closed, a whole new world of touch and caress, a murmur encompassing a whole language. I haven't known love since my father left and Manu rejected me and my mother abandoned me to find refuge in grief. Since then, I have been floundering, lost, and I only find anchor now in the arms of the man whom I have set out to seduce and who in my mind I have reimagined to be Manu.

I pull away after a bit.

'Kali…'

I open my eyes at the sound of my name uttered in an unfamiliar cadence in a stranger's voice. It takes me a minute to come to terms with the fact that it is Vinay, the landlord's son; that it is his lips that have been intimate with mine; that I am in an opulent bedroom where I do not belong and not by the stream with a boy from my not-so-distant past, which is now another life altogether, a sepia-tinged, salt-licked album of loss.

Reality smothers confusion-drenched passion and I run to my employers' bathroom, hang up my mistress's robe and flee downstairs, blindly chopping something, anything, to ease the ache that has taken over my body.

I hear his footsteps thundering down the stairs a moment later. He stands too close, his body radiating heat and desire, and I want to throw myself into his arms and beg him to finish what he has begun. I want to slap him, hurt him for not being the person I want him to be. I bite the inside of my cheek, hard, and it splits, my mouth filling with blood, wiping away the taste of his lips. I am angry with him. I am angry with myself.

My head is a jumble of warring thoughts: *I have cheated on Manu. I have just been with Manu.*

It wasn't Manu. Manu doesn't want me. Vinay does.

What have I begun?

I shouldn't be doing this.

I should, for my plan to work. My plan…

Vinay reaches out and trails a finger down my cheek.

I tremble.

'Go,' I urge, 'please. Radhakka will be here any minute.'

Already, through the kitchen window, I can see Radhakka's heavyset body making its laborious way up the hill, her weighty, measured tread. 'Please…'

But he takes me in his arms and I don't know whether my *please* means leave or stay. It's been so long since I have been held that I have to fight the urge to rest my head on the shoulder of this man who is not mine by rights; who is forbidden to the likes of me; who I don't really want but who is offering himself to me because I have made it so; who is there, so solid, so real. I want to take up his offer of comfort and forget the world, the sadness and hurt, the unworthiness and rejection that I lug around like an extra weight.

'Only if you promise you'll see me again.' His voice is thick.

'Yes,' I breathe, wanting. Wanting never to leave the solid strength of his embrace. Wanting him to be someone he isn't – a farmer's son, with rippling muscles and a cheeky smile, the boy who pulled my plait and carried my satchel and walked me home from school, the strong giant who ploughed fields and the gentle lover who brushed the hair out of my eyes before he kissed me among the reeds.

'Come this evening. After everyone's asleep. Come to the fruit orchard by the herb garden. I'll be waiting,' he whispers.

'Yes.'

He lets me go, disappearing just as Radhakka comes into the kitchen and smiles. 'Well, look at you! What's got into you, girl? Have you turned over a new leaf? Working already! Miracles will never cease.' She shakes her head as she deposits her bag on the counter and ties her sari pallu up in preparation for cooking.

I breathe a sigh of relief. Or is it disappointment?

I want Radhakka to know, to stop me before I take this further, to shake some sense into me – to be the mother figure I have been denied since my ma took to her bed.

And I want to hug the secret to myself.

I don't know what I want.

All the advice my ma had reiterated while I was growing up reverberates in my ears all as I wipe and dust, polish and mop, peel and chop, cook and wash up.

You think your plan is all that. You think you are very clever to have conceived of it. Get off your smug throne. You think nobody else has thought of this? You think other servant girls haven't made a play at other landlords' sons over the years?

Why would he want to marry you when he has you already, so easy and willing, and not even a landlord for a da backing you up and asking that he make an honest woman of you? Do you want to sink lower than you are already? Remember the promise you made yourself. If you pursue this foolhardy course and he leaves you high and dry, you will be everything you vowed never to be again, my conscience chides.

He isn't like that. He is kind, sensitive, romantic. A poet. He has waited for the right woman to fall in love with, and in his mind, I am that woman. I think he will do the right thing. He is principled, and unafraid to stand up to his mother. He likes poetry but he is not as passive as his father. He has the courage of his convictions, another part of my brain adds.

But then I think of my father, whom I adored, who loved me, who I thought would never abandon me, running away with another man's wife.

Men are fickle. They want only one thing. Don't believe anything they say. My mother's warning, oft repeated once she realised her daughter was maturing into a beauty, ringing in my ears.

I will not go that evening, I conclude, sometime during the long agonising hours before sundown, during which the household swells back to its normal population as every servant returns and the landlord and his wife arrive, the chauffeur hoisting an array of exotic-looking shopping bags behind them. Vinay has made himself scarce, sitting in the library no doubt, composing sonnets when not reading them.

Radhakka, Sumathi and I serve the evening meal.

No Vinay.

I am relieved. And I am worried.

Why are you hiding from me? I ask him in my head. *Regretting it already?*

It might not be about you at all, silly girl, my conscience scolds. *He might be keeping out of his mother's sight after their argument regarding the luncheon – have you considered that?*

In the grand scheme of things, you are still, despite what happened this morning, an insignificant servant. You do not own him yet. Perhaps you never will.

I will not go, I tell myself as I wash the dishes after supper, looking out at the gathering twilight, the sun setting in a medley of pomegranate, cerise and rose beyond the hill.

I will go and he won't be there. Why would he want me? I stare at my reflection in the mirror in the hall, breathing in the flavour of the waning day, flushed with hibiscus and marigold, zesty with the faint tang of lime, until Radhakka yells, startling me. 'What are you doing girl, standing there daydreaming? Are you talking to ghosts?'

The curtain of night draws to a chorus of croaking frogs and gossiping crickets. I clean myself in the lukewarm water left after most of the other servants have had their wash, shivering as my hands touch my body, which yearns for the caress of sturdy hands that have patted the flanks of buffaloes; strong masculine hands capable of such tenderness – a caress I will never have.

I change into my nightie having not yet arrived at a decision, my fingers trembling as they fumble with the hooks on my bodice, these trappings of modesty that I had sewn at my ma's urging, back when she cared about me.

Darkness hints suggestively, a murmuring drape.

I wait until snores reverberate all around me, the heavy, well-earned slumber of my tired fellow servants, their secret dreams and wistful aspirations colouring the pungent air in the room, rank with body odour and sweat. Then I get up, knowing that if I don't go, I will never forgive myself. Knowing in that moment that I am my father's daughter. A risk taker. Sacrificing everything for the possibility, the promise of a different – better? – future. Sacrificing myself.

I walk blindly, one foot in front of the other, hands stretched out, grasping for landmarks, until my eyes adjust to the gloom. The heady scent of night jasmine. Past the herb garden with its piquant aroma of coriander and mint, tulsi and chillies. Into the orchard. The fragrance of ripening fruit. Looming shadows of trees.

Something moves beneath my feet. I jump, and the leaves rustle, as whatever it is slithers away, before settling back into innocent inaction. I stumble further into the orchard. Nothing moves except my feet, and overhead, a sliver of moon and a sprinkling of straggly stars alleviate the inky darkness, black branches waving like phantom hands. A cooing and a rumbling. A silver flash briefly illuminating the desolate surroundings. The growling threat of thunder.

I am overcome by a sudden, piercing ache for that other time, when my love kissed me on a bed of reeds on the bank of a stream, to the drumroll of thunder, the drama of rain. I walk further in and wait, clutching at my nightie.

He is not here. Set aside your lofty dreams of becoming a landlady and lording over the world. You have thrown yourself at him, cheapened yourself, for nothing.

Fool, I hear the foliage beneath my feet hiss. *Why would he want you?*

I rest my back against the bark of a tree, breathing in the tart green fragrance of unripe mango, the pungent prickle of failure at the back of my throat.

You promised yourself you wouldn't feel small again, after Manu. What are you doing here then?

The bark shifts. I jump. Then I am enveloped. Musk and cloves. My lips taken captive, my body fitting into his.

'You came,' he murmurs before he kisses me.

'How could I stay away?' I gush.

And then he is laying me down, so very tenderly, on the carpet of sweet-smelling leaves, underneath the swaying canopy of fruit trees, in a dark, secret world, only ours, as the heavens explode and rain falls all around us, and he removes my clothes and his, gently, gently, and we move skin to skin, and I close my eyes and give in to the sensations swamping my body, imagining that I am doing this at a different time, in a different life, in a different place with a different man.

I understand then, in the salty, slippery feel, the musky scent, the throbbing taste, the arching waves of ecstasy, why my father left. Monsoon-washed earth and moisture-stippled bushes. The piquant, evocative night our stage. The drip and spatter of rain our backdrop.

Afterwards, we lie side by side, holding hands and looking up at the slice of star-dusted, cloud-splashed sky visible through the awning of branches. Vinay talks and I listen. He recites poems for me, narrates odes to me, composes love songs about me. He spins exquisite dreams.

'You are my treasure,' he says. 'I never believed this much pleasure was possible,' he says. 'We are made for each other,' he says. 'I love you,' he says.

I believe him.

Vinay is a poet, like his father. He lives in an alternate world where everything is possible, where insignificant servants can love heirs to magnificent fortunes. I know this and I have banked on it, taken advantage of his good nature. I have trapped him via his romantic ideals. I know that he won't abandon me and that, when the time comes, he'll stand up to his mother for me. I know he's a better person than Manu or my da ever was. So why can't I love him in return?

And so I lead my double life. During the day I am but a servant and at night I transform into the belle of the heir, the muse of the poet, the giver and receiver of pleasure. I embrace my secret close, a waiting time bomb, like, I imagine, my da nursed his in the days leading up to his disappearance. I shush that part of my conscience, the warning voice that screams counsel all day as I go about my chores.

I no longer look forward to Sunday mornings, when, in a previous, more innocent guise I would vicariously emulate the landlord's wife – instead I am actually doing something every night towards realising that elusive dream of *becoming* the landlord's wife.

I don't sag under the weight of hurt any more; it has lifted a little as my plan looks set to become reality. My plan – designed to get me out of misery and into power and, with it, happiness?

I listen to Vinay's poetry and I echo his sentiments, hesitatingly at first and then with more conviction as I become more at ease with the deceit I am so calculatingly carrying out, despite it being at odds with my overworked conscience.

'I love you too,' I say, adding, in my head, *Manu*.

And although it is as dark as the soul of a two-timing witch, I sense Vinay's smile and it sears my heart, branding it the murky blue of culpability, the same shade as the blood that flows in my da's traitorous veins.

And then it happens. What I have been waiting for. The catalyst that will speed things up, set them in motion, get me what I want…

When I come out of the bathroom, wiping my wet hands on my churidar bottoms, having been sick for the third time in twice as many minutes, Radhakka stops what she is doing and turns to look at me.

'Come here, girl, sit,' she says, indicating the stool beside where she is tending to the stove.

I walk up to the stool, heart pounding frantically, the remnants of the nausea I thought I'd extinguished churning my stomach.

This is it. Now it truly begins.

'What's the matter? Is it about the fish? I will get it done. I… I just haven't been feeling too good lately,' I say, not wanting to look at the fish. The unbearable stench of it drifts up to where I'm standing, mingling with the frying scents from the vat of oil where Radhakka is concocting plantain podis as a snack to accompany the landlord and his wife's mid-morning tea. Radhakka and Sumathi exchange a look before they both turn to examine me.

They know.

The amalgam of aromas makes me feel green. I want to be sick again, but I don't dare. Not now, with Radhakka and Sumathi staring at me like I have done something gravely wrong. Which I have.

I need to play this very carefully.

'Why am I in trouble?'

Much as I have wanted this to happen, I hate feeling ill all the time, like my brain is wrapped in wiry wool, like I am enveloped in fog, wading through thick clouds of unsettling odours, like my stomach is a whole other entity that seems to incite revolt at the littlest things. I have been stealing buttermilk from the kitchen at night when everyone's asleep, to try to settle my stomach. I have been eating mint leaves from the herb garden after seeing Vinay, hoping that will help, the night air smelling of intrigue and dalliance, coriander and tulsi, and the secret whispers that Vinay drops like jewels into my ear.

I have become adept at sneaking out of the servants' quarters late at night. I lie with Vinay in the shade of the mango tree in the thick, surging darkness, nocturnal animals whispering and hissing, slithering and croaking, hooting and calling around us. And after, I tiptoe back in, to my room-mates with their noisy slumber, their guiltless dreams, my nightie pulled tight around me. I drift into sleep with his scent on my body, his words ringing in my ears, his taste in my mouth, my body throbbing with remembered pleasure. For I do enjoy being with him, although in my mind I am not really with him but with Manu. I lead a double life in my head and I lead a double life with the servants and with my employers. And I cannot stop. Now that I have started this, I have to see it through.

'Child, do you have something to tell us?' Radhakka says now, her voice unusually gentle. She has never called me 'child' before. It's always girl this and girl that.

I don't deserve it.

Did Radhakka or Sumathi wake up one night and realise that I wasn't there? Did they get curious and wait for me to come back, smelling different, wilder, muskier, the scent of man and mulch, rotting fruit and forbidden desire, the truth of what I had done stamping a bloom on my cheeks, a stain on my skin – sweat and semen and leaves and rain?

I lower myself down slowly onto the stool Radhakka has pulled out for me. 'I…'

'How many weeks?' Radhakka asks gently.

'I haven't really counted.'

Radhakka bends towards me and tenderly touches my stomach. Tears sting my eyes. I want to throw myself into this woman's arms and sob my heart out, tell her of my crime, what I have done, what I am still doing. I abruptly, urgently, want someone to take this away, the responsibility, the gravity of what has happened, what *is*.

My foolhardy, impulsive plan has worked. And all of a sudden, I am filled with dread at what is to come. The truth is that the more I get to know Vinay, the more I know that he doesn't deserve what I'm doing to him. He needs a girl who will love him like I pretend to, a girl worthy of his sonnets, a girl who doesn't have a chequered past, with a love she cannot forget – a man she still yearns for.

Continuing to stroke my stomach, Radhakka looks at me, her eyes soft, sad. I have never seen her look like this before. 'Oh, Kali, you are but a child. Didn't your mother advise you not to get yourself in trouble like this?' She sighs hard, rocking on her haunches.

Sumathi is looking at me the same way as Radhakka, mixed, in her case, with relief that it is not she who is in trouble.

'Didn't your mother educate you? But still… It may not be too late. Who is he? Perhaps we can talk him into doing the right thing.'

He is doing the right thing. It is I who am not.

They know. Like I meant them to, wanted them to. And presently, via the servants' grapevine, everyone will know.

I haven't told Vinay yet. I haven't had the courage. But I will this evening. I have to. This is why I wanted the servants to know. So it would galvanise me into action, stop me postponing the inevitable, chickening out now, when it is far too late. I will tell Vinay that he is to be a father. I will tell him that the servants have found out. I will tell him that he needs to speak to his mother – and soon.

'Is it the driver, Ramu? Or the errand boy, Siddu? Tell us. We'll talk to him. Child, who is he?'

In response, I jump up and rush to the bathroom, the stool toppling in my haste. I retch over and over, the taste of bile and fear, as the rank consequences of my reckless plan catch up with me once more.

❖   ❖   ❖

I am exhausted. So weary. I want to sleep. I want it all to end.

'I don't want to tell him yet, not just now,' I plead.

'That's okay, you don't have to.'

'Oh but you don't understand. I *have* to tell him. Before the whole world finds out.'

'You don't…'

'Yes, I do. Ours is a small, tight-knit community of servants. Radhakka knows and so does Sumathi. By nightfall everyone will know. It will only be a matter of hours before the landlord's wife finds out. Already a couple of the servants are looking at my stomach instead of meeting my eye. I really have gone and done it, haven't I? I didn't think I had it in me. Turns out I am my father's daughter after all, capable of such cold-blooded, single-minded deceit…'

'Shhh… Look, take these pills and have a nap. It will all seem better in the morning.'

Why is nobody taking me seriously?

Frustrated, I lunge at the plate. Water spills, some of it on my hand, but the plate of pills remains firm. My aim is horrendous; my hands tremble, feeble, useless. What has happened to me? Being pregnant should not feel like this, as if I am reduced to a frail facsimile of myself.

Someone feeds me the pills, bitter in my mouth. The silvery slick taste of water. Perhaps this will stop the nausea at least. I swallow. Lethargic torpor drags my lids down. I will sleep. Just for a bit. Then, once I wake, I'll decide how to tell him.

Chapter 16
Jaya (Now) and Sudha (Before)

A Reflection in Still Water

Once she gets home from seeing Dr Meadows, Jaya makes herself a cup of tea and sits on the sofa with her mother's first diary, opening it to the next entry, losing herself once more in her mother's words.

﹡ ﹡ ﹡

Dear Diary,

I do it. I do exactly what I said I would. I shred Ravi's notes and chuck them in his face the day after my da slaps me for daring to say I will marry for love, thus throwing away my dreams of happiness, my fantasies of being loved for who I am.

When I come home, nursing a broken heart, a gaping wound, my ghostly twin shadowing my footsteps and my every thought, our house is empty. The cat is mewling. The dog rubs his nose in my palm and whines. Both animals haven't been fed.

Where are my parents?

I scan the fields, look up and down the path.

I feed the animals and then I stand in the courtyard, cuddling the cat, the dog bounding at my feet, scouring the empty fields, at a loss.

Have they gone away? Left me to fend for myself?

My chest hurts from the look on Ravi's face, from what I have done, to Ravi, to my parents and, all those years ago, to my brother.

Then Chikkakka comes down the path among the fields, a basket of fish balanced on her hip, her plump arms jiggling.

'Child, why aren't you at the clinic?'

'The clinic?' My heart is cramped by terror, a giant hand squeezing my ribcage.

'Don't you know?'

I close my eyes, breathe in the fishy air that reeks of panic. 'Know what?'

But I know of course. I know I am to blame. If they are ill it is my fault for upsetting them yesterday. Is there no end to my crimes? What more am I capable of? I seem to hurt everybody close to me, all the people I care about. What is it in me that is programmed to do this? I want to tear it out, fling it far away so it will not touch the people I love any more.

'Didn't anyone send word to the school?'

I want to shake her until the truth falls out of her like guavas from the tree.

'Please tell me.'

'Your da is very ill. Chest pains. They think he's had a heart attack.'

No.

I don't wait to hear any more. I run. All the way to the clinic in Sannipur, four miles away.

I collapse, breathless, worn out, dishevelled and muddy, at the entrance.

'Please,' I beg, falling at a nun's feet, barely managing to squeak the words out in-between giant puffs of gasping air. 'Take me to my father.'

When I enter the ward that houses my father, the odour of phenyl and pills, death and distress, mustard-seed bitter in my parched throat, she is asleep on his chest. Her grey hair, escaping the confines of her bun, is fanned out all around her, caressing my father's ailing heart, wishing it back to health.

My mother. But never completely mine. My brother's mother. The mother of the boy I killed.

Da's face is ashen, wiped of colour. His eyes are closed.

I sit there looking at the machine connected to his heart and will it to keep spiking, to not become one straight line.

I wait.

When I wake, it is dark. Cold.

Goosebumps on my arms. Pain-suffused moans drifting from somewhere.

I open my eyes. Blink. I can feel their collective gaze upon me. The power of it.

His face is pallid, hers watery. Both of them accusing.

Ma speaks. 'Look what you did. Your da almost died.'

And it is there, in her voice. The accusation. Clear as a reflection in still water. Like your brother. He could have died like your brother. Are you planning on killing us all?

There are no walls any more. They have smashed, dissolved, like the regret trampling my fragile heart.

My throwaway comment the previous evening, my fledgling attempt at stretching my wings, pushing against the boundaries I've found myself walled into all my life, has backfired.

But in an oblique, albeit painful way, it is such a respite that it is all out in the open. I know where I stand with them now. I need not expect them to love me like I want to be loved.

I understand that they don't trust me. That their love for me is spiked with hatred, layered with resentment, seasoned with loss, grief and misgiving.

I will marry the person my parents choose for me – if someone looks beyond my past and agrees to marry me, that is. For me, no loveless marriage will be as bad as living with the knowledge that my parents will never forgive me; that they will not see past what happened – that they cannot.

❋   ❋   ❋

Jaya closes the diary and sets it out of reach of Mr Fluff just as the cat jumps onto her lap, purring and moving about until he's comfortably draped across her legs.

Oh, Mum, Jaya thinks, *no wonder you were so reserved. No wonder you stayed clear of people, never having any friends. How could you trust anybody when your own parents treated you like a pariah? Mum, I take it you didn't marry Ravi. So who is my dad? Was your marriage to him loveless? Is that why you never mentioned him to me?*

The more she reads her mother's words, the more questions Jaya has. She gently dislodges the cat, picks up her untouched cup of tea and walks to the kitchen.

You were hungry for love and approval as a child and so, as a mother, you made sure I never wanted for anything, Jaya thinks as she pours the cold tea into the sink and puts the kettle on while opening a tin of tuna for the cat. She stares blankly at the grey, blustery evening that is gusting over the garden, painting the grass the inky velvet of wistfulness. *Oh, Mum.*

Chapter 17
Durga

A Decapitated Mermaid

Lathakka leaves, breathing many sighs of relief at having successfully delivered Durga into her grandmother's care. She tries to gather Durga into a goodbye hug, but Durga slips expertly out of her arms.

Once the rickshaw disappears down the hill, Durga's ajji leads her inside, past huge, dark, falling-down rooms smelling of mould and old age, secrets and past grandeur. No ghosts anywhere in sight. No madwoman either. And her ajji seems completely sane, neither possessed nor cursed nor raving. Durga doesn't know whether she is relieved or disappointed. All she feels is an overwhelming exhaustion.

Following in her ajji's wake, Durga gets a glimpse of high ceilings and crumbling walls that breathe magnificence and destruction, mildew and poignant reminders of splendour long past: a glint from a broken chandelier; a torn tapestry, threads trailing; a decapitated mermaid, her smooth body undulating in a lovely arc.

'The original kitchen burnt down. This was the pantry, which was mostly untouched by the fire,' her ajji says, turning a corner and coming to a stop. She switches on a light so the room they are in is awash with a golden glow, making everything, from the pots and pans to the marrows and the tubes of garlic and bunches of dried chillies hanging from the ceiling, seem magical and intimate. 'The old lawyer installed the gas range himself – nobody wanted to come and work here, of course, after what happened, with all the talk of curses and black magic. A couple of brave souls did venture in to do the repairs, in the very beginning, after much bribing, I'm told, but Kali was at her most aggressive then… They weren't quite brave enough to weather her tantrums. They turned tail and left, adding fuel to the rumours…'

Who is Kali? Durga wonders.

'Now nobody will come near it, not even if you offer them the world. The old lawyer kept trying until his death, and the current lawyer has also attempted to sweet-talk and bribe labourers into coming here. But, if anything, the tales surrounding the house have got even worse – which is why this place is the way it is, falling apart at the seams.' Her ajji takes a long breath. 'You'll be sleeping with me in the room just off here, okay?'

Durga barely has time to nod before her ajji says, 'That room and the one next to it used to be the servants' quarters – a room for the men and one for us ladies. I used to sleep there once. Now I've come full circle, sleeping there again.'

'You were a servant here?'

'In another lifetime. In those days, there were seven of us girls squeezed into that one room. I'm glad I have you now.'

'Are you really?' Durga can't help but ask.

Her ajji grins at her and Durga is once again amazed by how this woman's sharp edges soften to look so much like Durga's kind, curvy ma when she smiles. 'Ah… You are right to be wary, child. I have kept my distance, haven't I?'

What sort of question is that? *Careful – don't lose your temper,* her mother's voice warns in her head. But it's too late. Durga is too tired to be patient with this stranger who she will now be living with in this old, disintegrating mansion, populated with ghosts and curses and a madwoman. 'So you're okay with my dark colouring and my lower caste now, are you?'

The old woman puts her hands on her hips and assesses Durga. 'Feisty, are we?'

'I'm told I get it from you,' Durga says and her ajji laughs, a witch's cackle resonating off the crumbling walls and incredibly infectious. Durga bites her lower lip to stop herself joining in.

'To answer your question, I had no choice, did I? I couldn't possibly leave you in the clutches of that horrid woman who phoned,' her ajji says when she's stopped laughing.

'Gowriakka?'

'Yes, that one! "You are Durga's only living relative," she said. The cheek of the woman! "Last I checked my daughter and her husband were alive – ailing but alive," I told her.'

Durga's lips curve upwards of their own accord. She can't help warming to this woman who shares her dislike of Gowriakka. But she is not letting her ajji off the hook this easily. 'So you're having me stay only because Gowriakka bullied you into it?'

Ajji's lips set in a grim line. 'Nobody can bully me into doing anything, especially not that vile woman.' Then she looks at Durga and her face softens again. 'I wanted to have you, child. I've wanted it for so long but didn't know how to ask.' Her eyes shine and she turns away, rubbing at them with her pallu. 'My stupid pride,' she mutters.

In the kitchen, the cold, unloved, fusty scent pervading the rest of the house is replaced by the welcome warmth of spices, the piquant embrace of jaggery, sweetened milk and hot oil – the promise of a hearty meal. Durga's neglected stomach rumbles long and loud.

'You must be hungry. Wash your hands over there,' her ajji nods to indicate a bucket of water, a tap dripping into it. 'Then come and sit here,' she pats a stool in front of a wooden table, 'and eat.'

She sets a steaming plate heaped with food in front of Durga. 'I didn't know what you liked, so I made a bit of everything.'

And the thought that this prickly old woman has spent most of the day cooking for her makes Durga's eyes sting.

Thank you, she wants to say. *This is very kind of you.* She wants to show her ajji that her mother has taught her manners, brought her up well, lower caste or not. But she is so hungry that her mouth doesn't want to produce words when it can eat chapattis and potato with peas, brinjal masala and dhal, fish fry and fish curry, vegetable bhath and plain rice.

'There's payasam for afters.' Her ajji watches Durga as if she can't quite believe she is there, right in front of her.

'Your cooking is as good as Ma's and she's the best cook in town,' Durga manages between mouthfuls.

Her ajji laughs. 'You don't need to sound so surprised, child.'

'Thank you, that was really nice,' Durga says when she has polished off every single thing on the plate and has had two helpings of payasam.

'When was the last time you ate?' her ajji asks.

'I...' Durga thinks back to the previous evening, when she had flung the plate of Gowriakka's son's leftovers that Gowriakka had placed in front of her back in her face, getting an armful of slaps and a lecture on how food was precious; how she was spoilt and ungrateful (didn't she see all they were doing for her?); how she couldn't wait for Durga to leave.

'I can't wait either,' Durga had yelled, storming off into the night to sit on the veranda of her old house, now occupied by a new family who stared nervously at her.

'Oh, child,' her ajji murmurs although Durga hasn't said anything out loud. It is as if her ajji has peeked into Durga's mind and seen what is in there.

'I don't want your pity.' Durga sniffs.

She is so tired, her stomach full, her heart heavy. She wants to lie down, to cry. She wants her mother and not the bony grandmother she barely knows. She hates being this far away from her parents.

'I don't blame you for being angry.' Her ajji sighs and Durga is so surprised that she looks up at her to check if she's joking.

Everybody always blames Durga for being hot tempered – it's something she has accepted as fact.

'I am angry with myself,' her ajji is saying. 'I pushed your mother away.'

Something in her voice, like falling down a bottomless hole, a well without end, no respite of hitting water at the bottom, gives Durga pause.

'When she insisted on marrying your da, I said some horrible things, things that couldn't be unsaid. I lost her.' Her ajji takes a deep, shuddering breath. 'She came back with you. And she said, "Your granddaughter looks just like her lower-caste da. You won't want anything to do with her either, will you?" She knew just how to push my buttons – always has.' Her ajji's voice is the despair of a dehydrated man finally reaching the bottom of the well and finding only sand. Bone dry. 'I was ready to apologise, but when she said that, I got angry, my apology drowning in the waves of my rage. I said, "Yes. I don't want anything to do with your daughter." I wanted to apologise as soon as the words were out. But, as always, it was too late. Too many things had been said, too much hurt caused. I was too stubborn to go to her after, to say I was wrong, although I ached to see her and you, to get to know you. My vanity and obstinacy were my downfall.'

She opens her arms and Durga, for the first time since her parents ended up in hospital, allows herself to be held. Her ajji's arms are stiff and crinkly; she smells of wood smoke and old age, wisdom and stale sweat. And yet, in the echoing kitchen of a strange house far away from everything familiar, in her grandmother's arms, as her ajji strokes her hair, Durga finds the solace she would normally only get in her mother's arms.

'I caused the accident,' she says, finally letting out the truth that has been sitting in her gut like a stone swallowed from a launched catapult. 'It was my fault.'

'Oh, Durga,' her ajji whispers, patting her back.

'We were on Da's scooter, with me sandwiched between Ma and Da like always. Then I saw Baluanna across the road.

He had complained about me and I was angry. I aimed my catapult at him and Ma said, "No, Durga," and Da turned to look and that's when we went into the back of that lorry – only, a split second before that, Ma pushed me off the scooter to safety.' Durga's words dissolve in a crater of tears.

Her ajji holds her and rocks her.

'Ah, child,' she says when Durga has calmed down somewhat, 'we all do things we regret.'

'But I… I can't seem to do what is expected of me.'

'Well, you must get that from me,' her ajji mumbles into her hair.

Durga smiles then. She can't help it.

✳   ✳   ✳

Afterwards, Durga has a wash.

'I'll comb your hair tomorrow, massage it with coconut oil,' her ajji says. 'Now to bed.'

'Where is the madwoman?' Durga feels better after her meal and wash, her stomach gorged, her body smelling clean and lemony.

'Her name is Kali. She's asleep.' Her ajji looks worn out after her earlier confession and their shared tears.

Ah, so the madwoman is Kali.

'Where?' This room Durga is in is closed, windowless, perhaps because it was once part of the servants' quarters, but it doesn't feel claustrophobic.

'Kali's room is just down the corridor from here,' her ajji says.

Durga turns to her side, propping her head up on her elbow to look at her grandmother. She likes being here, she decides, in this room that her grandmother has somehow made cosy, a madwoman sleeping nearby, the wind occasionally howling at the walls like the wails of the ghosts this mansion is rumoured to be harbouring. It is exciting. It makes her forget – however briefly – her troubles – what she has caused to happen to her ma and da.

'Why did you come here?' she asks her ajji.

'I was lonely, child. Too proud to make up with your mother. And I knew Kali. I had liked her when she was a young girl.'

'You knew her as a young girl?'

Her ajji nods. 'Kali and I worked in the kitchen together, for a very strict lady called Radhakka… Well, Radhakka was stern, but she could also be incredibly kind…' Her ajji smiles, her gaze far away.

Durga is shocked as she processes what her ajji has said. 'Wait a minute… Kali used to *work* here? She was a servant?'

'She was so full of life then.' Her ajji's eyes get that faraway look again. 'That was such a long time ago, when we both had everything ahead of us.' She blinks. 'Anyway, you asked how I came to be here. Well, when her previous caretaker became too ill to look after Kali, and the old lawyer asked in the village for someone willing to take Kali – and this ruin – on, I was at my lowest point. The family I had been working for for many years were moving away. I had hardly any money saved. I couldn't afford to pay the rent on my cottage for long without any income coming in… The lawyer's plea got me thinking. I had known Kali once. I thought I understood what had propelled her into madness. I didn't really set great store by the rumours about ghosts and curses surrounding the mansion. And I thought I might as well look after her. At least I would have somewhere to live. I should have turned to your ma, I know, but I was too proud…' A long, deep sigh. 'However much I missed her and regretted our estrangement, however much I wanted to get to know you, child, I also didn't want to rely on the charity of your mother and her husband, the very one I had shunned and spoken against. I didn't want your ma to think I was making my peace with her only because I had no other option.'

Her ajji pauses, ruminating. Then: 'It's not so bad here, you know. It's worked out well for me. The new lawyer visits every so often, just like his predecessor – the one who employed me – used to. He makes sure Kali and I are comfortable and don't want for anything. And Kali doesn't give me grief most of the time. During the day, there are nuns to care for her. The nuns make sure she is sedated at night, so I can manage her by myself. Most nights, she sleeps through. And even when she does wake up, she is subdued, reflective, searching for something from long ago, thinking she is somewhere else.'

'Oh,' Durga says, thinking, *Will she wake tonight?*

'Don't worry, child – you're not in any danger. If I thought Kali was even the slightest bit dangerous, I wouldn't have had you here.'

'I'm not worried,' Durga says sharply. 'I'm not a scaredy-cat.'

Her ajji laughs. 'I gathered as much.'

Something taps on the ceiling above Durga. Ghosts wanting entry into this snug haven? The room smells of flaking walls and fresh sheets and impending sleep and old recollections. It tastes homely, of shared confidences and the promise of security.

'You said that you understood the reasons for Kali going mad?' Durga is fascinated by the madwoman and by her grandmother's history with her.

'We all muddle through our days, child, finding different ways to deal with what life throws at us. If I had endured everything Kali did, I would be mad too. She spends most days in her distant past when, I gather, she was happiest. Sometimes her mind stumbles on the painful parts of her history and she is upset. But then it shies away, back to better times.'

Something tumbles and skitters, above them. Her ajji cocks her ears, then smiles reassuringly at Durga. 'Just this old house settling, child. Nothing to worry about.' And then: 'I wanted to come and pick you up when word came about your ma and da's accident. But… she has nobody else, you see, old Kali. I've become attached to her. She and I… we grew into our adult selves together. She chose one path and I chose another. And look where we've ended up now… I couldn't leave her. She… Nobody will come here, apart from the nuns, the rickshaw driver who brings groceries every week and the lawyer. The driver doesn't count as he stays only long enough to drop off the produce. The nuns don't stay the night and neither does the lawyer. Kali needs me here at night, you see… I wanted so much to see your ma. But then again… I don't know if I could bear to see her in hospital. I neglected her, shunned her when she was healthy and whole. Shame on me…'

Her ajji swallows once, then again, her eyes shining. 'The lawyer pays me well and I have a tidy sum put away. So I've assured your townspeople that I'll pay your ma and da's medical bills when the money from the house sale runs out… When

I heard what happened to your ma, I was… I…' She gulps. 'And then when they sent word asking if you could come here… It was God, taking with one hand, giving with the other. I told your townspeople that I would recompense them for everything they had spent on you.'

Durga recalls Gowriakka's rage when Durga threw the plate of leftovers at her, how she'd said, 'We are feeding you out of the generosity of our hearts, you spoilt brat, and this is how you repay us?'

'Do you trust them?' she asks.

'What else to do, child? You have to trust someone. They will make sure your parents are well cared for.'

The thought of Ma and Da brings the ever-present ache to the fore. Durga dampens it down, tries to push it away. Overhead, a thump. 'Is this house cursed like they say?'

'Stuff and nonsense. We carry our curses, our phantoms, within us. Human beings inflict more damage than a thousand ghosts. We don't need madwomen or spirits to place curses – we do it ourselves by being horrible to each other. Bad spirits are conjured from lost hopes and ill feeling and a healthy imagination. No, this house is not cursed. It's just sad. Yearning for all that it once was. Stained and tainted by melancholy, reeling from the unfulfilled dreams of those who once lived here.'

No ghosts or curses, just a sad house with an old madwoman living in the past as a respite from the present, Durga tells herself as she drifts off to sleep, a part of her disappointed and hoping that her ajji is wrong.

Chapter 18
Kali

The Fugitive Star

When I open my eyes, I see stars framed within the window bars. They dot the sky, a rippling awning, sparkling like a young girl's smile when she falls in love for the first time. And then I watch as one breaks free, makes a run for it across the sky.

Go, little star, go, I cheer silently, even as I realise there's something I must do. I'm forgetting something crucial, but my mind will not cooperate, however much I rack my brain. It is only when the white speckled dust left in the fugitive star's wake fades into grey that I remember.

I did not make a wish.

* * *

I sneak out to meet Vinay just the same as always the evening after part of my secret is discovered by Radhakka and Sumathi. I let him make love to me, once, then again, before telling him the truth that is growing in my stomach, the truth that has burgeoned out of my dishonesty and treachery – this child I have created as a means to get where I want to be, who will hopefully bring contentment and a sense of belonging, power and, with it, entitlement, which will erase the insecurity that floats just below the face I show to the world. I hope this child will ease my restlessness and hurt and anger and upset, and allow me to love Vinay for himself and not as a substitute for Manu.

No pressure, little one.

Afterwards, we lie beneath the canopy of night-tinted blue branches, staring up at the constellation of stars glowing like secrets.

I am just about to open my mouth to tell him, when he grabs my arm, slick with our combined sweat, and says, 'Look, Kali, a shooting star. Make a wish, quick.'

An iridescent shower that puts the other stars to shame, winking and dragging shadows in its trail. I close my eyes, cross my fingers, one hand grasping my stomach, and wish with all my heart that every hope I have resting on this child is realised.

'What did you wish for?' I ask when the star has streaked across the sky.

He turns to me and smiles. 'Ah, if I told you, I might jinx it.'

And suddenly I am afraid. What if I have got him wrong? What if he refuses to make an honest woman of me?

Please, gods, please, I pray, even as I think: *Why will the gods be on your side, sinner, when you have knowingly trapped a good man?*

I gaze deep into eyes, liquid with love for me, and open my mouth, dragging the shadow that will determine what comes after across the bright light of our relationship. 'I am pregnant.'

He looks at me and blinks once. Twice.

Please.

Then his eyes light up. They glisten and gleam like shooting stars. 'Oh, my darling!' he says, gathering me into his arms. 'How wonderful! We've created a miracle.'

I bury my head in the crook of his arm, breathing in the sticky scent of our lovemaking and I sob, like I have planned. But I am only half faking.

He holds me like I am the most delicate treasure. He strokes my hair. 'Why are you crying?'

'I'm so relieved,' I whisper. And this once I am telling the truth.

He tilts his head so he can look at me. 'You thought I wouldn't want you?' Hurt clouds his eyes. 'How could you?'

'Your parents will not be happy.'

'I know. That's why I made a wish. Oops!' He covers his mouth.

I smile through my tears. 'You wished for babies?'

'Not just babies. I wished for babies with *you*. I wished for us to be a family. I'm not stupid. I know my ma wants me to marry that girl I was introduced to at the party. But I… You drive me crazy, Kali. There cannot be anyone else. Only you.'

'But that girl is perfect for you. You are of the same status and class. You match.' I spout the speech I have prepared, taking a gamble, hoping…

'Rubbish,' he scoffs.

It worked.

'Look,' he says, pulling me on top of him. 'Look how our bodies fit so perfectly. And with the baby too.' He touches my stomach gently. I rest my head against his shoulder and smile. 'We're made for each other, Kali. I believe that. I know my ma may not see it initially. But we'll convince her.'

'Are you sure?'

'Absolutely. I don't want to lose you. Lose this.'

'When?'

'Huh?'

'When shall we tell her? I… I was being sick and Radhakka and Sumathi guessed, although they don't know whose baby it is…'

'Tomorrow. We'll do it tomorrow – get it out of the way. I'll speak with Ma and Da first, in the morning, and then come for you.'

I shiver at the thought of what is still to come.

'I'm scared. Are you?' I ask, planting a kiss on the tip of his nose.

'A bit.' He shudders. 'It will not be pleasant. But I'll make it okay, I promise.'

We make love again, gently, tenderly, and although I try my hardest to focus on Vinay and the child we've made together, as my body builds up to waves of pleasure, it is Manu that I think of, Manu's face that shimmers in my mind.

✻ ✻ ✻

'I think,' I say to the woman beside me, 'it was the magic of the night. Vinay and I together without consideration of position or status, not landlord and servant, just boy and girl, stripped to the skin, lying under a drape of stars, with only the frogs and the owls, the snakes and the celestial bodies for company, the smell of ripe fruit and raw desire and burgeoning life. Or perhaps it was my pregnancy making me crazy. But I believed it would all work out.'

'Oh, Kali,' my companion says. 'How far we have come, eh? Travelled miles away from the ideal, haven't we?' Her voice contains decades of familiarity.

For the life of me, I can't recall who this woman is. But does it matter? I am so tired. So very weary. Weary of trying. Tired of living.

'That enchanted evening, the dream I had nurtured, of becoming the mistress of a huge mansion – not just any mansion but the one that had enthralled me from the first time I laid eyes on it, the mansion that dragged me out of my misery – was suddenly, alluringly within reach.' I sigh deeply, my whole body aching, 'I stroked my stomach and using yarn from spilled stars and secret wishes, consuming loom from shining eyes and glowing prospects, I spun visions of a future where I was the mistress, running the mansion better even than the landlord's wife. A future where *I* was the landlord's wife.'

My body is rocking; it is shaking. My mouth is open and my ears are inundated by loud, keening howls. My eyes are wet, my nose is running and I realise, with dazed surprise, that I am the one responsible for the noise. I grab the arm of the woman, and when I am able to speak, ask, 'What happened? Tell me, what went wrong?'

Chapter 19

Durga

Rickshaw Drivers Bearing Portents

Durga dreams of ghosts and curses, of rickshaw drivers bearing portents, of beady eyes and voices sheathed in scorn. She dreams of whispers trembling like a small, cold infant: *Naughty girl. Look what you did to your ma and da.* They balloon into growls, the infant's body elongating and filling, transforming into a haranguing monster.

She dreams that Lathakka pushes her forward gently towards the ruin. And yet Durga stumbles. Lathakka morphs into her da, who is turning away from her.

'Why were you naughty, Durga?' Da asks, his face a map of pain. He folds his long body into the rickshaw and waves as it moves away, stirring the settling dust into turmoil again. She blinks, the orange cloud between her and her da shimmering and stinging.

'Wait!' the crowd, which seems to have collected out of nowhere, chimes. 'He's leaving the naughty girl here?'

Please, Da, take me home. I will be good, I promise.

Durga dreams that she is home, ensconced in her mother's arms, knowing that she is loved. Their house smells of damp and daydreams and of the fish they had for lunch. She is searching for something, looking in forgotten alcoves and crevices of the house, inhaling the cobwebby scent of dust and mothballs, of old saris and forgotten fancies – listening to the rhythmic tap-tap-splash of water dripping through gaps in the roof and hitting the tin cans placed around the room to catch the leaks, the scuttle and scurry of cockroaches hiding in the grimy corners of the room that never quite see the light.

She is searching for her ma and her da, who are missing…

She dreams she is falling off her da's scooter, her catapult shattering, falling deeper and deeper into an endless chasm.

'Durga,' her ma cries. 'Come with me.'

'Come,' a voice calls. Not her ma. 'Why are you sleeping? We have work to do. Wake up. Wake now.' An urgent voice. Imperative.

Durga wakes. She is cold. Bereft. The loss of her parents curling in her stomach – an aching throb. She throws off the unfamiliar bedclothes. Blinks. Where is she?

Moonlight slants in from somewhere, casting the room in an ethereal glow. She sees a small, bony woman, fast asleep, her snores reverberating through the room, her mouth open. And then she remembers. She is with her ajji in the ruin.

'Are you coming or not? We are late. Radhakka will skin us alive,' the commanding voice from her dream grumbles and Durga looks up and shivers, the fear cramping her stomach and clinching her throat exiting in a terrified gasp.

There's a woman standing at the door to the room, framed in moonlight, looking right at Durga and yet through her, as if she is looking inside Durga to all her secret, ugly bits.

A woman who was beautiful once, Durga sees, but who has now gone to seed, like this house. She is sharp featured, her bearing regal. But her hair is matted around her face, and her mouth is pursed into an impatient pout.

'Come, Sumathi,' she says. 'What are you waiting for?'

The woman is calling Durga by her ajji's name. Durga looks to her ajji for guidance. But she is asleep, the sari pallu that she's used to cover her face awry, jumping up and down with every puffed and noisy exhalation.

Durga gets up.

'About time!' The woman – it has to be the madwoman – turns and walks away, very quickly, taking long, purposeful strides.

And without thinking about what she is doing, Durga follows, struggling to keep up, excitement and fear running through her.

There are no ghosts or curses, she tells herself. *None.*

She is walking blind, into shadows, the sliver of moonlight that had lit up her ajji and the madwoman having disappeared, her eyes not yet adjusted to the dark. She breathes in the smell of dirt and intrigue as the silky threads of cobwebs – *not ghosts, no* – that she has destroyed in her haste to keep up with the madwoman brush her face.

Durga slips out the front door and down the steps into the courtyard on the heels of the madwoman. The night air, fragrant with jasmine, strokes her cheeks. She stares at the thick, swirling gloom until the heavy black shade of night settles into shapes and offers up its silhouettes and its secrets. She gazes up at the ruin, a smoke-stained, jagged profile piercing the overcast indigo sky; an angry facade, scowling down, hiding the devastation within. All alone. Abandoned. Disfigured.

'Why are you angry? Who are you angry with? What happened to make you this way?' Durga whispers to the ruin, in the shivering, memory-infested dark, populated with the ghosts of the madwoman's past, which weave through the woman's wavering mind and spill out into the shadows that engulf her and Durga.

A clawing grip on Durga's hand. Durga jumps – terrified. In that moment, before reality shakes the dread out of her eyes, she believes all the stories she's heard about the old ruin and fancies that spirits have come to claim her.

'I used to work here, you know.' The madwoman's fishy breath on Durga's cheek, the smell of unwashed skin, mouldy clothes and ancient reminiscences. Her hand on Durga's, her skin papery and crinkled so it is like being touched by the past.

'You did?'

In the darkness, interspersed with the sorrowful calls of a lone owl, the madwoman's eyes gleam – onyx stones rubbed smooth by years of experience, enfolding decades of mystery in their depths. Her grasp on Durga's wrist tightens without warning, her gaze pressing, her rambling voice suddenly lucid, as she says, 'Cursed.' Staring right at Durga, willing her to understand. 'The males are cursed. All the males, all dead.'

A glow-worm twinkles in front of them, the sudden golden light stippling the madwoman's face.

'But Hari,' the madwoman's eyes shine in the gloom, the quicksilver hue of an electric sky on thundery nights. 'Hari.' She says the name reverently, a devotee hailing God.

Who is Hari? Durga wants to ask. But she daren't break the spell cast by the madwoman's recollections, her abrupt and disjointed bridging of the past with the present.

'Hari didn't die. He didn't.' The woman's voice, so devastated a minute ago, now rises in conviction, celebration.

Her smile is alive with the presence of the past. 'Listen, I'm going to tell you a secret. Come close.' A soft finger on Durga's lips. 'Not a word until I say so. This will be just between me and you.'

But just then the otherworldly moment, stolen from time, is shattered. 'Kali?' Durga hears. 'Durga?' Her grandmother is standing at the front door, peering out into the darkness, trying to locate the two of them.

Durga tugs at the madwoman's hand. 'What was the secret? Tell me quick.'

'Who are you? Where am I? Where is Manu? Where are my ma and da?' The madwoman is staring into space, lost once again, walking the fragmented paths of her past.

Then Durga's ajji is upon them, taking them both by hand.

'She woke you up, did she?' Her ajji says to Durga, her voice tender. 'Come to bed, child. You look like you've seen a ghost.'

'Ghost? What rubbish!' the madwoman snaps. 'There are no ghosts.'

And Durga and her ajji exchange a conspiratorial smile in the undulating darkness.

Chapter 20
Kali

Faeces on a Sari

'Come, Kali, let's get you washed and dressed.'

'No. I don't want to.' I shake my head until I am dizzy. This is how the inside of my brain feels like all the time. Muddled, lost. With bits of comprehension shining through.

Now there is something tugging at the edges of my memory. What is it? And then a swooping sensation in my chest as it comes to me. How could I forget this, my passport to acceptance and respectability, power and perhaps happiness or, at the very least, an easing of sorrow?

I touch my stomach. It is gaunt, turning inwards. Shouldn't there be a bump? Oh yes. It is too early to show yet. But it will show. And then…

And then there will be mayhem.

Unless…

Unless something is done and fast.

* * *

It is not long after the household wakes up that the routine morning noises – the whistle of the idli steamer, the clink of breakfast dishes being laid out in the dining room, the bhajans booming from the cassette player in the prayer room, the driver whistling as he washes the car in preparation for the day's rides, the gossip of the servants as they sweep and mop the floors of the mansion, the head gardener haranguing his workers for not taking better care of his precious plants – grind to an abrupt halt, rocked into an uneasy silence by the uncharacteristic screams, the shouts and the wails that float down the stairs and echo through the house.

I am chopping the coriander and mint I have fetched from the herb patch, glistening with dew, to dress the chutney.

A yell, then the landlord's wife's raised voice, shrill as a pressure cooker, piercing the ordinary morning, setting it apart, rendering everyone mute.

'What's happening?' Radhakka whispers, the ladle she's been spooning idlis out of the steamer with raised, her eyes stunned as they meet mine.

I chop too hard and slice my finger. There is blood everywhere, bright red gushing, mingling with and staining the lush green. Sumathi takes one look at the blood and swoons. Radhakka, startled out of her daze at the ruckus from upstairs, drags me to the tap, runs water on the wound, tears a piece off the muslin cloth used for straining the water in the idli steamer and wraps it around my finger.

Servants congregate in the hall, Radhakka, Sumathi and I among them, breathing in the spicy scents of breakfast, the headiness of sandalwood incense wafting from the prayer room, all of us cringing from the screeching, fingernails-on-slate sounds of war from upstairs.

Around me my fellow servants gossip in shocked whispers, conjecture mingling with horrified upset. 'Should one of us go upstairs to check?' they wonder while I watch and listen, the thrill of dread prickling my spine, raising goosebumps. In the end, the most senior of the servants knocks on the closed door of the bedroom the landlord shares with his wife.

A screeching, 'Go away,' is directed back at him and he walks back down the stairs, ashen faced.

I tremble like a leaf in a squall. I have never known the landlord's wife to lose her composure so completely before.

After what feels like an age, the door opens and the landlord's wife walks out, still in her nightie, another thing she has never done before, always dressing up, even just to greet us servants. She stands at the top of the stairs and her gaze, sore and swollen eyed, sweeps over all of us servants gathered at the foot of the stairs before it meets mine. It lingers on me for a long moment, so cold and filled with scorn that I shiver even more uncontrollably. Then the landlord's wife gives me a hard little smile, beckons to the senior servant to follow, and turns and shuts the door behind her.

'What was that about?' Radhakka muses.

I cannot talk. I am quaking too much.

'Look at the state of you, child, your teeth are chattering. Come.'

But before Radhakka can say or do any more, the senior servant comes charging down the stairs, right up to me.

'You are wanted upstairs.' Curiosity is rife in his gaze, his voice.

'There must be some mistake…' Radhakka begins, for once at a loss for words.

I squeeze Radhakka's hand, look once at the gathered servants, taking in their inquisitive, worried gazes, before walking up the stairs alone, knowing that by the time I have finished climbing, everything will change, and that the posse clumped at the bottom will be my allies no longer.

Vinay comes to me as soon as I enter his parents' bedroom and he takes my hand. He looks broken. Dark shadows ring his eyes.

The landlord's wife's eyes centre on our joined hands and then her gaze finds mine. It is cow dung smeared on a chappal, faeces on a sari. A look that sees right through me, to my traitorous heart, a look that asks how I dared think my trick of trapping her poet son into loving me would transcend status, conquer prejudice.

I am in the room where I first kissed this woman's son, wearing her perfume and her robe.

'Who gave you the right,' the landlord's wife says, pacing the length of the room, 'to steal my son from right under my nose?' Her voice, after the morning's outburst, is calm, but there is ice in it.

I want to deny everything, feign innocence. But I cannot get the words out. It appears that I am not as brave as I thought, my body quivering, my mouth struck dumb.

'Ma, we love each other…' Vinay's voice is weary, as if he has tried this argument before and lost, his gaze forlorn.

'I am speaking to her, Vinay. Doesn't she have a voice?'

Finally I am able to get the few dishonest words I have prepared for exactly this eventuality past the obstruction in my throat that tastes of fear. 'I love him. I love your son.'

The landlord's wife laughs, sharp, bitter, like a hailstorm on a dark night, ice cutting glass. '*You* love him. Like your father loved that whore and ran away? Whore for a father, whore of a daughter.'

'Ma, don't speak to Kali li—' Vinay jumping to my defence.

'You thought I didn't know? I know *everything* that goes on. I know why you and your disgraced mother came to *my* village. I took pity on you, gave you a job and you repay me like this?'

Her gaze travels to my stomach. I place a protective hand over it.

'You say you are pregnant. Ha. How perfect. Why didn't I see it? My son. The poet. What better way to win him over than to feed him the dreams he spins via his poems? What a beautiful and romantic tale! Orphaned servant girl – you are as good as an orphan anyway, with the parents you've got – falls in love with the prince. They have a baby together and live happily ever after.' She takes a deep breath but she is not finished. 'Do you know what this will do to him? To his reputation and ours? He is meant for greater things than being tied to trash like you.'

'Ma! No… I will not stand for you talking to Kali like that.'

As if Vinay has not spoken, the landlord's wife asks me, 'How far gone are you?'

'Twelve weeks,' I whisper.

'Not too late…'

'No. Never.' Vinay places an arm around my shoulder, pulling me close, shielding me with his body. 'I'm going to marry her, with your permission or not.'

The look of raw pain that replaces the coldness in the landlord's wife's face is enough to stun the room into shocked silence. If the landlord's wife had stripped bare, it would have made less of an impact than seeing her like this. Reduced. The regal stance, the imperiousness gone, her shoulders stooped with defeat, so she looks, for the first time, old. A small, crushed old woman.

The landlord stands. He lays down his glasses and walks up to his wife. Holds her. He looks at me and there is judgement in his usually complacent gaze. 'You've hurt my family. Driven a wedge through it,' he says, the first words he's spoken to me, despite the number of times I have dusted books in the library while he has been ensconced in his armchair, reading, both of us lost in reveries.

'I am sorry, Ma, Da. It was never my intention to hurt you. But I love Kali only her and we are going to get married.' Even though his voice wavers alarmingly, Vinay stands his ground.

'If you say so, son. But know that you have hurt your mother. And me. And that you have brought dishonour upon generations of Gowdas.'

'How? By loving Kali?'

The landlord's wife looks up at me then, her eyes shimmering like moonlight shattering into scintillating shards on the surface of a river in the dead of night. 'You're pregnant. You're going to be a mother. When you have children, you'll understand the extent of the pain you have inflicted upon us. I hope your offspring brings you as much injury as mine has me, if not more. I hope you are punished just as much as you are punishing me by doing this, and I hope you are hurt more. I hope you are destroyed like you have destroyed us. That is my wish for you.' And with those terrible words, the landlord's wife lays her head on her husband's chest, closing her eyes and shutting us out.

'Come,' Vinay says softly, taking my arm. Together we leave the room.

As the door closes behind us on the landlord and his beaten wife, I can't help looking down at the tableau of servants. Comprehension is dawning in Radhakka's and Sumathi's eyes. They take in Vinay's arm shepherding me, they see the closed bedroom door. And they avert their eyes, as if ashamed for me, ashamed to be associated with me.

Don't be like that. I am above you. Aren't I? So why do you look sorry? Why do you look like you pity me?

But Radhakka and Sumathi, my allies, my friends of a sort, ignore my unspoken plea and turn away from me.

A door closed.

And that is when I understand, for the very first time, that realising my plan may not necessarily get me the result I have hoped for.

Scorn, anger, disgust, envy and suspicion fight for prominence in the other servants' faces before they too look away.

The house reeks of sorrow, trembles with shock. It is as if someone has died. An inauspicious way, if any, to begin my new life as mistress of this house, with a curse from the woman I have admired and the disappointment of the landlord, the loss of the only friends I have had since I lost my da and my love, and the contempt of the servants among whose ranks I have felt so very much at home.

* * *

'How clean you are now after your wash. How beautiful you look in your new maroon housecoat!'

'I am not clean. I am dirty. I have been bad. I am cursed.'

'Shhh, it's okay. You are…'

'It's not okay. Nothing is as I imagined, as I hoped it would be.' I hold on to the hand of the person who is being kind to me, as if it is my lifeline, even as I stare at her suspiciously. 'Why are you talking to me? Being so nice to me?'

'Oh, Kali!'

'You will turn around tomorrow and hate me, won't you, like everyone else?'

'Of course not.'

'You say so now, but…'

'Kali…'

'Ma'am to you. I am the mistress of the manor now. The mistress…'

Chapter 21

Durga

Fruit-strewn Earth

Durga wakes to sizzling spices, the golden aroma of onions caramelising in oil. This time when she opens her eyes, she knows immediately where she is. The room she shares with her ajji is bathed in sunlight, her grandmother's sheets folded neatly on her narrow cot. She hears shuffling from the kitchen – her grandmother trying to be quiet so as not to wake Durga up.

Durga looks to the doorway where Kali had stood the night before, silhouetted in moonlight, calling her by her grandmother's name and beckoning her to follow. She thinks of everything the madwoman said, the secret she wished to impart. Was it all a crazy dream?

She gets up and stumbles into the kitchen, rubbing her eyes and saying, 'Something smells nice.'

Her grandmother turns from the stove and smiles. She pats the stool where Durga had sat the evening before and says, 'Wash your face and hands and then come and eat. Did you sleep well?'

'Yes,' Durga says. Then: 'Were the boys from this mansion cursed?'

Her grandmother's hand stills on the ladle. She turns to look at Durga, her thin lips almost disappearing, two vertical grooves joining all the other lines bisecting her forehead. 'Pay no attention to what Kali says. She had a very disturbed night. I woke once and settled her, made sure she went back to sleep. I didn't think she'd be up again. I'm sorry I didn't wake up and she ended up taking you on her jaunt.'

So it wasn't a dream.

'I enjoyed it,' Durga says and realises as she says so that it is true. 'She's quite something.'

Her ajji smiles, the lines flattening on her forehead, only to collect in bunches at the corners of her eyes. 'That she is.' She waves her ladle at Durga. 'So are you. And a brave girl too. Any other child would have cried loud enough to raise all the slumbering ghosts this mansion is rumoured to house at being accosted by a strange woman in the middle of the night.'

Warmth seeps into Durga's heart at this unexpected compliment. She turns away to hide the prickling in her eyes. 'I'll go wash,' she says.

'You do that and I'll have breakfast ready.' Her ajji smiles.

'Who is Hari?' Durga asks when she is sitting at the table, taking a sip of the steaming, spiced tea her ajji has placed in front of her, ready to tuck into her breakfast – sajjige seasoned with mustard seeds and sweet with shavings of coconut.

Her ajji sighs. 'What did she say?'

'That he did not die.'

'She hopes that's the case.'

'She seemed quite certain of it. She was going to tell me a secret when you found us…'

Her ajji sits at the table across from Durga and squeezes her hand. 'You have to take everything Kali says with a pinch of salt, child.' Then, pointing at Durga's heaped plate, she says, 'Eat. Your food is getting cold.'

Durga takes a bite. It is exactly like the sajjige her mother makes. Her whole being delights in the comfort of her mother's cooking – it is like her mother coming back to her, gathering her in a fond embrace. 'Did you teach Ma this recipe?' Durga asks and her ajji laughs, looking, despite the tired circles ringing her eyes, happy.

Faint creaking and groaning sounds reach them from somewhere within the house.

'Where is Kali now?' Durga asks.

'She's had her wash and her breakfast – two slices of bread with my tomato chutney and a boiled egg – the only thing she will eat in the morning. I took it up to her just before the nuns came.'

'The nuns are here already?'

Her ajji nods, smiling tenderly at Durga. 'You slept in this morning, which is no wonder after your journey yesterday and Kali disturbing you in the night.'

'Where…?' Durga begins but she is interrupted by a crashing sound, a roaring.

'No, no, no…' Anguished wails. Kali.

Then the kitchen door slams open and Kali pushes in, hair streaming around her face, which is distressed, tears gushing from her eyes. 'Fire… I…'

'Kali,' Durga's ajji says gently.

Two nuns, huge crosses pinned to white habits, heads covered by wimples and faces spouting identical anxious expressions, follow Kali into the kitchen.

'Sumathiamma…' one says while the other smiles, albeit worriedly, at Durga. 'And you must be Durga. Your grandmother has been looking forward to your arrival.'

Kali's wild eyes skitter and dart around the room until they hone in on Durga. And just like her mood turned the previous night, from upset to jubilant in a volatile flash, her face clears, the tears stopping, a beaming smile transforming it into something riotously beautiful.

'Manu!' she exclaims. 'I've been looking all over for you. Come.' She strides up to Durga and tucks her arm in hers. 'Let's go and play.'

'Durga, you don't have to if you don't…' her ajji begins, concern colouring her voice.

'I'll be fine, Ajji. I do want to.' Durga smiles as she is led away by an insistent Kali.

'We'll keep an eye on her,' the nuns say and their unlikely procession, an old woman and a young girl hand in hand, skipping in unison – Kali *is* actually skipping, having regressed into childhood, and Durga is only too glad to join in – with two nuns following, wearing rosaries and clutching bibles and medical bags, leave the kitchen.

* * *

'Here, this is a good one,' Durga says, handing Kali a V-shaped twig – her best find yet.

They are in the fruit orchard by the servants' wing, where the hill starts sloping downward. It is heady with scents, guava and mango, banana and cashew and jackfruit all vying for attention, the ground sticky with juice, carpeted with trodden produce. The air is thick with buzzing insects stoned on nectar, dappled light filtering in through the arching canopy of overgrown trees, aching with unpicked fruit.

'What are we doing, Manu?' Kali asks, her tremulous voice trusting and tinged with the innocence of a child.

'We're making catapults.' Durga grins, not minding being called Manu at all, happy to take the lead.

She glances over at the nuns, sitting in the speckled shade of a jackfruit tree, fingering their rosaries and bent over their bibles, smiling at Durga and Kali every once and again.

Her hands itch to train her catapult on them, but she had procured rubber bands from her ajji after having solemnly promised her to aim the catapults only at inanimate objects – not at birds ('Of course I wouldn't do that!' Durga had huffed), and especially not at the nuns, however tempting a target they might be.

How can Ajji read my mind so well when she's only just met me? Durga had wondered and her ajji had grinned, once again party to her thoughts, and winked. 'I was just like you, you know, a lifetime ago when I was a child.'

'So look and learn, Kali,' Durga says and she takes aim at a particularly ripe cashew, red to the point of rotting. Her stone hits the target and it splatters, juicy bits flying everywhere, the heady taste of cashew liqueur and triumph swarming Durga's mouth. The nuns look up and smile as one and Durga feels guilty for having wanted to use them for target practice.

'Wow, Manu.' Kali's eyes are alive with admiration and hero worship. 'You are amazing.'

'Your turn,' Durga says, marvelling at how a child's intent and open expression takes over the old woman's weathered, experience-mapped face.

'Do you have your target in your sights, Kali?' Durga asks.

Kali sticks her tongue out in concentration and closes one eye, legs slightly apart as she aims at a guava. 'Yes, Manu.'

'Then go for it!' Durga yells.

Both the nuns look up, their expressions uneasy. Durga crosses her fingers behind her back.

Kali lets go of the stone. It splats onto the ground a small distance away, hardly even grazing the guava. Kali flings the catapult onto the ground in frustration. Her face crumples and she lets out a long, low wail. Then she is lying face down on the fruit-strewn earth, hitting it with her arms and legs, heart-rending sobs cleaving her in two, a toddler having a tantrum. 'I can't do it. I can't do anything. I fail at everything.'

Durga crouches beside her, trying to pat her moving, jumping shoulder. 'No, Kali…'

The nuns are upon them in an instant, saying, 'There, there, Kali, come now.'

But Kali is focused on Durga, her tantrum forgotten, her face scrunched in puzzlement. 'Who are you?'

'I…' Durga begins, at a loss. Should she say she is Manu?

The nuns try and coax Kali into standing but Kali shrugs them off, her eyes on Durga. 'Are you… Hari?'

Hari again. Who on earth is this Hari?

'I…'

'Sudha,' Kali whispers and her gaze is far away, looking beyond Durga to the magenta-splashed clouds drifting serenely across the gold-rimmed sky. 'She said she would send word. But she didn't… She didn't.' Her voice is longing and patience, worn thin by decades of waiting. She grabs Durga's hand, her grip harsh, pressing. 'Where are they? Where are Sudha and Hari?' She looks at Durga, right at her, as if seeing her for the very first time. 'They left. But they didn't come back. Don't they know I'm waiting?' Plaintive. Sorrow bathed. Tear dyed. A query that rips right through Durga's heart.

'Come Kali, let's get you inside and cleaned up, shall we?' the nuns coax. And as if her plea has taken everything out of her, Kali capitulates, allowing the nuns to lead her indoors.

❋   ❋   ❋

'Durga, would you like a snack?' her ajji asks, coming up to where Durga is perched on a mossy bit of crumbling wall near the orchard, musing on what Kali said. Her ajji pats the disintegrating brick beside where Durga is sitting. 'This wall used to separate the main gardens from the herb and vegetable patch and the fruit orchard.' Her voice is wistful. 'And all this'–she casts her arms around–'used to be lush lawn, the borders profuse with marigold, jasmine and roses, the hedge delineating it from the drive, which was adorned with bougainvillea.' She sighs. 'How times change, eh! I would like to see the ruin restored to its former glory in my lifetime. That would be something.'

'Ajji, why is Kali the way she is? What happened to make her so? And who are these Sudha and Hari that she keeps mentioning to me?'

'Oh, Durga. It is a long, sad story. But I suppose now that you're here, you should know it.'

And sitting there, Durga listens to her ajji as she narrates Kali's story in her soft, age-tempered voice.

'I feel for them, all of them,' Durga says when her ajji is finished. 'But Kali – why is she here?'

'What do you mean?' her ajji asks.

A butterfly alights on a weed next to Durga, translucent wings dotted blue winking at her.

'Shouldn't she be in a clinic of some sort?'

Her ajji sighs. 'After the fire, when she was released from hospital, the old lawyer tried housing her at various asylums. But she fought against it; she kept asking to come here. She was wild, uncontrollable. No asylum or clinic would have her for long. And so the lawyer managed to get a nurse to stay here with her – the rumours about the mansion being cursed weren't as rampant then – with the nuns looking after her during the day. As soon as she was here, she calmed down. She was on her way to recovery when…' Durga's ajji pauses, pondering.

'When?' Durga prompts.

'Her husband… They thought he wouldn't survive the fire. But he did. The old lawyer took him to his own house when he was discharged from hospital – they were family friends, you see, and the lawyer worried that he wouldn't be able to cope with the devastation to his house and with what had happened to his wife. But Kali's husband gave the lawyer the slip one day. He hired a rickshaw and came here. And the lawyer was right. It was too much for the man to take, seeing his house reduced to this shell. He hanged himself.'

'In this house?' Durga shivers, looking at the ruin.

'Yes. And Kali found him… After that she lost what little hold she had on her sanity.'

'So the rumours were partly right,' Durga says, vaguely recalling the villagers mentioning a man's body swinging from the rafters. She shivers again despite the warm breeze caressing her body.

Durga can't help her parents heal – she is too far away. But she can do something about Kali's pain. Kali looked so distraught when she mentioned Sudha and Hari… Durga cannot get her plaintive voice out of her head. And now that she has heard Kali's story from her ajji, Durga understands why she is the way she is, and is all the more determined to help her…

'Ajji, Kali is convinced Sudha and Hari survived the fire,' Durga says.

'But how?' her ajji muses. 'Although… I remember hearing that their bodies were never recovered. The fire was quite catastrophic, mind you. A couple of servants' and guests' bodies were not salvaged as well.'

'Kali must know something, Ajji. She said Sudha and Hari went away and promised to send word. She is adamant. She told me about Hari yesterday and again today. Please, just talk to her.'

Durga's ajji beams fondly at her. 'I will, I promise. Seeing you here must have triggered some forgotten memory in Kali's wandering mind. You are a good girl, Durga, you really are.'

Durga savours this unexpected epithet, thinking, *See, Lord Krishna – Ajji said I am good. Now can you heal my parents, pretty please?*

'I'm not usually,' she says.

'You have a good heart, Durga, and that is all that matters,' her ajji says.

Perhaps different people see things differently. The townspeople had this idea of me as naughty. They thought I was a nuisance. So I behaved badly. Here I am liked. I am wanted. By Ajji. Even by Kali, who confides in me. This place is good for me, Durga decides, stroking the wall, velvety with moss, and lifting her face up to the sun, its honeyed light dancing on her closed lids.

Chapter 22
Kali

Dreams Flying like Dandelion Spores

There is a girl. Bringing back memories. Asking questions. Making me hurt. Making me want.

Want what?

I am waiting. Waiting to hear from someone.

Who?

I am getting married, this much I know. To the landlord's son, no less. A future I aspired to, convinced that I was destined for great things. All those dreams, flying like dandelion spores, now taking root and sprouting.

I am going from servant to boss and am growing the heir to this great estate in *my* womb. The wedding is not exactly what I had hoped for, but…

* * *

Vinay's mother is the one who sets out the conditions for our wedding: it needs to be very small, very quiet. She cannot bear losing face in front of their peers, she says.

'I will not be able to maintain the smile on my face,' she cries to Vinay. 'I will burst into tears in public, embarrassing all of us.'

'Why can't you be happy for me? I love Kali. She's the only one who makes me happy, Ma,' Vinay pleads.

Outside this closed room swarming with angst, I picture the servants conferring in melodramatic whispers, as they sweep, mop, dust and clean. I wonder how many of them have their ear pressed to the door, listening carefully so as not to miss a word. Later they will congregate in the kitchen, the various factions: the outdoor servants, the upstairs servants and the kitchen staff, all bound by intrigue, the scent of gossip, thick and sweet, rising above the curling steam from their well-earned tumblers of tea and the few grudging snacks Radhakka will provide, as they dissect the colourful lives of their employers and one of their defecting own.

'She was so unassuming,' they will say, shaking their heads and rolling their eyes at their own short-sightedness, staring at the empty spot beside the kitchen window where I used to prop myself with a tumbler of tea during these habitual chinwag sessions, 'and all the while she was conducting a clandestine affair with the boss.'

Vinay agrees to all of his mother's terms concerning *our* wedding.

'You could have checked with me,' I protest later, when we are on our own, keeping my voice even, not showing the extent of my anger.

'But you don't want a big wedding, do you?' he says. 'You said so once.'

Fool, fool, fool.

How had Vinay remembered that one conversation? What can I say to him now? *Yes, I did say that, but I didn't really mean it.* I don't want to seem petty, especially not after all the hurt and upheaval our declaration of love has caused, for which I am getting the lion's share of the blame. Justified, perhaps, but it hasn't been easy for me either.

No servant will look at me, not even Radhakka or Sumathi. They all stop talking when I approach, ignoring me, pretending I don't exist. I don't sleep in the servants' quarters any more, in a room with six other gossipy women, sharing the day's woes, imparting confidences and advice, lightening our load before easing into slumber, the air tinted blue with merged dreams.

I now sleep alone, in a room more than quadruple the size of the one I had shared with the other servants, in the second wing of the house, removed from everyone – no chatter, no laughter, only the tense dialogue between my conscience and my other, more grasping self, keeping me company.

I had moved out of the servants' quarters at Vinay's urging the day we announced our love to Vinay's parents. 'You can't stay with the servants. You are to be my wife,' Vinay had said, looking at me softly, eyes filled with love but now also carrying an undertone of pain because of the rift with his parents. 'This is to be your room.'

The room was bigger than the house I had grown up in and crammed with more furniture than I knew what to do with – a huge bed, when I was used to sleeping on a mat on the floor, a magnificent sofa, the gleaming cream of spun silk, a dresser, two wardrobes and an en-suite bathroom, all to myself.

My dreams were already coming true and how! Amazed tears sprouted in my eyes.

Vinay misread my expression. 'I know it's a bit isolated. But you'll only be here until the wedding. Then you can move into my room.'

'No, she can't,' the landlord's wife had declared. 'I will not have her on the same floor as me.'

'Don't be like that, Ma,' Vinay had said, far too gently in my opinion.

Despite being more than satisfied with my wonderful room, I wouldn't have minded being in Vinay's room either, with its view down the hill and into the village, so I could watch the villagers, wavering dots in the dust-glazed distance and crow, in the privacy of my head, over how far I had come.

'I will be how I want to be. You move downstairs with her when you are married,' the landlord's wife had huffed.

And just like that Vinay had given in to his mother.

'You should have been firm with her, Vinay,' I couldn't help saying later.

'How?' he replied, rubbing a weary hand over his eyes. 'This is harder than I imagined, Kali. I hate to see them suffer. I have hurt them so.'

'Why can't they just accept me? I am carrying their grand-child, for God's sake.' All the frustration I was feeling coloured my voice, making it sharper than I intended it to be.

'I knew they would be upset, but I thought they'd come round sooner… Perhaps because they're older, more settled in their ways, it's not so easy. Let's give in to this for now. At the moment, I think it's all a bit too raw for them.' His voice was beseeching, his gaze suppliant.

'Your mother is wily,' I wanted to say. 'I know, because I'm wily too. She is manipulating you like she does everyone, like I have manipulated you. Why do you think she has the village's good opinion when she scrupulously collects all that rent from the villagers?'

But once again I kept quiet. It was early days yet. I had won the most important battle. I would bide my time.

Vinay's feebleness where his parents are concerned, how he allows himself to be taken in by his mother's tears, her tantrums, grates on me. To be honest, I am surprised that he has stood up for me and for our union at all. Needless to say, we don't meet in the orchard any more.

'We'll wait until the wedding, my love.' Another of Vinay's appeals. 'We've already caused so much upset and if they catch us sneaking off…'

Funnily enough, I miss our clandestine outings, the poetry Vinay would whisper in my ear, the endearments he showered me with. I miss being feted and cherished. The truth is, I feel so alone. I had thought that once his parents agreed to our wedding, it would be plain sailing, that I would find happiness and contentment among the grandeur, the wealth. I hadn't counted on the reality being so removed from my expectation; I hadn't realised that even surrounded by extravagant fortune one could be so *lonely*.

I haven't said anything to my aunt or uncle or even my ma yet. I didn't go to visit with them last Saturday, the first after we told Vinay's parents of our relationship, as there were no wages to give them. Vinay arranged for the driver to send word that I was ill. But I'm sure that gossip has spread already, into the village and beyond, and that the driver had filled my aunt, uncle and ma in on anything they might have missed and likely plenty that never happened at all.

'It'll never work,' my ma had tutted that time I visited when the subject of Vinay marrying into the lower classes came up. 'It doesn't do to upset the order, the way things are. And whatever that young man says, it would cause the biggest scandal. Destroy both families… Like your da's actions.'

Our wedding is to be a small affair, not at all befitting the marriage of the most eligible man in the village and beyond. There is no grand party. No lights are strung up and down the drive. No marquees are erected. No invitations are issued. No music blares from loudspeakers. No smells of cooking, the busyness of a house decked out in celebration.

Our wedding is not even to be held at a marriage hall. A priest is coming to the house to do the deed.

'I have seen funerals that are grander,' the servants mutter, within my hearing.

'People are sent off from the world with more fanfare,' they sniff.

'This is more befitting to a wake,' they snigger, 'although there would be more people at a wake.'

I keep my head high and ignore them, like I have learnt from observing the landlord's wife.

My family, what's left of it after Da did a runner, have not been invited to the wedding. They are not welcome at the house – the landlord's wife has made that clear.

'I want to invite *my* family to *my* wedding,' I insist.

As she has since the day Vinay broke the news of our love and my pregnancy, the landlord's wife does not acknowledge me. 'We will not have her relatives here. If they come, I will not attend the wedding,' she says, addressing Vinay.

'Kali, please. Let it go.' Vinay looks at me with distraught eyes.

I don't want to let it go. I want to put my foot down. But I know that it is too soon. I am still technically in the landlord's and his wife's employ, still a mere servant. Once I am married, I will have my way, every time, never giving in, not even for the slightest thing.

In the end, there is only the priest, Vinay, his parents and me, with the servants collected in clumps, not a smile anywhere in sight. The landlord sits sullen, itching to get back to his poetry book, I know – yearning to escape into a world where his wife is not upset and his son is not marrying a woman who was, until this morning, his servant, a woman who carries his grandchild in the faint curve of her stomach. The landlord's wife squats swollen eyed, her dreams for her son disintegrating as the sacred fire crackles and burns as the priest throws rice into it and utters the mantras that bind Vinay and me together.

From the first time I set eyes on the landlord's wife, I had yearned to be like her, respected and adored. Instead I seem to have attracted everyone's ridicule, their scorn, while Vinay has escaped unscathed. I had wanted to be the boss. Now I am stuck somewhere between lowly servant and boss, not fitting into either world.

Things will change after the wedding, I tell myself. I dared to think I would be one of them, the big people. I will not accept that I might never be.

After the wedding, Vinay and I retire to our remote room on the second wing. Vinay holds me to him and we lie like that, my bump between us, gently pressing against him. There are no words.

The day after, I visit my ma and aunt and uncle. Vinay is supposed to accompany me, but his mother is ill and needs him.

'She was alright yesterday. How come she is suddenly ill now?' I can't help saying although I know I sound sour, horrid.

'Kali, please,' Vinay says, his gaze hardening.

'I'm sorry. I'm just upset. I really need you to come with me, Vinay.'

'Son,' his mother calls, in a wavering voice, 'stay with me, please.'

What did she do when she fell ill and Vinay was away studying? How did she manage then? This time I have the good sense not to speak my thoughts aloud, not wanting to alienate my new husband further. 'Vinay,' I plead instead, 'my family were not invited to the wedding. The least we can do is go there together and get their blessing.'

He looks at me, his eyes troubled. 'Please can you wait?'

No, I will not wait. I will not give in like he does. Change my plans to suit the landlord's wife. Dance to her tunes. 'I want to get it over and done with.' My voice is short, coloured with disappointment. 'As it is, my family must be upset and hurt at not being guests at our wedding. If we don't even make the effort to visit them, it's going to make things worse.'

'I'm not saying we won't visit. I'm just saying we'll go tomorrow...'

'What if your mother's ill again tomorrow? What then?' I am shouting now, but I don't care.

It isn't auspicious, the sensible part of me cautions, *to fight on the day after one's marriage.*

Well, abandoning one's pregnant wife to look after one's supposedly ill mother isn't auspicious either, the incensed part of me snaps and my sensible side retreats into hiding.

'I can't,' Vinay is saying, his voice desperate, as I turn on my heel and walk away. 'After what we have done... how can I leave her?'

Will it always be like this, for the length of our marriage? Will I always come second to his parents? I wonder as the car makes its way into the village.

The driver is quiet the whole way, which suits me just fine, but his silence is icy cold, radiating displeasure. How dare he judge me when I am his boss? And how dare he presume that I'll care what he thinks, even if he used to like me when I was a fellow servant? We used to joke and banter all the way into the village when he dropped me off on Saturdays and Sumathi always maintained that he fancied me. I can't believe that was only a short while ago – it feels like a lifetime.

I exit the car and walk right into an antagonistic crowd. Everyone in the village has gathered in clusters, staring and pointing. Penetrating, judgemental gazes focus on my stomach.

Chilli-hot whispers: 'Look at her, shamelessly swanning around, the whore who stole the landlord's son and dragged that esteemed family down to her level.'

Seething crowds, gossiping busybodies and drama seem to accompany every major transition in my life. My da's leaving, my arrival in this village with my ma and now returning as a married woman, all underlined by a host of onlookers, chorused by rumour.

I am so weary of this. *Surely I am not a good enough actress to get starring roles every time? But then, it is my acting that has won me this role of a lifetime, as the next landlord's wife…*

'Go away,' my mother screams. 'Why have you come?' She is slapping her chest and sobbing. 'Why bring this disgrace upon us?'

'I am married to the landlord's son, Ma.'

'Where is he then?'

This is why I needed you, Vinay. Your presence would have quieted wagging tongues. You being here would have given my visit legitimacy, like you did my baby.

I shut my eyes, woozy from the rank odour of urine and sweat and stale clothes that swarms the dense air in this cramped house, wishing I could also shut out my ma's shouts. 'He couldn't come. But I have. I've come to ask for your blessing.'

'I will not give you my blessing,' Ma yells. 'You… you're just like your father. A slut.'

I glare at my mother, now reduced to this reeking, wasted slip of a thing wielding words like weapons to reduce me too. 'How can marrying the man I love make me a slut?'

'Love. Your father said that too. Whore. You got pregnant before marriage.'

I bite my tongue, the taste of hurt and rage coppery red. 'I am carrying your grandchild.'

'Don't you *your grandchild* me… How could you give your virtue away after everything I taught you? Like that woman your da ran with. You are no better than your da. Aiyyo, why am I cursed with such a feckless husband and such a tart of a daughter?'

Ma is off, hitting her forehead, her chest – as always, making everything about her.

And yet I say, 'Ma…'

'Don't call me Ma. They say the mistress is ill with shock and distress. That she has taken to her bed. How could you upset your benefactors this way?'

'Ma, whose side are you on?'

'There are no sides. I did not raise you to behave this way, to slap away the hand that feeds you. I am ashamed at what you've done. You're dead to me.'

So my mother is taking the landlord's wife's side over her own daughter's.

I turn to my aunt, but she won't meet my eyes.

'Aunt,' I try. 'I've come for your blessing.'

My voice wavers, finally cracking under the hostility, the vitriol directed at me from the people I'd naively assumed would back me.

My aunt lifts her head and I recoil from the venom in her eyes. 'I gave you shelter,' she bites out, 'against my husband's wishes. I got you a job. And in return you invite this dishonour upon us.' And then she spits, a huge glob of paan-stained froth that just misses my body but lands on my chappals.

I do not react. I push back my shoulders – hold my head high. 'Goodbye,' I say. 'You've made your choice. And I've made mine. I will not be seeing you again.'

'Where's our money for last week, girl? Rent for your miserable mother?' my uncle shouts at my retreating back.

'You will be paying *me* rent. I am married to the landlord's son,' I snap, turning to glower at him.

'You will take rent from us, your relatives?'

'You have disowned me. You will get the rent notice like everyone else.'

The driver has deliberately parked very far away. I put one foot in front of the other, refusing to hurry, to appear as if I am running away, ignoring my screaming instinct to duck and cower from the boos and insults aimed at me from the hostile villagers. I ease into the back seat, trembling all over, the taste of humiliation and upset bilious green in my mouth. I shake in the car all the way to the mansion. The mansion which is now, by rights, mine.

Why does it feel like I have lost when I have won? Why does it hurt?

Things don't change after the wedding like I'd hoped. The servants will not do my bidding. And I will not have that.

'Who cooked this?' I ask when, two days after our wedding, I sit down for breakfast. The landlord's wife has taken to having her meals in her room, which suits me just fine. The landlord has his in the library. Vinay has eaten one dosa hurriedly and left to tend to his ma, who is still pretending to be ill and has called for him.

Servants bustle around me, Sumathi among them, pretending not to have heard me, not meeting my eye. I take a sip of my tea and spit it out. 'This tea is too sugary. You!' I bang on the table and Sumathi, who was collecting Vinay's plate, jumps. 'Make me another cup with half the amount of sugar.'

'Make it yourself,' Sumathi hisses, under her breath.

'Excuse me, what did you just say?' I snap, eyes flashing. 'Do you want me to have a word with my husband about terminating your…'

'N-Nothing, s-sorry,' She stands before me, head down, her hands fiddling with the pallu of her sari, like I have seen her do when Radhakka tells her off.

'I can't eat this. The chutney is too minty. And the sambar has too much salt and not enough curry leaves. The dosas are rubbery. Make me some upma for now. And make sure the food at lunch is actually edible.'

'Yes... m-ma'am.'

I can smell the shocked outrage emanating off the other servants, can sense the profanities directed at me. It is agonising to turn on this community who welcomed me so warmly into their midst and where I've felt so completely at home. But it needs to be done. If I don't establish my authority now, I will always be looked down upon, made fun of, ignored, treated like dirt. The servants will never respect me, never recognise me as their new mistress.

I wait, stroking my stomach, surrounded by the smell of coriander and cardamom, masala and regret; the bitter taste of lost friendships, broken ties and new enemies; the hot pepper flavour of heartache.

The tinny clamour of a dropped tumbler comes from the kitchen and Radhakka's raised voice with it, the sizzling of onions, the gushing of water, and I feel a pang for the familiar routine and posse of which I was once a part.

Was this worth it? The thought is in my head before I can stop it. *Don't go there. You have only just begun. You have a baby to deliver. There is no point having doubts, thinking this way.* To distract myself from my melancholy musings, I direct the attention of the new servant girl, hired in my place, who is doing the dusting, to hidden specks only I can see, until the tea I requested arrives and then my upma, placed before me by a suitably demure Sumathi.

Radhakka is deliberately keeping out of my way, no doubt having been advised to do so by the others, as she can't be trusted to not open her mouth and give me a good talking to, getting herself fired in the process.

I think of how she called me 'child' when she found out I was pregnant, how she bandaged my thumb when I cut it that morning when my world tipped and I moved out of her orbit. I had kept that bandage on for a few days after, looking at it and missing Radhakka, who had been more of a mother to me than my own in recent months.

I push down the sudden ache that takes me over and ask for more ginger in my tea, some green peas in my upma. Once they've done as I've asked, I take a few sips and bites and leave the rest. 'Still not to my satisfaction. I really must talk to Vinay about getting some more help. New blood will perk up this place. You're all getting too set in your ways.'

I can feel their collective glare although they keep their heads meekly bowed. It is the sting of a colony of wasps, the venom-tipped fangs of dangerous snakes, spreading through my body, rendering me toxic.

But it works. After that none of the servants dare cross me or ignore me, or grumble in my presence. They are deferential and subdued. There is no laughter, no banter among them like before. Which is as it should be, I tell myself. They are here to work after all.

Vinay is as loving as always, but there is now the burden of his parents' disapproval, which he lugs around permanently, pulling down the corners of his lips, sapping the colour from his cheeks, the twinkle from his eyes.

'Do you blame me for what happened?' I ask him when we lie side by side on the huge bed, not touching yet again.

He turns around and holds me close. He looks at me and his eyes are sallow reservoirs of pain. 'Please don't ever think that, Kali,' he whispers into my hair. 'I love you. I do. But I find all this… this hurt, this upset, my parents' pain, very distressing.' His voice breaks. And then he buries his head in my shoulder and sobs.

I lie there in that opulent room, too rich, I have begun to understand, for my tastes. All this wealth, it is like a kaleidoscopic feast of balloons enticing a child with the promise of happiness. But when the balloons snag on a pin, all that is left is air, so filled with nothingness, so insubstantial, that you gag on it. I look up at the vast ceiling as the man I tricked into marrying me sobs in my arms, his salty tears pooling round my neck and staining the pillow. I gaze at the ample sofa, where I have come to be on first-name terms with solitude; at the wardrobes, which are mostly empty, despite housing my clothes and Vinay's.

Vinay exhausts his grief and drifts into sleep, occasional moans escaping from his exhausted dreams in sputtering hiccups, and I stare at the splashed cream of the ceiling until I can hardly bear to keep my eyes open. They sting and they tear, the ceiling undulating in milky swells of bluish white. I will not close them, will not allow them to do what they want – to cry and vent like my husband has. I will not allow the question that has formed in my heart, that is yearning to burst from my lips, to leak from my eyes, exit.

Was it worth it? Was it?

*   *   *

'The girl, where is the girl?'

'Why, Kali?' A gentle voice, like the raindrop-jewelled breeze caressing the tops of mango trees.

I know this voice. Don't I? 'The girl... I need her. Where has she gone?'

'She's having a nap.' A familiar voice. But one I cannot place all the same. Like Sumathi's but tremulous, curdled with age. A voice I somehow implicitly trust.

'I have to see her. There's something I have to tell her. Something important.'

'I think you already did, Kali. She told me so. Durga is my granddaughter, you see.'

'Durga? I don't know any Durga,' I snap. And yet... There is something nudging the recesses of my memory. Something vital that has to be shared. Something seeing the little girl has awakened... I grab the woman's hand, look into her strangely familiar eyes. From somewhere I locate the words. 'Find them. Sudha. Hari. Please. Find them before it is too late. Bring them home.'

Home...

'Ow, you're hurting me, Kali. No need to get agitated and clutch my hand this hard. It's okay. We'll find them.'

'Find who?'

'Never mind. You need to rest now.'

'I... Tell me, now that I am the young master's wife, why do I feel so unhappy?'

She pats my hand. Her eyes are soft and liquid, like sunflower oil. 'It's...'

'I am lonely, so lonely. I never expected this, accounted for this. I thought everything would change after the wedding. But nothing has except that I feel more isolated than ever. Perhaps when my baby is born, the legitimate heir to the mansion, things will be better. Won't they?'

*   *   *

It is a boy.

I hold my baby, the heir to the Gowda name and fortune, in my arms. I trace his perfect features. 'Now you are here everything will change,' I whisper. 'For the better. They can no longer deny me the respect I deserve. I am the mother of a Gowda, the wife of a Gowda, and finally I will belong, instead of feeling like I'm stuck between two worlds, not part of either.'

'You are drinking from my breast,' I murmur to my son, when I feed him every night. 'You will be strong like me, not weak like your da.'

With every tussle between my mother-in-law and myself, I lose my husband. Lose him to his mother, to her illness, her assumed frailness; the landlord's wife making me pay, again and again, for usurping her in Vinay's affections.

'I had hoped they would come around, Kali,' Vinay says often, 'but with Ma being ill and so dependent on me, I just… I…'

I close my eyes, turning away from this man who wooed me with poetry and promises. I am angry that, in his desire to please, his craving for peace, *I* am the casualty. It renders me incapable of continuing the pretence of loving Vinay. It makes me lash out at him.

The party for the naming ceremony of my son, the first celebration at the mansion since the gathering welcoming Vinay home after his studies, is a grand affair. The mansion is lit up with a thousand lights. There's song and dance and celebration, food and drink aplenty. The landlord's wife gets up from her bed for the occasion. Proudly she shows her grandson off.

The landlord's wife had wanted to name her grandson Vinod. 'A fine name, your grandfather's name, Vinay,' my mother-in-law had said, not looking at me.

'He is *my* son and I want to call him Manoj,' I'd declared, holding my son to my breast.

'Tell her, Vinay, that the horoscope decrees that our grand-child's name begin with a V.'

'I want to name him Manoj,' I'd repeated. A name that was shared by the man I had loved so passionately: Manu, short for Manoj.

Vinay looked from me to his mother, distressed. I stood my ground.

My mother-in-law gave in eventually. On the condition that the naming ceremony be held her way.

Manoj. *My* chosen name for *my* son. One small battle won.

For the naming ceremony, I dress in my best sari, the one Vinay presented me with at our wedding. I weave flowers through my hair and wear the gold passed on grudgingly by his mother: 'We can't have them thinking she is being treated like a beggar.'

I look the part of a landlord's daughter-in-law. But the assembled guests do not look at me. It is as if I am invisible. They coo over the baby. But the baby's mother is ignored. So I make a point of talking to them, these dignitaries who will ignore me.

'Hi, I'm Kali,' I say, my head high, my back straight. 'It is *my* son's naming ceremony you are attending. He has been given the name I have chosen for him. Do you like it?'

Some of them blush. Others huff. Yet others grumble, even yell, 'Have you no shame?'

I smile serenely. 'You are the one who is a guest in *my* home,' I reply. 'How dare you insult me? Have *you* no shame?'

The servants are now doing my bidding, if not with good grace then at least with suitable solicitude and reverence. All except Radhakka. This will not do – I cannot have any of the servants, even Radhakka, refusing to acknowledge me as mistress. It might cause mutiny, lead to accusations of favouritism. I cannot take the chance.

'Not enough salt in the mutton. I wouldn't feed this to the dog,' I say coolly, knowing very well that Radhakka does not take well to criticism, having been at the receiving end of her grumbles on the odd occasion when the landlord's wife had complained about her food. 'We'll have to think about hiring a new cook.'

Radhakka looks at me then, for the first time since I'd left her tutelage to become her mistress. Her eyes radiate hurt and disappointment, and it is I who have to look away, busying myself with arranging the pleats of my sari, the hot press of curried spices and what might have been stinging my eyes, making them water.

What might have been? Your destiny was not to remain a servant but to be the boss. What's got into you? But I am not heeding the domineering voice in my head. I am thinking of the time I came into the warm, cardamom-and-ghee-infused kitchen – Sumathi was concocting kheer – sopping wet, having been caught unawares in a monsoon deluge. Radhakka had tutted, shaking her head at my foolishness. She had waddled into the servants' quarters, returning with a towel with which she had dried my hair. She had ordered a scowling Sumathi to give me ginger tea and some kheer ('Special treatment for your favourite again,' Sumathi had grumbled), and she had sat me down beside the hearth and combed my hair until she had worked out all the knots, like my mother used to once upon a time, and it was silky and dry, as was I.

I am sorry, I whisper to Radhakka in my head as she takes the serving dish of mutton back to the kitchen, her steps weary, her shoulders hunched. *So sorry.*

As the years pass, the precocious girl I once was disappears, a haughty woman appearing in her stead, a woman who looks down on everyone, who treats people like she herself is treated by her ageing, ailing in-laws.

During the long, lonely evenings when Vinay is off tending to his mother, my son is asleep, and I am starved of company and conversation, during the dragging hours of night when sorrows balloon and doubts nag, and spectres of what might have been raise their heads, I vow that I will not be made to feel small again, renewing the promise I'd made outside Manu's house the morning he rejected me, the sun warming the fields and winter taking up residence in my heart.

Chapter 23
Jaya (Now) and Sudha (Before)

Gulab Jamuns Drowning in Syrup

'What's that you've got there, Jaya?' Mel asks, peering over Jaya's shoulder. Jaya starts, guiltily shutting her mother's diary and tucking it underneath the open file on her desk. Too late. 'What language was that? Looked exotic!' Mel smiles.

Why did she start reading her mother's next entry in the office of all places? Jaya has taken to carrying her mother's diaries everywhere and in the blessed lull at lunchtime when the office emptied, she couldn't resist opening the older diary and taking a peek inside, starting where she'd left off. And once she'd begun reading, she couldn't stop.

'Kannada…' Jaya mumbles as she pulls some papers towards her. It's her lunch break after all. She's allowed to read her mother's diary if she wants to. Why is she sounding so defensive, even in the privacy of her own head?

She will not be able to relax now until she's finished reading the entry. Jaya wants to know why the landlord's car was lounging on the roadside by her mother's house. She is as intrigued by it as her mother was the day she stumbled upon it.

'Kannada you say? Never heard of it! You are a woman of many talents, my friend. I just stopped by to ask if you wanted a sandwich? I'm off to Sainsbury's?'

'No thanks, I'm fine.'

'Right, see you in a bit then.'

Jaya waits until Mel is out of sight, pulls the diary towards her and starts to read…

※　※　※

Dear Diary,

It's been a long time, I know. I've been busy, you see. Oh I have so much to tell you!

Let me start at the beginning.

And for me that is coming home from college to see the landlord Mr Vinay's noble car, glinting blue-black in the sun.

A few village kids are gathered around it, pointing and laughing at the chauffeur, who is stretched out in the front seat, his hands linked over his huge belly, massive snores reaching my ears despite the closed doors of the car.

'Go home,' I tell the kids, who ignore me and continue to nudge and whisper in each other's ears.

I pull my shawl low over my bosom and walk to our house, trepidation beating a booming rhythm onto my chest. I breathe in the scent of jasmine blossom and taste panic.

Why is the landlord here? What have I done wrong?

I pause outside the entrance to our house. Voices drift from within, and the unfamiliar aroma of sweetmeats, the promise of a feast – unusual in our frugal home – assaults my nose, making my mouth water and my starved stomach complain.

'What has Sudha done?' I hear Da ask, his voice the bitter core of a raw mango.

'Why would she have done anything?' A woman's voice. Relief washes through me.

'K-Kaliamma...' my parents stammer in unison. 'You must have heard the rumours. Our son...'

'But that was when she was a baby. Since then she has been dutiful, hasn't she?' Kaliamma, the landlord's wife, asks in a haughty voice that demands immediate subservience.

A pause, then Ma's voice, soft. 'Yes, she has.'

Flattening myself against the wall, I peer inside.

Kaliamma is sitting on the only bench in our front room and, in her finery, is as out of place as her opulent car is among the dusty fields. She does not drink the tea my ma has prepared for her or touch the disintegrating, lurid yellow laddoos, or the host of other sweets, placed on a mat in front of her like gifts to a disobliging god.

From where I am standing, I cannot see my parents, but I can hear their every word.

'Have you had any cause to complain about her? Tell me now, before it is too late.'

'Why?' Ma's bemused voice is raised deferentially in question.

'I would like to consider your daughter as wife for Manoj, my son,' Kaliamma says crisply.

I manage to douse the shriek of shock that threatens to explode out of my stunned mouth just in time.

'Su-Sudha?' Ma asks in a squeaky falsetto.

'My son has noticed her going about the village and has taken quite a fancy to her.' Her voice is forbidding.

My mind is whirling. Kaliamma's son? I can't recall ever having seen him. I know he exists but other than that…

I don't know what to think…

'She's pretty, I'll grant you that. Perhaps one of the prettiest girls around. But Manoj is my only son, the heir to a fortune. There are girls lining up to marry him… Yet he seems to have taken a shine to your daughter…' She says this accusatorily, as if it is my fault that her son has 'noticed' me.

A crow caws mournfully from somewhere among the trees. A cow moos, as if in response, from the fields beyond the house.

Should I go in?

I dither at the threshold, staying out of sight while I make up my mind.

Ma says tentatively, 'What about other landlords' daughters?'

'Are you making fun of me?' the woman roars and I take an involuntary step back.

Kaliamma is formidable, I have heard. I have also heard, via village gossip, of the other landlords snubbing the Gowdas because of what Kaliamma did. Have they gone so far as to prevent their eligible daughters from marrying this woman's son?

'Sor-sorry, I didn't mean…' Ma's voice trembles.

'I have come here to bestow an honour on you and your daughter and instead of being grateful…'

'Please…' Da says. 'We are sorry, please sit.'

'I will.' Her voice is as feisty as a stoked fire. 'Only because my son is interested in your daughter. Now the one thing

I cannot stand is gossip. The whisper of scandal. Tell me, before we take this match any further, is your daughter likely to bring disgrace upon our family?'

I picture Ma and Da silently exchanging glances.

After what seems like an age, Ma says timidly. 'I… I know you've heard the rumours, but it's best you hear what happened from us. Then you can decide.'

I press my ear to the cracked wall and absorb my parents' pain, ringing out through my mother's wavering voice. When she has finished speaking, there is a muggy hush populated with the horror of what I have done, of what I am capable.

'From what I can see, what happened seems to have made your girl more obedient than most. I've been asking around and haven't unearthed anything bad about her except for what you just told me and the usual jealous gripes and catty remarks one would expect. I haven't heard her name linked to any boys… She is bright, good at her studies, isn't she?'

'Yes.'

'When is she getting home from college?'

'She should be here soon.'

'I will wait.'

I wait too. I count to ten, as the uneasy quiet drags within the room, interrupted once by Ma trying to get Kaliamma to eat something and the brisk reply, 'No.'

When I get to twenty, I enter the house quietly.

'Ma, there's a car…' I begin as I have rehearsed and then halt as I look at Kaliamma, folding my hands and bowing, my voice trembling as I say, 'Namaskar, ma'am.'

Her eyes as she peruses me are the flashing hue of burning paper.

Does she know I have been eavesdropping all this while, loath to enter? Have the dog's friendly whines as he welcomed me with wet caresses of his loping tongue given me away?

Before the landlord's wife can speak, Ma intervenes. 'Kaliamma has come to...'

'Tell me about yourself, Sudha,' Kaliamma interrupts.

I am subjected to an interrogation that goes on and on: 'Are you a good cook?' 'Can you sing?' 'Dance?' 'Does obesity run in your family?' 'Diabetes?' – my parents keeping tab, hawk-eyed, from the sidelines.

When it is finally finished, when Kaliamma leaves with assurances that she will be back the next day with her son and husband in tow, I drink her cold, untouched tea and eat two laddoos and one chakuli without pausing to take a breath, despite the fact that my parents are watching, thinking, I imagine, 'Greedy girl, stealing food not meant for her, like always.'

Kaliamma returns with her son and husband the very next day like she promised, a stately entourage gracing our lowly house. I sit on display, on a mat in the middle of the room, trying to ignore the urge to swat at the flies that congregate on the onion bhajis and the vadas, the coconut chutney and the kheer and the lime sherbet that Ma and I have spent the morning preparing (Ma thought it best I stay back from college), laid out beside me on the mat.

I keep my head down, glass bangles clinking as I fiddle with the pallu of my best sari, vermilion threaded through with gold, my plait weighted with the jasmine and aboli garland Ma and I concocted after the snacks had been prepared, the fragrance of wilting flowers and roasted spices and an uncertain future, the taste of fear and worry and shame, raw in my mouth as my parents and Kaliamma negotiate my dowry and the terms of the wedding, if there is one. Between them they list my considerable faults – poverty, the deathly stain accompanying my birth, my lowly and humble origins – and my meagre assets: beauty and the fact that Kaliamma and Mr Vinay's son, Manoj, is taken by me.

Why? *I think and I peer up from under the cover of my pallu, just slightly, looking down again immediately, blushing as red as my bangles because he is staring right at me. Once my gaze is safely averted, I process what I saw in his eyes: bashful kindness and embarrassment. He is as discomfited by what is taking place as I am. And he is shy! Fancy that!*

He is only human, *I think as I squat there, demure and still, not daring to look up at any of them but studying their feet, which are directly in my line of vision, ensconced on our only bench, with me sitting down in front of them like an offering. Kaliamma wears intricately patterned gold sandals and her nails are beautifully painted, although brushed with a tiny layer of dust, which seems to cringe from her feet apologetically, like everything and everyone in her presence. The dust displays no such qualms concerning her husband and son, both of them wearing shoes, which*

I imagine are black, although the black is barely visible beneath the liberal coating of grime.

From what little I have seen, Kaliamma's son, in the matter of his feet and everything else, is quite unlike his mother.

Tuned as I am to reading people, having had plenty of practice deciphering my parents' every expression, I think that if this match goes ahead, and from the ensuing discussion it sounds very much like it will, the man I will be spending the rest of my life with doesn't seem that bad at all, although his mother might be a handful. But I am used to bowing and scraping, pleasing and obeying, doing what I am told, which is what is needed to keep in Kaliamma's good books I understand.

The future suddenly doesn't seem all that worrying. At least, I decide, it can't be much worse than what has come before.

And after that, the rest of their visit passes in a haze of relief, sweet as gulab jamuns drowning in syrup.

After Kaliamma, Mr Vinay and Manoj take their leave, confirming their approval of me as their daughter-in-law, once the dust in the wake of their posh car has barely settled, villagers collect in our small house, ostensibly to offer their congratulations. But all of us know that they have really come to discover why it is me who has been chosen as daughter-in-law to the most important family around.

'Beware,' they warn us, as they munch on celebratory laddoos and sip cardamom tea. 'The lady of the house is a shrew. She hosted a huge party to try and find a bride for her son. Invited all the dignitaries and landlords from near and far. But none of them were willing to sacrifice

their daughters to that family,' they declare with obvious
relish. 'After that Kaliamma had no choice but to hunt for
a suitable bride from among us commoners.'

'That woman drove her husband's parents to the grave.'
The so-called well-wishers noisily slurp down the kheer that
Kaliamma and Mr Vinay and Manoj had not touched.
'Who knows what she will do to Sudha,' they say, their eyes
wide with glee at visions of the fate that might befall me.

It is obvious that in the household I will be marrying into,
Kaliamma is the boss. That everything revolves around her say.

'She is a tyrant. She will bully you,' the villagers announce
happily.

'That's fine by me,' I want to reply.

I don't wish to run a household. I just aim to do what
someone asks of me, so I can fade into the shadows, where
I will do the least possible harm.

'No servant stays in that household for longer than six
months,' the villagers say, pushing away the dishes empty of
kheer and popping paan into their mouths. 'That woman
is as stingy as she is harsh.'

'They don't want any dowry,' Ma interrupts and the
villagers choke on their paan.

'No dowry?'

'None.' Ma's face relaxes in a rare smile, and she shares
an equally rare conspiratorial glance with me. 'They are
paying for the wedding. We are not spending a penny. They
are also buying all the saris, ordering them from Madras.'

'Really?' Much sputtering and spitting of frothy, greenish-
red paan sediment.

'Truly.'

The villagers depart soon after, a deflated procession making their drooping way down the fields.

'They're jealous,' Ma says as I help her wash the tea tumblers, the kheer plates. 'Their daughters have not made a good match. You have.' Her face lifts in a smile.

Even Da looks happier than I have ever seen him.

I am pleased that for once, when they look at me, they do not spy the past but gaze into the future. Although a cynical part of me can't help thinking that they are thrilled because they are getting rid of me, relieved at last of the burden of having to look after me, be good to me, when all the while I am a reminder of what they have lost.

* * *

Wow! Jaya thinks closing the diary and carefully placing it beside the other, newer one in her bag. She blinks, coming slowly back into the present: the murmur of voices, the peal of laughter, the clacking of computer keys, the meaty smell of someone's lunch mingling with the bitter aroma of coffee and the shrill bleating of two phones at once, ringtones clashing. She registers all of this but she is far away, many years in the past, sitting beside her bedecked mother as Sudha awaits betrothal to a man she doesn't know, preparing to join a family that she has decided cannot be worse than her own.

Is Manoj my dad, Mum? But you said my father was a labourer. Was that a lie? What happened to you? How did you get from being betrothed to the landlord's son to living out your life alone save for one daughter, thousands of miles away?

Chapter 24
Durga

Twilight-tinted Dust

Durga bids goodbye to the nuns while her ajji is with Kali, settling her for the night.

'Your ajji told us about your parents,' one of nuns says. 'We are praying for them.'

Durga nods, her eyes stinging, the ache to see her parents overwhelming her.

'They'll be fine,' the other nun says, patting Durga's hand.

Durga watches them walk down the hill, comforted that they are praying for her ma and da. As if they've read her mind, they turn, their placid faces smiling gently as they wave at Durga before resuming their journey to the village below.

※　※　※

'Ah, there you are, Durga,' Durga's ajji says, coming to sit beside her on the mossy, broken wall beside the fruit orchard. 'I spoke to Kali.'

Durga feels fingers of expectation tickle her spine. 'And? Did she say anything?'

The sky above them is the flushed rose of anticipation.

'She asked after you. And she asked me to find them – Sudha and Hari. To bring them home. You're right. I think there's something in what she says. I think seeing you triggered her memory somehow… So I called the lawyer and talked to him just now. He promised to go over the old records again, follow it up, just to make sure.' She grins at Durga.

'Yes! I hope Kali is right and Sudha and Hari are safe somewhere. At least then she'll have something to look forward to…' Durga jumps off the wall and performs a victory dance, her feet sinking into the twilight-tinted dust.

Her ajji laughs. 'You know, I've been taking Kali and her mumbling for granted. We needed you to come and jog Kali's memory, take her ramblings seriously and push us into doing so too. You're amazing, Durga – a very caring and special little girl, and I'm so proud to call you my granddaughter.'

Durga beams, her heart glowing. Being here, somehow, makes Durga want to be the person her ajji sees, the person the nuns see. A *good* person. And the person Kali sees – someone to confide in. A friend.

Durga has never had a friend. The girls in her hometown hadn't liked her because she was too much of a tomboy, but the boys hadn't wanted her either. She always felt left out. And so she got up to mischief. Her townspeople saw her as naughty and she behaved accordingly.

Her parents had always made her feel loved, precious. But she could never shake the feeling that she was somehow letting them down, especially when there was a complaint against her nearly every day.

But here… here she feels *needed*.

The hill is blanketed in pinks and greys, the soft blush of dusk slipping into night. A host of glow-worms twinkle and wink. Crickets chatter and a sudden breeze whispers confidences to dozing trees and tired bushes, making their leaves quiver with intrigue. And it occurs to Durga that, although she fears for her parents, worries about them, misses them, she is happy here. In this dilapidated ruin with two old women and the nuns, she feels like she belongs.

Chapter 25

Jaya (Now) and Sudha (Before)

The Saline Taste of New Beginnings

In bed that night, Jaya picks up the photographs she found with her mother's things. She turns the group photo over, runs her hand over the words her mother has written there: Gaddehalli, India.

She has looked the place up. Not much to it. It is a small village in Karnataka, she's learnt. The nearest town is Sannipur. On Google, all she sees when she searches for Gaddehalli is mud and empty space, yellowing fields, some houses and a vast black eyesore – a shambling ruin when she zooms in – on a hill. Is this village where her mother lived before she came to the UK? Where is the huge house from the photograph then? Is it the ruin on the hill? That's the only one that fits. So what happened to the house to make it that way? What's its story?

Jaya picks up the pictures of the boy. And again something about him tugs at her heartstrings. The slight pout to his lips, his pert little nose and laughing eyes, the way his mouth curls upwards… She blinks, trying to push away the strangest sensation: a potent mix of déjà vu and nostalgia. Looking at this little boy brings the grief concerning *her* boy sharply to the fore.

She sets the pictures down, closes her eyes and gives in to reminiscing about Arun. She is able to do so now, concentrate on the time she did have with him, without being dragged under by the swamping wave of grief and regret that always threatens. She thinks of how he would curl up into her, how his eyes would flutter just before he fell asleep, how sometimes his lips would lift up in a half-smile. She swallows the yearning to hold him just one more time, to kiss his downy cheeks, brush his wispy hair away from his forehead, marvel at the curl of his eyelashes and trace his delicate, unformed features. She reaches instead for her mother's diaries, seeking solace from Sudha's words.

※   ※   ※

Dear Diary,

Two days before my wedding my ma takes me aside. 'Do you know what to do when you get married?'

I nod, unable to meet her eye. I am an avid reader after all, having always preferred escape into other worlds as a respite from mine.

'It will hurt at first.'

I nod again, drawing patterns in the dust with my feet. She grabs my hand then, my mother who has never willingly touched me if she can help it. The evening is infused with the aromas of roasting ghee, caramelised sugar and sweetened milk. Gossip drifts on wings of laughter from inside our small house, now crammed with guests, extended relatives who have arrived from far-off villages to camp with us so they won't miss my wedding, which will, rumour has it, be spectacular, with important dignitaries from all over Karnataka supposedly attending. Ma and I are standing in the tiny courtyard, the dog circling us, mosquitoes biting, cool air – flavoured with the pink sweetness of twilight – teasing my hair out of my plait. 'Do as he says, as he wants.'

I nod again.

'Be dutiful,' she hisses, and her words are harsh, pressing. 'Be good.'

I look up into her eyes and it is there again, the memory of what might have been, the thought that if I had not done what I did, she might be gaining a daughter-in-law right at this moment and not losing a daughter: a daughter she can't quite fathom, a daughter who is also the enemy, a daughter who has stolen her most treasured possession from her. A daughter better absent.

She undoes the knot that is always in the pallu of which-ever sari she wears, a knot she ties every morning when she changes after her wash, containing the keys to the Godrej wardrobe that houses all our valuables – not that we have many. She unties it with fingers that shake.

'Come,' she beckons, and I follow, pushing past the people crowding our house, relatives I have barely laid eyes on before now, the tang of sweat and paan and hearsay trailing us into the cold, poky darkness of the annexe where the Godrej resides.

Ma opens the wardrobe with trembling fingers and unlocks the safe within it. She takes out a pouch. Blue velvet. Glowing like lust in a villain's eyes in the dank, windowless

*room thick with body odour and surprises. She caresses the
pouch gently, more tenderly than she has ever touched me.
Then abruptly she holds it out to me. 'Here.' Her hands are
unsteady. 'Take it,' she says sharply when I hesitate.*

*I hold the pouch, as soft as my mother isn't, and pull the
drawstring open, flinching from the shining, undulating
mass inside. Gold.*

*'There are two necklaces, a pair of earrings and four
bangles,' she says.*

'I don't... I...' I hold out the pouch to her.

*'It's for you.' She swallows. 'Please. Do not bring...
disgrace upon us.'*

*I know that she means 'more disgrace than what you have
already heaped on us'.*

*I understand then. This gold is a bribe for good behaviour,
like sweets given to toddlers for not acting out in public.
She is buying me off.*

*'Your da's health is failing.' Again the veiled implication
of how I had brought on his heart attack and how he has
never really recovered from it.*

*I wish they would say everything that is in their hearts
out loud, shout it from the rooftops instead of hinting at it,
using pointed jibes. Always implying.*

'Be good,' she repeats.

After that there is nothing left to say.

*I have stored the gold untouched in a safe my mother-in-law
gave me on my first day here at the mansion. 'Keep your*

possessions locked away from prying eyes and wandering hands,' she said when she entrusted the safe to me. 'God knows the servants have little enough without them having to resist temptation as well.'

I keep the gold in there. I lock it with the key and then tie the key in my sari pallu, just like my mother. I do not wear the gold ever. My husband and in-laws have given me plenty. Even if they hadn't, I would rather go bare than wear that tainted gold. I might have to give it back if I misbehave. When I misbehave.

Am I being cynical? Reading too much into a kind gesture? I don't know. But I'd rather keep the gold out of sight where it doesn't remind me of guilt, hurt, blame, sin, sorrow. What I want from my parents, what I have yearned for, is love. Instead I have a few pieces of gold. I'd rather not see that.

On my wedding day, I wake in the cottage I have lived in all my life, peopled with memories, seething with unvoiced recriminations and unspoken thoughts and wedding guests I have scarcely met before. I wake with the tear-speckled yellow wash of sadness bruising me.

I feel the ghost of my brother whispering over my shoulder: 'I will never get married.' Gently I shush him. Tenderly I push him away to his rightful place in a corner of my heart. Today is not a day for guilt. Today of all days I cannot allow it to win.

I lie there in that room heaving with relatives and all the expectations my parents have layered upon my shoulders. I am leaving. And mingled in with the poignant upset, I feel relief, which percolates through my body like a cool drink on a hot summer afternoon.

From the kitchen come sounds of cooking, the mint and coriander, lemon and coconut scents of a wedding breakfast being prepared, the ladies from the village who have volunteered to help trying and failing to keep the noise down as they cook and chop, draw water from the well and light kindling for the guests' wash before they deck up in their finery.

I look at my mother and father, asleep beside me – every inch of available space in the house being taken up by sleeping bodies. Their faces are calm in repose.

Goodbye, *I think.* Your faces can stay this way. They don't need to be creased with the effort of trying to be nice to me. I am leaving. No constant reminder of what I did. Not any more.

Ma opens her eyes, as if I have spoken my thoughts aloud. A blink, as the gravity of the day dawns on her. She smiles then and it isn't tinged with hurt, weighted with sorrow. It is a light, complete smile. A gift I will treasure always.

'We will come and visit you every week,' she says. 'After all, you are not going far. Just up the hill. We will come.'

Hesitantly she reaches out to me, laying a calloused hand on my cheek.

A first. My heart blooms.

'Be good.'

And I feel my blooming heart dip. Why is whatever I do not enough? Why do they worry so that I won't be good?

But my ma is not done – not yet. 'Give us a grandson as soon as possible.' And, her face grave, she adds, 'You know your in-laws will expect it too.'

After that it is chaos. Breakfast, which I can't eat for nerves. Getting dressed in the sari that my in-laws have presented to me.

And then we are setting out for the marriage hall, and there is my husband-to-be, Manoj, standing with his parents and smiling at me. And then the priest is reciting the mantras, and Manoj and I are repeating them, we are walking around the consecrated fire and I am married.

It is the wedding of the decade, everyone agrees. My mother-in-law has made sure that the celebration of her son's nuptials is the grandest function in the entire state. She's invited landlords and politicians, society bigwigs and gossip queens from all over Karnataka. And everyone who has been invited attends.

'They've come to gloat,' I hear Biramma whisper to Chikkakka. 'To celebrate the fact that the heir to the most desirable estate around is marrying a mere commoner. The wedding spread is a bonus of course.'

Afterwards Ma holds me close for the first time in my life. Properly close without leaving that sanctified space for my dead brother, tears in her eyes. Da pats my back, tears in his eyes too.

It is a day of firsts. The saline taste of new beginnings and sentimental endings. And then it is over and I am leaving

*with my in-laws and my brand new husband to my married
home on top of the hill.*

*Later, alone in the bedroom with Manoj, I have had my
shower and changed into the modest, high-necked, long-sleeved
nightie that my mother has chosen for my wedding night. I
had deferred to her in this matter too, like with all others.
Manoj is sitting on the huge bed that dominates the massive
room, wearing only a pair of shorts and a vest. I avert my eyes
from the expanse of hairy flesh on display, feeling the blush
starting from the base of my throat and suffusing my face.*

*'Give us a grandson as soon as possible. Be good, be
dutiful.' My mother's words come back to me. She had
repeated them over and over as she packed my trousseau,
as she said goodbye.*

*I am overcome by feeling: bashfulness and embarrassment,
fear and worry at what is to happen, what is to come. This
morning I woke in my childhood house knowing exactly
what was expected of me, how to behave with my parents.
Now, here, in the intimate proximity of this man who is now
my husband, I don't know what to do. I am overwhelmed.
Nervous. Will I be able to do what is expected of me? Will
I make this man happy? Or will I disappoint him, like I
do my parents every day, just by being me?*

*My new husband envelops me, very gently, in his arms,
as if I am precious, breakable. 'Do as he says, as he wants,'
I hear Ma's voice in my ear, above the drumming of my
panicked heart.*

'You are very beautiful,' he whispers, drowning out Ma's voice.

I stand rigid within the circle of his arms. Should I hug him back? Should I tell him he is handsome? I open my mouth, but it is dry, the words I am searching for lost somewhere within its parched folds.

'I fell in love with you the first time I saw you,' he sighs into my cheek, lifting the straggly hairs that have escaped my elaborate wedding hairdo, created by the make-up woman my mother-in-law hired to transform me into a bride worthy of the Gaddehalli Gowdas. 'I was in the car. You were walking back from college, your head down, another girl tailing you closely and yet not walking with you. To be honest, what caught my eye was something in the expression of the other girl – I saw that she was making fun of you.'

I look up at him wondering when this was, my shyness forgotten.

'As I watched, the girl overtook you and put her leg out to trip you up. But she must have miscalculated, because she was the one who fell down, not you.'

Ah, I remember now. It was Kumari, who lived down the road from me and loved nothing better than tormenting me all the way home.

'What won my heart, Sudha, was your reaction,' Manoj says, smiling at me warmly.

My cheeks flare as I become aware once more that I am in the embrace of a barely clothed man – my husband!

'Instead of walking away, you actually helped the girl, who was fingering her ripped churidar bottoms and crying.

You gave her your shoulder to lean on. And I thought you were the loveliest girl I had ever seen, both inside and out.'

I am not, I want to say. You don't know me. In fact I don't even know myself, I want to say. But my voice is still in hiding.

'After that I took to driving past at the same time every day. I would watch you walking home, your nose buried in a book more often than not, despite the fact that it attracted derision and teasing, and try to garner the courage to talk to you... I never managed it, although I rehearsed it a million times...'

I find my absconding voice. 'You... You were too shy to talk to me?'

He nods, smiling. 'I too love books. I too forget the world while I am reading. What do you like to read?'

'Fiction!' I say, forgetting that Manoj is my husband, that I am in his arms, that it is my duty – according to my mother – to please him. 'I love stories, any stories. Novels are where I can lose myself and find myself too.'

His eyes light up. 'I feel exactly the same. I knew it from the first time I saw you. Something about you... I knew we were soulmates.'

I blush, but I am also completely awed. I was prepared to endure a loveless marriage, to do my duty by the stranger I was wedded to. I did not dare hope to connect with him, to have the same interests as him, to talk books with him. And yet that is what we are doing.

Am I allowed to be this lucky?

I think of Ravi then, of the vulnerable nape of his neck, visible above his yellowed shirt collar, of how I had yearned to reach out and touch it. His notes, R and S entwined within a heart. His love-filled gaze hardening when I tore his notes into shreds and flicked them at him.

I hurt everyone I care for, I want to warn my husband. You'll do well to stay away, I want to say.

'I wanted to marry you, only you,' Manoj is saying. 'But my mother… She sets great store by family name and reputation. The Gowda name means everything to her…' For the first time a note of bitterness creeps into my husband's gentle voice. 'She had this grandiose idea of merging two influential families – she wanted me to marry a landlord's or a politician's daughter. I would look at them, these dolled-up, artificial women, whom I couldn't envision having a conversation with, and think of you. I wanted you. But my ma… Once she gets an idea into her head, I've found it best to let it run its course. No point running up against it – she'll do everything in her power to get her way.'

I feel his sigh rise up in his chest and escape his mouth in a weary exhalation. 'I learnt early on that my father and I, we are just pawns in her pursuit of power and recognition…' I understand then that in this way too he is like me, soliciting his mother's approval, starved of her affection. 'My ma wants our family to be lauded and welcomed into the exalted circles of fellow landlords like it was before. This has been her overriding ambition all my life. But no matter how many advances she makes, the other landlords will never forget what happened, what she did, who she is. This only makes her even more determined to be accepted…' He sighs again, frustration mingling with upset. 'I'm sorry, Sudha, I must be boring you and on our wedding night too.'

'No,' I say. 'Not at all.'

I can feel his smile, the warmth of it, against my hair as he rests his cheek upon my head. Without my realising, I have become quite comfortable in his arms.

'Like I said, I wanted to marry you from that very first glimpse of your lovely face through the window of my car. When the landlords and other bigwigs refused to allow their daughters to marry into our family, after my mother had finally conceded defeat, I went to her, told her about you – the prettiest girl in the village and also the one with the best reputation. She had no ground to stand on, no bones to pick with my choice. The rest is history…'

I can feel his words reverberating from his chest before they fall out of his mouth, pressed as I am against him. I can't recall ever having been this close to another human being since sharing my mother's womb with my brother.

My brother…

I have to warn Manoj. 'I am not lovely inside, like you seem to think I am.'

To my surprise, he smiles. 'You're not?'

'No,' I insist, needing – suddenly – to show myself to this man, warts and all. He has been honest with me; he has bared his heart to me. He deserves the same courtesy. And after that, if he wants nothing to do with me, I will accept that as my due.

'Haven't you heard the rumours?' I ask.

'About what happened to your twin?' He is looking at me like I am the most valuable treasure in the world.

Nobody has looked at me like that. Nobody.

And somehow his gaze hurts.

'You know? And you still...'

'Sudha, from what I've heard, it wasn't your fault...' His voice is soft.

'I don't know what you've heard. This is the truth.' And I tell him everything, all my secret parts that I have only previously shared with you, Diary. I tell him what I did to my brother. I tell him about Ravi, and how I caused my father's heart attack.

When I finish he is silent. I don't dare look at him. I know that his gaze will not be tender any more. It will be replaced by that wary look I am so accustomed to seeing on my parents' faces.

'It wasn't your fault,' he says after a while, his tone gentle as an infant's dream.

I look up then. His gaze, if anything, is softer than before.

'How could they let you carry this burden of guilt all these years?' His voice is now the purplish maroon of a fresh bruise, the growling sweep of a raging ocean.

He means what he's saying. He means every word.

'But you don't understand. I hurt everyone I care for, even if I don't mean to... My parents, Ravi...'

Why am I doing this? Warning my husband that I inadvertently hurt my loved ones, warning him away, on our wedding night?

'My darling,' he says. That endearment: the caress of a feather on skin; the flicker of moth wings.

I can't bear it. 'I don't know what I'm capable of,' I whisper.

'What you are capable of is immense love and forgiveness.'

'You're making excuses for my behaviour.'

'You haven't done anything wrong to make excuses for,' he says. 'I love you, Sudha.'

Love. What I've desired all my life. Now offered, so easily, by this man to whom I have exposed my heart in all its complicated messiness. The only person to be party to the real me. My husband. This man who appears unfazed by what I have done, unperturbed by what I am capable of, who seems willing to take me as I am, everything *I am, even the bad bits – especially the bad bits – and offers me his love in return. This man in whose eyes I see a different me – the girl I have always desired to be. An ordinary, book-loving girl, not defined by her actions in her mother's womb. A girl who is loved!*

For the first time in my life I feel comfortable in my skin.

I rest my head against his shoulder, hard, unfamiliar and yet more reassuring than my parents' embrace.

His mouth on my cheek, my eyes, my mouth, raising goosebumps and urgent need, wet, hot.

We make love. And I am able to be outside myself, to forget about duty and guilt and penance and repentance and find another side to myself. A Sudha who gives and receives pleasure. Afterwards he holds me. His skin against mine. The scent and taste of love. And I realise that there's nowhere else I'd rather be. For the first time in my life, I am happy. So incredibly, completely happy that I worry something will happen, that something will go wrong.

* * *

After a miserable childhood, Jaya's mother had finally found happiness in her married home, but she was suspicious of it. *You had a right to be, Mum,* Jaya muses, as she drifts off to sleep. *For where was your husband, this man who loved you, when you were bringing me up?*

* * *

Jaya dreams of a boy running through the blackened rooms of a hulking shadow of a house.

He gambols in the sun-lapped courtyard, picking up huge clumps of rain-soaked earth, revelling in the gloopy feel of it, marvelling at how it turns his fingers vermilion. He giggles, his laughter echoing through the empty, gaping walls, sending spotted snakes scurrying, chasing away the feathery ghosts, making the crows cackle and dance among the collapsing, weed-plagued walls.

He jumps in the puddles left over from the rain and the grimy water arches up in a fountain that is almost taller than him. His body is wet, coated with mud. He is a superhero, a painted warrior. He is like the god Krishna, but he is red, not blue. His trousers are splattered, dripping. He tugs at them.

No, he hears.

He is a baby, fast asleep in his cot, his features not yet defined. His face pale. His lips blue. A baby who won't wake. A baby who is cold. So very cold.

No, no, no, no. Jaya wakes, her heart hammering. *No…*

Chapter 26
Durga

Sun-washed Instant

The next morning Durga finds Kali in the orchard, looking down the hill towards the village and mumbling to herself. The nuns sit close by and smile and nod at Durga as she lowers herself down onto the fruit-spattered grass beside Kali.

Kali turns to look at her, squints. 'Who are you, little girl? What are you doing here?'

'I'm Durga. Sumathi's granddaughter.'

'Granddaughter? Surely Sumathi is not that old? She's the same age as me, isn't she? She must have married early…' Then, after a pause. 'I did too, come to think of it. Why don't I have any grandchildren?'

Kali looks to Durga as if expecting an answer. Her eyes are deep pools of confusion. Durga is overcome by an urge to wipe the perplexed expression from Kali's face, set things right. 'My ajji has talked to the lawyer and they'll try and find Sudha and Hari…'

Kali's eyes widen and her face goes pale. She rocks back and forth, shaking her head. Unkempt, lanky grey tendrils whip her face. 'Sudha, Hari, they…' Her eyes shine and gleam and a single tear falls onto her ravaged cheek. 'I miss them all.'

'I am so sorry,' Durga whispers.

But Kali's attention is snagged by a movement at the base of the hill. 'Look – what's that?'

Tears forgotten. Pain brushed away in a sun-washed instant.

A balloon of dust weaves haphazardly at the bottom of the hill. Durga narrows her eyes against the late-morning glare and focuses. A bicycle smothered in the tangerine fog coughed up by its wheels, snaking down the path to the village. Small and compact and completely unexpected. 'I wouldn't have noticed it if not for you. Wow, you have sharp eyes,' Durga says.

'I am the mistress. I need to know everything that goes on, so all of my senses have to be in top form,' Kali snaps. 'And this is how I hone my eyesight.'

'How?'

'By seeing if I can make out any villagers going about their business.'

'But they're so far away!'

'Mere dots.' Kali grins gleefully at her. Then: 'Shhh… quiet. Now what do you hear?'

'Birds chattering.'

'And?'

'The breeze sighing through the branches above us.'

'Good. What else?'

'Hmmm…'

'Listen carefully.'

'Ajji humming in the kitchen.'

'Ajji? Who's Ajji?' Kali scrunches her nose, leaning close to Durga.

And Durga is overcome by a burst of affection for this woman with her untidy hair and stale clothes, old remembrances and quirky observations, the mercurial mind that flits like a butterfly in search of nectar, never still. Durga loves conversing with her – not knowing which whimsical direction her mind will take, where it will lead to next.

'Sumathi is my ajji,' Durga says.

'Who's she? Never mind. Now don't you hear the flick of pages as the nuns read their bibles?'

Durga strains her ears. 'No, I can't.'

Kali laughs and it brings to mind rainbow-hued balloons let loose upon a sky the colour of contentment. 'That's because they weren't turning any pages while you were listening, silly.' And immediately she asks, 'Do you believe in God?'

'I believe in Lord Krishna.'

'Good choice.' Kali nods approvingly.

'Why?' Durga asks, curious.

'Lord Krishna's not perfect. So he'll understand us humans, our messy mistakes, our repeated follies.'

'Yes. You're right. You're very wise.'

Kali laughs, but this time her laughter is as brittle as a heart stretched to breaking point. 'I am very far from wise.' Her voice is engulfed in sadness, the joy leached from it.

Durga changes the topic quickly, to stop Kali from descending completely into melancholy. 'Do *you* believe in God?'

Smells of boiling rice and roasting coconut and frying fish drift from the house. Her ajji must be cooking lunch.

'On days like today, when I sit here and look down the hill to the village and up to the horizon, when the air is warm and sweet and alive with birdsong but not too hot, when I can feel the sun on my face and appreciate what I have, I think I do believe in God, yes.' A beat then, she asks, 'Are you happy, child?'

'My parents are in hospital. I'm worried about them.'

'Worries. We all have them. But are you happy right now?'

Sitting there in the gilded sunshine, a chorus of birds crooning from the copse of mango trees, beside an old woman with a wandering mind, Durga decides that she is. 'Yes,' she says and smiles at Kali.

'When I was a girl,' Kali says softly, 'I used to dance among the fields, breathe in the scent of ripening paddy, spy on Manu, lie by the stream among the whispering reeds, enjoying the breeze, the ripple and gurgle of flowing water. I lived in the moment. Then life happened and I changed. I never thought I would find that girl again but sometimes, on days like today, I do – never for long, mind – but it is enough. It makes me happy.'

And Durga looks at Kali, her face momentarily peaceful and thinks, *How can the villagers be afraid of this woman? How can they think she will curse them?*

Kali blinks, sighs. 'I am tired,' she says. 'I'd like to rest.'

She stands up and walks towards the nuns and Durga follows.

'Thank you, Durga,' one of the nuns says, as the other links her arm through Kali's, who meekly allows herself to be led, 'for keeping Kali company.'

'I enjoyed it,' Durga says.

Durga's ajji pokes her head out the front door. 'Lunch is ready,' she calls.

'Your Durga is such a calming influence on Kali. Kali is the most peaceful she's been in a while,' the nuns tell her.

'That's my granddaughter.' Durga's ajji beams.

Durga basks in the pride in her ajji's voice when she says 'my granddaughter'.

Kali closes her eyes and lifts her face heavenward. It looks as if she is praying.

The nuns lead Kali – her eyes still closed – indoors.

'You know, Durga, I was secretly worried that you would hate it here. But you've fit in like you were always meant to be here. And you've brightened this place up just by being. Kali is happier, as am I.' Durga's ajji comes up to her and pats her head.

'So are we,' the nuns say from the doorway, smiling at Durga.

Durga's heart feels full to bursting. 'This is new for me. I have always been labelled naughty,' she says.

'You are *not* naughty. You care,' her ajji says firmly. 'Too much perhaps, which is what gets you into trouble sometimes. You have to learn to think before you speak and act. But that will come. Everyone makes mistakes. I've made some huge ones. Pushing your mother away – and you too – when I desperately wanted to keep in touch, because of words I spoke when I was angry. But I have learnt from my mistakes, as you will too. That is the whole point of life, child.' Warmth lilts in her ajji's voice, rendering it musical. 'Durga, you have the best heart of anyone I know.'

Durga closes her eyes and lifts her face skyward like Kali had a few moments earlier. She feels sunlight dancing on her eyelids and warmth seeping into every corner of her being. And Durga glows, feeling loved.

Chapter 27

Jaya (Now) and Sudha (Before)

The Buttery-almond Taste of Luxury

The gold your mother gave you just before your marriage, Mum. A bribe, Jaya thinks as she picks up her mother's diaries from under Ben's pillow, where she had tucked them just before she fell asleep. *How could your parents be so awful to you?*

Rain spots the window, framing a drizzly grey morning, the jaundiced sky splashed with leaky inkpots of clouds. Ben is arriving early tomorrow morning and Jaya cannot wait to see him, show him her mother's diaries, talk to him. She checks the bedside clock. There's just enough time to read one of her mother's entries before she needs to get ready for work. She opens the first of the diaries to the right entry and dives in.

* * *

Dear Diary,

Every week without fail my parents visit me in my married home. They sit like sculptures in the main hall, dwarfed by the grandeur around them, intimidated and awed by their daughter's new home. They look out of place, insignificant.

I am swamped as usual by the complex potpourri of emotions they invoke in me, the familiar smoky taste of anger and hurt and love all mixed up in my mouth. I want to protect them and I want to lash out at them. They gawp when the servants call me 'young mistress'.

My mother-in-law bustles in and orders the servants about. 'Get masala tea and bondas and the Mysore pak as well,' she snaps. 'This tea has too little sugar,' she yells. 'Who made it?' she demands. 'Where is the chutney to go with the bondas?' she bites out.

The servants dance to do my mother-in-law's bidding, appearing even more browbeaten than my parents. I know what my parents are thinking: 'How does Sudha put up with this shrew of a mother-in-law? Everything everyone said about Kaliamma is true. In fact, she is even worse than they say.'

My mother-in-law's fiery temper and her high-handedness stem from her overpowering desire for the Gaddehalli Gowdas to be known and revered far and wide. She is ruthless. She wants everything her way always. But what she is, what she wants, is all there, right in front of you. Nothing is hidden or implied. What my parents don't realise is that I much prefer my mother-in-law's directness. It is such a relief after years of trying to decipher and dance around and pander to my parents' veiled allusions, their accusatory insinuations.

'You seem to have settled well into your new home,' they say when my mother-in-law leaves me alone with them.

My mother, looking me up and down, says: 'You've put on weight.'

'Have I?'

I know what she is really saying: overeating as usual? Like you did in my womb at the cost of your brother?

My father: 'When are you giving us a grandchild? Make it soon and make sure it is a boy. She expects it too, you know.'

'She' meaning my mother-in-law.

'And don't get too fat – they might send you back home and find another, prettier, more fertile bride. Remember there is no worse fate than being the discarded wife of a man who has married again.' My father bites into a bonda and chews noisily. 'Far better to be a widow.'

'Your da's health is weakening. We'd like a grandson before we die. We always longed for a son…'

Pointed, weighted silence.

That look, mirrored in both of their gazes, once again bringing the harsh truth of what I did to the fore. However hard Manoj tries, I will never be able to overlook my transgressions – not as long as my parents keep up their weekly visits.

Snug in the unexpected but wholly wonderful love of my husband, I am beginning to forget how I used to feel in my parents' house. I am starting to relax, to come into myself. I do what my mother-in-law expects of me and get through the days, counting down the hours until evening, when Manoj returns home from overseeing the smooth running of the properties and businesses that he will one day inherit, and we can retire to the bedroom, into a cocoon of our own.

'Make sure the servants do as they are told. Be firm,' my mother-in-law warns.

There are so many servants that I keep mixing up their names. Yet they don't seem to mind. They tremble with fear at the mistress but are so kind to me, the 'young mistress'. I still look behind me when they address me so, not quite able to equate that moniker with me.

'You are too soft with the servants,' my mother-in-law admonishes. 'Don't apologise to them if you get their names wrong! For God's sake, behave like a boss otherwise soon they'll be ruling you.'

When my mother-in-law is away shopping or doing charitable works in a bid to outdo the other landlords' wives' showy generosity, I quickly finish what she has asked me to do and spend the rest of the day with my father-in-law, Mr Vinay, in his room on the second wing. We sit side by side, surrounded by timeworn books, old ghosts and festering remorse, not talking but at ease in each other's company, breathing in the mildewed aroma of fleeting stories and bygone lives. My father-in-law is a quiet man, lost to this world and living in another one, a realm flavoured by his poetry and his regrets. He is unperturbed by his wife's tantrums, her constant, overwhelming need to be endorsed by high society.

'Shut in his rank room, which reeks of body odour and distress, damp and despair, no matter how many times I get the servants to clean it, no matter if the windows are left open all day and night,' my mother-in-law complains of her husband.

'He's been like this since his parents, my granddad and grandma passed,' Manoj has sighed, burrowing his face in my hair as if drawing comfort. 'No amount of medication or counselling has worked – he refuses to leave his room in order to get help, so we have to bring the physicians and counsellors here. It's as if he's given up on this life, like he's already joined his parents up there, wherever they are.'

'That's why he was so distant, so removed, when he visited my parents' house when our betrothal was sealed,' I say.

'Ma had to literally drag him along with threats and cajoling. The same for our wedding. He gets anxious if he's away from that room of his. I don't know what's in there that assuages him, but he seems to find a measure of calm only in that room.'

I sit with my father-in-law during those afternoons my mother-in-law is away and the house settles into an uneasy, waiting hush without her constant bluster to rouse it. Fragrant air, scented with fruit and spices, drifts into the room from outdoors and is smothered by the fug inside, the sweetness leached out of it until it is limp, saturated with pain. When I sit with him, among the fraying tomes and assorted debris of his life, he nods without looking at me, staring out the window as always, the ubiquitous book open in his hands, his glasses sliding down his nose. He nods again when I leave. Other than that, he gives no indication that he knows I'm there.

Slowly, as I get used to the rhythms of this vast house and the lives being led within, those of servants and owners alike, I try and push aside that careful girl I have trained myself *to be, always watching myself, perpetually worried I will do something bad. I teach myself instead to live in the moment. I do not want to be like my father-in-law, who is not with the present because he is overwhelmed by past regrets, yearning to go back and right the wrongs he inadvertently made in the brash thoughtlessness of his youth. I do not want to be like my mother-in-law, neglecting to love and show affection, because she is chasing after the elusive approval and acceptance of a whimsical, superficial community.*

Gradually, I grow to believe that I am the woman I see in my husband's eyes; I trust the assurance he repeats every night before we both drift off to sleep in a tangle of limbs, the taste of love moist on our lips: 'You did nothing wrong, Sudha. You are not wired to hurt those you love, whether unintentionally or knowingly, as you seem to think. You make me so happy. I love you.'

But when my parents visit, it all comes back in a rush of bitter black bile and gagging nausea.

They eat loudly and with relish. They look around the room, assessing the gold ornaments, the baroque staircases, the servants scurrying. The spiced sandalwood scent of opulence. The buttery-almond taste of luxury.

'Hope you're being good. You'd be silly to lose all this.'

After they leave, I sob noisily, unable to control the tears that flood my mouth, tasting of salty gruel. The servants gawp. My mother-in-law comes and yells at them. 'Have you got no work to do? What are you staring at? One of you go and get Manoj sir, go on. He's working in the office in the annexe.' And to me, in the same harsh tone, strident as a bristly broom attacking grime, she says, 'What are you making a scene in front of the servants for? This is not how we behave.' 'We' meaning the Gaddehalli Gowdas.

She ushers me into one of the rooms leading off the living room and closes the door. 'What's the matter?' she asks and her voice is softer.

'My parents... They...' I hiccup, but I can't say any more. Manoj comes rushing in, breathless. 'What happened?' I am too upset to answer.

'Her parents happened,' my mother-in-law says drily before leaving the room to allow us some privacy. She is being very understanding, or perhaps she is just disgusted by my tears. 'Make sure your eyes are dry and clear when you come back out. Keep your head high. We don't want to give the servants any more fodder for gossip,' she warns as she leaves.

Manoj holds me.

'I have upset your ma. There's nothing she hates more than the servants blathering about us,' I manage between hiccups.

'Oh don't worry about Ma. She'll get over it. There have been worse rumours about our family. She knows by now that gossip is the flip side of the renown she so wants for us. People will invent something to talk about, especially about families such as ours, and if she chases veneration and respect, she has to take gossip in her stride. Now tell me – what did your parents say?'

'They... they... it wasn't so much what they said as what was implied... I...'

'Oh, Sudha. If you want, I'll tell them not to come any more.'

'No. I want to see them.'

'But, Sudha,' he says, gently wiping my eyes. 'Look at what they reduce you to.'

'I… I love them. It's just that I can never appease them. I look at their faces, etched with loss, and I feel instantly, completely guilty. I am responsi—'

'You are not. Don't even think it.'

'But I can't not, Manoj. My parents, whom I love the most apart from you, are hurting and they always will be because of what happened when I was born. My brother's loss is what defines us, what binds us. Whether they mean to or not, subconsciously my parents blame me. And I blame myself. When I made a good match, married you, I thought it would be enough to right what I did to them… I was foolish to assume so. I'm beginning to realise that no amends I make will annul the past and allow us to begin again, with no bad marks against me.'

'You don't have to make it up to them because you did nothing bad.' Manoj voice rings with frustration. 'I wish… This is why I stay clear when they come to visit. I know that what they feel is so ingrained that it can't be changed. But I get so angry and upset on your behalf.' He sighs deeply. 'I understand your pain at not living up to your parents' expectations. You are angry at them for not loving you unconditionally, but most of all, I think, you are angry at yourself for fostering their expectations, for not being able to say no to them, for wanting to please them.' He takes a *breath. 'I wish you would allow me to talk to them, to tell them how you feel, like I have offered to countless times…'*

I pull back and look up at him, my husband. This man I did not choose, but who loved me from the first moment he saw me, loved me with a conviction that hasn't changed, despite knowing who I am, and what I have done. This man who has given me the one thing I have always yearned for: unconditional love.

How on earth did I get so lucky?

'How do you know exactly how I feel?' I ask.

He showers my face with kisses, tasting my tears on his lips.

Maybe I don't deserve this. But I will enjoy it while I can.

'Because I feel the same,' he says, his voice as fragile as a bubble floating in a bower of thorns.

I think of his mother, busy running events and sitting on committees and courting favour with the other landlords at the expense of her son. I think of his father spending more time with spectres from his past than with the lad who is his future. I picture Manoj as a little boy, wandering the vast rooms of this palatial house, peopled with servants to cater to his every whim. Having everything he wants except the one thing he desires above all else – his parents' love. A lonely boy in a gilded mansion. The ultimate cliché.

My twin will never know love. He will never know how cool air aromatic with the promise of summer rain feels on a sweaty face, how happiness tastes. He will never know grief or sorrow or loneliness, or how guilt smells, hot, red, the cutting ferocity of a resounding slap. He will never know how it is to be speared by the accusatory gaze of your parents, to cringe from the reflection of your failings in your parents' eyes, to grow up without love, the love that is lavished in abundance on a sainted memory. He will never know what it is like to envy and perpetually exist in the shadow of a person whose non-life is paired with his, a person who has been dead for every single day that he has been alive.

My twin is not here.

But this man is. This man who knows, like me, what it is to yearn for love, long for approval. Who understands what it means to live up to what everyone expects of you and what you expect of yourself – the constant conflict, the maintaining of a facade. This man who loves me.

I am here.

And we will comfort each other, two lonely people who have been seeking love all our lives.

'My parents were asking when we were going to give them a grandson,' I say, in a bid to wipe the desolation from Manoj's eyes.

It works. He smiles and it is the rippling, translucent swell of honey.

'I am happy to oblige,' he says.

'Don't you have to go back to work?'

'Mmm…' he mumbles from where he is kissing my neck.

'The servants…'

He peppers my shoulder with kisses. 'They will gossip anyway. Why don't we give them something concrete to talk about, while at the same time appeasing your parents…?' His voice is the heady caramel drag of burnt sugar. His mouth finds mine, and then there are no words. Only love.

* * *

The more she reads about her mother's parents, the more angry Jaya is with them.

'Dr Meadows,' she pictures herself telling her therapist at their next session, 'my anger at my mum was misdirected. In actual fact, I am raging at her parents. They were horrid. Smothering my mother with recrimination and blame from the moment she was born. Putting pressure on her to give them a grandson as soon as she was married! I wan to shake them until they see sense!'

Outside the drizzle has cleared, the appearance of a watery sun chasing away the downcast clouds.

What would your parents have thought of me, Mum, their only grandchild, and a girl at that? Did they know about me? What happened to them?

Mum, Jaya asks of Sudha in her head as she tucks the diaries into her bag and gets ready for work, *what happened to destroy that happiness you found with your husband?*

Chapter 28
Durga

The Sweet Wings of Faith

The phone rings while Durga is out playing with Kali, who is in a very jovial mood. The air around them is alive with the sounds and smells of summer – birds singing, moths with yellow-gold wings flickering, the buttercream fragrance of aboli and jasmine – and syrupy with spices, nectar and warm mud. Being with Kali is like going blindfolded into a strange new place, Durga thinks. You never know what's going to happen next, what you are going to experience.

'Can you answer that, Durga?' Her ajji's voice drifts over the shrill, insistent ring of the phone to where Durga is crouched beside Kali. Kali was tugging at Durga's hand, in the process of pointing something out, but she is distracted now and staring, unblinking, down the hill and beyond, at something only she can see. The phone stops ringing then starts up again.

'Durga?' her ajji calls.

'Kali, I have to…' Durga begins.

Kali makes a gasping noise and violently pulls her hand away from Durga's grasp and takes off down the hill, surprisingly agile, with both nuns in pursuit.

And Durga rushes inside to answer the phone.

'Hello?' Durga breathes into the mouthpiece just as her ajji rushes in from the bathroom, wiping her hands on the tea cloth slung across her shoulder. Seeing that Durga has picked up the receiver, her ajji sits down across from her with a basket of green beans, which she then proceeds to top and tail.

'Is that you, Durga? Not there two weeks and already you are the boss of the house, answering the phone?' Gowriakka's severe voice makes Durga want to choke, her good mood dissipating like shadows in the harsh glow of torchlight. She lifts her leg and kicks hard at the stool beside her, toppling it.

Her ajji looks up sharply, first at Durga and then at the phone. 'Who is it?' she mouths, as she snaps the head off a green bean.

Durga's leg hurts and tears stab at her eyes.

'Is your ajji there?' Gowriakka's voice is as dry as kindling.

'If you are expecting her to say bad things about me,' Durga yells, biting hard on her lower lip, tasting blood and distress, 'she won't. Unlike you, she *likes* me.'

'I don't have time to waste debating with you, Durga,' Gowriakka hisses. 'Is your ajji there or not?'

Durga's ajji is beside her. She puts one arm around Durga and takes the phone from her with the other. 'I am here. What do you want?' Her voice is cool.

Nestled against her ajji, breathing in her musty smell of sweat and worn clothes and comfort, Durga tries to shut out Gowriakka's voice. Why is she calling anyway?

'Oh?' her ajji says, and her voice is suddenly soft, breathless.

In the absence of the stool that Durga has kicked aside, she lowers herself and Durga with her gently onto the floor, which is littered with dust and onion skins, garlic and potato peelings, that have escaped the ministrations of her broom. 'Both of them?'

No, please, Lord Krishna, no. I have been good. I am sorry I had horrible thoughts about Gowriakka just now.

'Yes, yes…' A pause while her ajji listens to what Gowriakka has to say. 'Oh. I see…' Another longer pause. 'I can't come. But I will send Durga. We'll make sure she gets onto the bus if one of you meets her at the bus stop on your end?' Her ajji takes a breath while Gowriakka replies, then, her voice cutting, she snaps, 'No, she won't run away. Whatever gave you that idea? She will get on the bus this afternoon and you will make sure to collect her at your end – and let me know once you have.'

Her ajji sets the phone down so hard that it rocks on its stand. 'I defy anyone not to be naughty in the presence of that awful woman. I haven't even met her and I feel like shaking her until her head falls off. Good job she was on the phone, or I wouldn't have been responsible for my actions. She was the one who made the comment last time about me being your only *living* relative. Insensitive woman!' Her ajji pauses, then, softly, she says, 'Durga?'

Durga has covered her ears with her fists, shutting her eyes and curling into a ball, hoping that this will somehow protect her from what is to come.

Please, Lord Krishna.

She feels her ajji's green-smelling hands cupping her face, tasting fear on her lips, crimson, metallic. 'Come, child, we have lots to do. I need to call the rickshaw driver, and you have to pack. You need to go back for a bit. Your ma and da have woken up.'

Durga's eyes fly open, fixating on her ajji's face.

'They have?'

'It seems they were put into a medically induced coma, so as to recover from their injuries. And they are going to. Your da woke the day after you left. The left side of his body is paralysed and he has lost his hearing and sight on that side, but the doctors are positive he is otherwise fine. His speech is slurred and difficult to understand, but that is to be expected...'

'And Ma?'

'Your ma woke today, asking for you. In fact, they are both asking for you. It seems the first word your da said, although it was so unintelligible that he had to write it down – with his good hand, thank goodness that he is right-handed – was *Durga*.'

Durga sniffs and swipes at her nose and her eyes with the back of her elbow.

'Your ma lost one of her legs, Durga. And she won't be able to have any more children it seems.' Her ajji's voice snags, then lifts with determined cheer. 'But she will recover. They both will.'

Durga flings her arms around her ajji and sobs, all the guilt and hurt flowing out of her mixed in with relief that her parents are alive. 'I did this. I did.'

'No, you didn't. It happened. It was meant to be. They are fine. They have woken up and are asking for you,' her ajji says, hiccuping as she sobs along with Durga. 'You go and see them and give them my love. And after they have seen you and are reassured you are fine, you make sure to come back to visit your old ajji. I wish I could accompany you, child, but I can't just now, as you know. I will talk to the lawyer, see if he can find someone to stay here for a while, so we can both be with your ma and da while they recuperate – that's a promise.'

'What's all this racket?' Kali huffs, striding into the room. 'You would think someone had died in here! What are you two doing on the floor for God's sake? Can't you see it's dirty? What is this place coming to!'

And Durga and her ajji laugh through their tears, tasting salt and tentative hope, wafting on the sweet wings of faith.

Chapter 29

Jaya

Haunted Lives

Jaya picks up the post from the mat with one hand and Mr Fluff, who is rubbing against her leg, with the other, as she lets herself into her empty house, her mother's diary entries at the forefront of her mind. She didn't read or even pull out her mother's diaries at work at lunchtime, although she was sorely tempted, deriving solace instead from knowing they were in her bag. She has come to rely on her mother's words – the story of Sudha's life before Jaya. But she must have been preoccupied for more than a few colleagues, their faces creased with concern, had asked if she was okay, wondering perhaps if she was slipping back into the depression that had plagued her after Arun's passing.

The cat purrs as he burrows into her shoulder and she takes comfort from his warmth, his energy. She sets him down on the kitchen floor, the post on the island, and opens a tin of cat food. After filling his bowl, she cracks the window open and looks out into the night, the shadowy garden spun silver in moonlight, alluring as a face glimpsed in silhouette. She sees a startled fox, orange eyes gleaming, debating whether to continue foraging or run; the ginger cat that is Mr Fluff's nemesis, that doesn't belong to her and Ben and yet owns their garden, now sprawled languidly on the roof of the shed; the trees, just waving outlines; the ashen sky with its tantalising sliver of moon and its dour burden of rainclouds.

Somewhere someone laughs. Jaya breathes in the smoky aroma of her neighbour's dinner, charred meat and caramelised onions, wafting in through the open window, the faint bars of a song being played carrying on the evening breeze, the soft music of wind chimes in someone's garden.

Mr Fluff, having wolfed down his supper, barrels through the cat flap into the garden, intent on chasing the intruder daring to bask on *his* roof. Jaya turns away from the window, stretching her muscles, cramped from hunching at her desk all day. She contemplates making a sandwich but has no appetite, does not feel like food. What she does feel like is tea – a nice strong cup. She picks up the kettle and her gaze lands on the post. As the kettle boils, she riffles through the day's letters. Flyers for pizza, a plea from an estate agency, the *Guardian* and… a thick brown envelope, official looking, a bit frayed at the corners. She picks it up. It is addressed to her mother and has been forwarded on from her mother's old address by the family currently renting it. Her mother who has been dead almost eighteen months! Her mother who has been foremost in Jaya's mind recently.

What a coincidence!

Foreign stamps. Postmarked India. She turns the envelope over but there is no clue as to who sent it. She looks at the address again, penned in a neat hand, running her fingers over her mother's name: Sudha Gowda. She is strangely reluctant to open the envelope, to see what is tucked so densely inside. Reading her mother's diaries, her intimate notes to herself, is one thing. But a letter… A letter someone else has written to her mother. A private message meant for her eyes only.

But she is dead.

The grief hits Jaya sideways, owning her. She puts her arms around her stomach and keels over, trying to rein her pain in. Now that she is getting to know her mum, she is finally able to mourn properly for her, her sorrow riddled with remorse.

She takes deep calming breaths and stands back up, bringing the letter to her nose and sniffing it. It smells of earth and loss, of memories and pain and haunted lives.

Oh how fanciful she is, standing in the dark in her lonely house, thinking a letter can smell of feelings. Somehow sensing her anguish, Mr Fluff comes in and purrs and she picks him up, holds him close. He paws at the envelope, mewls. In a split second, Jaya decides. She rips open the envelope, pulls out the sheaves of sand-coloured paper, the first of which is what looks like a cover letter, printed in English. The rest of the pages are handwritten in messy Kannada script.

She reads the cover letter first.

Dear Sudha Gowda,

I am pretty sure I am writing to the right person here. The Sudha Gowda formerly of Gaddehalli?

Gaddehalli. The name her mother had penned on the back of the group photograph.

I am Mr Guru Kumar, senior advocate at the law firm Desai and Sons, Sannipur. I handle the estate of Mr Vinay Gowda of Gaddehalli, India, and it has come to my notice that you are one of the beneficiaries in his will.

Vinay Gowda. Where has Jaya come across that name before? Ah, he was the landlord, wasn't he? Manoj's father; her mum's father-in-law.

I am sorry for the delay in contacting you. I have only recently taken over the practice following Mr Desai's demise last year. It was assumed that you had perished in the fire, which is why Mr Desai didn't think to look for you, and nor did I for that matter, until recent events made me think otherwise.

A fire? And what recent events?

I enclose with this letter a note from Sumathiamma, the carer of Mrs Kali Gowda, wife of Mr Vinay Gowda.

Kali – the landlord's wife. The Kaliamma that Jaya's mother mentions in her entries. Sudha's mother-in-law, the stern woman whom the villagers warned Sudha against… She is alive. Jaya feels a tingle tickle her spine, goosebumps owning her body. Why didn't she write the letter to her daughter-in-law then? She must be indisposed to need a carer. Perhaps she narrated the letter to her carer…

I also enclose my phone number and the number of the house in Gaddehalli in case you have any queries.

If you are not the person I am looking for, please forgive this intrusion.

Yours sincerely,

The letter is signed *Guru Kumar* in the same careful handwriting as the address on the envelope. Jaya's fingers tremble as she turns her attention to the remaining pages, penned in Kannada; the handwriting untidier than her mother's diary entries, with words crossed out and scribbled over, as opposed to the solicitor's professional missive, typed in English.

Dear Sudha,

I am Sumathiamma, from the village. I don't know if you remember me. I used to live in the cottage beside Chikkakka's – the Chikkakka who used to roll beedis. You would come by every Saturday to collect some for your father. You always said hello to me if I was in the courtyard. Many years have passed since and I know life has a tendency to wipe detail from memory, especially if it is a memory you don't particularly cherish. And you weren't exactly happy in the village, were you?

This lady knew her mother growing up, Jaya thinks, tasting tears, salty yellow, in her mouth.

The lawyer, this new one – he is very efficient, mind, not like old Mr Desai – tracked you through your passport and other records. He said it is easy enough to do nowadays.

You did not change your name, which is why the lawyer was able to find you so easily. You still felt some connection, then, to your past – to here.

Mr Desai should have thought to do this earlier. But I can understand why he didn't. He was Mr Vinay's oldest friend and was very cut up after the fire and, later, his friend's death. And he believed, like the rest of us, that you and

Hari were dead, lost in the debris, as your bodies were never recovered. We should have put two and two together when the rumours started of course. You had good reason to take advantage of the chaos after the fire, to pretend to be dead.

Jaya pauses, her breath catching in her throat. Her mother pretended to be dead? What rumours? And who is Hari?

Anyway nobody thought to question it. To search for you. Until recently, that is, when my granddaughter came to stay here at the big house. I still call it the big house – old habit – when it is nothing but a sorry ruin now.

Something about Durga – my granddaughter – jogged Kali's memory and she insisted that you survived the fire. I would have ignored it even then, see, as another of Kali's ramblings, but Durga was adamant that Kali meant what she was saying and nagged me into action. And thus, this letter…

Sudha, as I said, the big house overlooking Gaddehalli, the Gowda legacy, is in shambles, lying unloved. This house, it needs life. Love. Someone to restore it to its former glory.

The hazy ruin Jaya saw on Google when she looked up Gaddehalli. That *is* the mansion in the photograph her mother saved!

And Kali… I look after her, see. She's not been herself since the fire, her grief at the loss of everything she held dear so huge that the only way she can deal with it is by sidestepping her own mind.

Sudha, I know Kali wasn't the friendliest of women – hard and bossy – but she is no longer so. She cared about you.

*She still does. She asks after you. And after all she has lost,
if she could know, somewhere in her mind, that she didn't
lose you too, that would be wonderful.*

*Of course, Sudha, we will understand if you don't want
to come back. You ran away after all. You had your reasons.
You have stayed away.*

*But, Sudha, so much time has passed. Nothing is as it
was. The scandal caused by the rumours surrounding you
died down as quickly as it started, eclipsed by the devastation caused in the fire's wake. In time, other scandals have
taken precedence.*

*Nobody remembers any more, except Kali, every so often,
an old woman living out her days in a ruin that still carries
the imprint of long-ago splendour.*

*Sudha, it is safe to come back now. Please do. Kali is
waiting.*

Jaya stares at the sheets of paper, crumpled where she has
clutched them too hard and freckled with dark, wet drops.
Her mother caused a scandal and pretended to be dead to
escape the repercussions. This is why she never mentioned
India, never went back. What did she do?

Jaya turns the last sheet over. There is nothing more.

She looks out into the night. The garden is in shadow,
bathed in silky darkness, punctuated here and there by the
warm golden glow of the street lights. A dog barks and a man
whistles, 'Here, boy.'

Inside it is quiet, the pensive silence of stunned surprise.
The cat is curled up on the sofa.

You were meant to get this, Mum.

If you had, would you have gone to India? Or pretended nothing had happened to rock your world and continued as before, burying the call of the past? Would you have told me? Or kept this from me? Hidden it like you have everything else?

Outside cars whoosh and growl in the distance, their owners eager to get home to their supper. Jaya reads the letter again, thinking, *Is this your doing, Mum? You were a staunch Hindu, believing in the afterlife. Are you watching from there, orchestrating all of this? If not, why I am getting this letter at the same time I've been reading your diaries?*

What happened in that house on the hill that made her mother run away and stay away all her life? And who is Hari? Is he – could he be – the boy in the pictures her mother treasured, the boy Jaya has repeatedly dreamt about, the boy who morphs into Arun?

Oh, Mum. How could I have gone through my life knowing so very little of yours? How could I have been so self-absorbed?

Jaya glances at the clock. It is evening here but afternoon in Chicago. Ben must be packing. His flight home leaves in four hours. She realises that she cannot wait until he gets home. She wants to talk to him now.

'Jaya?' Ben's voice is ringed with concern. 'What's the matter?' His apprehension is an indication of just how much their relationship has suffered since they lost Arun, Jaya thinks. She doesn't call Ben when he's away any more, which is why, when she does, Ben panics.

'A letter came today,' she says, 'addressed to my mum.' She looks at the letter in her hand, the brown of the envelope smudging to a glossy mahogany where it is embellished by her tears.

'A letter meant for your mum?' Ben repeats, his voice still crackling with worry.

And standing beside the window, the cat purring softly on the sofa, Jaya reads the lawyer's letter out to Ben, and then Sumathiamma's – Ben waiting patiently as she haltingly translates the Kannada sentences.

He is silent after she finishes. Jaya listens to his steady breathing bridging the distance between them and a memory – sharp, vivid – ambushes her. A Saturday evening two weeks after Arun's birth. Waking in their bedroom, awash with the rose glow of the setting sun, mellow pink rays playing on the faces of her husband and her son, their beloved profiles identical in sleep, mouths half open. She had lain there and watched them, her family, the smell of milk and talc, sweet reveries and contentment caressing her nose, as the sun had set, shrouding the room in darkness, and Arun had woken and started to cry.

'What now, Jaya?' Ben asks and Jaya blinks, loath to let go of the recollection.

'I suppose I should go to India, meet with Kali and Sumathiamma and this lawyer, see this house – the house from the group photograph Mum saved?' Her voice lilts at the end, a question.

'Do you *want* to go or do you just feel you should?' Ben asks.

Jaya pauses, considering his question. 'Now that I'm reading my mum's entries, I just… Ben, all my life, I've been obsessed with history – my mother's and mine. I always felt there was something missing. And these dreams I've been having…'

'Of the little boy in the photos? You've had more than one?'

'Yes. They're so vivid. And somehow I get the feeling they take place in India. Although I've never been there...' She swallows. 'And Kali, the woman my mum mentions in her diary entries – her mother-in-law – is living in this house whose picture my mum saved! I would never forgive myself if, after all the years of haranguing my mother for her past and mine, I don't take the chance to meet someone who might be related to me...'

'Jaya, it sounds to me like you do want to go to India, discover for yourself that bit of your mother's past.'

Yes, Jaya thinks as she listens to Ben's gentle voice swilling in her ear, she means to go to India, the country that spawned her enigma of a mother. She will visit Gaddehalli, the house on the hill, the picture of which her mother saved. She will meet with Kali. And she'll understand why her mother left, why she pretended to be dead, if this Sumathiamma is to be believed.

'Yes,' she whispers into the phone. She wants to experience the India that shaped her mother and then pushed her away so she lived out her adult life as a hard-working shell in a cold country thousands of miles away.

'I could come with you?' Ben suggests.

Jaya has never believed in the afterlife. The extent of her dabbling with religion has been accompanying her mother – reluctantly – to the temple a couple of times. But now... Ben's offer... For the second time this evening, she feels a thrill tingling her spine.

It is you, Mum, isn't it, arranging this from the afterlife?

'Your work? The business?' she asks around the lump in her throat.

'This client I've just won for us is one of our biggest and will keep us going for the next year at least. I can afford to take a step back now, allow Mike to take charge, do the technical bit. I'll continue to liaise with the clients of course, but I can do that from the UK or from anywhere in the world really. I was planning to take a break anyway, Jaya – I've been working non-stop for months now.'

'You said you had to go to California?'

'Oh they can wait. If not, we've lost one. It doesn't matter. *You* do.'

She opens her mouth. Tastes tears and love. She thinks of how she had crossed her fingers when replying in the affirmative to Dr Meadows' question: 'Does he love you?', when all the while she was thinking: *I hope so. I hope it's not too late.*

He loves me, Dr Meadows. He does. It's not too late for us.

Jaya hopes there will be time, during this sojourn into her mother's past, to repair the cracks in her relationship with Ben, to seal them. She hopes there will be time to find each other again and to tentatively begin the process of moving on, of looking to the future.

I have collected enough regrets. I don't want more.

The cat comes up to her, rubbing his warm body against her legs, as if sensing her plans to go far away. He looks up at her, green eyes posing a question. *What about me?*

'What shall we do with Mr Fluff?' she asks.

'Mike will have him in a heartbeat,' Ben says immediately.

'Perfect.' Jaya picks up the cat and drops a kiss on his furry head.

'I'll be there tomorrow morning and then we can book tickets and sort everything out.' Ben's voice is animated with the hope that is surging through Jaya's being.

A trip together. When was the last time they went away? Their honeymoon to Morocco. Two weeks of sun and sand and laughter and love. After that they were working, saving, growing a family, starting a business. She tastes faith, spangled silver, as she says, 'I love you, Ben.'

'I love you too.' His voice is music and love, glossy caramel.

Chapter 30
Kali

Imminent Squall

'Ma? Da?' Where are they? And where is Manu? 'Manu?' I call, my voice plaintive, quivering in the darkness. Where *is* everyone? And then, with a start, it all comes back. There's a wound somewhere on my body, I can't pinpoint where. A festering wound, exuding hurt. Oh, how it hurts…

✻   ✻   ✻

My ma dies soon after Manoj is born. My aunt and uncle move away, God knows where. Despite their derision when I went to visit them in the village the day after my wedding, I had invited my family – my mother, aunt and uncle – to the naming ceremony of my son, their grandchild and grandnephew. They did not come. After that I gave up. If they didn't want to see my child, then I didn't want to see them.

When my mother passes away, my aunt and uncle do not invite me to the cremation. I only find out when I hear the servants whispering and demand to know what's happened.

'You order us about,' I hear Radhakka grumble, 'and you don't even know your mother is dead.'

'Come here,' I yell at Radhakka so fiercely that Vinay looks up from his rice and fish curry. 'What did you say?'

'Nothing, ma'am.' Radhakka will not look at me. The *ma'am* is a snort.

This woman who used to save some jalebis for me every time she made them, knowing they were my favourite. Who made a concoction out of milk and honey and ginger to combat sickness and nausea when she found out I was pregnant. This woman who held my hair away from my face while I was being sick.

'Tell me,' I scream.

'Your mother is dead.' Radhakka stares fixedly at the floor.

Vinay comes round then and wordlessly gathers me in his arms. I shrug him off with more force than necessary. 'Not in front of the servants,' I hiss and somehow the hissing turns into sobs, which I manage to control until I stumble to my room and shut the door.

In the privacy of my opulent room, surrounded by the luxuries I have earned at great cost, I mourn. For my father absconding. For Manu rejecting the gift of my love. For my ma going to pieces when my da left and then disowning me when I married Vinay, for her not laying eyes on her grandchild and dying without my even knowing. Most of all, I sob tears of regret for the woman I have become. Bitter, angry. A woman whom Vinay looks at with shock and anger and baffled hurt, his eyes, which used to darken with love, now widening with incomprehension, his perplexed gaze asking me what I also want to ask myself: 'Where have you disappeared to, Kali? Who is this woman left in your place?'

Where is that curious, starry-eyed girl who used to hide behind doorways eavesdropping on her boss? The girl who admired the landlord's wife and wanted to be like her, commanding respect and awed affection. Who instead has to make do with fear, the smell of it – rancorous, stinging, like pepper powder mixed in with chillies.

'Why won't you talk to Grandma and Grandpa?' my little boy asks, his hot, insistent palm in mine, his upturned innocent face bemused.

'Ask them. Go on. Ask them why they will not talk to me,' I snap, eyes flashing.

He drops my hand, his lower lip wobbling dangerously at my tone and runs to his nanny, hiding behind her skirts.

It was Sumathi's job to be nanny, the one she was qualified for, having been a wet nurse and nurturer before she started working at the mansion, but I hired another girl from the village to look after Manoj. Sumathi quit soon after. 'I would have loved your son like my own,' she'd said when leaving, adding the grudging 'ma'am' as an afterthought. *You know that,* she was implying.

To tell the truth, I was relieved when she left. If all the servants who had been here when I was a servant left, so much the better. Although it was tempting, I knew not to fire them.

It would be one step too far, even for me. Instead, every day, I hoped for a communal relaxing of memory. But scandal has its own reach. And the memory has never eased.

I can never quite wipe the whiff of disgrace from my clothes, no matter how many times my servants, old and new, wash them. Over time, I've if not accepted then come to tense terms with the ignominy stalking me, the other landlords looking down on me. What I find harder to come to terms with is Vinay's depression, his weakness, the way he has collapsed into himself since his parents passed, becoming a shadow flitting through the mansion, a ghost haunting the second wing.

My mother-in-law passed on first. To Vinay's lasting regret, and despite the care and solicitude he showered upon her, his mother never quite recovered from the blow of her son's lowly marriage to me, a mere servant, and from her subsequent loss of face. Strong as Vinay's mother had once been, she went downhill rapidly after our wedding and was dead before Manoj turned five. After she passed, her husband wilted. Six months on, he was dead too.

'Your da has made a will,' my mother-in-law had sniffed on her deathbed, addressing Vinay, not looking at me but saying the words loud enough so I would hear. 'Everything goes to Manoj.'

'Oh, Ma, don't talk so. You have years to go yet,' Vinay had said, completely missing the point.

But I hadn't overlooked the barb I knew was intended for me. I understood that I was just the carer of the heir. I would never belong. This house that I loved, this house that was now the only thing, besides my son, that meant anything to me would never truly be *mine*.

I left the room then, my head held high. I caught my mother-in-law's smirk, even through her wheezing, those lungs that refused to do their job. She was having the last laugh as always, her whistling lungs sounding out an encore.

The villagers are wary of me. Despite the years that have elapsed, I am still the servant who usurped the mistress, who sent the virtuous woman to her death. My mother-in-law's saintliness grows in direct proportion to the passing of time. Slander follows me like a loyal pet. I can smell the servants' distrust – it is the stormy blue of an imminent squall.

I try not to care. Now that my in-laws have passed, *I* am the matriarch and there is no stopping me. I have dreamt of this, worked towards this, for what feels like forever: being the wife of the landlord, the man whose family has owned this village for generations.

By marrying me impulsively, Vinay lost more than he gained. And the love he had so boldly stepped up for, the only thing he stood up for in his life, is gone. It has trailed away like the sparkling dust left in the wake of the shooting star that we had both wished on once upon a happier time. Vinay and I haven't slept together in years. He refused to leave our room – the room on the second wing – to move upstairs to his parents' bedroom with me. When I broached the subject a good few months after his parents' passing, he stared at me, shocked, silent tears streaming down his face.

'Please don't, Kali. Give my ma the peace she deserves in the afterlife.'

'I'm just thinking of moving into her room. I'm not…'

'Please.'

I moved into his old room instead, like I had dreamt of doing once, with its huge window that looks down the hill to the village. But when I peer out that window, instead of crowing about my high position, my wealth, like I once imagined I would, I am filled with yearning for an ordinary life. One where I am not maligned and disliked. One where I am a different, kinder person, more like the girl I once was. One where I am the wife of a farmer, *Manu*, beloved and content, kneading chapattis and boiling rice, helping out in the fields and looking after my children. One where I am not the cold mother of a son who shrinks from me and quakes in my presence, much like the servants do.

I look at Manoj, his fearful eyes afraid to meet mine, and irritation wars with love. I had hoped that my boy would bring me the recognition I craved. I created him purposefully. He was the means by which I would achieve everything.

But I have failed and when I look at him that is all I see. I snap at him, am prickly with him, and the more I do so, the more he retreats into his shell. I seem unable to tell him how much I love him. I cannot bring myself to open my arms and gather him to me, hold him without reservation, love him without boundaries. I have forgotten how.

I watch him sometimes from the window of my room. I see my only son running to his nanny, dust rising in a peach cloud behind him, his shirt flapping around his skinny brown body, face alight with joy. He throws his arms around his nanny, smiling up at her, eyes sparkling and I have to turn away, hug myself until I feel able to push the screams that want to escape, the keens that keep on coming, back inside so I can maintain my dignity, the facade of a proud landlord's wife who will not stand for nonsense.

Vinay refuses medical intervention. He will not leave his room, that dank space tattooed with his remorse, his hurt, to accompany me anywhere, least of all to hospital. He declines to see the doctors I bring round.

The only person Vinay will see is his oldest friend – the family lawyer, Desai. Desai, who is always civil to me but never close, spends hours in Vinay's room. The lawyer has even convinced Vinay to go for walks with him on the hill once or twice.

Over time most of the books from the library have migrated to Vinay's room, crammed into every available space, the scent of dust and silverfish and sonnets and melancholia in the air, the taste of wistfulness and lost hope and old paper. I get a servant to tidy up and the next day the room is back to how it was, littered with poetry books and stray bits of paper, Vinay lost in an oversized armchair in the middle of it all, as much an old relic as the tomes open and spilling around him.

Late at night, as I try and fail to sleep, a worm of insecurity uncoils, wrapping itself around my brain. 'Ungrateful, conniving bitch,' it whispers in my mother-in-law's cutting voice. 'You don't deserve this.'

I feel like giving up altogether. Running far away, starting anew, in a different guise. After all I am a genius at reinventing myself.

Where are you, Manu? I picture him as he must be now, father to three strapping youngsters who look like the Manu I remember: forever young, champion skimmer of stones, with another luckier woman leading the life I was once convinced I was destined to inhabit. The nocturnal air whispers jasmine-perfumed reassurances, and I push the thought away. *I* am the lucky one. I have all this. This is what I wanted. I must go on. *Otherwise,* another, softer voice chimes in my head, *it would all have been for nothing. Nothing.*

I get up and go to the bathroom, splash some water on my face.

Are you happy, Da, I ask my absent father in my head, *with the choice you made? Your actions caused so many ripples, changed so many lives. And here I am now.*

I look in the mirror. My face is just the same as always, although my eyes do not shine with the innocent hopes I once nurtured. Instead they are hard, calculating. I used to be a girl who wanted very little. A love story, like in my favourite book. Marriage to a boy I loved. The adoration of my da. The pride of my ma. I had it all, except the marriage to the boy I loved, which was still to come. And then it all changed. One rash action by my da, or perhaps a calculated, selfish one, and my life and my ma's was devastated, as was the happy-ever-after I had been hoping for.

And now I have only gone and done the same. Selfishly, like my da, like a child in a toyshop denied one thing and hankering after another, I tried to grab the mansion as a consolation prize, and with it a man who was sensitive, a man who cared, perhaps far too much. A man who'd had nothing bad ever happen to him and thus dared to look for the very best in people, so he was very easy to deceive. I took Vinay's love and I manipulated it. I took his heart and shattered it. And like my da before me, I ruined Vinay's family. I destroyed it so I could get what I wanted. I took wilfully and I have not given back.

I walk to the wardrobe and fling it open – silk and comfort, perfume and shimmering iridescence. When I first got married, my belongings would not have taken up a third of one of the compartments of this vast closet. Now my clothes, many of them unused, spill around me, enveloping me in soft luxury.

I pull out the small carrier bag tucked in a corner at the very back and open it. The aroma of loss and despair, betrayal and rot and neglect – old tales and older lives, nostalgia and reminiscence. I close my eyes, and just for a moment I am back in the village where I grew up, the afternoon we packed our belongings and left – the sun-dappled fields, the dog's howls, the villagers gathered to bid goodbye, some crying, my mother wailing loudest, me dry eyed and numb hearted, stunned by Manu's rejection, not really caring what I was throwing in the carrier bag supplied by my aunt, my mouth thick with the taste of memories and homesickness, although we hadn't left yet.

I dig through my belongings from another life and find what I'm looking for – the tattered book that I stole from my school, the love story that filled my head with ideas, that I lugged with me even when my own love failed. I have saved it. Hoping.

Hoping.

This book is imprinted with the hopeful visions of the young girl I was, infused with my glittering dreams for the future, carrying the weight of all my expectations. I take it out and I shred it to pieces like I have wrecked Vinay and his family.

It doesn't make me feel any better. I despise the woman who stares back at me from the mirror. The woman who was once a naive girl who wanted love and adoration, who *still* yearns for love and adoration. The woman with her hard eyes and her stern, unyielding mouth. The woman who will stop at nothing to get what she wants, no matter how many lives she crushes along the way. The woman who is like her father – selfish and grasping but perhaps even worse.

I looked down on my ma for taking to her bed after my da left. But at least the only person she harmed was herself. Unlike me.

Unlike me.

I have nothing to show for my life except what I have done to Vinay and his family, and that thought terrifies me. And this is why I try my hardest to maintain Vinay's legacy, to restore the mansion back to its earlier glory, so I can give that back to him at least: the respect and pride the Gowdas once commanded. The irony that he doesn't care, not any more, is not lost on me of course. But if I could get the mansion, the Gowda name, to what it was before, I could go some way towards righting the wrong I did. My mother-in-law couldn't fault me for this at least from where she's keeping tabs on me in the afterlife.

Like Vinay's mother, I have a flair for business. I have expanded all of our companies. Our properties have flourished, grown. Reigniting the grandeur of the Gowda name on the other hand – I am working on that. I've tried socialising over the years, invited landlords and politicians. They come. But they do not stay. Conversations are stilted. And Vinay and I are never invited back, never part of the elite circles in which my in-laws were seamlessly included.

But I will not give up. This is now my fantasy, my dream, my wish, my hope, my prayer: I will make sure the Gowdas are accepted into the folds of high society the way they once were. Manoj will make a good marriage, have many children. The family name of the illustrious Gowdas will live on. I will show Vinay how the Gowdas are thriving, make him see how happy his ma would be, watching from the afterlife. I will convince him that she would definitely have wanted this, forgiving him anything, even his marriage to me, because of where the Gaddehalli Gowdas are. And Vinay will understand. He will finally be relieved of the guilt he feels for sending his parents to an early grave because of his decision to marry me. He will get better, and we will grow old together, he and I, surrounded by our many grandchildren, heirs to the Gowda fortune.

You are getting fanciful in your middle age, a voice chides in my head.

It could happen. I dreamt up a plan to ensnare the heir to a fortune and look where it took me.

Yes, look where it's got you – brimming with loneliness in a huge house stuffed full of people waiting to follow your every command.

* * *

'Sudha, when will you give me an heir? People are talking,' I yell.

The woman smiles and I see that it is not Sudha. It is never Sudha.

'An heir. I want an heir…'

A clamp of foreboding. A pang of fear. An attack of nerves. I am scared. Petrified. Why? 'Sudha. I…'

Something shifts in my head. Something clicks. And then I know. Sudha is not here. I know this just as surely as I know my name – Kali – and what I did. What it led to. Sudha is not here. None of them are. The sting of smoke and betrayal. The sweep of fire and destruction. A shiver. A release. The taste of brine. The stench of urine. The sensation of hot wet creeping down my thighs.

Shame trickles through me, reeking of ammonia. I bend down to clean myself. But I find I don't have the strength, my trembling arms failing me, my body rendered fragile, refusing to do what I want.

I was once the boss of all I surveyed. I had servants dancing to my tunes. I made them dance and how! Now I can't even control the workings of my bladder.

You deserve it.

Yes. I do.

Chapter 31
Jaya

One Crazy Ride

Jaya and Ben pick up their hire car from the airport and, armed with directions from Sumathiamma, drive straight to the house that Jaya's mother ran away from all those years ago, in the midst of a fire.

✳   ✳   ✳

Sumathiamma's voice on the phone had been high pitched and tremulous with excitement and emotion.

'I'm Jaya. My mum was Sudha Gowda,' Jaya had said.

'Was?' A soft, sad exhalation.

'She passed away nearly eighteen months ago. Heart attack.'

'I'm so sorry to hear that.'

'You said in your letter that you knew her?' Jaya had asked.

'I did. A sweet girl, eager to please. Beautiful too. Inside and out…' Sumathiamma's deep heartfelt sigh had echoed down the phone line.

'She was… She became a very different woman.'

'I can imagine,' Sumathiamma had said.

'I… My husband and I… we'd like to come there, to see this house you describe. Meet with Kali.'

'That would be wonderful! When were you thinking of coming?' Her enthusiasm had reverberated through the line, making Jaya smile. 'Come straight to the house – I'll send word to the lawyer.'

And thus it had been decided.

* * *

'Wow,' Ben says as their car is see-sawed by hurtling vehicles overtaking from all sides. His face is screwed up in concentration, the veins standing out in his hands where they clasp the wheel fiercely as he tries to keep the car from careening into the rubbish-swathed ditch beside the road. 'This is one crazy ride, Jaya.'

Ben's expression is open and awed as he turns to smile at her before hunching forward to right the car, which is almost pushed off the road by a speeding bus, crammed to bursting with passengers. He looks younger than he has in ages, she thinks. His T-shirt is soaked through despite the air that rushes in through the open windows of the car, tasting of summer and adventure.

* * *

When Ben had returned from Chicago and pulled Jaya into his arms, she had stiffened at first. But then she'd thought of how she had failed her mother, refusing to see the extent of her mother's love for her because she was looking backward, into the past. *Ben is here now. With me. He loves me. And I love him too.*

She'd relaxed into his arms and they'd made love for the first time since Arun passed. It had been passionate and emotional, hungry and breathless, as they'd discovered each other again, their bodies older and changed in subtle ways, marked by grief. He'd kissed her Caesarean scar and they'd sobbed in each other's arms, sharing their loss – another first.

Afterwards, she had shown him the diaries and the photographs, translated her mother's entries for him – the ones she herself had read so far. Ben listened quietly and seriously, his face raw, eyes stark, as he processed what her mother had been through, the muscle in his cheek – which throbbed in direct proportion to how upset he was – working overtime. It had been therapeutic to discuss Sudha's entries with him, to unburden the guilt she felt, the hurt on behalf of her mother.

Before leaving for India, Jaya had called Dr Meadows, filling her in on what had happened so far and on her decision to visit Gaddehalli with Ben. Dr Meadows had dropped her professional mask enough to say, 'Good on you, Jaya,' her usually unflappable voice ringing with approval.

*   *   *

And now, here they were, she and Ben, in her mother's birthplace, alive with heat – a stifling, humid slap – and vendors hawking piles of tender coconut, newspaper cones of peanuts and hillocks of syrupy sweetmeats from beneath striped awnings propped up by coconut fronds.

They drive past huge houses, barricaded with iron gates and high walls, topped with glinting, multi-coloured shards of glass, to deter burglars Jaya surmises. She thinks of the much-thumbed group photograph with Gaddehalli written in her mother's handwriting across the back, experiencing a thrill as it dawns on her anew that they are actually here, within reach of Gaddehalli, driving towards it, and a pang that her mother is not here, doing this with her.

'The matriarch in the group picture must be Kali, and the bald man she's propping up must be Vinay,' she muses to Ben.

'So the younger woman in the picture – think she could be your mum? She's slight like your mother,' Ben says.

Hollow-eyed mothers beg for food, thrusting pleading hands into the open windows of cars stuck in traffic, infants clinging to their legs, babies strapped onto concave stomachs with sari slings.

'I've been wondering the same thing,' Jaya says, shouting to be heard above the roar of the breeze permeating the car. 'The woman's face is hidden by the little boy whose pictures my mum saved. Who is the little boy? And where do I come into all of this? I assumed I was born after Mum came to the UK. Even so, I wish she'd dated her diary entries so I had some idea.'

They are out of the city now and the traffic has eased to the point that theirs is the only car navigating the potholed road. Ben lifts one palm off the steering wheel to squeeze Jaya's hand before turning his full attention – and both hands – to conveying them safely to the place so intimately linked to Jaya's mother.

'We'll find out soon enough, Jaya,' Ben says, before letting out a stream of expletives and braking hard. He manages to avoid hitting a cow that has ambled onto the road right in front of them just in the nick of time. The cow turns its head towards them, serene eyes, the boundless brown of sun-caressed earth, regarding them mildly through the grimy windscreen. Then it opens its mouth in a yawn and, with a wet flick of its tongue, licks the windscreen in a wide arc, before sauntering away with a soulful moo. Jaya meets Ben's gaze and they start laughing as one. And as Jaya shares this magical, mad moment with her husband, the difficult few months that have led up to this point fall away like droplets dispersing from leaves after a storm has passed.

When he's managed to get his laughter under control, Ben starts the engine only to turn it off again. A posse of dogs have followed the cow's example and have taken over the road, trailed by a hen and her brood of chicks. While waiting for the road to empty of animals, Ben leans over and kisses Jaya. When they sit back in their seats, a crowd has gathered outside their car, staring and pointing.

'I love it when you blush, Jaya!' Ben grins as he starts the engine and their car edges past the crowd, now shaking their heads at Ben and Jaya while conversing loudly among themselves.

*   *   *

People defecate next to the road, clothes lifted to expose shrivelled skin; women chat companionably as they wash clothes in the gushing river, the water silvery green as it skips over shingle and tumbles past boulders, naked children jumping from rocks with dripping hair and turmeric teeth.

The air gusting through the car smells of spices and stories, of hunger and desire. It is tinted with sunshine, embellished with dust and flavoured with moisture-soaked, adrenaline-painted, nausea-tinged anticipation.

'This is some country, Jaya! Your mother… She must have missed it so. I've only just got here and I already know I'll be visiting again,' Ben says, a contented grin, the likes of which she hasn't seen for a while now, gracing his face.

'Oh?' she asks, smiling at him.

'Yes, I'm definitely coming back. With you in tow of course.' He raises his eyebrows, mock challenging. Then, his voice grave, he says, 'And yet your mother never returned.'

Women cook on an open fire, twigs and newspaper topped by dancing gold flames, their mud pots wearing a crown of steam. Teenage boys ogle giggling groups of girls, whose faces are obscured by colourful umbrellas they use as shelter from the unrelenting sun. Coconut trees, haloed by sunlight and dotted with the black shadows of nesting crows, wave languidly as their car goes past. Women hawk jasmine garlands, white wreaths smelling of the incense Jaya's mum used to favour.

'I wish Mum was here with us now,' Jaya whispers, her gaze snagging on a seething, packed black mass, a hill of decaying rubbish that has been taken captive by flies.

* * *

The village, when they finally come to it, is just a sprinkling of cottages, exactly as Jaya had viewed it on Google, basking drowsily among bleached fields in the soporific heat, the house that her mother once lived in and whose photograph she'd saved glowering down from the hill above. People gather outside their cottages to watch their car, curious eyes, open mouths, heads shaking, pointing fingers.

'Why are they doing that?' Jaya says, a sudden, forbidding tremor making her shiver despite the heat.

'Doing what?' Ben asks.

A vendor gapes at them from behind mounds of rice and he too shakes his head when Jaya meets his gaze. 'Ben, it's as if they're warning us not to go up the hill.'

✴   ✴   ✴

The hill is very steep, the drive riddled with stones and roots, making for a jerky ride. And finally they are at the top, rendered breathless by the view, the countryside they have just traversed spread out below them, a medley of rust-rimmed gold. The house itself is huge but battered, radiating neglect, having collapsed in on itself like an old hero, now vanquished, proudly wearing the scars of battles past. Ben whistles, long and low. On the right side of the front entrance is what looks like an overgrown fruit orchard. Ben parks in the perfumed shadow of fruit trees – mango and jackfruit, guava and cashew. A tremulous chill takes Jaya's body hostage. 'Ben, I know all these trees; I can identify every single one. How?'

He switches off the engine and puts his arm around her. She rests her head on his shoulder, breathing in his familiar, beloved scent, but she can't stop shivering. Now that she's actually here, she is strangely loath to get out of the cosy cocoon of the car, wary of what's in store for her, what she is going to find. To postpone the inevitable, she pulls the group photo out of her bag, and together she and Ben scrutinise it again. And gradually, as Jaya looks at the people in the photograph like she has done close to a hundred times since she found it, trying to glean clues, she stops shaking, comes back into herself.

'The matriarch – Kali? – her proud face, her air of privilege.'

Ben nods, yes.

'The young man – Manoj possibly?'

'Yes, it has to be,' Ben says.

'And the woman beside him – this woman whose face is hidden by the child who morphs into Arun in the dreams I have of him – she must be my mum.'

A stab of recognition. But… How?

She shudders, closing her eyes.

'What is it, Jaya?' Ben's voice is concerned.

'I… I just realised… In my dreams, the boy was playing in the mud in front of *this* house.'

'Our subconscious works in strange ways, Jaya. You saw the photos of the house and the boy among your mother's belongings. You looked up Gaddehalli and saw the ruin on Google. And it surfaced in your dreams…' Ben's rational voice cuts through her fear, her confusion.

The front door of the house opens and a head pokes out, attached to a bony body draped in a worn sari, a tea cloth flung across one shoulder. Sumathiamma must have been watching for them and seen their car arrive.

Jaya places the picture back in her bag carefully and turns to Ben.

'Ready?' he asks.

She nods and, taking a deep breath, gets out of the car, the sticky heat hitting her afresh. Sweat collects in the grooves of her face and travels down her body, a salty baptism to this new country.

Sumathiamma comes towards them, beaming. When she smiles, her face transforms into that of a much younger woman. She nods to Ben, saying, 'Welcome,' in English.

'Thank you. Delighted to be here,' Ben says and Sumathiamma giggles.

She turns to Jaya. 'I didn't understand a word of what he said. *Welcome* is the only word of English I know. You will have to translate for me from now on.'

She takes Jaya's hand in both of hers. 'You are so like your mother.'

Jaya closes her eyes, rocks on her feet. Ben puts his arm around her to steady her.

'Sorry, I know it's all a bit too much.' Sumathiamma sounds worried.

'No, *I'm* sorry.' She smiles at Sumathiamma. 'It's just... overwhelming. Being here. This place where my mother lived once.'

'I cannot begin to imagine,' Sumathiamma says gently. 'But you are here now and we are delighted. The lawyer is coming tomorrow to meet you. You must be tired after your journey. Come inside, have something to eat.'

What dramas were played out here, Jaya wonders as she and Ben follow Sumathiamma into the sorry carcass that was once the largest mansion for miles around, *behind a curtain of wealth, the shimmering screen of elevated status? The scandal caused by Mum that Sumathiamma referred to in her letter – did it take place here?*

'Kali is having a nap – she was distressed this morning and had to be sedated. She'll wake in a couple of hours. Plenty of time for you to eat and freshen up before you meet her,' Sumathiamma says.

The damp, rotting smell of death, the musty, desperate taste of a thousand previous existences, hits Jaya as soon as she walks through the front door of the ruin, the echo of what was once reverberating off the cavernous space. She senses the whispered presence of stories, the thrill of lives lived, loves lost and cherished, the flash of dancing flames, the burn of fire and smoke, the hopelessness of ash and devastation.

There is grief and there is *grief*, she thinks. Their house in the UK is steeped in sorrow, awash with Arun's loss, but this one... this grand, dilapidated mansion radiates despondency and anguish from each weed-ambushed stone, each moss-stained, disintegrating tile.

She can swear she hears the silenced screams of smothered lives; she can feel the air glisten as it comes alive with the ghosts of happier times.

'Are you coming?' Sumathiamma calls from somewhere up ahead.

'Yes,' Jaya says and resolutely wipes her face to rid herself of these thoughts.

'You okay?' Ben asks, his eyes shining with concern.

No, I am not.

She nods and starts walking, beckoning Ben to follow. She sees a little boy skipping through the many rooms, his gleeful laughter, the texture and essence of innocence, reverberating through these broken walls, the empty, distraught rooms. She takes a step and something moves. Something tangible, slithering, alive. She yells and jumps backward, bumping into Ben, both of them almost tripping over the leaf strewn, rotting threshold, as a snake glides right past them. Jaya's scream echoes and ricochets across the blots of tragedy that stamp the passageways of this wrecked house.

Sumathiamma comes running back towards them. 'What's the matter?' And then, smiling reassuringly as she notices the tail end of the snake disappearing into the mulch across the threshold, she says, 'Oh, just a rat snake. It's harmless. On the lookout for frogs.'

'*Inside* the house?' Jaya is shocked.

'Come, the kitchen is better, I promise. No snakes in there. Or any other animals for that matter – except ones I have cooked.' She looks up at Jaya and grins cheerfully.

The kitchen is a magical haven, smelling of spices and comfort, dried vegetables hanging from the rafters, pots bubbling on the stove, a scarred wooden table taking up most of the space, enveloped in a warm glow from the sun angling in through the windows.

'Forgive me for writing to your mother, Jaya,' Sumathiamma says as she places a plate of steaming gram-flour-coated vegetables in front of Jaya and Ben, alongside a bowl of coriander and mint chutney. 'You see, I asked the lawyer to show me the letter he wrote before posting it and I decided that dry little flyer would never convince Sudha to come back. If anything, it would push her into hiding further.' She laughs as she piles their plates high and, nodding at Ben, mimes *eat*. Ben needs no encouragement and dives right in.

'Eat some podis, child,' Sumathiamma urges Jaya, placing tumblers of tea beside her and Ben.

Jaya bites into a podi dipped in chutney. She closes her eyes as the explosion of spices hits her throat, chasing away the emotions aroused in her from entering this house. 'This is divine,' she says and Sumathiamma glows brighter than the light bathing this cosy room.

Ben has polished off every morsel on his plate. There isn't even a smear of chutney left. He grins at Sumathiamma. 'Delicious!'

'I don't need you to translate that!' Sumathiamma smiles happily at Jaya and piles more podis onto Ben's plate.

Ben laughs. 'At this rate I won't be able to fit into the car for the drive back, but who cares, these are heavenly,' he says, tucking in.

Jaya takes a sip of the tea, savouring the sweetness of the cardamom, the kick of ginger, as she listens to what Sumathiamma is saying.

'"Sudha does not want her inheritance," I told the lawyer. "She ran away from it. She is not one of those grasping people who'll come running at the mere mention of a will, a bequest. I know the girl," I said.'

Jaya feels tears smart her eyes. She wishes she had known the Sudha Sumathiamma was recalling.

'I cajoled him into including my letter. "This will make her come, if anything," I said.' Sumathiamma's eyes shine with sudden tears. 'I'm sorry it's too late.'

She leans forward and folds Jaya's hands into her own calloused ones. 'But I'm glad you are here. And I'm sure Kali will be too when her troubled mind registers your presence.'

'You intimated in your letters that my mother did something, caused some scandal?'

Sumathiamma's eyes widen. 'Don't you know?'

'No. She was very closed about the past.'

'Oh. I would have thought… seeing as you are…'

'But she kept diaries. I've been reading them.'

'She doesn't mention anything in them?'

'I haven't read all of the entries. I only found the diaries recently, while going through her things. I… I can't read more than one entry at a time. She didn't have the best childhood and it is hard… I need time to process her words.'

'I think you should first read what she has to say. *Everything* she has to say. Once you've finished reading, we'll talk. You see, all I have are rumours. Hearsay. I can guess at her reasons for what she did but that's all it will be. A guess. It's better you find out what your mother has to say first.'

Jaya turns to Ben, who is looking from her to Sumathiamma, and translates their exchange for him.

'What she says makes sense, don't you think, Jaya?'

'Yes.'

'You'll meet my granddaughter, Durga, soon too. She's arriving this evening,' Sumathiamma says, pride staining her weathered voice.

'The little girl who urged you to pay heed to Kali's ramblings?' Jaya asks.

'Yes, that's my granddaughter.' Sumathiamma beams.

'I can't wait to see her,' Jaya says and Sumathiamma rubs her palms together with delight.

'Me too. She's been visiting her parents – they've been in an accident.' Sumathiamma's face clouds over. 'I've missed her,' she says. Then, smiling gently at Jaya, she says, 'I can see both of you are quite worn out. Why don't you rest and later, when you're feeling up to it, you can meet with Kali?'

'That sounds perfect,' Jaya concedes, noting the dark circles under Ben's eyes, which must mirror her own. Being in this house, ambushed by sensation, has taken it out of her. She cannot think – she just wants to be, Ben beside her, their door closed to the world.

As if she has read Jaya's thoughts, Sumathiamma says, 'Let me show you to your room.'

Their room is small but snug. Windowless but not oppressive. 'This used to be the male servants' room. Hence no windows.' Sumathiamma is apologetic. 'You're right next to us – Durga and me. We have no windows either – ours was the female servants' room.'

'I love it.' Jaya smiles, just as Ben says, 'It's perfect,' and sets down their suitcase.

'Ironically the only rooms intact downstairs after the fire were the pantry, which is now the kitchen, the servants' quarters and the room off the library, now Kali's room, which is just down the corridor from here. I have heated up water for you to have a wash. Shout if you need anything,' Sumathiamma says and she leaves, quietly pulling the door closed behind her.

Ben gathers Jaya to him, sealing her lips with his own. And she loses herself in him, the tensions of the day easing.

Afterwards they lie side by side on the bed, and Jaya reads her mum's next entry out loud, translating for Ben as she goes, a thrill passing through her as she realises that the events her mother is describing took place while she was living here...

Chapter 32
Sudha

The Tune of Fate

Dear Diary,

Life was looking up for a while. I was getting used to being loved.

Then I found out I was pregnant. It was joy, sheer fulfilment – the tangible essence of our love overwhelming my body, ambushing my limbs, rounding my stomach. Then I lost the baby, proving the gods and my parents right, my dead brother whispering from his perch beside my right ear, 'What did you expect? You took my life. This is only fair.'

Manoj held me and consoled me, as every night I keened for our lost child.

'I hurt everyone and everything I love,' I sobbed.

'Rubbish,' Manoj said, massaging my back.

'Thank goodness we didn't tell your parents or mine – get their hopes up.'

'Sudha,' Manoj said when I had finally exhausted my grief, replaced with a sore numbness. 'We will get through this. Together.'

And so, Manoj and I try to get through it.

I get pregnant easily. It is keeping the child conceived out of love, so much love, that is hard. Every time I get pregnant, I hope that this time the gods will allow my baby to live. To thrive. And every day that passes without my experiencing the constricting pain that signals the beginning of the end, I thank the gods.

But it arrives of course. Without fail. Six weeks in, seven. That agonising, terrible pain. My whole body protesting as my baby is wrenched away. Again.

I know that I have to pay. That this is my punishment. But how many times? Oh, gods, how many times?

The faith-tipped anticipation. And then the unbearable loss. Wrenching grief the red of chastisement, the blighted black of a sinful heart. The sort of darkness that has no hope of lightening.

Manoj and I have, secretly, without our parents' knowledge, consulted all the specialists in the fertility field.

'There's nothing wrong with you,' the experts say. 'Rest, eat well and healthily and you should be able to carry a baby to term the next time you get pregnant.'

I rest. I eat healthily. I get pregnant. And, a few short weeks later, I miscarry.

Every week my parents visit. They look at me with hope in their eyes, which dies when they read my face.

'When are you going to give us a grandson?' they ask.

They are specific of course. They want a boy. The boy I denied them. It is their right. My duty.

'We are at death's door, our bodies failing, our various ailments worsening,' my parents complain. 'There is only one wish left before we die. To hold our grandson in our arms. What's taking you so long?' Disdain and disgust, scorn and pleading tint their voices ink-blot navy.

They do not know about the miscarriages. I have managed to keep them quiet.

'People are talking,' they say and beside me my mother-in-law goes very still.

Hearsay and wagging tongues have been instrumental in the ignominy of the Gowdas spreading far and wide. And now dishonour is trailing us again.

Although she pretends not to care, I sense my mother-in-law's quiet desperation, notice how her face sets in a grimace and her eyes quiver when she hears the malicious murmurs following us at the market: 'There go the women from that doomed house, cursed when the servant married the heir and drove his parents to their deaths. Of what use is all that wealth if they can't pass it on?'

'The Gowdas of Gaddehalli will die out,' the villagers predict, nodding sagely, gleefully. 'The sins of the parents visited upon the children.'

The villagers, with their casual malice, fuelled by their poverty and their envy, will not let my mother-in-law rise above what she did. *It could just as easily have been one of our daughters,* is what they are thinking when they see her in her finery, with her chauffeur-driven car and her bevy of servants. And for this they will not forgive her.

My mother-in-law's back has begun to stoop, her face lined no matter how much powder she cakes it in, her mouth permanently creased in a frown.

'How will the Gowda name flourish if there is no grand-child to carry it on? How long do you expect me to wait? It has been four years. Give me a grandchild or I will find another bride for Manoj,' my mother-in-law declares, all her frustration and rage at the gossip mongers making her lash out at me.

'Ma, I will not marry anyone else. I love Sudha. She is the one for me, child or no child.' Manoj's voice rises to a bellow, the first time I have heard it so.

Servants gather at the door, their shadows blocking out the slip of light at the doorjamb and creeping inside via the small gap under the door, yellow black. The room reverberates with the hollow pulse of hurt and recrimination.

'Don't lie, Manoj. How can you be happy without a child? We cannot have this. We need an heir to carry on the Gowda name.'

'*You* need a grandchild. *You* need the Gowda name. Da doesn't care and neither do I. Sudha matters more to me than your stupid family name.'

'I rue the day I welcomed this girl into our home. She lured you with her pretty face, and I went along with it. I should have paid heed to the villagers when they told me that Sudha was cursed, her womb barren because of what she did to her brother.'

'Ma, no, don't you dare!' Manoj strides towards his mother, hands clutched into fists by his sides, his face suffused.

My womb barren. I hug my stomach and sway on my feet. *Please, gods, I am sorry for what I did. So sorry. What more can I do to appease you? I just want to hold a babe, my babe, Manoj's babe, the product of our love, in my arms. Please.*

'Hit me, son, like you want to. Go on!' my mother-in-law mocks, at the same time as I manage to find my voice and yell, 'No, Manoj.'

I cannot bear this. I can't stand seeing my husband this way, undone by anger and hurt, this man with whom I have found the happiness I did not think was in my reach.

Gods, you have allowed me a shot at love, given me Manoj and you think I don't merit any more happiness, is that it? I agree with you, I do. But what has my husband done to earn this sentence too? When his only crime is that he loves an unworthy woman?

He is a good man. He deserves a happy family with a fertile wife and lots of adoring children. He deserves better than me. But he seems to want me. Please, gods, for his sake – one child is all I ask.

If this rift with his mother exacerbates, I worry that history will repeat itself, and that Manoj will turn into his father, smothered by regrets, his future arrested by the aching reach of a fractious past.

He looks older already, hollowed out. He is suffering. He doesn't deserve this.

And despite my mother-in-law's prickliness, her bossiness and quick temper, she does not warrant being scoffed at and derided because of my failings.

For a while after my marriage, when I discovered love and found happiness, I dared to believe that I had paid for what I had done in my mother's womb. I even began to believe Manoj's oft-repeated assurances that it was not my fault.

But when I suffered my first miscarriage, I knew. How could I think that I was safe, that I was blameless? I was cursed by what I had done. I was tainted. But because *I* am, it doesn't follow that this family who have taken me into their fold should suffer the same fate. They don't need to be punished for what I did, for the baggage I haul from my past, just because my present has intersected and merged with theirs.

What to do? There must be something I can do. But I can't countenance what.

So I continue as before, hoping and praying and bargaining with the gods; loving Manoj, getting pregnant and losing my babies.

Then one day a servant comes running, out of breath, to where I am lying on the sofa, recovering from my latest miscarriage.

'Please come quickly. Your mother fell down the steps at the temple when she went to pray for a grandson, it seems. She is hurt badly and in Sannipur hospital.' The words slip out in one huge panting gasp.

The chauffeur takes me to the hospital, driving faster than he has ever done before, with me praying all the way. Praying like I do every time I feel the dragging pains, the vice-like hand cramping down on my cursed stomach, wrenching my babies away from me.

Please, I beg. *Please, gods.*

Ma is a pale, bruised shadow, hooked to machines. It jolts me, seeing her like this, reduced, vulnerable.

She is weak and delirious, her hot hands grasping, her leaking eyes beseeching, over and over, 'A grandson, Sudha, please. Give me a grandson before I die.'

'I will,' I say, howling inside.

I return home defeated. And I do the only thing I can think of. I pray, even though the gods do not mind my prayers.

I pray and then, as the evening bleeds sunset pink into night, weeping dewdrops upon shadow-choked leaves, it comes to me. Perhaps my prayers are not enough. Perhaps, like the Catholics intercede with God via Mary, I need someone to intercede for me. Someone who has guaranteed access to the gods.

I pick the servants' collective brains. I pay them to discreetly scout the neighbouring villages for sages. I keep this secret even from Manoj. I don't know what he will think of my idea. And I don't want him talking me out of it.

I am desperate. What if my mother dies before she realises her longing to hold her grandchild in her arms? I will never forgive myself if I am not able to do this for her, to go some way towards appeasing her for denying her a son.

And what if my mother-in-law goes ahead with finding another wife for Manoj like she threatens to, more and more often nowadays? I know there are hundreds of girls willing to marry him. He is handsome, kind, so very loving and, for now, he is mine.

'Sudha,' my mother-in-law had taunted, when she and Manoj almost came to blows over her suggestion that he remarry, 'don't you agree with me? Will you be so selfish as to stand in Manoj's way, prevent him from having the future, the children, he deserves?'

'Don't listen to her poison, Sudha,' Manoj had yelled, pulling me close.

And yet every night when he holds me and loves me, assuring me that we will be okay, that it will all work out, professing how much he cares for me, I think, *You would be so much better off with a proper woman, one without a tainted past and a cursed present, one who does not inadvertently hurt everyone she loves – one who has the means to be the mother of your children.*

I know Manoj loves me. I know he wouldn't look twice at another woman. But I also know my mother-in-law. She is nothing if not tenacious. If she gets an idea into her head, she executes it, no matter how long it takes or how preposterous it sounds. I wouldn't put it past her to trick her son into marriage with another woman. And as much as I agree with her that Manoj would be better off with someone else, I am selfish enough that I will do everything I can to pre-empt my mother-in-law's plans.

I love Manoj. I couldn't bear losing him, the only bright spot in my life, the reason for me to keep on living when my babies are not.

'You are not a victim,' Manoj told me once. 'You survived living with your parents, hoisting the burden they placed on you. You are strong. Stronger than you know.'

I am not going to give Manoj up this easily. I will try every means at my disposal to keep him.

The servants return with news of a visiting sage, the wisest guru this side of Karnataka, camping under the Bodhi tree in the outskirts of Sannipur. A sign – the guru visiting just when I need him. It is meant to be.

I decide to meet with him the very next day, when Manoj is away overseeing one of the properties and Kaliamma is out visiting a hotel where it is rumoured the Chief Minister's wife is staying. 'If I make her acquaintance, the landlords' wives will come flocking to me,' Kaliamma declares that morning before leaving, having decked herself out in a dazzling turmeric sari and all of her considerable jewellery.

I go to the wise man bearing gifts, trying not to think of them as a bribe. Fruit and brass likenesses of the gods, coconut burfi and sandalwood incense, money and gold-embroidered cloth in exchange for a baby.

The guru has a beard that brushes his bony knees. His eyes are syrup and wisdom, his skin grooved with the insight that comes from communion with the gods.

I prostrate at his feet amid the smell of blistering air and burnt earth, dry leaves and raw hope.

'Please'–the diaphanous silver taste of faith, fragile as a child's heartbeat, in my mouth–'can my womb be filled with a babe that I carry to term? Can my husband have an heir to carry on the family name?'

The guru envelops me in his profound gaze – the inside of a mountain, the bottom of the sea. 'No.'

'Why not?' My voice is saturated with salty upset, violet with desperation. 'Please.'

He is silent for a long time. Then: 'I will pray to the gods on your behalf. Come back tomorrow.'

All that day and evening, I clutch hope close to my heart, prayer filling my mind. *Please, gods. Please.* The next day I return with more gifts, my heart echoing my footsteps, dragging heavy with expectation, anticipation, dread.

The guru is meditating when I arrive and I wait, tasting heat and spices, breathing in sweat and dust. Above us, from among the sprawling branches of the tree, birds sing of old crimes and fresh beginnings and stirring secrets.

The guru opens his eyes, unsurprised to find me there waiting. His smile is as benevolent as a blessing (a good sign?). 'You will be allowed a child. Only the one.' His words are as grave as the hush before time, in a space unpopulated with life. 'But you will have to pay.'

My body starts to shake, seemingly without input from me, rocking violently like earth beset by tremors. I swallow a couple of times before I am able to squeeze the words I want to say out from my uncooperative tongue. 'How will I pay?'

After what feels like an age, the time it takes for mountains to sink into the sea, for children to grow into their adult avatars, the guru speaks. 'Asking for a child against all odds will destroy you.'

Birds fly off the tree above, a flustered rustle and flapping of wings, and my mouth fills with the bitter taste of impossible choices. The guru closes his eyes, meditating as he awaits my decision. My body hasn't stopped swaying, a pendulum rocking to the tune of fate. I swallow, trying to garner saliva into my parched throat.

I think of my mother-in-law, so desperate for an heir that she is willing to endure her son's animosity by replacing his sterile wife with a fertile woman who will sire a grandson to carry on the Gowda family name. I think of my ailing mother, who is even now in hospital after suffering a fall when she went to pray for a grandson. My parents, whom I have wronged, and who expect a grandson as recompense for my sins against them. If I were to go back to them, disgraced, a barren woman, shunned by the family into whose fold I was wedded with so much fanfare, no longer a wife, not even a widow, but someone worse – a woman with a cursed womb, a woman who has failed in her primal duty – it would devastate them.

I think of Manoj – so loving, so kind. So deserving of parenthood. And I think of my craving to hold my babe, one that I have created with my love, Manoj, in my hands. I yearn to be a mother, to love my child like I was not loved. Unconditionally. With my everything.

I have no choice, not really.

'I will take that chance,' I whisper to the guru, my voice wavering only very slightly on the last word, a full stop at the end of the sentence that could, with just a small downturn pull, be a comma.

'Are you sure?' The guru's voice is the turn of centuries, the grumble of the earth as it rotates on its axis, making its unwavering way through another in a constellation, a super eon of days.

'Yes, I am sure.' This time there is no indecision in my voice. It is definitely a full stop, no commas in sight.

'Here,' the guru says, digging in the folds of his robe, holding a cloudy bottle out to me, 'take one tablespoon of this potion with milk and honey, twice a day.'

'Thank you.' I bow deeply, hands folded.

The guru smiles and it is the miracle of the sedate blue firmament exploding into the transcendent palette of an arching rainbow.

I turn to go and grind, abruptly, to a stop.

There is a snake blocking my path. A cobra, head poised, watching me. Hissing. About to strike.

An omen.

'Come,' the guru says from behind me, the gravity of millennia, the weight of the past and the inevitability of the future in his austere voice.

The snake lowers its raised head, slithers past me to the guru, deftly climbing up his body and wrapping itself around his neck.

'You will have one child,' the guru intones, stroking the snake, which stares at me with beady eyes that gleam and spark with foreboding. 'And it will destroy you.'

I walk away, dazed, the guru's words ringing in my ears, the potion tightly tucked within the folds of my sari.

That evening, I grind some of the potion into milk thick with almonds, spiced with cardamom and laced with honey, and, despite the trepidation that is making my stomach writhe with the dance of a thousand snakes, I drink up every last bit.

As much as I want a child for myself, I also yearn for a child to bring to fruition my loved ones' hopes, their expectations. I will believe anything, drink anything, if it means my baby will stay in my womb.

As the days pass and my mother gradually recovers from her fall, I feel something inside my womb again. A quickening. The day my mother is released from hospital, I find that I am pregnant again. I keep vigil. One week. Two. Four weeks. Six. No pain.

Please, gods.

Every evening, after visiting my recuperating ma at my child-hood home, I go to the temple. I pray that this baby will survive. And somehow, perhaps because of the wise man's prediction, I know it will. I also know that I will never get pregnant again, or if I do, that I will lose every child but this one. I know this because of the wise man: *You will have a child. Only the one.* I know it because I know my body and I know myself.

I have felt cursed my whole life with two notable exceptions. Manoj, my love, is a blessing. This baby is another. I know I will not be afforded more. I don't desire more. If I carry this child to term, if it is healthy, I am content. I am replete.

And so I treasure this pregnancy, every moment of it, even the sickness, the nausea. I cherish it all.

Please, gods. Let me be destroyed as per the wise man's predic-tion and not my family. Not this child. I will not ask for more. Let this child live.

Eight weeks. Ten.

At twelve weeks, I tell Manoj. He is beside himself with joy. We keep watch. We pray.

Sixteen weeks. Twenty.

Twenty-five weeks.

I can no longer hide my bump from my mother-in-law, whose face relaxes somewhat, the multiplied lines easing beneath their mask of make-up.

I release the breath I seem to have been holding for months. I have won this round with my mother-in-law, at least for the time being. With this child growing in my womb, Manoj is firmly, completely mine again.

I refuse to countenance the wise man's words, echoing in my ears, lodged in my heart, decline to give in to the fear that rises within me like the head of a snake, its clairvoyant gaze flashing, forked tongue flickering, poised to strike.

Twenty-eight weeks.

When I visit my parents, they discover my burgeoning secret. My mother feels my stomach with her claw-like hands. My baby responds to her touch, jumping obligingly. Already an accommodating child.

'Definitely a boy in there,' Ma says, her eyes lighting up.

Da nods, satisfied. *A boy,* his expression pronounces, *after all these years.*

And I caress my bump and pray that I can finally give them what they want, that I can at long last pay off their debt, although a contrary part of me wants to scream, 'What is wrong with a little girl? What was wrong with me? Why was I not enough? Why have I never been enough?'

My mother-in-law wishes for a grandson as well, to serve the dual purpose of carrying on the Gowda name and quieting the rumour mill.

When I go for my check-ups, I look at the doctor's face, trying to read the sex of my child in his expressions. I wish they would tell us the sex of the child here in India like in other countries. But they don't, they won't, because of the risk of female infanticide.

I have always wanted to be loved unconditionally. I would like the same for my child, and yet I am subjecting it to conditions even before it is fully formed. I am willing it to conform even from the confines of my womb just like my parents did with me.

I want this baby to be the answer to everybody's wishes and desires. I know that in aiming to please all of my relatives, I am letting my baby down already. This child who is laden with expectation even before it arrives into the world.

Personally, I couldn't care less what sex this child is. Although sometimes, just sometimes, I want a girl, just to prove everyone wrong.

'Once you are born,' I tell my child every night, just before drifting off to sleep, Manoj snoring softly beside me, 'I will not burden you with my insecurities, my guilt, my anxiety, my desire to please. I will not drag you down with duty. I will love you completely, more than life itself, and hope that it is enough. I already do. You are loved, regardless of who you turn out to be,' I whisper, stroking my bump, the baby moving trustingly under my palms, 'You are loved.'

Chapter 33
Jaya

A Tilting, Falling-apart Castle

Jaya sets down the diary and takes a deep breath. She rubs a palm over her eyes and discovers that her hand is trembling, her face wet.

'Wow,' Ben says softly, 'your poor mum!' His eyes sparkle and shimmer, reflecting the hurt Jaya herself feels on behalf of her mother.

Again, she takes out the photograph she found with her mother's belongings. 'If the younger woman is Mum, and I'm pretty sure it is, then she did have a son. The longed-for boy – the answer to everyone's prayers. The happy, smiling cherub whose photographs she saved. It makes sense.'

'Yes,' Ben whispers.

Jaya runs her finger gently over the little boy in the picture. 'So then, what happened to him, this boy? And Mum had me later, so that wise man was wrong about her having just the one child, wasn't he?'

'Of course he was wrong,' Ben says gently.

'And the doctors were right. Once Mum carried one baby to term, it must have been easier with the next. How horrific it must have been for her, suffering all those miscarriages and lugging the weight of all that expectation when she finally did carry a child to term. I ache for her.'

'Yes, she seems to have been hounded by expectation all her life.'

'Ben, the more I read, the more questions I have. Is Manoj my dad? And the little boy… My big brother… Did he die in the fire?'

'Jaya…'

'It seems that Mum lost a child too. She would have understood what I was going through if…'

Her eyes fill and Ben pulls her to him, kissing her tears, her lips, salt and comfort. And they lie in each other's arms, Jaya's head swirling with images: her mother prostrate in front of a man with a snake draped around his neck, her mother pregnant, she herself pregnant, her hopes for her unborn child swelling like her belly, an inert little boy, his cheeks an unearthly cream, his lips blue. A boy who will not wake up…

Ensconced in her husband's arms, Jaya closes her eyes, tiredness and jet lag catching up with her. She dreams of a little boy frolicking in the dust, fashioning glutinous orange cakes, dancing stick people, a tilting, falling-apart castle out of wet mud. Then the boy's face changes, becomes smaller; his features alter, lose definition, and he mutates into a baby that cries for its mother. He wails and wails but she does not come. She does not. She is being consumed, burnt alive, vermilion flames lapping greedily at her body, staining her soul the charred black of culpability.

Jaya wakes with a start and it takes her a few minutes to establish where she is. The room they are in is shrouded in a deep golden glow. Beside her, Ben is fast asleep, his arm flung across her stomach, his face vulnerable in repose. She plants a kiss onto his warm cheek, which smells of slumber and musk, and gently disentangles herself from his embrace. He grunts dissent, eyelids fluttering, then rolls over and is deeply asleep again.

Sumathiamma smiles at Jaya when she stumbles into the kitchen, rubbing the vivid dream of the little boy who morphs into Arun from her eyes.

Sumathiamma is kneading dough and there are more pots bubbling on the stove, the kitchen heady with smells – the tartness of tamarind, the potency of crushed chillies, the syrupiness of coconut milk flavoured with vanilla – mingling in a piquant potpourri.

'I thought I'd make chapattis to go with the vegetable korma,' Sumathiamma says. 'Did you have a good rest?'

Jaya nods, smiling, although her mouth aches with the effort. Reading her mother's latest entry, combined with the dream she just had, has left her feeling fragile. 'Ben is still sleeping.'

Sumathiamma nods. 'Kali is awake and in the orchard. She seems to be in a good mood. Are you up to meeting her?'

'Yes.'

'When Ben wakes, I'll let him know where you are. I think he and I are developing quite a system of communicating via signs,' Sumathiamma laughs.

* * *

Jaya tastes the unfamiliar flavour of heat and spices as she walks to the orchard. Kali is running among the trees, humming to herself, her bare feet sending the leaves carpeting the mud into a tizzy, her nightie flapping around her, two nuns keeping watch nearby.

Kali is tall, her bearing regal, her face beautiful despite her unkempt hair, her wild eyes. Jaya nods to the nuns and they smile a greeting. Kali looks up as Jaya approaches, pausing under a mango tree, her hand looped around one of the branches.

'Who are you and what are you doing here?' Kali asks, her voice haughty, entitled.

Jaya scans Kali's face carefully, trying to find some resemblance to herself. She doesn't know if she is disappointed or relieved to find that there is none.

'I… I'm Jaya.'

Kali's face scrunches up as if she is mapping Jaya's name to a list in her head. 'I don't know any Jaya…' And then her face clears. 'Ah, you must be the new servant, come to replace Sumathi.'

This woman, with her mop of white hair and her sunken, troubled eyes bears only a passing resemblance to the authoritative lady from the picture Jaya found among her mother's belongings. Jaya feels a great sadness for Kali, who had so much and lost it all, this woman who haunts the cobwebbed corridors of her past, preferring that to the present, her mind ravaged by a life that has not been good to her, withered by the whimsical depredations of time.

'No, I... I'm...' What should she say? Should she mention Sudha?

But Kali has lost interest in Jaya. She is playing with the bark of the mango tree, mumbling to herself.

Jaya starts walking past Kali, meaning to talk to the nuns, ask them how best to converse with Kali. But Kali's hand whips out, clutching Jaya's upper arm, her nails digging into Jaya's skin. She is frantic, shaking her head this way and that, her long white hair dancing around her anguished face.

'Too late now,' Kali yells, her voice a manic shriek, her face very close to Jaya's, a whiff of body odour mingling with her breath, which smells of tea and fennel seeds. 'Far too late. How could I have been so foolish?'

The nuns are there in an instant, extricating Jaya from Kali's grasp, soothing Kali. 'It's okay. You're okay.'

Jaya stands there, heart beating frantically as birds sing from among the branches of the trees above them. A sudden puff of warm, moist air sets the scrub next to Jaya sighing in an abashed flutter.

'No, you don't understand,' Kali screams. 'If only I... Oh, if only!' Her crazed eyes are bloodshot as she wrings her hands to indicate the urgency of whatever it is she regrets she did not do.

And without even thinking about what she's doing, Jaya says, softly, 'I understand. I too wish I could go back, do things differently. How I wish it were so...'

Kali stops struggling, going limp in the nuns' arms, her restless eyes focusing on Jaya. And Jaya sees that she has beautiful eyes, almond shaped, the colour of flowing honey. Kali's gaze is direct and unsettling. It seems to look right into

Jaya's blame-wracked soul, tainted with guilt for having been an indifferent daughter to her secretive mother. And then the gaze liquefies – it dissolves in a flurry of sparkling silver, as Kali extends an age-spotted hand, cupping Jaya's cheek, saying softly, in a voice choked with warmth, 'Sudha.'

Jaya sobs then. And Kali sobs right along with her. An old woman and a young one, both crying for the sins of their respective pasts, mistakes they both wish they could rectify.

'Sudha,' Kali says at last, awe colouring a voice that is hushed, reverential. 'You came back.'

Jaya does not have the heart to correct her. And then, as if a light has switched off within Kali, she is lost to Jaya, mumbling about mint leaves and shooting stars and the feelings that poetry arouses, agitating about coriander and chutney and gushing blood. And Jaya stands beside this woman smelling of mothballs and memories and tries to read the secrets of Kali's past, of Sudha's past, of her own in this woman's face, inscribed with the time-worn lines of experience.

Chapter 34
Durga

Honeyed Chequerboard

Durga gets off the bus in her grandmother's village, eager to be back, not dreading it, like she had last time. Unlike her previous visit, she is alone and unchaperoned, and it feels fitting. In these few weeks, she has grown up, grown into herself. She knows who she is now, and she is no longer defined or swayed by the labels people seem only too eager to bestow upon her.

The village feels familiar and alien all at the same time. She blinks, disorientated, as the apricot smog settles, and a crowd emerges in its place, pressing around her, bringing with it the fetid reek of body odour and pickled vinegar, the tang of stale spices and agitated earth and nosiness. Durga grins, taking comfort from the fact that nothing here has changed, especially given the recent upheaval of all the constants in her life changing so suddenly and irrevocably.

'Back again so soon?' the rickshaw driver says. 'You've not had enough of curses and madwomen?'

'Do I look cursed to you?' Durga ask between sneezes as the dust and odours tickle her nose.

'Definitely.' The rickshaw driver flashes paan-stained teeth.

'You truly must be mad,' the villagers sigh, jerking their heads in the direction of the ruin, 'to go back up there again.'

'That place must cast a strange spell,' they mutter, eyeing her curiously.

'The place is neither haunted nor cursed. It is just sad,' Durga says, repeating the words her ajji had said to her on her first night in the ruin and feeling a flash of pleasure that she is soon to see her and Kali again.

'Beware. You were only there for a few days last time,' the villagers warn, chewing paan and nodding their heads wisely. 'The ghosts might have decided to stay hidden while you were there – who knows, perhaps you repel ghosts?' They look her up and down, trying to discern what it is about her that appears to deter spirits.

'Or perhaps you just slept through their haunting,' someone says and they all laugh.

'You are very brave,' they murmur grudgingly, their gazes admiring as they take her in – the girl who not only rubbed shoulders with ghosts and mad people and curses and survived intact but is returning to them.

'Or foolish,' one of the oldies slurs, spitting noisily onto the dirt right next to Durga's feet.

'Lots of activity over there today – a posh car went up the hill a couple of hours ago.'

'Did it?' Durga asks, intrigued. Who can it be? Oh well, she'll find out soon enough.

'I've fixed that flap,' the driver says when she climbs into the rickshaw. 'Mind you don't rip it again.'

'Only if you share the laddoos in your tiffin box, hiding beneath that magic seat of yours,' she quips and he laughs.

'There were two people in the posh car,' he says between gasps as he cajoles his vehicle up the hill.

'Oh?'

'It hasn't come back down yet.'

'The lawyer visiting perhaps?'

'No, I recognise his car. He comes every other Wednesday. And he always stops in the village to pay me for the groceries first.'

'Well I have no idea,' Durga says, sitting back to stare up the hill at the ruin that she has missed more than she thought she would.

'So why are you back here then?' the rickshaw driver asks and Durga feels comfortable enough with this wiry, superstitious man, to tell him…

*   *   *

Seeing her parents at the convent-run recuperation centre they had been moved into from hospital had been a shock. They had both lost weight, and her da especially, with one side of his face and body collapsed, looked distressingly different, diminished. But… They'd been alive and awake and extremely glad to see her.

'My Durga!' her ma had said, touching her eyes, her nose, stroking her cheeks, her shoulders, her arms. 'You've shot up in just a few weeks and you seem, I don't know, changed!'

'I have changed,' Durga had said, managing to keep the smile on her face, although she'd wanted to break down and bawl at the state of her parents, 'for the better. I am no longer naughty.'

Her mother had smiled, her fatigued eyes sparkling. 'Oh, my darling, how I have missed you! You were never naughty, just impulsive.'

'That's exactly what Ajji said!' Durga had exclaimed.

And Ma had patted the seat beside her. 'Come, sit here and tell me all about her.'

*   *   *

Her ma and da had tired easily and had been trying their best to come to terms with their disabilities, putting on a brave face for Durga's sake. And Durga had tried to be brave too, working hard not to let her shock and upset at their injuries show, denying the tears that threatened to spill every time her da tried to speak. And in doing so, she'd understood just what her ajji had meant when she'd said, 'You will learn to think before you speak and act.'

She *had* learned. Whereas before she would have said exactly what she was feeling and displayed every emotion – whether anger or annoyance or glee – on her face for all to see, at the recuperation centre she'd refused to allow the distress she felt at her parents' condition to play on her face or spill from her mouth in unconsidered words.

The nuns at the recuperation centre had been as kind and patient as the ones looking after Kali. The centre – catering to patients with every kind of disability – was nestled in a vast field complete with a vegetable garden, a flower bower and a fruit orchard, worked on by those patients who felt able to do so.

'We are so lucky, Durga, to have escaped with most of our faculties intact,' her ma had said often. 'I realise that anew every time I look around me.'

Yes, Durga had thought. *I'm lucky to have my parents back. And, I suppose, even though it was horrible and shouldn't have happened, the accident made me bond with Ajji, who also loves me.*

*   *   *

Durga had soon settled into a routine with her parents. In the morning, when her da was taken for his exercise and remedial session, Durga had spent time with her ma. In the afternoon, it was her ma's turn and Durga had watched over her da while he slept, exhausted after his rigorous morning. But Durga had been able to see that her parents worried for her and about her, and it was taking its toll on them, impeding their recovery.

Three weeks in, Durga had said to her ma gently, 'I know you and Da are anxious about what being here is doing to me, you're upset that you can't care for me like you want to. I am fine, honestly, but you don't seem convinced and it's hampering your recovery. I… I'll go stay with Ajji for the remainder of the holidays.'

Durga's da had been at his session with the doctor and Durga and her ma had been sitting on cane chairs on the veranda, looking out at the lush garden: buttercream and magenta and tangerine blossoms basking in the humid kiss of sun.

Tears had shone in her mother's eyes as she'd cupped Durga's face and smiled at her. 'Wow, Durga, you were always caring but when did you get so perceptive? I am so proud of you, of how you have coped, are still coping.'

'Will you speak to Ajji?' Durga had asked then, like she'd been doing on and off since she'd arrived. Her mother had kept saying that she wasn't quite ready. That there was too much happening in her life to cope with even more emotion.

'She yearns for you. She is sorry.' Durga had tried again.

The cat that had turned up one day at the centre – no one knew where it had come from – and adopted the residents for its own, had jumped through the low wall of the veranda then and landed on Durga's lap, burrowing into her, bringing the smell of wet grass and ripe fruit. Durga had stroked its straggly, damp fur, and it purred contentedly in response.

'I know. I'm not angry with her or upset, not any more. In fact, I'm grateful to her for having you when we were in hospital. And being with her seems to have changed you, matured you.' Durga's ma had sighed. 'I put what happened between your ajji and me to bed long ago, Durga. And I am sorry too, for what I said and did, for running away from her and not reaching out when she needed me. What hurt most was that she didn't want to know you. She does now. Turns out she always did.' She'd beamed at Durga, her face radiant, the new lines that had been etched into it since the accident disappearing briefly. 'She is my ma and I love her. I always have, even when I was estranged from her. I will speak to her to tell her that you are coming to stay.'

Durga had grinned then, feeling lighter than she had since she'd arrived at the recuperation centre, as she'd pictured her ajji picking up the phone in the high-ceilinged kitchen of the ruin, warm with spices, strips of amber sun transforming the dirty floor into a honeyed chequerboard. In her mind's eye, she'd seen her ajji say, 'Hello?' her nose scrunching up the way it did when she asked a question. Then she'd seen her ajji lowering herself slowly onto the stool that Durga had kicked in a fit of anger at Gowriakka, one hand clutching at the telephone as if it was a lifeline, the other placed on her heart, tears rushing down her face as she made long overdue peace with her daughter.

'Make sure you tell Ajji everything you just told me, Ma.'

'Oh, Durga!' Pride had bloomed in her ma's eyes. 'When did you get so wise?'

'Spending time at the ruin, Ma – it taught me so much. I understood that labels are just something people slap on you when they don't know any better,' Durga had said, thinking of Kali.

'Sweetheart.' Ma's voice had been the music of birds drunk on sunshine.

'You see, Ma, Kali might be shunned and feared. But she's chosen her madness because that's the only way she can cope.'

Her ma had been sniffing and smiling at the same time.

'And me. Despite what you said, I was starting to think there was something bad in my very core. But I'm not bad – I know that now. I helped Kali, you see. She was able to confide in me, talk to me.'

'Oh, sweetie, people find it hard to accept when someone is even slightly different from them. You are high-spirited and very intelligent. You were bored in our little town, which is why you got up to mischief.' She'd smiled fondly at Durga. 'And if everyone was the same, the world would be such a boring place. I called you Durga after the principal goddess because she is invincible. And you are too. You make your da and me so proud and we thank God every day for the gift of you.' She'd paused. 'Why did you think you were bad?'

'What I did. To you and Da.'

'Sweetie, that wasn't your fault. If anything, it was Da's. He was the driver. He shouldn't have turned around. And mine, for I shouldn't have drawn his attention to what you were doing. And you would have missed hitting Baluanna anyway as we were moving.'

'Yes.' Durga's sigh had caught on a sob, the futility of everything that had happened, her ma losing one of her legs, her da the use of the left side of his body, hitting her afresh.

'Lots of people lose their lives; plenty of families lose their loved ones. It could have been much worse. Look around you, Durga. We are the lucky ones to have been spared,' her ma had said, gently wiping Durga's tears with the pallu of her sari.

'So I'll speak to your ajji, make my peace with her and also tell her you are visiting. Perhaps you can leave on Saturday, when Lathakka comes to see us? She can put you on the bus that goes into Gaddehalli. And the rickshaw driver could take you from there, eh?' Her ma had smiled fondly at her. 'It's only for a few weeks, until we are able to manage by ourselves. Then we'll look into renting a small place near your school, and we'll all be together again.'

And so it had been decided. Her ma had spoken to her mother, Durga's ajji, over the phone, a long, tearful and ultimately happy conversation, and afterwards her mother had glowed, looking better than she had since the accident.

* * *

And now Durga is back, telling the rickshaw driver her story, aching to get to the ruin, meet with Kali again and find solace in her ajji's bony yet comforting arms.

'Wow, you are quite something,' the rickshaw driver says when she has finished.

'I miss my ma and da so much, but they are better off not having to worry about me. And I do love being with Kali and my ajji.'

'I would still be wary of the ruin. All those rumours… there must be something in them. Watch your back at all times, girl.' Sweat beads the rickshaw driver's face, his earnest eyes round as potato bondas. 'I will make sure to check up on you when I come by with the groceries.'

They are three quarters of the way up the hill, at the bend in the overgrown road. 'Stop here,' Durga says, making up her mind impulsively.

'Why?' the driver asks, his eyes meeting hers in the mirror.

'I'll walk from here. I want to surprise my ajji.'

'You sure?'

'Positive.'

'Bye then. I'll be up there Friday morning with the groceries. Try not to get cursed or possessed until then and if you want to escape, just say so.'

Durga laughs as the rickshaw driver waves jauntily before turning his vehicle around and she begins to trudge up the hill towards the ruin, this monstrosity that has somehow transformed, for her, into a haven. She didn't realise just how much she'd missed this ugly, dilapidated building and its ageing inhabitants until she set eyes on it again. She stops and moves her satchel from one shoulder to the other. She misses her parents – it is an ache in her chest, constant, unwavering. They will be having dinner now, with one of the nuns feeding her da, half the food falling out of the collapsed side of his mouth.

She worries about the future, and now that she is away from her parents, no longer required to be brave for their sake, all the anxieties she has been keeping at bay crowd to the fore. Most importantly, despite her mother's breezy declarations of renting a small cottage for them to live in once Durga's school starts, she knows money will be an issue.

Durga has eavesdropped on her parents' late-night conversations when they think she is asleep, peppered with all the worries they keep from her. The money from the sale of their house is running out. The recuperation centre, while heavily discounted, still requires payment for medical and sundry costs. What will they do when the money runs out, with Da unable to feed himself, let alone work, and Ma unable to walk? Durga's ajji had offered to help with bills that first night in the ruin, but even if Durga's ma, who is just as stubborn and prideful as *her* mother, accepted Sumathi's help, the money wouldn't last long…

Durga shudders, trying to shake her fears away. Something will work out. It has to. *Please, Lord Krishna.*

She licks her lips and tastes salt and sweat. Now, a few paces on, she regrets sending the rickshaw driver back. What possessed her to walk up the last quarter of the way? She misinterpreted the distance to the ruin – it had looked deceptively close but it is not so, not on foot anyway. She is tired and her tummy rumbles ominously. She's still got some distance to go. Her ajji will be waiting with a plate full of food, she knows. But she is hungry now.

She looks down the hill. The rickshaw is almost at the bottom, a pulsing blob – the driver must have zoomed down. She digs around in her bag and pulls out the tiffin box filled with conjee and pickle that her ma had insisted she take that morning. There are a couple of bites of conjee left and she eats them. The cold conjee is gluey, and without the tangy, spicy pickle to make it palatable, it sticks in her throat. There's no fruit she can sink her teeth into. She thinks of the orchard at the top of the hill, the cashew she had burst with her catapult, the remembered taste of ripening mangoes and juicy guavas making her stomach cramp. She would like to pluck a cashew, plump and yellow, from the tree. She imagines biting into its lush flesh, feeling the syrup ease her dry throat and line her empty stomach.

She had forgotten how hostile the ruin appears from the outside. No wonder there are so many stories abounding about it. It gives off a cold, unwelcoming aura, seeming to issue a bleak warning to anyone who dares venture near it. A warning that had put Durga off when she'd first arrived with Lathakka. How terrified she had been then, her head brimming with tales of hauntings and curses! And how very different the reality had been – the fun she had had with Kali, the comfort she had received from her grandmother.

She starts walking with renewed vigour, wanting to touch the ruin – to see if, up close, it holds the same charm for her; if, despite its forbidding exterior, it will offer the succour it gifted her the last time she was here. When Durga is almost there, a few steps away if that, she stops to gather breath and imagines the look on her ajji's face when she catches her unawares.

Her ajji must be worried by now. *Where is Durga?* she must be thinking. *What has happened?* And just as she is about to call Durga's ma, Durga will walk in and say, 'What have you cooked for me, Ajji?' and her ajji will clutch at her heart and feign shock and upset, while beaming at Durga and saying, 'You almost gave me a heart attack, child. Now wash up and eat and then fill me in, tell me all.'

Durga smiles and looks up at the ruin, a frowning silhouette of navy against the rose and nectarine of the setting sun and blinks. Was there a movement just then, in the abandoned top floor where no one goes?

Goosebumps erupt on her bare arms. And again, a movement. Something fleeting, catching the corner of her eye. White, ghostly, floating at one of the windows at the top. Are the rumours true after all?

Durga stares, mesmerised and terrified, and right into the eyes of the most beautiful woman she has ever seen. A pale, ethereal vision.

Then the vision turns away from the window and begins gliding through the rooms, billowing swirls ballooning in her wake, white flowing all around her. Floating past the windows, moving down.

Durga is rooted to the spot. Fear takes her whole being captive.

Where are her ajji and Kali? What has the ghost done to them? Is she next?

She opens her mouth to scream, but her voice is gone – there is not even a whisper to be found in her dry throat. Durga's panicked mind recalls the rickshaw driver's words when he'd first brought her and Lathakka here and she'd scoffed at his tales of hauntings: 'Oh it happens alright. When the time is right.'

The apparition glides placidly, closer and closer to where Durga stands. And finally Durga's body cooperates. Her legs move at the same time as her throat.

'Help,' she screams and turns to run, tripping over a large boulder sitting right beside her leg. She is aware of falling, her whole body jarring in a resounding thud, a scream shaking out of her, going on and on and on, until the blessed abruptness of stunned black hits.

Chapter 35
Jaya (Now) and Sudha (Before)

Flailing Limbs

Once Kali is led indoors by the nuns, Jaya, waiting for Ben to wake, sits on the disintegrating wall beside the orchard and reads her mother's next entry. She will translate it for Ben and they will go over it together later but right now, with Kali having recognised her – or, to be more precise, her mother in her – and with the house that shaped Sudha's decision to run away right in front of Jaya, all she wants is to burrow herself in the cocoon of her mother's words.

* * *

Dear Diary,

We have all been invited to an exclusive party, touted to be 'the event of the year' in the circles my mother-in-law aspires to.

I am thirty-six weeks pregnant. I was out of sorts all last night, unable to settle, to sleep. And now I'm aware of a constant pressure on my bladder. The baby is quiet in my womb. Not moving half as much as it used to. I have not said anything to Manoj yet, not wanting to alarm or worry, hoping that if I rest all morning, I will be up to attending the party. It is just a niggle, I tell myself, something I ate.

My mother-in-law is looking forward to this party. She has been for weeks. She was beside herself when we got the invite.

She'd come to find me in the kitchen, where I was drinking buttermilk spiced with ginger, mustard seeds and red chillies, a new craving. 'Do you know we've been invited to the private do of one of the biggest landowners in South India? Only a select few families asked. We've made it, Sudha. We've finally made it.' Kaliamma's eyes had been alight, her face beaming in a way I hadn't seen before.

She'd been so much more relaxed since the fact of the baby, her grandchild, became reality, as envisaged by my flourishing stomach. She no longer shouted at the servants as much. The whole house was happier, breathing easier in her presence. I had even heard the servants humming to themselves as they went about their work. And now this – companionably sitting next to me, talking to me, a smile on her face. My mother-in-law was changing, becoming more human. I could often now catch a glimpse of the girl she was before she transformed into the domineering, hard woman I have always known.

I had grinned back, delighting in her joy. It meant so much to her. To be welcomed into the capricious folds of high society. To finally shrug off the stigma of her past mistakes. I'd wished I could shrug off the stigma of my mistakes as easily. Perhaps this baby…

'This is because of him,' my mother-in-law had said, nodding at my stomach. 'My grandson. The heir to our

family name. Not born yet and already heralding good things for us Gowdas. They all know that our family is the richest around and it doesn't do to snub us for long, especially now we are thriving, producing heirs…'

There won't be heirs plural, I had thought, rubbing my belly, sending love to my babe, even as I'd swallowed the surge of panic rising bilious in my throat, the wise man's words reverberating in time with my baby's happy kicks.

'It is a boy, isn't it? It has to be.' My mother-in-law's face was vulnerable suddenly. 'Otherwise you can just try again until you have a boy. Once you carry one baby to term, it is easier the next time.'

There won't be a next time, I'd thought, tasting desperation, harsh black on my lips. Please, please be a boy, I'd pleaded with my baby, who danced within me oblivious.

Why was everything I did subject to conditions? I was so happy to be carrying this baby to term and yet, even as I'd enjoyed my pregnancy, I'd also been constantly praying, perpetually wishing that this baby was a boy.

But then I was just as bad as everyone else, investing so much upon this child, wishing it would chase away the reek of the past and usher a fragrant future.

Now that the day of my mother-in-law's much-anticipated party, her springboard into the world she has longed to be part of for so long, is here, I don't feel good. I have rested all morning, and yet I feel drained.

Manoj comes into the bedroom to get changed into his suit. 'Are you coming in that?' he says, grinning at me, cosy in my favourite nightie. 'I don't mind, honest. I think you look sexy. But I don't know if Ma will approve…'

The thought of getting up and dressed is too much.

'Will it look too bad if I don't attend? I'm not feeling a hundred per cent.'

'What's the matter?' Manoj asks, concern budding on his face.

'I'm fine,' I smile. 'I just don't feel up to socialising, that's all. I want to lie in bed with a book.'

'But it's Sunday.' Manoj's voice is soft with worry. 'It's the servants' day off. And Ma has given them the rare evening off as well because she thought we would all be away, so they won't be back until tomorrow…'

My mother-in-law has managed to coax my father-in-law into attending the function too, the first time he will be leaving his room and the house since the occasion of my wedding to Manoj.

'That's fine. I'll be fine.'

'I could go into the village now, get someone to come in and stay with you?'

'No, that's not necessary.' I inject my voice with as much enthusiasm and calm as I can. If Manoj goes to the village hunting for a servant, my in-laws will be late for the function.

I know how much this party means to my mother-in-law, how her heart is set on making the right impression. If they are late arriving, it will give the wrong message. They may not be invited again, thus ruining my mother-in-law's chances of ever being fully accepted into the hallowed echelons of high society. As it is, I am causing upset by not attending – I do not want to make it worse.

'I'm sorry, I should have said earlier. But I thought that if I rested, I would feel up to coming along…'

'Sudha, don't apologise. I was busy trying to finish the accounts and I didn't even notice that you looked peaky. I'm so sorry…'

'Manoj, I'm fine. Just tired.'

'I'll stay with you,' Manoj says, his voice determined.

'But the chauffeur is off too…'

Manoj had insisted he would drive us to the party so the chauffeur could have a well-earned day off. My mother-in-law cannot drive; she has never had reason to learn. My father-in-law's eyesight is failing and he can't drive any more either. Not that he would: he hasn't driven since he became housebound following his parents' deaths. If Manoj stays back, everyone has to. And it is not fair on my mother-in-law.

'You all please go. I feel bad enough that I'm not feeling up to attending. No reason why you shouldn't… I know how much this means to your mother. I don't want to…'

'You are more important than all the functions in the world,' Manoj says fiercely.

I manage a laugh, although even the small effort required to do so takes it out of me. 'Look. There's no point in all of you staying back.' I don't add: And your mother will never forgive me for it. *'All I plan to do is go to bed and have a rest. You'll be twiddling your thumbs if you stay. Please go.'*

'Shall I call the doctor?'

'No. I'm just tired. I'll go to bed and I'll be fine.'

'If you're sure.'

'Certain. It's one afternoon. What can go wrong?'

Turned out plenty could… But I didn't know it then.

'Manoj,' I say softly, as he fastens his cufflinks, his apprehensive eyes never leaving mine in the mirror, 'your mother will be angry…'

'Please don't worry about Ma. I'll convince her. Are you sure you'll be okay?'

'Positive.'

'We'll try and come back as soon as we possibly can.'

He leaves the room, closing the door gently behind him.

I hear raised voices, my mother-in-law yelling, 'Why didn't she tell us earlier? What is this nonsense at the last minute?' And then a note of hysteria entering her voice, 'What will we tell them?'

I close my eyes and wait until her tantrum eases.

'Sudha,' she screams. 'Come here at once.'

'Ma, no, she is…' Manoj begins, his voice sharp, stopping mid-sentence when he sees me.

I hobble to the door and out onto the landing. My mother-in-law is decked in her most gaudy sari, all the many jewels she owns twinkling from her neck and arms.

'Are you sure you'll be alright on your own?' she asks and I am so surprised that shocked tears sprout on my face.

'I'm not taking any chances where my grandson is concerned,' she says, in the same strident tone but I can see anxiety shining out of her eyes.

'I'll be fine,' I assure her, like I have Manoj.

'Do you need a doctor?'

'No. I just need to rest.'

She scrutinises me carefully, then nods. 'If you are sure.'

This is the first time she has given in so gracefully when things have not gone her way. Looks like pregnant women bearing Gowda heirs get special leeway, even in the case of my unyielding mother-in-law and her must-attend social events.

My husband, his eager mother and reluctant father leave after a thousand assurances from me that I will be perfectly fine after a nap.

'I don't feel good about this…' Manoj protests until I push him out the door.

'Go.'

I shut it behind him and rest my head against the wood, closing my eyes. I wait until I hear the car – parked right beside the steps leading up to the front door by the chauffeur before he left – accelerate down the drive and then, like I had promised Manoj, I climb the stairs, very slowly, and go to bed.

I dream that I am being dragged down. Someone is holding my stomach and pulling. Pulling hard.

'Stop,' I yell. 'Let go of me.'

But the grip only intensifies. Whoever it is is squeezing so hard it hurts. It hurts.

'Please,' I want to scream. 'Please stop.'

But I find that I cannot speak. Even my breath is being squeezed out of me.

I wake. I am covered in sweat. My nightie is wet. The bed is wet. And the clamping feeling is real. Something is clasping my stomach, not letting go.

Oh no. Not now. I am all alone in the huge house.

The phone, I think. The phone.

I have foolishly left the portable handset – which Manoj had pressed into my hands before leaving, extracting a promise to keep it with me at all times – downstairs. I picture it lying on the side table by the front door, where I had placed it when I waved goodbye to my husband. I sit up. But the pain pushes me back down. Why hadn't I thought to bring the receiver up with me?

I try again. But the pain is coming in waves, insistent, almost non-stop. I understand then that I am in labour. It has begun. My waters have broken. I am well into it.

I try to walk. I cannot. The thought of going downstairs is more than I can fathom.

And who will I call? The phone number of the people who are hosting the function that Manoj and his parents are attending is on the invitation, which is also downstairs, beside the phone book containing my doctor's number.

I try to move towards the door. I go on all fours. But tremors of agony overwhelm me and I can't go far. The only thing that helps is holding on to the bedpost while the pain rocks me. The nauseous green smell of fear. The pungent copper taste of blood.

Outside, the smack of thunder, slanting sheets of rain hitting the window and exploding in ruthless silver splashes.

I give in. I let the pain claim me. I do as it instructs. When I feel it envelop me, I push.

The baby wants out.

I have waited for this baby. I have longed for it, prayed for it, and conducted a deal with God via the medium of a wise man wearing a writhing cobra necklace for it. I am not giving up now.

I will deliver this baby. I will bring it into the world, safe and hale. I will.

I hold on to the bedpost, on all fours and I push.

⁕ ⁕ ⁕

'I'm going to wash and change,' Sumathiamma says, peeking her head out the front door while wiping her hands on the tea cloth that rests permanently on her right shoulder.

Jaya jumps, closing her mother's diary and blinking as she comes back into the unfamiliar present. The sun is lower down the horizon, level with the hill and less potent. The village, a tapestry of russet and emerald spread out below Jaya, basks serenely in its gilded embrace. Jaya's top sticks to her back, the breeze that caresses her face carrying a hint of jasmine, the flavour of cashew and the promise of evening.

'Your husband is fast asleep and Kali is too. The nuns have left for the day. Durga is due any minute; in fact she should have been here by now. I hope everything is okay.' A skein of worry threads through Sumathiamma's voice as she scans the hill for the rickshaw that is bringing her granddaughter.

'I'm sure she's even now making her way here,' Jaya says, her voice feeling rusty, as if it has not been used in a while.

'Look out for her, will you?' Sumathiamma asks and Jaya nods her assent.

After Sumathiamma goes back inside, Jaya decides to explore the mansion, unable to sit still since reading her mother's entry, her head full of her mother's words, her heart heavy for her mother experiencing childbirth in an empty house – *this* house – all on her own.

She debates whether she should wait for Ben. But he is doubtless sleeping away his jet lag, having spanned three time zones in less than a week and might not wake up until the morning.

Jaya walks carefully through the countless rooms upstairs, where it is clear nobody has been for some time, looking out for snakes, staying away from doubtful-looking, suspiciously moving piles of decomposing leaves.

How ironic that she has left her own house empty, leaking grief, haunted by happy memories and the loss that overshadowed it, to travel here, to a similar one, gone to ruin.

Outside the wind picks up, rattling the shattered windows of this empty shell. A high-pitched screech, the rush of wings, displaced air flavoured with earth and mouse droppings in her face. She screams, and as it comes back to her, amplified, steeped with hysteria, she sees the bat swinging from the cracked ceiling. And once more, something stirs, a feeling.

I've been here before.

When? How?

Is she remembering a past life? Ghosts? She shivers. *Get a grip.*

Sweat has dried on her skin, mingling with her perfume. A pungent, acidic aroma.

Why did she get this feeling of déjà vu in this relic that breathed sadness and exhaled legends, fragments of past lives etched into its ruined tiles?

What was my mother hiding? Why did she flee this place, never to return? Why did she choose to live out the rest of her years behind a mask as lifeless as this ruin? Who was my father? Who am I?

She is level with one of the windows when she trips, losing her footing. She puts her hand on the sill to steady herself and something attaches itself to it. Something red. She recoils, almost falling over again.

Blood?

No. Just paint. Paint that is peeling off the windowsill in lanky, wet strips. And then movement, in the corner of her eye.

What's the matter with you? Pull yourself together already!

Something moves again, a persistent glint in her peripheral vision. She swivels, almost falling out the window. A weaving dot is pulsing up the hill.

She stands back. Out of sight. The dot flickers, disappears, then comes into view again, moving closer. And closer.

Jaya blinks, shakes her head, walks slowly, deliberately, to the next window. And the next. The dot comes towards her, unwavering. And then she sees it is a child. Only a child. She lets out the breath she didn't know she was holding. Her body is spotted with goosebumps.

The child comes closer. A little girl. Walking determinedly up the hill. Sumathiamma's granddaughter, Durga – who else could it be?

Jaya walks past the windows in an effort to find the stairs, so she can get to Durga, thank her for insisting Sumathiamma take more notice of Kali's ramblings, giving Kali not only the time of day but interpreting what she was trying to say – the reason Jaya is here.

Durga is wearing a blouse and skirt, both of which are too small for her by the looks of it. She is hefting a heavy satchel on her back. Beyond her, the sky is the colour of churned mud as the sun prepares to set.

Ah! At last Jaya finds the stairs. She steps carefully, looking out for creepy-crawlies. When she reaches the ground floor, she dithers, unable to find the doorway, unsure of just how to exit this mausoleum.

When Jaya does stumble outdoors, squinting in the shadowy, fuchsia-spattered light that heralds the impending dusk, the little girl opens her mouth, her eyes wide with terror as she shrieks, turns to run and collapses in a wretched heap of flailing limbs.

Chapter 36
Durga

Do Ghosts Wear Jeans?

Her body hurts. Everywhere. She is aware of gentle arms enveloping her, a scent, unusual, of summer in a foreign land.

With difficulty, she drags her eyes open and finds herself looking into the most beautiful eyes she has ever seen. They are a soft, shimmering brown. Beyond the eyes she sees the spectre of the ruin, silhouetted in the gathering darkness. And then she understands. She is being held captive by a ghost.

She gathers saliva in her sore mouth. 'Are you a ghost? Or an angel?' she whispers.

The ghost laughs, a tumbling cascade.

Durga sneaks a proper look at this superior being. And finds a small yet endearing flaw. Are ghosts allowed them? Worry lines fan from the ghost's eyes, which are crinkled in laughter like butterfly wings. Her hair – for it is definitely a lady ghost – is a mass of spilling ebony. She is wearing a long flowing white top and jeans. The white top was what she saw, Durga realises, billowing around the ghost. It had appeared as if she was floating. Do ghosts wear jeans?

Durga has to admit that she feels quite solid, not like an apparition at all, her soft body warm and extremely human. Durga even thinks she detects a hint of sweat mixed up in her balmy, ethereal scent.

'Durga,' she hears, a familiar voice, pierced with concern. 'What happened, child? Where is the rickshaw driver? I was beside myself with worry…'

Her ajji kneels beside the apparition, stroking Durga's face. She smells of soap and hot water, kindling and washed skin.

'It's my fault. I went exploring and… she took me for a ghost.' The vision holding Durga speaks haltingly, as if she is going over each word in her head first – picking the right ones and rejecting the rest. Her voice is as lovely as her face, the Kannada words dropping hesitantly out of her mouth in a strange, melodic accent.

Durga's ajji smiles fondly at her. 'Silly girl. You know there are no such things. This is Jaya. She and her husband arrived this afternoon.'

The posh car the villagers and the rickshaw driver mentioned…

'Jaya is here thanks to you, child,' her ajji is saying.

'Me? How…?'

From somewhere down the hill comes the faint sound of dogs barking.

'We'll tell you everything, but first let's get you inside so we can look at where you're hurt and feed you after your long journey,' her ajji says.

Propped between her ajji and Jaya, Durga slowly hobbles inside, to the kitchen.

✳   ✳   ✳

'The lawyer wrote to me – well, my mother actually,' Jaya says, her accented words flowing like an exotic song. 'And so did your grandmother.'

'You did?' Durga asks her ajji, surprised.

'You did your bit by making us search for Sudha,' her ajji says, stroking Durga's back and smiling fondly at her. 'Once we found her, I had to do my bit.'

As they speak, Durga wolfs down bisi bele bath and mosaranna, chapattis, vegetable korma and curried lentils with spinach, finishing it all off with a tall tumbler of curd spiced with ginger and chilli, and sago payasam for afters. She is warm and content, the aches in different parts of her body, jolted by the fall, no longer hurting as intensely now that the food is working its magic inside her. She is sitting on the stool, her ajji beside her, in the snug golden glow of the kitchen, her head pillowed by her arms as she listens to what Jaya has to say.

'My mother passed away eighteen months ago – the lawyer and your ajji weren't to know that. Her post was forwarded to me. I read your ajji's letter and I had to come…'

'Sudha was your mother?'

'Yes.' Jaya's voice is like the mournful strands of a violin, sounding out an elegy. 'My mother was very closed, an intensely private person. I didn't know anything about her past, growing up. But recently I found her diaries and I've been reading them and then this letter arrives…' She shudders. 'Do you believe in destiny?'

'I do,' Durga's ajji says.

The branches of the mango tree outside the kitchen tap against the window shutters in the soughing breeze.

'I can't believe my mum spent a portion of her life here and I knew nothing about it until recently.' Jaya sighs.

'She was very gentle was Sudha, a quiet, introverted girl,' Durga's ajji says. 'That poor thing. First her parents, and then to have Kali for a mother-in-law! Talk about bad luck. But she coped very well I heard. They actually got on, after a fashion, Kali and Sudha.'

'If both Sudha and Hari survived the fire, where is Hari?' Durga asks and both her ajji and Jaya turn to look at her.

'I found some of his pictures among my mother's things – at least I think it's Hari. But I don't know what happened to him. I haven't reached that part in the diaries yet.'

The males are cursed, Kali had said to Durga her first night here. *But Hari didn't die. He didn't.*

'Mum kept so much from me,' Jaya is saying in the pensive quiet. 'A whole other life. And I'm still trying to figure out where I come into all of this.'

'You will. Now that you are here,' Durga's ajji says gently, patting Jaya's hand.

'It's like your ma is telling you her story from the afterlife,' Durga says to Jaya. 'What a blessing, to have found your mother after you thought she was gone forever.'

A tall white man with hair as yellow as Durga's ajji's podis stumbles into the room, rubbing his eyes and blinking rapidly as he takes them all in.

Jaya smiles up at him, her rosebud mouth curving like a papaya and he grins back, his face softening as he looks at Jaya.

'Ah, Ben, slept well, did you?' Jaya reaches out and squeezes his hand, pulling out the stool next to her. 'Come, sit. And this,' she says, grinning warmly at Durga, 'is Durga. It's thanks to her that we're here.'

'Durga.' Ben holds out his hand. 'A pleasure to meet you.' Her palm is dwarfed by his as he shakes it vigorously, grinning at her.

'Durga, thank you so much for listening to what Kali had to say and setting into motion the events that brought us here. You are absolutely amazing.' Jaya says.

'She is,' Durga's ajji agrees, beaming at Durga.

'Thank you, Durga,' Ben says. 'I'm so happy to be here. Your country is stunning and your grandmother is an exceptional cook.'

Jaya translates for Durga's ajji and she glows, saying, 'He must be hungry? I'll heat up the food.'

'It's warm enough,' Jaya protests, but she is already standing up.

And even as Durga is aware of happiness, shiny as the mist-washed slate of sky at dawn, the yawn she has been trying hard to suppress bursts out of her in a loud, cavernous exhalation.

'Right. To bed, young lady,' her ajji says.

'But…'

'We'll talk more tomorrow. You've had a long, action-packed day and your body is telling you it needs sleep. Come on…'

'Goodnight, beautiful ghost,' Durga whispers in Jaya's direction and the tuneful laughter that bursts out of Jaya follows Durga all the way into bed.

Chapter 37
Kali

A Golden Halo

A summer's morning. Sunshine warming my face. The scent of dew and powdery earth.

A little girl, bright eyed, asking questions. A woman with her who is familiar. How? Where do I know her from? When I see her, I taste the past. Tantalising. Evocative. She holds hands with a man whose hair is the colour of baked sand. A golden halo. I think of the golden day when I held my grandchild and was able to look into the future…

'As soon as I pushed the front door open, when we returned from the party hosted by the Shettys, I knew. It was the smell. Blood and pain and sweat and hurt and newness. The sensation of a house easing. Settling back into calm after something momentous had happened.' I pause, thinking of that time, the taste of hope and fear on my lips.

'And then?' A voice sweet as peda, soft as the comfort of a pillow after a long day.

I blink. Come back into the present. A little girl, looking at me, eyes open and innocent and sparkling with the promise of all that is to come.

'And then, just as Manoj bounded up the stairs, calling to Sudha, I heard it. A wail. A mewling. And I ran, stumbling up the familiar steps…'

'And?' the girl prompts.

'Sudha was lying on the bed, eyes closed, blood everywhere. Red on white sheets, like kumkum on a bride's powder-caked forehead. Her eyes were closed, her face drawn and very pale. And beside her, nestling in the crook of her arm, rucked red face and swaddled body – a baby. Tiny. Perfect. I looked at Vinay, who for once had not retired to his room but followed us upstairs. He was peering over my shoulder, his face creasing in one of his very rare smiles, even as he tried to catch his breath. He looked at me and in his gaze, I spied our shared memory of another birth, the advent of the boy who stood beside his wife, looking down at his child in stupefied wonder, now a father himself.' I rub a hand across my eyes and it comes away wet. 'That enchanted, stormy evening, as I held my grandchild in my arms for the first time, I sampled hope, and I… I spied a future that was more beautiful, and happier, than all that had gone before.'

Chapter 38

Jaya

Marshmallow Horizon

'The doctor said that you can't have any more children, Sudha,' Kali says, looking right at Jaya. 'So who's the little girl?' She nods in Durga's direction.

Jaya looks at Kali, speechless, as her mind frantically processes what Kali has said. Finally, from somewhere, she manages to find her voice. 'The doctor did? Are you sure?'

'No more children,' Kali says, 'but that's okay. We have Hari.'

Hari. The boy in the photographs.

Jaya's legs no longer feel able to support her body. She is aware of Ben's arms around her, bolstering her, but it is as if that is happening to someone else, another Jaya, in an alternate universe.

She has bitten her lower lip so hard that her mouth is filled with the taste of pennies, clotted red with fear. 'If Sudha couldn't have any more children, then who am I?'

Kali looks at her vacantly. 'Who are you?' she repeats, her nose scrunching up in befuddlement. 'And who is this man?' She stares at Ben. 'Why are you loitering? Don't you have work to do?'

'She might have got it wrong, Jaya,' Ben whispers into her ear.

'I… I'd taken the wise man's warning to my mother with a pinch of salt. But if a doctor said so…'

'She's confused,' Ben says reassuringly.

'Sudha,' Kali queries plaintively, squinting at Jaya, 'is that you?'

'Kali,' Jaya tries, 'do you know how Sudha managed to have a little girl, after… after Hari?'

Kali's face crumples. 'Hari,' she cries, 'Hari…'

Huge sobs rack her body. She is wild, flailing, hitting out at everyone around her.

Ben shepherds Jaya and Durga backward, away from the agitated Kali as the nuns tend to her and soothe her. Even though Jaya knows better than to set great store by Kali's words, something about what Kali has said feels right. The prophecy of the wise man that her mother believed in so completely for one. The blood on the sheets that Kali mentioned when they came back from the party and found Sudha had given birth – so much blood. And Sudha's own conviction that she would only have the one child…

So. Who am I then, Mum? Did you steal me from someone?

The entry where her mother describes giving birth all alone in the mansion was the last in the first diary, the one written in Kannada. Jaya had translated it for Ben the previous night, both of them distressed on behalf of Sudha. The next few entries are in the newer diary, written in English, Sudha's adopted language.

Durga squeezes Jaya's hand, asks her in her soft, sweet voice, 'Are you alright?'

Since Durga's dramatic arrival the previous evening, Jaya has delighted in her company, taking comfort from the girl's vivacious presence, her spirited enthusiasm, her infectious giggles – the way she remains unfazed by Kali's mood swings, her occasional histrionics. Although she's been here less than a day, Durga has brought lightness and life to the mansion.

Jaya looks up at the sky. Clouds chase each other across the marshmallow horizon. Two birds hover, side by side, as if poised for something.

Mum, what was it you kept hidden so carefully, even taking it to the grave with you, lest I find out? All those times I asked you what you were keeping from me. All those times we fell out because I was frustrated by your secretiveness. What were you afraid of? What didn't you want me to know?

I am terrified. Afraid to read the entries in your English diary. Afraid to discover whatever bombshell it might reveal.

Afraid to find out what destroyed you.

'Jaya?' Durga is looking at her, her worried gaze mirroring Ben's.

Jaya squats down so she is at Durga's eye level. She holds the little girl's hands in hers. 'Durga,' she says. 'I need some time alone with Ben to read my mother's diary and find answers. Will you tell your grandmother that we're going upstairs, and we'll be down in a bit?'

Durga nods solemn assent.

*   *   *

'This house and our home in London are so similar,' Jaya says to Ben when they are upstairs, her voice echoing in the empty space. 'Both missing the past, enduring the present and craving a sunnier future.'

She pictures Arun's nursery, the Winnie the Pooh motifs – painted so carefully and with such hope by a couple with a growing bump and dreams for a radiant future.

Jaya takes a deep breath, pushing away the ever present loss, and she is back once more in the gold-tinged, wildflower-painted, sun-smothered country and the house that both shaped her mother and chased her mother away – where Jaya hopes she will find out who Sudha really was.

'I know this will sound corny, Ben, but… this ruin speaks to me, its broken walls breathing time-worn tales, even as it guards the confidences it has hoarded for generations.'

Ben nods, looking at her curiously. 'You've felt like that since you entered this house, haven't you? It's as if you have some innate connection to it.'

'Yes,' she whispers.

'This house has such character,' Ben says, patting one of the bricks lightly, fine red dust coating his hand. 'It's seen so much. So many lives, happy, sad, despairing, lost, contained within its walls.'

'It's crying out to be transformed.' *I have lived with ghosts and I know when they are ready to leave. They've bided their time here, but now they need to be given a good farewell.* 'You know when Sumathiamma was saying this morning about how the previous lawyer, and this one, both tried and failed to get builders in to fix this place because of the rumours of hauntings and curses?'

'Yes?'

'I thought about how to convince them otherwise and then, when she was telling us about her daughter, Durga's mother, I had an idea…'

And she shares with Ben the plan hatched while talking with Sumathiamma, a plan that has grown in her subconscious all morning, feeling gratified when she sees his face light up, her vision for this house reflected in his eyes.

'Wow, Jaya, that's it! You're brilliant!' He pulls her towards him for a kiss.

Together they picture this mansion restored to its former glory, the high-pitched, innocence-seeped voices of children, the incessant barking of dogs, the drone of cars grumbling up and down the hill, kaleidoscopic saris catching the light, onions sweating, spices frying, pots sputtering, oil sizzling as lunch is prepared, the daily drama of lives being led reverberating through its rooms, a sparkling coat of fresh memories painting the timeless interiors.

Then they sit beside the ruin's crumbling walls, breathing in the dank aroma of mulch and earth and Jaya opens her mother's newer diary, tasting sunshine and anxiety as she gathers the courage to read her mother's words, to find out what happened to upend Sudha's desperately earned love and happiness.

She wants to know where she comes into her mother's story. Did her mother have to lose Hari, Kali, Manoj, her parents, everything and everyone she held dear, in order to gain Jaya? Was this the prophecy the wise man forecasted? Is that why her mother was distant with her?

Taking another deep breath, Jaya reads her mother's words to Ben…

Chapter 39
Sudha

Stinging Tentacles

Dear Diary,

How I have missed you!

For a few years now, I've told myself I didn't deserve to talk to anyone, not even you.

But now… I think I'll go mad if I don't set things right at least in the privacy of my own mind. And the perfect way to do so, I've always found, the best way to array my thoughts in order, is by writing to you.

Yes, I know. I am not writing in Kannada any more. The voluptuous, musical language of my past. I am writing instead in English – steady, plain, reliable. This is my punishment. I will write to you because I feel I will lose my mind if I don't, but as recompense for giving in to this cathartic impulse, I have relegated Kannada to that secret part of my heart that contains my loves and my wounds, my regrets and my dreams, what I had once hoped for and what I have lost.

Enough time has passed now that I can look back. Make sense of what I did. It will hurt, but it has to. I deserve it.

I, of all people, do.

So here we go. I will rewind to the happy times. I will begin again there.

The three years following the birth of my child are unequivocally the happiest of my life.

I know of course that I am living on borrowed time. I know I will have to confess sometime. I open my mouth to do so often but then close it again. I cannot find in me the strength to undo what I have so rashly done.

One moment of madness, one lie, its reaches spreading far and wide, miring me deeper and deeper into its charade, wrapping me firm in its stinging tentacles…

Regardless of my inner turmoil, Hari grows, a cheerful child thriving in the warmth and affection of all the adults in his life. My mother-in-law is the happiest I have ever seen her. Finally, after years of hankering after it, she has been accepted into the smarmy and slick world of the landlords, although I often wonder why she wants so badly to be part of this community that is so fake, backbiting, fickle. Judging only by wealth and status.

She hates them. But she wants to be part of them.

My mother-in-law – a medley of contradictions. As strict and severe as the bun into which she subjugates her hair, and yet as soft as cashew burfi when it comes to her grandson, for whom she will do anything. She has changed so much since Hari's birth. She is softer now, kinder, even to the servants. And she is much nicer to me.

When my in-laws and Manoj came home from the party that fateful, rainy Sunday to find that I had given birth, Manoj had summoned the doctor, while hugging the baby and me, and rebuking himself for having not been there for me while our babe was being born.

The doctor decreed that I needed to be hospitalised immediately. But I would not be parted from my child.

'You need to be in hospital. You are weak from blood loss – why do you insist on doing everything for the baby yourself? All the servants are lining up to look after their new master, so you can have a rest, get your health back,' my mother-in-law snapped. 'A couple of the servants are experienced midwives. They will look after my grandson even better than you can.' My mother-in-law was direct as ever, tact famously lacking.

'No, I'll do it,' I insisted. 'I don't want to miss anything, not even the smallest part of my baby's life.'

I will not have any more children; I will not get this chance again, I thought, picturing a wizened face with a long beard, a cobra coiling around a grooved neck, a solemn voice predicting doom and destruction.

'Sudha, you need to be hospitalised,' the doctor reiterated.

'You heard her. She doesn't want to come to the hospital. Do what you need to here, bringing in nurses and equipment if necessary,' my mother-in-law informed the doctor tersely.

'Thank you,' I said to Kaliamma, moved to tears.

'Oh give me my grandson; I haven't had a turn cuddling him yet. Look at you, swaddled like a larva, aren't you cute?' Kaliamma had crooned at the baby, and Manoj and I had exchanged dazed glances, unable to believe this soft woman emerging from within the brusqueness of the enigma that was my mother-in-law.

'What shall we call him?' my mother-in-law asked.

'You name him, Amma,' I said.

My mother-in-law had beamed then, in a way that lit her up from inside.

She gave her grandchild God's name. Hari.

The doctor requested a meeting. 'I'm sorry, Sudha, you cannot have any more children,' he said, fiddling with his shirt, not looking at any of us.

I pushed away a vision of the wise man, his grave voice professing disaster. I held my precious blessing a wee bit closer, breathing in his soft, pure scent of innocence and perfection.

My mother-in-law nags me often about my possessiveness of Hari. 'He's growing up, Sudha, you need to learn to let go,' she admonishes. 'Why do you insist on doing everything for the child, from changing him to bathing him? You never let him out of your sight even for a minute, even when others, like me for example, are playing with him and perfectly capable of looking after him. It's as if you can't trust anyone but yourself to do a good job with Hari.' And then, in a softer voice, she adds, 'I understand why – after all you went through, you want to protect Hari. But smothering him with attention will do him more harm than good in the long run, making him too dependent on you. It needs to stop.'

Manoj humours me, but even he has started to gently nudge me. 'Hari is going to start school soon, Sudha, then what will you do?'

'Oh, Manoj, I…' I open my mouth to tell him then. But I cannot continue. I can't.

'Look,' Manoj says, his voice tender. 'I know you worry he will be taken from you. That it will be penance for what you think you did. You worry that you haven't paid enough, that you might lose him because of what happened with your brother…'

The tears glistening in my eyes overflow, staining my cheeks. Hari climbs up my body, my nimble little acrobat, throwing his arms around my neck, burying his face in my hair. 'Ma, why you cry?'

'I understand,' Manoj says. 'But…'

'I know,' I say, hugging my boy fiercely, dropping kisses on his hair, his face.

He giggles. 'Ma, tickly.'

Manoj pounces on us and we collapse on the bed, all three of us tangled, our laughter reverberating through the room and wafting outside, causing the servants to smile as they go about their chores and my mother-in-law to yell, 'What's going on in there?'

I have gone some way in righting the wrong I did to my parents.

'We can die happy now,' they say often, their smiles beaming like torchlight during a power cut as they hold Hari like they never did me. Hari has their seal of approval – they pay him the ultimate compliment. 'He looks just like Sudhir,' they say. Sudhir. My twin. My sainted, hallowed and now seemingly reborn twin.

It is at Hari's third birthday celebration that our world implodes. The party is the grandest the mansion has ever known. There are entertainers wielding balloons, magicians and clowns galore. Children chase each other through the rooms; they play hide and seek in the vast grounds. Despite its size, the mansion is overflowing with people; they spill onto the gardens, where the marquees are set up.

I rush about making sure that the guests are being well looked after, that they have enough food and drink, while also keeping an eye on Hari. Manoj is in one of the rooms leading off from the library, keeping the old fogies entertained with his father, who has been cajoled out of his room for the occasion by my mother-in-law.

Hari tugs at my hand.

'Ma,' he says and my heart liquefies as I squat down right there in the middle of the chaos to look into his butterscotch eyes. 'I want wee wee.'

He's only recently started to talk in full sentences – a bit late as my parents have pointed out a million times, imply-ing that I am doing something wrong, as always. They are here somewhere, flitting about, lost among all the extremely important people my mother-in-law has invited.

'Come on then,' I say to my beautiful son, and I am leading him to the bathroom when there is an almighty commotion – the thunder of pots tumbling in the kitchen.

I rush to see what's happened, dragging my boy along. I spy my mother-in-law heading towards the kitchen from the opposite direction, lifting her intricate, gold-embroidered sari with both hands so it doesn't sweep the floor as she runs with the sprightly gait of a much younger woman.

'Ma,' my boy says. 'Wee wee.' He is fiddling with his trousers.

'One minute,' I say and pull him along to the kitchen.

The overpowering aroma of spilled spices and fried masala ambushes us, greasy yellow and staining the tiles, the walls. One of the serving dishes is broken and there is curry everywhere. The servants stand stunned, fear and shock written all over their faces.

As she always does in an emergency, my mother-in-law coolly, efficiently assigns all the servants their jobs, then dons an apron, tosses me one and, despite our finery, we start mopping the floor, the servants who have been designated to help clean following our lead.

I am taken unawares by a fierce burst of admiration for my mother-in-law. She's bossy and annoying, short-tempered and irritable; she's also extremely gentle and incredibly patient with Hari, and now she is on all fours, cleaning the kitchen in the middle of a party milling with luminaries she has spent years trying to impress and who have only recently accepted her into their fold.

Manoj comes to the door of the kitchen and pokes his head inside.

'All under control. You keep them entertained, be a good host, go,' my mother-in-law yells as she goes back to wiping the tiles.

Manoj winks at me and I smile, then he is gone.

Afterwards, when the floor and walls are spotless – no trace of curry, no turmeric stains or lurking spices – we wash our hands and take stock of the food.

'Good job we always cook too much,' my mother-in-law says grinning. 'Look at you in your apron,' she laughs, her uncharacteristic exuberance bringing to mind the limbless languor of a summer afternoon. Relief of a crisis averted is making her more open than usual. 'Better get back to our guests, eh? They'll be wondering where we are. But to be honest, the people I was talking to were so boring, I was glad of an excuse to escape ...' She giggles, and she sounds like a bashful young girl, her infectious peals setting me off.

And it is then that it happens. Ice dousing my mirth.

I look down. Frantically scan all around. While I have been averting one crisis, there's been another, bigger one looming. I have not let my boy out of my sight once all these years, from the moment he was born that tempestuous Sunday afternoon. And today of all days, when the mansion is full of people, I lose him.

'Hari,' I shout, 'where is Hari?' noting but not caring about the hysteria tinging my voice nightmare blue. My eyes desperately scan the surroundings for my little boy with his tousled hair and earnest face, wearing new khaki trousers that are slightly too big for him.

My mother-in-law meets my gaze. 'It's okay, Sudha. Someone will keep an eye out for him.' Her voice is trying for gentleness but is laced with impatience. She is itching to get back to the party, play hostess. She doesn't understand. How could she?

'Don't worry,' she says, humouring me, when she realises how upset I am. She is trying to be kind despite wanting to yell at me to get a grip. This unusual generosity, combined with the terror that is overwhelming my body, makes me want to howl right there in the kitchen with the festive sounds of the party wafting in: the clink of glasses, the chuckling banter.

Where are you, Hari?

Please, gods, please.

A balloon pops with a loud bang, a child screams and I flinch, the metallic crimson taste of panic and exploding secrets in my mouth.

Before I can stop her, my mother-in-law pops her head round the door, calling, 'Has anyone seen Hari?'

'No.' I am hyperventilating, I know, but I can't help it. The last thing I want is for the world to be alerted to Hari's absence and to start looking for him. *I* need to find him, gather him safely to me before the inevitable happens. But I can't seem to move from where I am standing. And even if I did, where would I begin to look for him? And what if, the moment I leave the kitchen, he comes in here in search of me?

Oh, why on earth did I do what I did?

Without even thinking about it, I have clutched my mother-in-law's arm. 'No,' I plead.

She pulls her arm away from my clasp none too gently, her small reserves of patience exhausted in the face of what she thinks is my irrational distress. 'Look, Hari has done what children do and run off to have a little play. It's fine. In fact, it might be good for him to be away from you for a few minutes. He can't get lost – the house is too full of people. He's chosen the perfect time for his little adventure actually. Someone will find him. Stop overreacting so.'

My mother-in-law's irritable words wash over me in a wave of dread. All I can hear is Hari's little voice in my ear, 'Ma, I need wee wee.' All I am thinking is, *Not now. Please, gods, not like this.*

Everyone has started looking for Hari, but I find I still cannot move. I stand there in the middle of the kitchen my mother-in-law and I have just cleaned, the smell of phenyl overlaid with curry assaulting my nose, tearing my eyes.

My mother-in-law shakes her head and makes to leave the kitchen. She is at the threshold when there is a roar.

Pained. Booming. Human.

The servants rush to see what the uproar is about.

'Just what I need – another disaster, more damage control,' my mother-in-law sighs. 'Why do these things have to happen at the most inconvenient times?'

'What are you gawping at?' she yells at the servants. 'Get to work.'

I am glued to the kitchen floor as speculation abounds among the servants in a fluster of excited whispers, even as they go back to frying the starters and heating the main courses as per Kaliamma's instructions.

'No,' I hear. 'No, no, no.'

I recognise that voice but not his tone. It is a voice that has whispered sweet endearments in my ear, thick with desire, soft with love. It is a voice that has caressed me and cherished me. But never in all these years have I heard it like this – saturated with pain, unmoored, spilling loose from the depths of his soul.

I bite my lower lip hard to stem my terror. The sweet, hot, coppery taste of blood fills my mouth.

It is happening. What I have kept at bay for so long. All my life I have conformed, done what was expected of me. I have tried to please, lied to please. And now it is all catching up with me…

'Sudha,' I hear. 'What have you done? What is the meaning of this?'

My mother-in-law stands just outside the kitchen, like me rooted to the spot. Guests are pointing, bewildered, but she has abandoned her role of hostess and is not pandering to them. The smile has slipped from her face and I can see the swell of tears in her eyes. I have never seen her cry before, I think, inconsequentially, my mind cringing from what is happening even as it accuses: *You are responsible for all this.*

'What's happened?' my mother-in-law wonders. The sound that escapes her mouth is barely a whisper, as if cowed by the events that are running away from her, browbeaten by her gentle son's unaccustomed anger and hurt.

People swill around me, beside me. 'What's going on?' they ask, puzzled.

I do not hear them, my ears echoing with the grave warning of a robed man sitting cross-legged under a Bodhi tree.

Among the tumult, Manoj comes into view holding Hari in his arms. And everything is lost.

Chapter 40
Kali

Soup of Memories

'Oh, why? Why on earth didn't I see it coming? How could I have been so foolish? So very foolish.'

'Kali, calm down…'

'I will not calm down. Let me go. Let me…' I try to struggle, to hit, to kick, but my body refuses to cooperate, my arms feeble, my legs not holding me up. When did I lose control over my own body? I who used to control properties and servants but refused to see what was happening right under my nose.

A loud moan and my legs give way, my throat hoarse, my eyes dripping as everything catches up with me…

* * *

'Sudha,' my son calls. 'What have you done? What is the meaning of this?'

I have never known Manoj to sound like this. In that moment, hearing my son's voice, so very familiar and yet so very strange, bearing down upon me, I know somewhere in my heart that life as I know it is about to change.

Somehow, as my son comes into view, his face contorted in anger and upset, my grandchild giggling in his arms, the world recedes: the sounds of the party, the bewildered faces of the guests, pointing fingers and shocked whispers. My naked grandson, wet, draped in mud. Squirming in his father's arms. Laughing, even though his da, my son, is crying. Saying, 'Da, Dada, put me down…'

My naked… Not grandson, no…

I blink.

Not grandson… Granddaughter…

Granddaughter?

I stand there, trying to comprehend what has happened, while my son cries, sobs, pleads, 'Sudha, where is Sudha?' thinking, as scarlet rage owns my body, *Now I know why she was so overwhelmingly possessive, why she kept him with her all the time.*

Him? Not him. Her. Her.

My grandchild's laughter morphs in that mercurial way of children into tears. He – she? – is sobbing, along with her father. 'Da, Dada, I want Ma, Mama, I want my mama.'

I am aware of swaying, of my legs giving way. I hear gasps. And then I am falling. Descending into blessed black. Wiping out everything. Giving me a second chance. To start all over.

To go back to that point when I hid in the library and heard the landlord's wife say, 'He's come back with ideas in his head of marrying for love.' The moment when I saw my reflection in the glass alongside Vinay's face in the photo frame I was dusting and decided that we fit, we made a good match. The cheek, the preposterous ambition of a young servant girl daring to dream big, a dream that I still find hard to believe I achieved.

Or to go back even further, to the time I moved to my aunt's village, nestled in the shadow of the mansion, when my aunt pointed to it, that rain-studded, loss-stained, heartache-infused evening and told me she'd found me work there...

Several times in the future when my broken mind, with its soup of memories, snags on this moment, I will hope to freeze time. Reverse back to this instant. *Say no, I don't want it. Say no.*

How could I have known how my life would change? I was wowed, swayed by glamour. I was hoodwinked. Enchanted. Lost.

※   ※   ※

'Lost. I am lost. I don't want to be here. I want to drift in the hallways of my youth, that safe period of time when I knew how to give and receive love, before my world turned upside down for the first time, when my father ran away... You, whoever you are, take me back. I want to go back. To before. I don't want to think of this horrible time. Please. Give me something to sleep. To forget. Please.'

Chapter 41
Sudha

The Hollow Bruise of Panic

Dear Diary,

I stand in the kitchen of the house where I have known more affection in a few years than in the entirety of my life before I came here. I stand there, breathing in the smell of phenyl my mother-in-law and I used to clean the floor mixed with spices and boiling oil, where one of the servants is frying the samosas to take round the guests, as my world detonates around me.

I stand there as I hear the shouts, the uncomprehending moans, filled with pain and hurt, of my husband, who has always loved me unconditionally, who has taken me as I am, and who has taught me to push aside my self-loathing and to love myself like he loves me.

And in return, I have deceived him. My husband, who has given me everything, including my sense of self. Who convinced me that I am better than what I am and treated me so. Who brought out the best in me.

I have lied to him; I have lied to a father about his child.

That rainy afternoon when I delivered my child – all alone in that empty museum of a house, the dead souls of those long since departed cheering a new life into the world – when I finally held my babe up to the voiceless chorus of the celebrating spectres, I was ambushed by love and a fierce desire to shield her.

I looked at her tiny body, her cherubic face, innocence and faith, eyes shut tight against a capricious world, and I made a decision.

I lied.

I didn't give my husband, my in-laws, my parents the opportunity to prove me wrong. I didn't feel able to take that chance. I couldn't bear to see the disappointment in my parents' gaze when they beheld their beautiful granddaughter – the disappointment that I have grown up with.

I held my baby and kissed her soft head as outside the rain lashed the countryside, transforming the trees into whirling dervishes forecasting doom.

I knew I couldn't have more children. I was losing blood at an alarming rate. I understood that my body wasn't designed to give birth to more than this lovely, perfect little girl. But my mother-in-law would insist on an heir. She would do anything to get her way, including getting another, more fertile woman for *my* husband, overriding Manoj's will, tricking him into subordination.

My mother-in-law, and my parents, would make my perfect child feel unwanted, second-rate, like I had felt all my life prior to Manoj. My girl would think, like I had, that she was not enough. I saw her whole life unfold before my eyes, mirroring mine. She would always try to please. Always seek to reassure, to make up for the fact that she wasn't a boy, spending her life trying to right something she had no control over.

I didn't want that for her. I didn't.

I wanted her to be loved and feted and adored like I hadn't been. And at that moment, exhausted by labour, overwhelmed by love and protectiveness, I could think of only one way to give her this gift. And so I hid my child's gender from the world. And once I made this decision, once I said 'him' instead of 'her' to Manoj, my in-laws and my parents, I couldn't turn back.

Over the years I tried to tell Manoj the truth, several times, but the words died every time I opened my mouth. I couldn't bear to have him look at me in disappointment, his loving gaze dimmed by my treachery, his distraught eyes reflecting my parents' judging, disenchanted stares. Every morning, when I dressed my child in boys' clothes, doubts bombarded: *What will you do when she is older, when she starts puberty? How will you keep this up?*

But I had shut my ears and shut the questions out, taking comfort from the soft, innocence-infused presence of my child. And the lie sat like a stone on my heart, haunting my eyes, draining me.

One moment. One lie. One rash decision that would change the course of all our lives.

I cannot face him. I can't face Manoj. And so I turn, ask the flabbergasted servant to move aside and stand by the vat of bubbling oil. I take over the frying of the samosas to give me something to do.

I am a coward to the last. Afraid to face my husband even as I ache to hold him and our child, gather them both to me. I am shaking as I try to concentrate on the samosas, my insides battered by the hollow bruise of panic.

Please.

I am hoping for a miracle. I am seeing the wink Manoj gave me as he popped into the kitchen and saw us scrubbing the floor, his mother and I side by side, on our hands and knees in our finery. I am thinking of my mother-in-law's uncharacteristic, high-spirited, infectious laughter that had set me off in giggles too. My family. The family I gained. Now about to be lost forever.

Will it ever be the same again? Can it be, after I have broken my husband's trust like this? Can he ever believe anything I say after this?

He is here, in the kitchen. He is holding our child and he is looking at me. Tears streaming down his face. Our naked child wiggling in his arms. His face... That look.

He opens his mouth, all the bluster gone. 'Sudha.' My name is a lament on his lips. 'Why?'

I turn to him and somehow, in doing so, the vat of oil in which I was frying the samosas overturns. Oil everywhere, on the stove, on the floor, blistering, sparking, igniting, glowing, spreading, catching. One of the servants throws water on it and it explodes in a fountain of slick, blue-crowned orange.

Dazed yells. Screams.

I feel the heat lapping at my legs, my skin erupting in bubbles where it has been splashed by hot oil, but I can't take my eyes off him. The man I love, and who has loved me, unquestioningly, unconditionally. The man I have deceived. The man holding our child. Around us and between us mayhem, topped by golden flames, a yellow-tongued navy cloud, roaring crimson cries, the sensation of choking.

Black heat, burning welts, searing red, salty blue smoke, wails, panic, hurt, terror.

Flames lick the space between us, my husband's face, our child's face dissolving in the shimmering, grease-soaked air.

Smoke, suffocating. Heat, burning.

Shouts. Screams. Sobs. Moans.

A weight pinning me down.

With great effort, I drag my eyes open. Swirling darkness stinging. Columns of black smoke throttling. Debris swirling. The sensation of drowning in heat, of bathing in an inferno. The scorching taste of fear and ash.

My eyes smart; they water. I close them again. And then, even as my nose is choked by heat, my throat asphyxiated with embers and anguish, my chest clogged with pain, it comes back to me. My child. My husband. Where are they?

Oh, gods, I think. *Please, gods.*

The wise man's words: *Asking for a child against all odds will destroy you.*

Please.

I try to move, make to crawl. There's something trapping my leg. I pull, I yank, creeping forward, dragging my body behind me. I need to find my family.

I tug, and then all of a sudden I am free. I look back. The thing restraining me was a person. Unmoving. One of the servants. Banni, I think.

And then it dawns on me in a horrified shudder. Banni is dead. I shake my aching, muddled head as if by doing so I can shake away the knowledge that people are dead. Because of me.

Please, gods. Not my child. Not my husband. Please.

I drag myself forward on my hands and knees. Somehow I gather the energy to sit up and then stand. My feet wobble, but they manage to hold me up. Just.

They are not in the kitchen. Neither my husband, my child. I stagger forward into one of the rooms adjoining the kitchen. A few steps and I trip over a body. Familiar. Loved. Those features that I've wished would relax in a smile that does not carry the weight of the tainted past, a smile that is not burnished by grief, suffused with expectation. My father.

I bend down. Hold him with my guilty hands. He's scorching to the touch. But unmoving. Not a whisper of a breath. He's gone. My mother is next to him, her head lying on his chest as if listening to the secrets his heart holds, like she did when I visited them at the clinic when Da had his heart attack.

She's gone too. I choke on grief, gag on sorrow. I caused this. I have killed them as surely as pointing a gun at their hearts and pulling the trigger.

You will be destroyed. The snake-strangled voice of a man who bargained with God on my behalf reverberates in my anguished ears.

People push past, hacking coughs escaping their covered mouths, urging, 'Sudha, we have to get out, come with us.'

I ignore them, thinking, *They survived. Please let Manoj and Hari be alive.*

I have to find them. I do.

Please, gods.

I doggedly move forward, step by punishing step.

Please.

Smoke holds court, a harsh miasma of smarting, charred blue.

Please let them have escaped.

I see his hands first. Long, slender fingers. Hands that have taught me to love. Hands that have wiped my tears. Hands that were always in motion.

Now still.

I bend down. Lay my cheek on his. It is boiling. But there is no movement. No trace of breath.

'Manoj,' I sob, shaking him. 'Please, Manoj.'

And then, as if in answer to my prayers, a small, plaintive shadow of a wail. Gently I move Manoj, not daring to hope, but wishing all the same. Praying.

Underneath my husband, wedged beside his shoulder is our child. Sobbing, coughing, crying. Alive.

'Hari.' A prayer, a granted wish, absolution. 'Hari.'

I gently untangle my babe, hold her close. By shielding our child from the press of smoke, my husband has saved her. I kiss her all over. She is hot, her skin blistered. But. She is here. In my arms. Breathing. She is here.

Movement behind me.

I turn.

My mother-in-law. Gasping.

She opens her mouth, coughs.

Her face wild. Mouth twisted.

Her gaze alights on me and then on Hari. Then she sees Manoj. Inert. Unmoving.

'Is he...?'

My mother-in-law grips my hand with hot, urgent fingers. 'Why, Sudha? Why?'

How do I explain? How to say anything at all when grief is bitter, burning yellow in my mouth, when my actions have cost me my love, when I am responsible for all this loss, this destruction? When my husband lies unmoving beside me, when I have just walked away from the bodies of my parents. What to say?

My mother-in-law nods as if she somehow understands despite my silence. 'You have to go now. Take Hari and go.'

'But Manoj...'

She coughs. 'Too late for Manoj, but not for Hari and you.'

'No.'

'Yes.' Her breath is becoming laboured even as she looks into my eyes, imparting urgency, 'Take Hari and go. I'll follow, I promise.'

'Come now…'

Hari coughs. And coughs.

'Go.'

Hari choking.

'Please, Amma,' I beg. 'Please come.'

'Vinay… I'll look for him…' my mother-in-law wheezes, 'then I'll come. You take Hari and go. Here.' She digs inside her sari skirt, into which she's had a pocket sewn so she always has money for emergencies and tucks a purse into my free hand.

In the midst of the devastation that I have caused, I am overwhelmed by my mother-in-law's generosity – and her practicality. I open my mouth but can't find the words to thank her. She nods, squeezing my hand. We don't need words when grief for the man we both love binds us. I tuck my mother-in-law's purse into the identical pocket I have had sewn into my sari skirt, following her example, where I always keep my diary (your predecessor), along with a choice few pictures of Hari so they are with me at all times.

My mother-in-law shrugs off all the gold she is wearing, which is substantial given she was decked out in all her finery for the party. 'Take it. Leave the village. Go far away. Then send word.'

I hesitate.

'I'll be fine. Go.'

I swallow. Salt and smoke. Hari has not stopped coughing.

I squat down and hold Manoj. My husband. My love. I lay our child's body against Manoj's still one. I fold my palms together and ask my mother-in-law for her blessing and make Hari do the same, despite the fact that my babe is swaying, set to faint.

Then I turn and run, stumbling, gasping and gagging on sobs and smoke. I run away with my child in tow.

Chapter 42
Kali

Frayed Curtain Dangling

'Come, Kali, it's time for your wash.'

'I don't want to wash. There's smoke… Fire. No… Sudha… she escaped. I saw her. Where is she?'

'Sudha? You mean Jaya?'

'Who's Jaya? Where's Sudha? She came back. It took so long. But she is here rousing memories.' Always beside me now, the dense fog of memories and regrets: swirling tendrils of pain, unfulfilled wishes and unattainable dreams. 'Seeing Sudha, it's brought it all back.'

'It's alright, Kali.'

'*Nothing* is alright. Where's Vinay?'

'Huh?'

'Vinay… I saved him. I watched my daughter-in-law leave with my grandchild, sending a little prayer their way and then, despite my lungs screaming, my body rebelling, my heart seizing with grief, despite wanting to throw my arms around my son and lie there with him and let the world combust, I dragged myself forward and went in search of my husband.'

My chest clouded with ash, my eyes stinging. 'Vinay was in the library, stretched out beside the armchair his da used to frequent, arms flung out as if to encase every single one of the precious poetry books that had not made their way into his room. Breathing. Just.'

The air is a leaden blue thump of gagging breathlessness. It is cinders and grit and flames and singed hopes and scorching devastation. 'With my last reserves of strength, I managed to drag him out the main door to safety and then I fell in a faint, in the burning air, for the second time that day, for only the second time in my life.'

I can't breathe. Why is it so hard to get a lungful of fresh air, untainted by smoke, unmarked by guilt, unsullied by the smouldering brand of my actions? 'I ruined Vinay by marrying him, and then I saved him when it mattered. Does that make us even?'

'Yes, it does.'

'No. Nothing will undo what I did to him. *Nothing*. I thought that by becoming the landlord's wife, I could control my destiny, wiping away what had gone before. I thought I could keep hurt at bay, manipulate love, earn adulation and praise.' A gurgle, a convulsion. I realise with some surprise that I am crying. 'I manipulated the innocent affections of Vinay, crushing his gentle heart as surely as Manu had crushed mine. I used my child like I had used my husband, both pawns in my game to win power, admiration, respect.'

The shudder of a thousand lost instants claims me, moments where I could have taken a different turn, become a different person, rerouting destiny, setting it right. 'I lost everything and everyone I cared for. The house for which I sold myself. My son. My opinion of my daughter-in-law. My version of my grandchild. Myself.'

'I am sor—'

'I don't know who I am any more. What have I got? Nothing. Not even control over my body or mind nowadays – my brain feels like someone has set fire to it, my thoughts disappearing like flame-licked smoke. But… I did save Vinay's life. There is that. So where is he then? Where is my husband?'

'He…'

And then it is in front of me, the knowledge undulating before my eyes, swaying like… Like…

I tremble and quake. My teeth chatter within unsteady lips, my voice the hiss of air from dying breath. 'Vinay's gone, isn't he? I wanted to restore the house and the Gowda name to its former glory – for him and also, I admit, for me. I cherished dreams of Vinay and I reaching a truce in our old age as the Gowda name flourished. Instead I let it go up in smoke. And then I pulled Vinay from the fire, when he was willing to die with his poetry tomes, and he had to endure more loss, see the mansion at its worst, his son, his grandchild, his hopes for the future destroyed. I saved him, and then I lost him.'

The torn end of a frayed curtain dangling from the ceiling on the ground floor…

This house but… the splendorous mansion I fell in love with wrecked. Ruined by my greed. My want. My horrible, destructive ambition.

The taint of flames, the mark of sin, the reek of charred lives.

Bumping into Vinay's body sagging from the ash-coated rafters.

My endless, horrified scream echoing down the hill...

My mind slipping, sliding, spiralling away from my culpability, my guilt...

Chapter 43
Sudha

Insipid Imitation

Dear Diary,

Alongside money, in the purse that my mother-in-law, the woman whom I betrayed, gave me even as she urged me to leave, I find treasure. A photo of all of us – me, Manoj, our child, my in-laws – taken a few months previously in front of the house, back when we were all happy and whole and my festering lie had not exploded in our faces.

I hold the photo to my lips, kissing each of my loved ones in turn, lingering on Manoj, and then I carefully put it away so I don't ruin it with my tears. My fierce mother-in-law kept this with her at all times, cherished it, cherished us.

Oh, Amma, I am so sorry.

Why didn't I think to tuck some pictures of all of us into my skirt pocket? I have some of Hari, but none other than Kaliamma's group one of Manoj. If it wasn't for Hari, I would go back inside the burning building and urge Manoj, plead with him, shake him, apologise to him, love him back to life.

I use the money my mother-in-law gave me, despite my duplicity, the destruction I caused, to rent a cheap hotel in Ballegapur for us. After two days – three? I have lost track – I go back. Not to the village, as I cannot bear to see the damage I caused, coward that I am, but to the hospital in Sannipur, knowing that, if anything, my loved ones will be there, hoping against hope that I somehow got it wrong and that Manoj is still alive and in there, recuperating. I cover my head and the lower part of my face with the pallu of my sari. I dress my child in girls' clothes, like she is meant to be clothed, so we are not recognised.

'I am a friend of the family,' I tell the nurses.

'Oh what a tragedy,' they console as they take me to see the survivors, Manoj and my parents not among them.

My father-in-law lies unresponsive in the emergency ward. He is not expected to recover. My mother-in-law is in another ward, this one for mentally disturbed patients. She has a room to herself.

'She was agitating all the other patients, so we thought it best to keep her separate from everyone else,' the nurses sigh. 'It's best if you leave your child here with us,' they say. 'Kaliamma may not be in the best of moods and might upset your little girl.'

Once in my mother-in-law's room, I close the door, pull down my sari pallu to reveal my face. 'Amma,' I say, 'it's me.'

But she looks right through me and rocks back and forth, her legs pulled up, her chin resting on her knees. In just a few days, she has lost weight, is a slight, insipid imitation of her earlier self. Her hair is loose, her face more lined than I have ever seen it. She smells rank, of unwashed body and distress. I bite back my tears and the urge to touch her, to fold her into my arms like I do my little girl.

'Who are you?' she asks after a bit. She flicks out a hand and grabs my palm, her fingers gripping my hand harshly, urgently. 'Why are you here?' Her eyes dart around. 'What have you come to steal?'

And then she looks right at me, her gaze hard and manic, overlaid with shadows. 'What more do you want? You have taken everything. Everything.'

She drops my hand like it has given her an electric shock, emitting high-pitched screeches and hitting herself repeatedly.

Nurses arrive to tend to Kaliamma. And the weakling that I am, the spineless deserter, I run from the room, from the wreckage and upset I have caused.

As I collect my little girl, I ask the doctor in charge, who has arrived to tend to Kaliamma, what is to happen to my in-laws.

'Mr Desai, the lawyer who handles the estate, was away on family business in Rajasthan but is now on his way back,' he says.

I've told him I am a distant relative, dumbfounded by what happened to the Gaddehalli Gowdas. He commiserates with me about the young generation, Manoj and Sudha and the little boy Hari, succumbing to the fire. I am relieved that the truth about who Hari really is has not become public. Yet.

'The lawyer called to make sure Vinayappa and Kaliamma get the best treatment, no expense spared,' he assures me, noting my upset and turmoil. 'The Gowdas have plenty of capital in property and shares, it seems, so please don't worry. They will be well looked after.'

The smell of phenyl and medicine stifles me. My child pulls at my hand, her palm warm and soft, grounding me even as I try to shut out Kaliamma's screeches, her voice echoing in my ears, 'You have taken everything.'

Knowing that my in-laws are to be taken care of – the in-laws who shared their world with me, which I then so callously snatched from them – I grab my child and run.

Far enough away that I can outrun the past. What I have done. What I brought upon myself and everyone I cared for.

With the gold I was wearing the night my world went up in flames, and the gold my mother-in-law gave me when her house was burning and her mind was still intact, I move with my babe to Delhi. I find work there as a maid. Like my mother-in-law did all those years ago in a mansion that she was to gain and lose, taking her sanity with it.

The lady I work for is a hard taskmaster, but she is fair. She reminds me of my mother-in-law. I try to push all thoughts of the past away and concentrate on my child's future. I make myself indispensable at work. In time, all the other maids leave, but I stay.

When my employers move to the UK, they take us along. I work hard. I keep my head down. I bring up my child. I push memories away. I survive.

So many times over the years I am tempted to go back. To that one place where I had found, against all odds, the acceptance and love I had sought all my life. The place I demolished with one impulsive falsehood.

When the ache for what I lost grows too strong to ignore, I take out the picture my mother-in-law had bestowed on me, her last gift to me in the midst of the smoking cinders of her hopes for our collective future. A photo of me and my love with our child and his parents, in front of the mansion. An image of happy times stolen from fate, bookended by prophecy, underscored by a lie.

I have penned the address of the house that gave me so much on the back of the photograph, as if, by writing it down I am visiting it in my mind. I have written the address in English, the language of my new country, the language that I have made my own, eschewing Kannada, the language in which I dream, the language that belongs to the secret past, the language which, nevertheless, I have taught my daughter to read and write and speak, just in case…

Just in case.

I have written down the address of the house: Gaddehalli, India. It hurts too much to write anything else.

I see my husband in my dreams. I see them all.

And then I wake to my pallid world, where the only colour I have, my daughter, distances herself from me because she senses that I am keeping her story from her.

'Who is my dad?' she asks. 'What are you hiding from me?'

My astute daughter picks up on my restraint, knowing that I am not telling her everything but not knowing enough to ask the right questions. She is Kaliamma's granddaughter after all. Bright and resourceful like her. My daughter who cannot deceive, unaware of the deception I once indulged in, of which she was the innocent, unknowing accomplice.

I am tempted to tell her now she has matured into a wonderful adult, one who makes me proud every single day.

But I haven't. I won't. What use is the truth when it will only cause hurt?

I watch her carefully, but she seems unaffected by what happened in the first three years of her life. And I want to keep it that way.

I knew I wouldn't get away with my deception forever. But once I started I couldn't stop. It ran away with me, my lie, developed a life of its own, blowing up in my face and that of everyone around me, devastating them, sparing me.

Why did I get to live? This is a question I ask myself often.

I do not deserve to be spared. But perhaps *this* is my punishment, to live with the consequences of what I have done, to spend every moment of every day repenting, missing, saturated with loss.

And I also think I was spared so I could do my best by my daughter. She makes it worth the while. I am grateful for her.

I named my daughter Jaya, meaning victory, so she would become victorious, rising out of the ashes, the smoke permeated, fire-branded, flame-licked debris of everyone's hopes and aspirations.

And she has.

Chapter 44

Jaya

The Taste of Past Lives

Oh my goodness, Jaya thinks, shock waves rocking her body. *Oh my goodness.*

She doesn't realise that she is shaking until she feels Ben's arms around her, his voice in her ear, 'It's okay, Jaya.'

'Oh, Ben! This is why I recognised all the trees in the fruit orchard, why I dreamt about mango and mud, why I felt a connection to this house. It was speaking to me, telling me I had lived here once.' Her voice comes out in winded puffs.

She had walked the span of this black, smoke-tainted ruin, rising from a red hill amid yellowing fields in the middle of nowhere, and yet she hadn't made the connection that she had lived here as a little boy, although she had experienced the shivers of déjà vu, the slippery ache of nostalgia.

'I felt restless all my life. I was fascinated by the past. I felt hounded by it. I knew there was something missing… What was missing was the little boy I had once been, his phantom presence visiting me in my dreams, morphing into Arun. I always woke with tears in my eyes.' She exhales deeply. 'I understand now that I was crying for two little boys: Arun and the boy I was once upon a time, a boy of my mother's creation, a boy who vanished the day of the fire when he took off his muddy clothes and ran into his father's arms…'

'Oh, Jaya…' Ben holds her gently, patiently allowing her to speak, to spew the thoughts crowding her head, wanting release.

'Once she ran away from here, Mum reinvented herself like she reinvented her child – me! – as a boy in a previous life. To counteract what went before, she only looked forward. She focused on me. She was constrained all her life, lugging the load of everyone's expectations. And yet, she never once weighed me down with the burden of her expectations.'

Among the age-worn, fire-slicked stones which housed her mother once upon a time, and where she was conceived and had spent the first three years of her life as a little boy called Hari, Jaya laments the choices her mother felt pressured to make, the path her life took. 'When I was older and kept my distance from her, she never asked that I call or visit. She never once made me feel guilty when I didn't. She always gave the impression that she was self-sufficient, content, and how it used to irritate me! I thought that she didn't really need me! That she was happy, regardless of whether I visited or not, called her or not. How callously self-absorbed I was!'

'Jaya, you couldn't have known…'

Jaya takes a deep, gasping breath. 'I should have tried, Ben. *Now* I understand that she was putting on an act for my benefit. So I could go about my life without feeling guilty, burdened by her loneliness. For she must have felt lonely. Lost in a country that she had adopted but that was never really hers.'

I am sorry, Mum. So very sorry.

Jaya swallows. 'I could be myself, warts and all, with her, because she loved me unconditionally. That's why I had the freedom to rebel against her, rail about her, ignore her. Only now, too late, I recognise what a prized gift that was. A gift that Mum bestowed so freely at the cost of being ignored and neglected.' Jaya stumbles on a sob. 'Oh, Ben… How I wish I had told her, shown her how much I loved her. I wish I'd told her that she was my anchor, the springboard from where I could experimentally stretch my wings, leap into the world and experience all it had to offer.' The sticky air, which smells faintly of mould, feels slimy on her skin, wet with heartache.

'She knew, Jaya. I promise you, she knew.'

Mum, you went to the grave with your secrets. But you left some photographs behind, tucked carefully into the back of an old, fraying album cataloguing my school life. One of them a snapshot of all the people you had loved. A reminder of everything you lost. A photograph given to you by Kali in the precious moments before she lost her sanity, her hold on the present. A photograph that would one day, almost a year and a half after your death, lead me to the home where you were happiest, where you found yourself and lost almost everything you held dear with the exception of me.

And you left me the greatest gift of all. The legacy of your words. You left me the truth of my past and yours; you left me the real you, Mum, the person who was waiting all this while to come out from behind that impassive facade, the person you denied me to protect me.

I thank you for this treasure, Mum.

'There were never any pictures of me as an infant and toddler. I asked Mum why there weren't any and she said that she hadn't owned a camera then,' Jaya says to Ben as he holds her. 'Now I understand that there *were* photographs – of a happy little boy called Hari, the bearer of his family's dreams.'

Ben gently wipes away her tears with a disintegrating tissue that he has salvaged from one of the pockets of his jeans.

Ben. The father of the child they'd lost. The keeper of *her* hopes and the owner of *her* dreams. Her lover. Her best friend. Such a comfort now, when she desperately needs solace.

'Mum didn't change in two ways even after she donned a fresh avatar in a different country: she kept a diary in her old life and in her new one. And she saved pictures obsessively – a moving, living record of the child she gained at great cost, pictures I only discovered after she passed.'

'She must have been so worried, Jaya,' Ben says softly, 'that she would lose you too.'

'Yes.' Jaya wants to keen long and loud, an elegy for the pain her mother carried within her, for all her mother suffered.

'She was plagued by fear that she hadn't paid for taking her brother's life, even after she lost everyone but you. She trusted in a punishing god who would extract an eye for an eye. There was that prophecy too. And so she saved pictures of you and Hari – you in a previous avatar.'

'She had pockets sewn into her sari skirts in the UK too, a tradition she picked up from Kali. This was why, when I went snooping, I found nothing, because whatever was of value to her – her diaries, the pictures – were in there, with her at all times.'

'Yes,' Ben murmurs into Jaya's hair, holding her as she cries.

'How Mum punished herself! Small wonder her heart caved in much too early. If only she had told me, shared herself with me. If only we had come here together…'

Jaya pictures herself and her mother bonding during the course of the journey to India and into her mother's past. Meeting with Kali together…

Would her mother gasp in distress at the state of the ruin and of Kali? Laugh with surprised joy when Kali recognised her? Sob when Kali said her name with warmth and deep affection?

Sudha was always contained, so very controlled. She carried herself so carefully as if she would disintegrate if she showed even the slightest hint of emotion.

Now Jaya understands.

I love you, Mum. I fancy you can hear me, here in this ruin, infused with the odour of mud and memories, the taste of past lives and secret wishes, where once upon a time you were happy.

A soft breeze brushes Jaya's face, tender as a caress, carrying the whiff of curry and coconut oil mingling with a faint tang of sweat – her mother's smell.

You kept the truth from me so I could look ahead, Mum, and not be held back by the past, like you were. But I have been guilty of doing just that.

I need to move on, to look forward. I need to take charge of my life, live it to the full. Otherwise I will be stranded, stuck, like Kali, my grandmother (my grandmother!), who is lost in the past and like you, Mum, so apart from life.

I will have more children and in their rounded faces, in their sparkling eyes, in the curve of their cheeks and the arch of their shoulders, I will find you, Mum.

Thank you for everything. For giving me of yourself through your diaries. For opening my eyes to what once was and what is left and what I have to live for.

'I'm sorry, Ben,' Jaya whispers, 'for pushing you away.' Her voice is as tremulous as the patter of drops scattering from rain-stippled branches.

'You're here now,' he murmurs into her ear. 'In my arms. Right where I want you.'

'I know now what Mum wanted of me – all she wanted of me: to be happy and free of restrictions, free to be myself. She would want me to look forward, to not be hindered by what came before, like she was all her life. She would be delighted that I met Kali, and I think she would be pleased that I reconciled with Hari. She would be happy that I'm here, at this house where *she* was happiest. And I know that she would be very pleased with the plans we have for it.'

'She would,' Ben says.

'But I know she would be happiest with the plans I have for us.'

'What plans do you have for us?' Ben asks.

'A big family – four children at least.'

He laughs, and on his lips she tastes their future, sun-caressed gold, a bud unfurling.

*   *   *

'Thank you for going to the trouble of finding my mother and for your letter,' Jaya says to the lawyer. Ben and Jaya had watched him arrive from the upstairs window, Jaya still in the process of digesting what she had discovered from reading her mother's diaries.

'My pleasure, ma'am,' the lawyer says formally.

'Please, call me Jaya. And this is my husband, Ben.'

They sit on the wall by the fruit orchard, the languid mid-afternoon air drunk on syrup and birdsong. Sumathi-amma, Durga and Kali are all enjoying an afternoon nap. The nuns are at prayer, using the kitchen as a makeshift chapel.

The lawyer runs a hand across his moist brow. A fly buzzes, hovers.

'What exactly did you have in mind for my mother, assuming it was she who had received your letter and agreed to come here?'

'Um…' The lawyer waves a hand around him, his Adam's apple bobbing in his sweat-soaked, hairy throat. The collar of his cream shirt is stained urine yellow. 'This estate…'

'Yes, about that, I've been thinking… I had a long chat with Sumathiamma and it sparked an idea. I've talked to Ben and he thinks it will work. I want to run it by you and see what you think. I know you're acting on Kali's behalf …'

'No,' the lawyer says gently, 'I'm acting on yours.'

Jaya looks up, shocked. 'Mine?'

'You must know by now about the scandal Kaliamma caused by marrying Mr Vinay?'

Jaya nods, exchanging a perplexed glance with Ben – Sumathiamma had told them about it that morning.

'Mr Vinay's parents cut Kali out of the will. This is solely his estate and it goes to his issues and *their* issues, which means it goes to you.' The lawyer smiles at her.

'Oh.' She swallows, trying to assimilate what he has said. 'Okay. Here's what I thought…'

When Jaya has finished outlining her plans for the house, the lawyer is silent, stroking his stubble. A bead of perspiration clings to the tip of his nose.

Jaya slips her hand inside Ben's, threading her fingers through his.

'It's a brilliant idea,' the lawyer says finally, smiling widely, and the drop of perspiration falls off his nose, absorbed into the humid air.

They sit there, Jaya and Ben and the lawyer, budgeting and forecasting, until sizzling sounds and spicy scents begin to drift from the kitchen.

'Come inside, all of you, for a snack,' Sumathiamma calls from the front door.

Kali bounds past Sumathiamma, weaving past Jaya and Ben and the lawyer into the orchard, her speed belying her years. She squeals as she chucks handfuls of leaves at Durga and the nuns, who have followed her outside, her face blooming with laughter, Sumathiamma's summons falling on deaf ears.

Chapter 45
Kali

Dragonfly Wings

I am lost. Wandering the rooms of my disjointed memory, the way I once roamed the rooms of the mansion I stole. Every once in a while something comes, a flicker. A shard of memory. Tantalising. I try to grab it, and it is gone, elusive as dragonfly wings glimmering golden blue in the summer sun.

Days pass in an absent whirl. Nothing lingers long enough for me to process, to hold in my fleeting mind. Sometimes there is an echo of the mysterious, intangible past. Like now: this woman beside me, wearing a wispy orange dress like a guru's robe. A woman I think I know. She comes in the wake of a little girl who talks to me, asking questions, sparking aches and bringing to the fore long-forgotten truths. This strangely familiar woman's hair cascades down the sides of her face in glorious waves. Her face is young, unlined and yet marked by those small traces that sorrow leaves behind, that intense grief imprints. She has tasted loss, I can see.

'Ajji,' she says, her voice as gentle as the ocean after the gale has passed, as wistful as summers long past, nostalgic as the jarring echoes in grown men's growls of the children they once were.

Why is she calling me Ajji? I am nowhere near old enough to be anybody's grandmother.

She rubs her face with her hands, spreading sweat all over it. I stare, fascinated by her shimmering face, beads of sweat gleaming on it like tears.

'My mum was Sudha. Your daughter-in-law,' she says.

And that name… that name ignites a pang somewhere within me.

'Don't you wish for a chance to go back in time? I do… all the time.' She leans across and rests her palm on my knee. A wedding ring glints from her finger. I used to be married once, I recall with sudden clarity. But nothing else comes, just that one fact.

'Sumathiamma told me about the girl you were once. Funny, spirited, a fabulous mimic. She told me how Radhakka once came up behind you while you were imitating her and you thought you would be in trouble, but Radhakka surprised you all by laughing.' Her lips lift but her eyes are sad.

Memories arrive in a whirl of images, startled awake like doves dozing in the rafters spooked into flapping around in squawking circles. A thickset woman asking me to eat, holding me while I am being sick, smiling fondly at me. Radhakka.

My eyes are blinded by the twin cataracts of remorse and nostalgia. My mind shies away from the well of pain that has opened up within, engulfing me, drowning me. A keen escapes my mouth and alarm tints the woman's black eyes silvery blue.

'I am sorry, Ajji. So sorry. I know it hurts.'

RENITA D'SILVA

'You don't know anything,' I bite out fiercely. 'You don't know the half of it.'

I close my eyes and start to rock back and forth. And just as soon as the rage has come, it dissipates.

'I'm sorry I upset you. I'll get help,' she says, standing up to go, her voice violet with distress.

A picture in front of my eyes. A big house rising like hope on top of a hill. Where a girl who lost her father to his selfish want and her mother to grief and her love to circumstance finds refuge. She concocts a ruthless plan to gain the house. And in the process, she loses so much. So much.

Images. A baby boy. Who grows into a handsome young man whom I am afraid to love. A woman, his wife, whom I grow to care for. Then... another baby boy. Who is... Who is... Who is not.

Flames dancing.

A fire that destroyed everything.

Everything.

After that, there was only the taste of loss, the smell of burning. Dreams once nurtured going up in a wisp of smoke. The ghosts of the past, haunting, beguiling, damning, dangling enticing slivers of what could have been, holding court over my wretched heart, wreaking havoc with my charred mind.

I grab the hand of the woman beside me. 'Wait.'

She is young. Hauntingly familiar. She stirs recollections of a past that I had hoped would glide triumphantly into a stellar future.

I look closely at her face. That patrician nose. Those soulful eyes… They remind me… They bring back…

Laughter. A little boy running through the rooms of the mansion, his mother in pursuit. *Hari, come here, you little devil.*

'Hari,' I whisper.

'I'm called Jaya now,' she says.

Tears quiver in her eyes. One falls down her cheek onto my hand.

I watch it dissolve, moist, soft. Bringing to mind babies. And love.

I longed for a grandson to carry on the family name. But now this young woman emerges from the embers of my derelict dreams, the ashes of my ambition, the smoke-stained brick and mortar of all that was: a huge mansion and I, the queen of all I surveyed from the top of the hill. She is beautiful. She has Sudha's lips and chin, Manoj's nose and his gentleness. And yet she is her own person. Her face glows with the light of a future unmarked by the past.

And briefly my confused mind, muddied and cracked by all that has gone before, plagued by flames that stole everything that mattered, littered with stray thoughts like tendrils of smoke from a dying fire, is clear and looks ahead, like it did once before when I held this girl as a swaddled infant whom I named Hari. I spy a future where the Gowda name is carried forward by a woman who was once the boy I pinned all my hopes on, and the tired house, unloved and abandoned, carrying memories of loss and destruction and doused hope, is alive again, with laughter and promise and love, with Vinay

RENITA D'SILVA

and his mother and father looking down from where they are, finally content, my wilful actions – which caused everything that followed – forgiven, my sins laid to rest.

I reach out a hand that trembles and quakes, creased like much-folded paper, with skin that hangs limp, and cup the woman's chin. Memorise her features.

Jewels sparkle on her face. They twinkle and shimmer. I reach out to touch them. They are wet, insubstantial, like the thoughts that crowd my mind, only to disappear – poof – when I try to grab them, hold them in place. I wanted to do something. What was it?

There is a young woman. Familiar. 'Who are you? Why is your face wet? Go wash it, child.'

I am ready for bed. Where are all the servants? This woman with her damp face will have to do. I clutch her hand. 'Take me to bed. Where is Vinay? Is he in bed already?'

A memory... Vivid. Scorching.

A man who loved me with all his heart, loved me in a way my guilt-blemished, greed-tarnished soul couldn't fathom, hanging from the smoke-blackened rafters of a destroyed house.

Cavernous pain. A fiery blaze in my head.

I open my mouth and scream as loud as I can to drown out the searing pain, the blistering upset.

The woman opens her arms and envelops me in them, whispering, 'It's okay, Ajji.' She smells of exotic fruit and comfort.

Sudha holding me. Sudha...

'Run, Sudha,' I plead. 'Take Hari and go. I'll come later. I just have to find Vinay and then I will come.'

'Ajji…'

'Go, Sudha – take Hari. And send word please.'

'I'll get help and be right back,' she says, and then she runs away from me, her turmeric dress swishing once, twice before the splash of colour disappears, leaving behind peeling, flame-licked walls the dingy beige of crumbling hope.

Chapter 46
Durga

Bible-wielding Shadows

'Thank you, Durga,' Jaya says.

She is looking much better now than she did this morning, when she'd appeared in the kitchen while Durga and Ben and Durga's ajji were having breakfast. She was panting and breathless, worried that she had upset Kali. They had all run to Kali's room, but when they got there, Kali had been asleep and snoring gently, her face calm and looking so much younger with the lines ironed out by slumber.

'Kali saw something in you that triggered her memory,' Jaya says now. 'If not for you, I… I wouldn't be reunited with my grandmother.'

I was reunited with my grandmother here too, Durga thinks.

They are perched on the broken wall by the orchard. Durga's ajji squats beside her, her gnarled hand resting on Durga's back. Kali is in the orchard, the nuns beside her, habit-clad, bible-wielding shadows. Kali plucks fruit and squashes it with a splat, giggling every so often – today she is, once again, a little girl trapped in an old woman's body.

I know your story now, Hari, Durga thinks, unable to equate the mysterious boy who kept cropping up with this beautiful woman before her. How would it feel to discover that you were once someone completely different to the person you have always believed yourself to be – a different gender even! She cannot begin to imagine.

And as if Durga has asked the question out loud, Jaya says, 'I… I dreamt about him.' A longish pause. 'Hari. But I never made the connection. Never remembered that it was actually *me.*'

Ben puts his arm around Jaya, gathers her in his embrace. 'See even now I am saying *him* when talking of Hari. He is somehow apart.' Jaya chokes on her words.

'You didn't want to remember,' Durga's ajji says softly, patting Jaya's hand. 'You kept going back to the point when your world shattered, changed forever, but you couldn't go any further.'

Grit swirls in the spiced air, sticky with humidity, infused with the scent of wild garlic and overripe fruit. 'Yes.' Jaya rubs her palm across her cheeks, blue drops glittering on her skin like grief-tinted jewels. Her fingers tremble as she takes a tissue out of her bag and blows her nose. 'And my mother… You know, I always wondered why my mum died so young. That heart attack… completely unexpected. Now I understand that it must have been because of everything she was keeping inside: the grief, the guilt. Her heart just gave way.' Jaya sniffs, pushes her shoulders back, pulling herself together. 'Durga, you are a very special girl. If not for you, we wouldn't be here. Ben and I think this house needs love; it needs to be cherished, restored. And for that, labourers need to come here. We've talked to your ajji and the lawyer too and we all think that you are the only one who can convince the villagers that this house isn't haunted; that the rumours are just that: rumours.'

Sumathi nods her assent vigorously, smiling at Durga.

Durga grins, her heart blooming at Jaya's compliment. She rubs her hands together. 'That's the kind of challenge I like.'

Her ajji and Jaya and Ben laugh in unison, and in the orchard Kali stops what she's doing to yell, 'What are you laughing about? Get to work! Don't you know we have a party to prepare for?'

'How did she read my mind?' Jaya says. 'That's what I was going to say next. We'll have an open house, invite the villagers here – after we've cleaned it up a bit, and once you've convinced them, Durga, that there are no ghosts. And once they've been here, *they'll* spread the word.'

'What a good idea,' Durga's ajji says.

'We've also been thinking… This house, it needs a purpose, a fresh start. It's languished in the past for too long. Durga, your ajji told me about your ma and da. What if, instead of moving into a rented house, they came here? Ben and I have gone over the accounts with the lawyer – we can afford to employ more nuns, a few doctors and nurses and turn this building into a recuperation centre like the one your ma and da are at presently, although this will be a free one.'

The blood coursing through Durga's body is the texture of prayer, the consistency of faith, the essence of anticipation, her whole being blossoming and yet at the same time shying away from hope. *Please,* she thinks.

'Before the fire,' Jaya says, 'Kali had expanded the family business and properties considerably and invested judiciously so there's more than enough money coming in for repairs and to run this place as a charity for the foreseeable future. This house could be a refuge for people like your ma and da, who can't work because of tragic circumstances and would be destitute otherwise. Your ajji is happy to stay on, and if your ma and da agree then they could be on the books too, paid a salary for overseeing operations here. What do you think?'

Durga throws her arms around Jaya. 'Thank you!' she says.

She basks in the glow of Jaya's smile.

'You don't mind leaving your friends behind and going to school with the village children?' Jaya asks.

Friends? What friends?

Durga thinks of the villagers here, who are already in awe of her for not only staying at the ruin once but returning to stay again. She thinks of the bedraggled village children, some of whom think she is possessed of the special ability to repel ghosts. She thinks of the rickshaw driver who, in the course of her journey here, has become an ally. Much better here than staying in a town where she is 'naughty'. Her ajji beams at her, and Durga knows that she is thinking the same thing.

'I don't mind at all.' Durga grins at Jaya. 'I love it here, and I'm sure Ma and Da will love it too. And I am beginning to love Kali, who is even naughtier than me.'

As if on cue, Kali yells, 'Enough already. Stop nattering and get to work. What am I paying you all for?'

They laugh, Ben too, although Durga can tell he hasn't understood much of the conversation.

And standing there, in the navy shadow of the ruin, Durga formulates plans for her future and that of her parents and her grandmother in her head even as she chuckles. She is properly elated for the first time since the accident, which, she understands after the conversation with her mother, wasn't anybody's fault but an unlucky combination of circumstances.

She imagines her ma and da's expressions when she tells them of their new home, their awe when they see the ruin, so huge and marvellous and full of potential. She pictures her ma and da and ajji and herself sitting in the shade of the fruit trees, the perfumed breeze caressing their faces as they look down the hill upon fields sparkling green and gold after the summer rains and in her mind's eye Durga sees the good part of Da's face lift in a lopsided smile.

Chapter 47
Jaya

The Kannada Word for Grandmother

Jaya talks to Kali, telling her of her plans for the restoration of the ruin. She tells her about Arun, and of how she and Ben lost their way for a bit but have now found each other. She tells her of their intention to have a big family, starting as soon as possible.

She tells Kali that she is going to resign from her job and that she and Ben plan to divide their time between the UK and India, how Ben will need to travel often but he can do that from India just as well as from the UK and how Jaya won't be lonely when he does for she will be here with Kali and Durga and Durga's parents and Sumathiamma.

Afterwards, her throat dry and hoarse, she sits companionably beside Kali, who is still, her eyes closed, her face turned upwards to the sun. No restlessness, no mumbling.

The air is aromatic with the ripe smells of summer; it is laid-back, carefree days and roses singing from arbours.

Kali opens her eyes, tugging urgently at Jaya's wrist. Jaya squats down in front of her grandmother, trying to read what she wants to say in her gold-flecked, often lost but now gratifyingly luminous eyes, which are focused on Jaya.

'Ajji,' Jaya says gently. The Kannada word for grandmother.

Silver tears sprout in Kali's bright eyes and sparkle on her eyelashes.

She extends an age-worn, trembling hand and cups Jaya's face.

'You are beautiful,' she says, her voice a tender, love-filled embrace.

And then she blinks, the light going out of her eyes, her gaze turning puzzled.

Perhaps, Jaya thinks, wiping away the moisture that has collected in her eyes, somewhere in Kali's disorderly mind, she knows who Jaya is. Perhaps she does.

There have been moments like this before now too, moments when Kali has seemed coherent, appearing to grasp what Jaya has been telling her.

And the thought gives Jaya hope.

Letter from Renita

First of all, I want to say a huge thank you for choosing *A Mother's Secret*. I hope you enjoyed reading it just as much as I loved writing it.

For me, what I adore most about being a writer is hearing from readers, finding out what they thought of my stories. So please do let me know, either via a review, through my website or my facebook and twitter pages. Also, if you'd like to keep up-to-date with all my latest releases, just sign up here:

www.renitadsilva.com/e-mail-sign-up

Finally, if you liked *A Mother's Secret*, you might also like my other novels, *Monsoon Memories*, *The Forgotten Daughter*, *The Stolen Girl* and *A Sister's Promise*.

Thank you so much for your support – it means the world to me.

Until next time,

Renita

@RenitaDSilva
RenitaDSilvaBooks
www.renitadsilva.com

Acknowledgements

A big thank you to everyone at Bookouture, especially Oliver Rhodes, Natasha Hodgson and Kim Nash.

Thank you to Lorella Belli of Lorella Belli Literary Agency for everything you do. I am so lucky and privileged to have you championing my books.

A *huge* thank you to Jenny Hutton for seeing right through my initial drafts to what the story can really become. You are the best, Jenny.

Thank you, Natasha Hodgson, for the title and copy, for your wonderfully detailed edit and for your support and guidance. You are amazing.

Thank you to Emma Graves for the *beautiful*, evocative cover.

Thank you to all my lovely fellow Bookouture authors for your support and friendship, especially the amazing Angie Marsons, Caroline Mitchell, Sharon Maas, Rebecca Stonehill and Debbie Rix.

Massive thanks to all the wonderful book bloggers especially Joseph Calleja, Julayn Adams and Jules Mortimer, and all my Twitter and Facebook friends, for your support.

Thank you to Margaret Ilori, Perdita D'Silva and Levin D'Souza for patiently taking the time to answer my many questions.

Thank you to my husband and my children for your patience and understanding. A special thank you to Tanya for suggesting the name Mr Fluff.

And thank you, reader, for talking the time to read this book. I hope you enjoy it.

Author's Note

This is wholly a work of fiction. The villages in this book are a combination of various villages from different parts of India and the place where I have set them may not necessarily have a village like the one I have described.

I have taken liberties with Gowda weddings in order not to complicate the plot. There are a lot of rituals – pre and post wedding – that I have skipped for the ease and smooth flow of the story.

I apologise for any oversights or mistakes and hope they do not detract from your enjoyment of this book.

CPSIA information can be obtained at www.ICGtesting.com
Printed in the USA
LVOW07s0240140416

483573LV00023B/393/P

9 781910 751947